Anne PERRY

TRIPLE JEOPARDY

HEADLINE

The right of Anne Perry to be identified as the Author of
the Work has been asserted by her in accordance with the
Copyright, Designs and Patents Act 1988.

First published in 2018
by HEADLINE PUBLISHING GROUP

First published in paperback in 2019
by HEADLINE PUBLISHING GROUP

1

Cataloguing in Publication Data is available from the British Library

ISBN 978 1 4722 5723 9

Typeset in Adobe Garamond by Palimpsest Book Production Limited,
Falkirk, Stirlingshire

Printed and bound in Great Britain by CPI Group (UK) Ltd, Croydon CR0 4YY

Headline's policy is to use papers that are natural, renewable and recyclable
products and made from wood grown in sustainable forests. The logging and
manufacturing processes are expected to conform to the environmental
regulations of the country of origin.

HEADLINE PUBLISHING GROUP
An Hachette UK Company
Carmelite House
50 Victoria Embankment
London EC4Y 0DZ

www.headline.co.uk
www.hachette.co.uk

To Victoria Zackheim,
for her friendship and immeasurable help

List of Characters

Daniel Pitt – a recently qualified barrister
Jemima Flannery – Daniel's sister
Patrick Flannery – Jemima's husband
Cassie – Jemima and Patrick's elder daughter
Sophie – Jemima and Patrick's younger daughter
Sir Thomas Pitt – Daniel's father, head of Special Branch
Charlotte – Lady Pitt, Daniel's mother
Rebecca Thorwood – an American heiress
Tobias Thorwood – her father
Bernadette Thorwood – her mother
Philip Sidney – works in the British Embassy in Washington
Impney – chief clerk at fford Croft and Gibson
Toby Kitteridge – a senior barrister at fford Croft and Gibson
Roman Blackwell – a private enquiry agent and ex-policeman
Mercedes Blackwell – Roman Blackwell's mother
Marcus fford Croft – head of fford Croft and Gibson
Miriam fford Croft – his daughter
Sir John Armitage – a British diplomat
Morley Cross – works at the British Embassy in Washington
Judge Ullswater – a judge
James Hillyer – a barrister

Mr Partington – works at Foreign Office
Mr Edgeley – a prosecution witness
Mr Stains – a prosecution witness
Miss Wescott – a postmistress in St Anne, Alderney
Dr James Mullane – a GP in St Anne, Alderney

Chapter One

Daniel rang the doorbell, then stepped back. He realised with amazement that he was suddenly nervous. Why? This was his parents' home, the house he had grown up in. At twenty-five, he still returned quite often for dinner, for communication, for comfort and pleasure in conversation, even sharing some of his thoughts, and perhaps an experience that had been important to him. What was different this time?

What was different was that his elder sister, Jemima, was back from America with her husband and very small daughters, Cassie and Sophie. Daniel had not seen Jemima for four years, and he had not met Patrick Flannery at all, or his new nieces. Both his and Jemima's lives had changed radically in that time. He had sat his degree at Cambridge, then passed his bar exams, and was now actually practising the law he had dreamed about so long. Jemima was married and had lived in New York, and now Washington. 'Idealistic and naïve' she had once called him. Of course, he had changed a little, but she might have changed a lot. It was a relationship he had always taken for granted. It was comfortable; they could disagree over important things, and trivial

1

and silly things, because they knew that underneath, everything that ever mattered between them was unbreakable. She was three years older than he. She had been there all his life.

Did he resent the fact that she had married an American, and so had gone to live there? Not really, if it made her happy. She was bound to marry someone, and loyalties shifted, grew in time to include others. She had bossed him around when she was nine and he was six. He wouldn't tolerate that now, although she would probably try because it was an old habit. She would accept defeat gracefully – wouldn't she?

But he had missed her. It was a relationship that mattered: their growing up together, with all the good experiences and, more importantly, the difficult ones. He could remember vividly the day they had been measured against the door, and for the first time he was taller than she. It was a reversal of roles. For twelve years she had protected him, or it felt like that. Now, his father had explained, he must protect her. But that was not always necessary. His mother did not need anyone to protect her. If she was angry, she was the equal of anyone, and not afraid at all! Sometimes Jemima was like that, or meaning to be.

Nowadays one could cross the Atlantic very quickly, in a mere five days! But five days there, five days back, and the visit: it was a long time to be away. Too long during exams time for him to have visited her. And too expensive on a student's budget.

Would she have changed? Would he find that the old ease and comfort was gone? That was what he was afraid of.

He was reaching out to pull the bell a second time when the door opened, but instead of a servant, his mother stood in the entrance. She was a handsome woman, quite tall, and with the auburn light in her hair that he had inherited. She was over fifty now, and there were touches of grey, but her vitality had not faded in the slightest. That change he would find painful to accept, but it was far in the future, if ever.

'Daniel!' She threw her arms around him and held him tightly for a moment, then stepped back. 'Come in! Jemima is dying to see you, and of course you must meet Patrick. And Cassie and Sophie! You'll love them, I promise!'

He had no overcoat to hang up. It was August and London was too warm for a jacket, even at this time of the early evening. He followed his mother into the withdrawing room, where the door at the far end was still open to the evening air and the last light shimmering on the leaves of the poplar trees. It was all so incredibly familiar he could have left here only this morning. His father was there, standing with Jemima and the man who must be her husband.

Jemima came forward. She was familiar, too, and yet she had changed in slight ways. Her hair was still the same, darker than his, and curly like their father's. She was quite ordinarily dressed, in slender pale green, yet she looked lovely because there was an inner happiness in her that gave her a special grace. He wondered if she would find him changed and wondered in what way: still tall, of course, and slim, his brown hair still unruly and his face neither handsome nor plain.

Automatically, he held his arms out and she walked straight into them and hugged him hard. Then, as quickly, she stepped away and turned. 'This is my husband, Patrick. Patrick, meet my brother, Daniel.'

Patrick Flannery was tall, roughly the same height as

Daniel, but there the likeness ended. His hair was black and his eyes very blue. His features were less regular than Daniel's, and had not their sensitivity, but the humour and individuality in them made him attractive. 'I've heard so much about you from Jemima. I'm happy to meet you at last.' His voice had the softness of his Irish forebears clearly overlying the American accent.

'Welcome to London,' Daniel said quickly, taking Patrick's hand and grasping it.

'Thank you,' Patrick replied. 'I thought New York was big, but this is . . . enormous.' He said it with a smile to rob it of any offence.

'Lot of villages all run into each other,' Daniel replied. 'We'll have to show you around. Take a trip down the river, perhaps. Or up it?' He glanced at Jemima to see if she approved the idea.

'I've got it planned,' she said with a smile. 'But there's two more people for you to meet before we have dinner. Sophie's sound asleep and Cassie's half asleep, but she was determined to stay up to say hello to her uncle Daniel. Come with me . . .' She held out her hand. Her face was shining with pleasure and pride, and nervousness.

'Excuse me,' Daniel said to his parents, particularly his father, to whom he had not even spoken, and followed Jemima obediently.

Upstairs, Jemima showed Daniel baby Sophie in her cot in Jemima and Patrick's own room. The child was fast asleep, her soft downy hair dark against the pillow. Wordlessly they gazed at the baby, then smiled at each other and tiptoed across the corridor.

In the nursery, the first room Daniel could ever remember as a tiny child, Jemima pointed to the bed. A very little girl

4

had fallen asleep sitting up there, and had toppled sideways on to the pillows. She had dark hair, almost black, and soft flawless skin. He would have guessed her to be three, even if he had not known.

Jemima kneeled down beside her and woke her gently, before Daniel could tell her not to disturb the child.

Slowly she sat up, then looked past her mother to stare at Daniel. She had not her father's blue eyes. Hers were soft grey like Jemima's, and like Thomas Pitt's.

'Hello, Cassie,' Daniel said, stepping forward. 'I'm Daniel. It was very kind of you to stay up so I could meet you.' He was not sure whether to hold out his hand or not.

She blinked a couple of times. ''S all right,' she replied. 'We came all the way to see you. In a big ship.'

'How exciting,' he said. 'I've never been in a big ship.'

She smiled slowly, and a little self-consciously, half turning away and moving an inch or two closer to her mother.

'Please will you tell me about it, one day?' Daniel asked.

She nodded. 'My daddy is a policeman . . .'

'That's funny, so is mine,' he replied.

She looked at Jemima again. 'Is that your daddy, too?'

'Yes. We're all family. Your family,' Jemima answered.

Cassie sighed and gave a wide smile.

'I think it's time you went to bed, young lady.' Without waiting for argument or even likely argument, Jemima tucked her up and looked over Cassie's head at Daniel. 'Tell Mama I shall be down in about ten minutes. Don't wait dinner for me. And . . . thank you . . .'

'She's gorgeous. They both are,' he replied.

Jemima held her child a little closer. She was clearly asleep again. 'Thank you,' she whispered, pride and relief shining in her eyes. Had she really imagined Daniel would be

5

anything but completely enchanted, and just a tiny bit envious?

Daniel went out on to the landing and down the stairs again. Jemima had changed, but not radically. As a little girl, she had never wanted dolls, but she had held toy animals with just that same tenderness. It was strange which memories were indelible.

He relayed to the family Jemima's message about not waiting for her, but of course they did. The time afforded Daniel the chance to speak to his father. Now, in 1910, Pitt was in his early sixties, very grey at the temples, but it suited him. He was still head of Special Branch, that part of the services that dealt with antiterrorist activities within the country. It had been formed originally to take care of the Irish Fenian bombers. Much of his work was secret, as it had always been from the time he had left the regular police. He had been knighted for services to the Crown in the last year of Victoria's reign, but even his own family did not know exactly what those services had been. In spite of his openness in so many things, he kept his professional secrets close. He answered questions with silence, and a smile, and Daniel tried to do the same.

'How is it going with Marcus?' Pitt asked conversationally. He was referring to Marcus fford Croft, the head of the legal chambers to which Daniel was attached, as a new and very junior lawyer.

Daniel liked Marcus. He appreciated his quirky personality – 'eccentric' was almost too mild a word – but he worked with him very little, and most cases he was allowed to be involved with were pretty pedestrian and boring. He could not admit it to his father, however, whom he knew had gained him the position. It was one that could become exciting, prestigious and highly rewarding, if he proved to be both dedicated and skilled enough.

Daniel smiled. 'Nothing as exciting as the Graves case,' he said ruefully, mentioning the case that had exercised him earlier in the summer. It was a double-edged remark, said with humour, and remembrance of the very real fear the Graves case had caused, touching all of them with a vision of terrible loss. Even Sir Thomas himself faced ruin if Russell Graves had been allowed to publish his false and incendiary accusations. 'But I don't need that again.'

'Most cases are pretty ordinary,' Pitt answered. 'But they are of intense importance to the people concerned. They'll get bigger and more complicated as you refine your skill. You don't want one beyond your ability.'

Daniel hesitated a moment. Was that a memory of the darkness of the Graves case that he saw in his father's eyes? He had shown it very little at the time, but he must have felt his world collapsing around him. Daniel had let the relief carry him like a flood tide away from the pain. Perhaps his father had not? He should remember that. Cases that went wrong hurt a lot of people, and all of them were worthy of consideration.

Jemima returned from upstairs, they all went into the dining room and dinner was served. Conversation became very general, pleasant but not remarkable. Jemima told them about their apartment in Washington, the neighbourhood, and the climate. Patrick said little about his job, but with obvious affection described his family, brothers, sisters, warm-hearted mother, eccentric father, numerous aunts and uncles.

Daniel listened intently, not only because the narrative was colourful and charming, but because the people of whom Patrick spoke with such love were Jemima's new family, so different from the one she had left in England. Pitt had no family at all. He was an only child, and both his parents were dead before he married. It was a story they did not repeat.

Charlotte had one living sister, and Emily was a big part of all their lives, as were their cousins. Did Jemima miss them?

They touched only on happy memories now, but all the way through, Daniel had the impression that Patrick had something else weighing on his mind.

He learned what it was when they were walking alone in the garden in the pleasant, rose-scented darkness.

Daniel was thinking how to broach the subject, when Patrick immediately took it out of his hands.

'There was another reason I came to England,' he said after only a moment or two. It was as if he knew time would be short, and he had something to say that was very important to him.

'Oh? Something to do with me? Or you want me to speak to somebody?' Daniel asked, trying to keep his voice friendly and non-committal. He did not mention that he had noticed Patrick's preoccupation.

'I want you to have something to do with it,' Patrick said, his voice already thickening with emotion. 'I need to tell you the story from the beginning or it doesn't make sense.'

'If Jemima comes out—'

'She won't. She knows I'm going to tell you.'

'She didn't mention anything . . .'

'She wouldn't,' Patrick said quietly. 'But she cares about it, I think as much as I do.'

Daniel leaned against the trunk of one of the silver birch trees and waited.

Patrick cleared his throat. 'One of the oldest and most socially important families in Washington is the Thorwoods. Not politically, but they are very highly thought of, and philanthropists to many good causes, especially to the police.' He hesitated, perhaps to see if Daniel understood their importance.

'I see.' Daniel nodded. 'Go on. The Thorwoods . . .'

'They have only one child, a daughter named Rebecca,' Patrick continued. It was growing darker and Daniel could hardly see his face, but he could not miss the urgency in his voice. 'She's twenty. She's got money, position. She's very attractive in a quiet way.'

Daniel wanted to interrupt and tell Patrick to get to the point, but with an effort he controlled himself. Patrick had said this would be a long story.

Patrick went on, his voice becoming more strained. 'Just over a month ago, she woke in the middle of the night, in her own bedroom, to find a strange man there. He assaulted her, ripped off her neck a valuable diamond pendant, tore her nightclothes.'

Now Daniel was listening in horror.

Patrick's voice was tight. 'She screamed several times and tried to fight him. He struck her pretty hard. As he was fleeing, her father met him in the corridor and tried to catch him, but he escaped down the stairs. Mr Thorwood went into Rebecca's bedroom and found her hysterical, bruised, and with minor cuts where the chain of the pendant had torn her skin. She was terribly distressed, I . . . I don't know what else he may have done to her . . .'

Daniel could imagine it. It must have been terrible, unforgettable. 'But how could I help?' he asked in some confusion.

'Tobias Thorwood recognised the man, because it was

9

someone he knew,' Patrick replied. He was standing rigid now; this much was obvious even in the darkness.

'So, you arrested him? Or the police did?'

'No. We couldn't, because he was a British diplomat. Philip Sidney. He fled to the British Embassy, and we couldn't get in there. It's legally British territory.'

'Oh . . .'

'And he's pleaded diplomatic immunity, now he's back here in London.' Patrick's voice trembled with anger.

Daniel could understand perfectly. In fact, he felt the same emotions himself. It was an appalling thing to do, and outrageous. He knew all the arguments for diplomatic immunity and the protection of countless diplomats abroad, but it was certainly not meant as an escape from punishment for offences like this. He was embarrassed for his country, humiliated that such a thing should be told to him by his own brother-in-law, and he had no defence for it whatever. 'I'm sorry,' was all he could think to say.

'Of course,' Patrick said quietly. 'I knew you would be, but I want to do something about it. I'm not sure how. But if he could be charged with anything, and come to trial, all sorts of questions could be raised. Why did such a man have this post in Washington? Why, if he is innocent of the assault of Rebecca Thorwood, did he leave without any preparation, such as ending the rent of his apartment? He took only his clothes, eluding the police to leave the embassy at night and collect his things from his apartment. Then he went to New York, and straight on to the next ship leaving for Southampton. That looks like running away, doesn't it? Why?' Patrick's voice in the near darkness was tense with emotion. 'Surely the accusation of assault and theft would have to arise if he were in court for any offence committed in England? We've

10

just got to get him to trial.' He did not ask Daniel outright to help, but it was threaded through his words.

Daniel thought about it. He could understand Patrick's sense of outrage. He would have felt it if an American had committed such a disgusting act in London, and then fled home, pleading diplomatic immunity. 'Tried for what?' he asked slowly. 'He's been in America for the last few years, hasn't he?'

'Yes, but the British Embassy anywhere is British territory,' Patrick said, 'as is any country's embassy. If he had done something there . . .' He stopped, looking at Daniel intensely.

'I suppose it would . . .' Daniel wanted to be cautious. This was far outside his experience, and yet he felt the same anger, pity and outrage at the injustice that Patrick did.

'Will you help?' Patrick asked. 'If there is something you can do?'

'Yes – yes, of course I will.'

Patrick turned towards the light from the drawing-room windows and Daniel could see his face was lit with a wide, warm smile. He did not need to say anything.

Chapter Two

Daniel left quite late and Jemima noticed how much more relaxed Patrick seemed to be. It was their second night here, and all the old warmth and familiarity had wrapped around her. She saw in the new ease in Patrick that he was beginning to feel it too. She had not realised how much it mattered to her. Had she been aware of his nervousness at her bringing him to meet the one member that had not gone to New York for the wedding? It was not Daniel's choice, of course: he could not miss his exams. But it still left him a stranger to Patrick, apart from Jemima's frequent references to him.

Now they were upstairs with the bedroom door closed, and the rest of the house was quiet. Jemima had checked on Cassie, and watched her for a few moments, sound asleep, her doll in her arms. Sophie, too, was quietly sleeping. She was such a good baby.

Then Jemima changed into her nightgown, ready for bed, her hair loose around her shoulders. Patrick was standing in front of the closed curtains. She had been worried about him. She had not known when she first went to New York that there was a certain amount of prejudice there against the Irish. She had noticed it only slowly: one incident, then another; and small signs, such as a notice in a boarding-house window that Irish and Jews were not welcomed in the establishment. Prejudice is so much more apparent when it is not your own. It had struck her like a slap across the face that her charming, funny and brave husband was unacceptable to some people because he was of Irish descent. He himself would never deny it. Loyalty to one's own people is only strengthened by other people's attacks. In a way, you are defined by the decision to abandon your heritage, or to double your loyalty when it is attacked. Patrick doubled it. She had wanted him to; she would have been bitterly disillusioned had he not done.

And yet she, too, felt a loyalty, sharply reawakened by returning home to the long-familiar Englishness in the house in which she had grown up. Perhaps she could not have described it in her memory, but it was all so familiar when she saw it again. There were the watercolour paintings of English scenes, her father's books on the shelves, not in order of size, but of subject. And there were her mother's casual, informal arrangements of garden flowers, all sorts together, but to Jemima, it always worked. She was ashamed that it was a young Englishman from the British Embassy in Washington who had attacked Rebecca Thorwood. It felt like a betrayal of all that people like her family held dear.

Jemima clearly remembered Daniel being born. She certainly could remember him at the age Cassie was now. It startled her how protective of him she was. She would never let him know, of course. That would embarrass him, and probably her, too. It would upset the casual ease of their relationship, and the balance of power. He was the man, and felt a certain superiority in that, which she would certainly not grant. She was the elder, though the difference had years ago ceased to matter at all.

'Did you tell Daniel?' she said.

'What?' he replied, not certain what she was asking.

'About Rebecca . . . and the assault on her.'

Patrick came over and climbed on to the comfortable bed. 'Yes, of course. We need as much time as possible to act. We won't be here more than a month. I can't afford to be away for more than that. I've probably taken this year's holiday and next year's as well.' He leaned across and touched her gently. 'I'm sorry, sweetheart, but this really matters. Have you seen Rebecca lately?'

'Yes . . .' Jemima answered quickly. Anyone who had seen Rebecca at all must have noticed the difference in her. She was now pale, intensely nervous, speaking softly, and only if she was directly addressed. Jemima knew that she slept little and ate without appetite or pleasure. 'I know,' she added, 'she must feel as if nobody cares, except her own family. What did Daniel say?'

'He'll help.' Patrick smiled, and there was amusement in it as well as pleasure. 'He's pretty decent, your brother. A newly minted lawyer, for sure. And careful! Very English!'

'Of course, he's English!' Possibly Patrick thought both her father and her brother very Establishment figures but Jemima knew all about the unconventional background of Sir Thomas Pitt, head of Special Branch.

Her father was so familiar to her, she had found him comfortable as far back as her memory stretched, but then he had been a very ordinary policeman. A tall, gentle man, with untamed hair, which was always too long, and clothes that were always untidy, their collars crooked and the pockets full of things he might need one day: pencils, packets of peppermint bull's-eyes, scraps of paper, small balls of string! And a woollen scarf in winter.

Inside, he was the same man as Sir Thomas Pitt, who looked like a gentleman and had always behaved like one. And spoken like one. He was the son of a gamekeeper, but he had been educated alongside the son of the manor house to provide the boy with a spur to success. Instead, it was the gamekeeper's son who had outstripped him.

But Patrick didn't know that. He certainly shouldn't know that Pitt's father had been transported to Australia as a punishment for poaching, a crime of which Pitt had never believed him guilty, but which had been impossible to prove. She did not know how long ago he had stopped trying.

Maybe she would tell Patrick that, but not yet. Loyalty kept her silent. Once in a great while she had seen the sadness in her father's face, and knew that it was from a hurt that never totally went away; successes he would have shared, but his mother, too, had died long before that.

She pushed those thoughts away. 'What are you going to do?' she asked Patrick.

He looked at her enquiringly.

'About Philip Sidney? What an honourable name! He doesn't deserve it,' she answered with sudden heat.

He looked totally confused.

'There was another Philip Sidney,' she explained. '*Sir* Philip Sidney, and he was one of my heroes. About the time of Queen Elizabeth, I think. There was a situation where a lot of people were dying, after a battle. They were very short of water. Someone came to him and offered him a flask. He was dying and he said to take it to another man near him who might live.'

Patrick was watching her; the tenderness in his face startled her. She turned away, tears in her eyes, but she reached out a hand to him and he held it too tightly for her to take it back. Not that she wanted to, and it was very comfortable not to be able to.

'You're right,' he said. 'The name is far too good for him. I resent his having it. And soiling it. I'm sorry I have to expose it, but I do.'

'I know. But how?'

'I'll find a way. The Thorwoods are over here, you know?'

She stared at him. 'You didn't tell them there was any hope . . .? How could you? They'll expect something, and there isn't anything more that . . . is there?'

'Don't you ever finish a sentence?' he asked.

'Don't change the subject! What did you tell them?'

'I didn't tell them anything,' Patrick replied. They both knew the Thorwood family quite well, in spite of the vast difference in wealth and social station between them. Patrick had had occasion to help Tobias Thorwood professionally on several occasions. Jemima had met Rebecca at an exhibition of British portraiture at the British Embassy. She had seen Rebecca alone in front of a portrait of Anne Boleyn, looking puzzled. Jemima had spoken to her, offering an historical explanation of Henry VIII and his six wives, and then his three children, who had inherited his crown, one by one, lastly the brilliant and long-lived Elizabeth.

They had toured the rest of the exhibition together and become friends from then.

'The Thorwoods being here has got nothing to do with me, or Philip Sidney.'

'What then?'

'Aunt May Trelawny.'

'Aunt May . . .'

'Trelawny,' Patrick repeated. 'She was Rebecca's godmother. She lived somewhere in the Channel Islands and died recently.'

'Not Cornwall?' Jemima said. 'Trelawny – it's a Cornish name. Why is Rebecca here now when you are pursuing Sidney?' Jemima was suspicious, and she knew she sounded it.

Patrick's smile was definitely twisted. 'I suppose it could be Cornwall. And Rebecca is here in her role as heir.'

'I'm sorry. That's very sad,' Jemima replied. 'Whatever the estate is, if Rebecca cared for her godmother, I'm sure she would rather have her alive. It's another blow. Poor Rebecca.'

'I know where they're staying in London. You could go and see her – as long as you don't say anything about Sidney, of course. I hope he won't dare show his face.'

'Hardly! London's a very big city. It's difficult enough to find anyone if you want to, never mind if you don't. Except if you know where they live, or what parties they go to, or clubs and things.'

'I shouldn't think Rebecca would be going to any parties. But it's important they be here. If I manage to find something to charge Sidney with, and get him tried . . .'

'Patrick,' she said gently, trying not to sound as frightened as she felt. 'Are you sure this is right?'

'Right?' he said with surprise. 'Do you think it's right that Sidney get away with it, Jem? He broke into Rebecca's home, entered her bedroom in the middle of the night! He assaulted Rebecca in her own bed! Ripped her nightclothes and tore the pendant off her neck, the one that her aunt May left her, a diamond, although that's not the value of it to her. It's because it was Aunt May's. He stole it right from around her neck and she still has the scar. Heaven knows what else

17

he would have done, if she hadn't screamed. He ran, and Tobias Thorwood saw him. There's no doubt who it was. Tobias saw him quite clearly.'

'I know! That's not what I meant.' She tried very hard to keep her voice level, but she was deeply distressed for Rebecca. She could hardly even imagine how Rebecca had felt, and was still feeling – the nightmares she must still have. Jemima had never for a moment forgotten how kind Rebecca had been when she was new in Washington. She had been a stranger to America, only just beginning to find her way in New York when Patrick was offered a promotion and the corresponding raise in salary if he moved to Washington. Jemima was proud of him, and certainly pleased for him to get a raise in money. She was not used to managing on relatively little. She had tried desperately hard not to let him know that, but the financial struggle was never very far from her mind.

But the change had been a difficult one, especially with a small and very demanding baby. It was Rebecca Thorwood who, ever since the meeting at the exhibition, had been the friend who was never too busy to help, too impatient to listen, or too full of judgement to be gentle with Jemima's tears or forgetfulness, or the occasional bout of longing for the familiarities of home.

Now Jemima wanted not only what was just, but what would give Rebecca the chance of healing, whether that involved punishment for Philip Sidney or not.

Patrick was waiting, and not with a lot of patience. 'What did you mean?'

She shut her eyes so as not to see his face and be distracted. She was still very much in love, even though she knew him better and better every day. She knew his quirks; she did not see them as faults. There was still something magical in seeing him come home every evening, and hearing his laugh, waking up beside him in the morning.

She chose her words carefully. 'Are you sure that exposing what happened is really best for Rebecca, I mean in court? If you accuse somebody and take them to trial, they have the right to a defence. The only other person who knows what this was is Rebecca . . .'

'So?'

'So . . . what is he going to say? She did know him, Patrick!'

'Are you suggesting that she let him in?' His voice was incredulous.

'No! I'm not suggesting it, but his defence might. He isn't going to fold up and keep a gentlemanly silence! Not if he's the kind of man who'd break in in the first place. He could say she invited him, and then changed her mind and screamed!'

He raised his eyebrows. 'So, he tore the necklace off her throat and ran? Please, Jem, that's hardly a defence.'

'No, it's an attack in return. But are you willing to take that risk? Or, more to the point, are you sure Rebecca is?'

He looked startled. He started to speak, and then changed his mind, as if realising she was thinking of something they had not touched on yet.

'I know Tobias wants justice for her,' Jemima tried again. 'But at any price? Has he even realised anything of what she feels? I've tried to imagine, but I can't!'

'Wouldn't you want to see Philip Sidney punished if he'd done that to you?' he reasoned.

'I don't know! I might think I did, until it came to telling everybody about it.'

19

'But it wasn't her fault!' he exclaimed indignantly. 'She's utterly and completely innocent in all of it!'

'And helpless, in her nightclothes, and lying in bed—'

'Exactly! How could she possibly be more innocent?'

'Or vulnerable, or helpless, or passive?'

He looked at her sharply. 'What are you saying? That it is somehow her fault? That she should have taken some kind of . . . precaution? Like what? Gone to bed with all her clothes on? You're being unreasonable, Jem.'

'No, I'm not! Or, yes, perhaps I am. I'm trying to put myself in her place and think what I would want,' she explained. 'I'm perfectly sure I wouldn't want to be known as the woman who lay passively while a man broke into her room and tore her clothes and ripped off her necklace and have to sit there while other people's imaginations go . . . everywhere. I don't want to be thought of as a victim!' She felt her frustration with him rising, crossing over into anger. 'I'd hate it! Even if people weren't thinking that, wondering if I was telling the truth, or if perhaps I'd let him in.'

'She didn't! That's ridiculous!'

'And people's imaginations are never ridiculous?' she said with amazement. 'We think nobody knows what we're imagining, that it's private.'

'It is!'

'Oh, please! It's written on your face half the time. And it slips out in little remarks you think nobody understands, when there are only men present.'

'You've never been there where there were only men present.'

'I've been there when there are only women present!' She saw the smile melt away, to be replaced by perception, and then clear self-mockery. 'And so has Rebecca,' she finished.

20

He remained silent.

'I know Tobias thinks she'll feel better if Sidney is punished, and he may be right. But what if he isn't? He can't take it back.'

'Don't you think he will be right?'

'I don't know! But if it all comes out in trial, Sidney's going to want to deny it.'

'He can't. Tobias saw him there. Tobias is a very important man. Everybody respects him.'

'In Washington. Over here, they respect Sidney.'

'They won't when they learn what he did!' Patrick said with contempt.

'Patrick . . . my darling . . . people in London are exactly the same as everywhere else: they believe what they want to.'

'So, you shouldn't accuse important people, because people would rather believe them than you? No wonder they get away with it and know they will. That's probably why they do it in the best places, and will go on doing it!'

She saw the disgust in his eyes and it hurt. She knew the prejudice he had experienced. At least, she knew a tiny bit of it. Her name was now Flannery – obviously Irish – and she had been turned away from one or two places. It had confused her at first, then given her a curious sense of pride in being Patrick's wife and belonging to his family, his clan, even if by marriage rather than birth. Finally, the fury had come that anyone should be treated that way. Maybe Cassie and Sophie would have it one day; then Jemima would tear the offenders to bits.

She knew Patrick felt it with a mixture of pride and pain. And he had watched her to see if she would take it or crumble.

Her father was a gamekeeper's son, convicted of a petty

theft – had he felt that sting of humiliation, too? Had there been anyone to protect him? Yes, there had been his mother, and then, later, Jemima's mother, Charlotte. Woe betide anyone who had hurt Thomas then! She put up her hand and touched Patrick's cheek, very gently. 'If it was me in that position, I hope I would try to make the decision imagining I knew the price and what it might do, whether he pays it or not. I don't know whether she's thought it out.'

'But you do believe her?' he insisted. 'You don't think she let him in?'

'No, of course I don't. But I know she knew him, and really quite liked him. That's why it hurts so much.'

Patrick bent forward and kissed her.

At least temporarily she forgot about Rebecca, even though she knew that had been his intention. She would start worrying about whether anything would come of the issue tomorrow.

Chapter Three

The next morning Daniel went up the steps and walked into the office of fford Croft and Gibson with a sense of urgency. He had not slept well after the evening at home, seeing Jemima again and finding all the old familiarity little changed. Under the new wife and mother, and all the responsibility that that brought, the old Jemima was still there, just lightly covered: the sense of laughter and the ridiculous, of adventure, the curiosity that he knew so well.

But this morning, the weight of Patrick's story about Sidney's crime lay heavily upon him. The revolting nature of it was bad enough, but the injustice of his escape by claiming diplomatic immunity was worse. It was cowardly, deeply offensive, but legal. There were reasons for this immunity to exist. Diplomats in foreign countries were highly vulnerable. They could be blamed for offences of which they were innocent, but easily convicted; in a sense, held to ransom. It was up to them to behave in such a manner that they were above suspicion. No country could afford to have its diplomats blacken their reputation; that there should be deceit, corruption, petty crimes or unpaid bills, let alone something intimately violent and offensive as this.

Not only did Rebecca Thorwood deserve better, Daniel wanted Philip Sidney punished for embarrassing and disgracing Britain, and all other diplomats who represented it, in America or anywhere else. It scorched him, and he longed either to find a way to disprove it or, on the other hand – and regrettably far more likely – to see Sidney punished, even if it had to be accomplished obliquely.

'Morning, Impney,' he said to the chief clerk.

'Good morning, sir,' Impney replied with a deferential nod. 'Mr fford Croft is not in yet. Would you like a pot of tea, sir? I can have it ready in five minutes.'

Daniel thought for only a second. 'No, thank you, Impney. Is Mr Kitteridge in?'

'Yes, sir. If I might say so, there is no one with him yet. He has about half an hour before his first appointment.'

Daniel gave him a warm smile. 'Thank you, Impney, you are a jewel.'

'Thank you, sir,' Impney replied gravely, but his eyes were bright.

Daniel went straight to Kitteridge's office and knocked on the door. He put his hand on the knob and then hesitated. It would be a bad start to asking his advice if he walked in without waiting for an answer. He knocked again.

'Bring it in, Impney!' Kitteridge said from inside.

Daniel opened the door and went in, closing it behind him. 'Good morning.'

Kitteridge looked up from his desk, faintly surprised. The senior barrister was a few years older than Daniel, comfortably into his thirties. He had an odd face: not handsome, but lit by a very obvious intelligence. His hair was well cut, but still unruly, as if it did not quite fit his head. It was when he stood that one could see his unusual height. He was even taller than Daniel, who was over six foot, but in contrast to Daniel, Kitteridge had no grace at all. He seemed to be all elbows and knees.

'Pitt! Sorry. I was expecting Impney with the mail. What is it? You look full of . . . what?'

Daniel walked over to the chair on the other side of Kitteridge's desk and sat down. 'I've got something of a dilemma.'

Kitteridge gave a twisted little smile, but it was out of amusement rather than any sort of condescension. That misunderstanding Daniel no longer had, not since the Graves case. 'So, you want to share it with me?' Kitteridge asked.

A few months ago, Daniel would have been put off by that remark, but he had seen another side of Kitteridge, or perhaps glimpsed would be a better word. It was there, and then gone again, self-protective. 'Yes,' he agreed. Then he took it a little more respectfully. He considered Kitteridge a friend, but definitely a senior friend in the law, and in the company, at least for now. 'I need your advice,' he began.

'Legally?'

'And morally. I think I know what the answer is, morally,' Daniel replied.

There was a flicker of humour across Kitteridge's face. 'Which means the exact opposite. You are *sure* you know the answer morally. You don't know how to accomplish it legally.'

Daniel took a deep breath. 'Yes, exactly,' he admitted. He decided to go on before Kitteridge interrupted. He wanted to engage Kitteridge's sense of outrage before coming to legal difficulties. 'A British diplomat in Washington is accused of breaking into the bedroom of the daughter of a distinguished

25

family. He assaulted her physically, tore her nightclothes, stole a valuable necklace, with a diamond in it, off her neck, and then escaped, but not before her father came to her screams. He saw the intruder and recognised him; they had met socially.'

Kitteridge was looking far more interested now, but he did not interrupt.

'The intruder's name is Philip Sidney and he ran—'

'Sidney?' Kitteridge said in surprise. 'You mean that? Philip Sidney?'

'Yes. You know him?'

'Not personally. Hardly my social sphere.' There was rich amusement in Kitteridge's face, but also a noticeable trace of regret.

'You think well of him?' Daniel leaped to the conclusion.

'I did,' Kitteridge admitted. 'If this is true, that rather shatters it. Pity.'

'Tobias Thorwood, the father, swears the intruder was Sidney, and his daughter, Rebecca, bears it out, shaken as she was. He really knocked her about a bit, and ripped the necklace off her violently enough to tear her skin. He escaped back to the British Embassy and immediately claimed diplomatic immunity. Then he left the country.'

'Horrible,' Kitteridge agreed, pulling his face tight with distaste and unmistakable sadness. The disillusion clearly hurt him.

'I'm sorry . . .'

'So, what do you want to know?' Kitteridge said, suddenly more sharply. 'What is there to say? He took diplomatic immunity and escaped. He was not charged, therefore not found guilty. You would be betraying him if you said anything, and you couldn't possibly prove it, especially over here. Sorry, Pitt, but if he did it, he's got away. To his shame and I suppose our embarrassment.'

'What if he committed a crime on British soil, and was charged with it?' Daniel asked.

Kitteridge's eyes narrowed. 'You mean after he arrived back here? How long ago did all this happen? He must be crazy!'

'No, not here, but technically on British soil, like at the embassy in Washington.'

'Is that very likely?' Kitteridge clearly did not believe it.

Actually, neither did Daniel. 'I know. But if he did?' he pressed.

'Connected to the assault and the theft of the diamond? Does he have the diamond? Has he tried to sell it? That would be pretty convenient.'

'No,' Daniel admitted. 'I know he took it, but I don't think anyone knows what he did with it.'

'You know he took it?' Kitteridge said with a lift of his eyebrows. 'You mean *you* know, or that Mr Thorwood told you?'

Daniel winced. 'My brother-in-law told me that Tobias Thorwood told him that Sidney took it.'

Kitteridge blinked. 'Your brother-in-law?' His eyes narrowed. 'Daniel, what else have you left out? What exactly is this all about?'

Daniel realised how incoherent he had been, trying to draw Kitteridge in before telling him the more doubtful parts of the story. It had been instinctive rather than deliberate. Now he realised it and was annoyed with himself for being so clumsy. 'Sorry,' he said seriously, principally sorry to have done this so badly. 'Patrick and Jemima are visiting from Washington. He's police out there. Irish-American.'

27

'Ah, I begin to see,' Kitteridge said, shaking his head. 'And he is outraged!'

'Aren't you?' Daniel challenged him.

'If it's true, yes. And embarrassed.'

'Don't we have to do something about it?' Daniel asked.

'No, I don't think so. I don't think there is anything you can do,' Kitteridge said with genuine regret. 'I'd like to think the diplomatic service would get rid of him, and make sure that it becomes well known as to why.'

'Yes, so would I,' Daniel agreed fervently. 'But Tobias Thorwood can't accuse him without any proof, not publicly. It has to come out in court. Otherwise, no newspaper is going to publish it. Sidney would have him for libel. And who knows what he would say about Rebecca?'

'You have a point,' Kitteridge nodded. 'So, what is left for you to ask me? You seem to have got it all thought out. It's wretched. But you can't bring the man to answer the law here, for a crime that he may or may not have committed in Washington, and for which he sought and got diplomatic immunity. I imagine he's lost not only that job, but any other in the service, or position in society at all.'

'No one will know, except if there was someone who advised him to leave, and I presume now has helped him. But even if someone has offered Sidney help, he may not know what Sidney did. He might even think he's innocent.'

'He might even be innocent, Pitt! No proof, no crime, in law. And from what you've said so far, there is no accusation, except what Tobias Thorwood has said, and if he has any sense, not publicly!'

Daniel had come to ask Kitteridge what he thought of what Patrick had suggested, or at least implied, but now he was undecided about it. Was he in a way betraying something

Patrick had not intended? Suddenly the idea of bringing Sidney to court on some other charge and then confronting him with the theft and assault in Washington looked far-fetched and bizarre.

'Pitt!' Kitteridge said sharply. 'Are you planning something about this? Don't be a quixotic idiot. You don't have anything but what your brother-in-law told you – Patrick, is it? Do you actually know anything at all about it?'

'Jemima does. She knows Rebecca . . .'

Kitteridge sat up straighter. 'Jemima is your sister, I presume?'

'Yes. Sorry if I didn't say so.' Daniel was aware he was presenting this badly, letting emotion get in the way. He had seen clients do it, and he had expected better of himself.

Kitteridge slumped again. 'And you are afraid that Patrick is as quixotic as you are, and he may . . . help . . . the evidence along a bit?'

Daniel was caught. That was exactly what he feared, but he was very loath to admit it to Kitteridge. It would be more or less something admitted to a stranger against his own family. The fact was that he had never met Patrick before, and he had shared many cases, at one level or other, with Kitteridge. They had seen horror and tragedy, evil on many levels, courage, skill and love, felt all the emotions that go with them, but that still did not make this completely all right. 'I think . . .' he started out, then stopped.

Kitteridge's expression conveyed the complicated exactness of his feelings.

'All right!' Daniel admitted. 'Yes. I don't know him. I've known Jemima always, but people change, especially girls, when they fall in love. Whether you believe Patrick or not,

29

there's no question at all that it was a wretched crime, and a cowardly way of getting out of answering for it.'

'It seems he has been—' Kitteridge began.

'Oh, for heaven's sake!' Daniel lost his temper. 'Stop being so . . . so like the vicar's maiden aunt! It was disgusting! In every way. He has terrified Rebecca, confounded her father and distressed her mother. And in case you have overlooked it, he has also shamed and disgraced us – Britain – in front of the Americans. We'll all go down in people's estimation for that.'

Kitteridge looked startled. Then he began to laugh very quietly.

Daniel's voice turned to ice. 'What is so amusing about that?' he said sarcastically.

'You are,' Kitteridge replied. 'If your sister is anything like you, I look forward to meeting her.' Then the light and humour vanished from him. 'Unfortunately, none of that is a legal argument. Which you ought to know as well as I do. For heaven's sake, go and persuade her of it. Didn't her husband, Patrick or whatever his name is, know that? Washington isn't the Wild West. I know it's actually very civilised, for a young country.' Kitteridge still looked grim, in spite of his flippant remarks.

'Of course, it is,' Daniel agreed immediately, 'but the underbelly of any city can be pretty rough. London is as bad as any.'

'Brings some pretty revolting images to mind,' Kitteridge said with distaste. 'But the Thorwood family is hardly the underbelly, nor is the British Embassy.'

'You're trying to evade the point!' Daniel accused.

Kitteridge cast aside all pretence and became utterly serious. 'Are you afraid that Sidney is going to escape punishment for his behaviour, and thus blacken Britain's reputation in Washington, and anywhere else that people know about it?' He drew a deep breath. 'Or is your real fear that your brother-in-law is going to try to get round the law by creating false evidence to bring Sidney to trial here, for a made-up crime, so that you can expose the real one?'

Daniel bit his lip. Kitteridge had read him precisely. 'Yes, I suppose so, but I can't let it go!'

'You mean Patrick can't?' Kitteridge amended.

'Could you?'

'I have to accept the inevitability, but I have no choice,' he replied.

Daniel stood up. He was more hurt than he had expected, disappointed in Kitteridge, because he had grown to like him, but even a little frightened because he needed help in his situation with Patrick and he felt out of his depth. 'Accept it quite easily, it seems,' he said coldly, and went out of the door, almost bumping into Impney carrying a tray of tea.

'Sorry, sir,' Impney said, although it was in no way his fault.

Daniel was ashamed of that. Young men, newly qualified in the law, seemed rather often to think they were superior to Impney, who although a clerk and not a barrister, probably knew far more than most of them, and carried it with more grace.

'It was my fault,' Daniel said quickly. 'I wasn't looking where I was going. Probably because I really think I don't know where I'm going!'

'A difficult case, sir?' Impney enquired sympathetically. 'Would you like to take your tea in the law library, sir? I might be able to point you to something in there that could be of assistance. Mr Kitteridge is very familiar with it, but

31

I have been here even longer.' He gave a slight, knowing smile. He liked Kitteridge, but he was aware of his oddities as well. No doubt, in his quiet way, he was aware of everyone's. He gave the word 'devotion' a whole new meaning.

'I have nowhere else to try, at least not yet,' Daniel replied. 'Yes. Thank you.'

'Yes, sir.'

Ten minutes later, Daniel was sitting in the library, a large comfortable room with walls lined with law books going back at least a century. The silence was peaceful and pleasant. But Daniel felt that the library had nothing else to offer. He was becoming aware of having behaved rather badly or, if not that, at least to no purpose, which amounted to almost the same thing.

The door opened and Kitteridge came in, closing it behind him. He looked even taller than usual, and like a scarecrow, minus the straw.

'Does he expect you to do anything about it?' he asked without preamble. 'Except bail him out if he gets into trouble?'

'What?'

'This brother-in-law of yours,' Kitteridge said impatiently. He sat down in the chair opposite Daniel. 'I've being trying to think of anything . . . any legal way . . . of helping, and I can't. I can't afford you to get into trouble. We've taken long enough training you to be useful – I don't want to lose you now.'

Daniel smiled in spite of himself. 'Graciously put, Kitteridge. You are all charm.'

Kitteridge was quite aware of Daniel's sarcasm. He knew his own awkwardness and hated it.

Daniel was immediately sorry. 'But as you pointed out,

charm doesn't always work.' He watched Kitteridge's face and saw the shadow of pain disappear from his eyes.

'I still haven't any ideas,' Kitteridge replied. 'But I'll work on it.'

Daniel thanked him quite sincerely, if not for any help, at least for the friendship.

That evening, Daniel went to visit Roman Blackwell. He was not at all sure if it was a good idea, but time was pressing, and Patrick would be looking for ways to trap Sidney. Blackwell was something of an adventurer, both inside and outside the law. Just before the Graves affair, a few months ago, Daniel had rescued Blackwell from the gallows by proving him, against all the odds, innocent of a particularly mean-spirited crime. One of Blackwell's greatest virtues was his generous and long-lasting gratitude, and in the Graves affair he had proved it.

The law regarded him as a scoundrel. Daniel saw him as an inventive man with a strong, if individual, morality, but scant regard for the law.

Blackwell was at home and welcomed Daniel into the richly colourful and extremely untidy house he shared with his mother, Mercedes Blackwell, known as Mercy. It was an appropriate abbreviation, as long as you took into account her volatile temper and eccentric sense of right and wrong. She was fierce, sentimental, and outwardly afraid of nothing. Only in her fear for Roman's life had Daniel seen that shell break.

Now he followed Blackwell through the hallway, past the crowded coat stand, the paintings on the wall and the views of corners offered by many mirrors. The sitting room was the same, filled with mementoes of foreign travel and relics from other cultures. The colours were purple and crimson, and extremely comfortable. In August, the fire grate was concealed by an elaborately framed tapestry screen.

Blackwell signalled Daniel to sit down, and then sat in one of the other chairs and put his hands through his wild black hair, making it stand even more on end, and sighed. He was Daniel's side of forty, probably, but only just.

'You have a problem,' he announced. 'It's writ large in your face. Explain it to me, and tell me why you can't solve it yourself, and then why my solutions won't either. Or I'll tell you. If the law could unravel it, you or Kitteridge would do it. And if it were the wrong side of the law, you wouldn't touch it, right?'

'Just about,' Daniel admitted.

'Can Mercy know?' He always referred to his mother by name, rather than relationship.

'Certainly. The crime has already been committed.'

'In the view of whoever you are defending?'

'No, I'm for the prosecution . . .'

Blackwell's eyes opened wide. 'You're what?'

Daniel described the attack on Rebecca Thorwood.

Blackwell's face was highly expressive of his disgust. 'I don't see your problem. The father saw him and recognised him. Is his word not good?'

Daniel then told him about Sidney's use of diplomatic immunity, and his flight to England.

'Repulsive,' Blackwell agreed, 'but perfectly legal. What are you planning to do? See if he's done it before? Reasonable. A man doesn't suddenly start behaving like that.'

Daniel hadn't even thought of that, but Blackwell was perfectly correct. He sat upright with a sudden surge of hope.

Blackwell smiled and rolled his eyes. 'Unimaginative,

34

Daniel,' he said quietly. 'How long was he in America? You want something that happened here. Perhaps that's why he went? Did you think of that? Might have left home for the "colonies" for the age-old reason. Want me to take a look?'

'Yes. Yes, please,' Daniel said immediately. He should have thought of it himself. People don't suddenly behave so abominably. It builds up. There are signs for those who look for them. 'I'll see what his reputation is. Someone will know.'

'Leave it alone,' Blackwell said sharply, leaning still further forward. 'You don't know the right places to go. You'll only get into more trouble.'

'And you do?' Daniel asked sceptically.

Blackwell's face lit with a wide smile. 'No, but Mercy does!'

Daniel thought back to Mercy's help in the Graves case. He had not asked her where the information came from, perhaps because largely he did not want to know. That did not really satisfy his conscience, but it did answer his legal need to be honest in court. Mercy was still a handsome woman, maybe a little short for magnificence, but perhaps not? She had a presence, even without height. Her hair, black but with a dramatic white streak, hung beyond her waist when loose; piled up on her head, it was a veritable shining crown. Her face was bold: high cheekbones and magnificent eyes. But it was her intelligence that held the attention, and the fierceness of her emotions. Her loyalty was absolute, her convictions deep, her humour outrageous. Some people were terrified of her because she did not forget an injury. But then neither did she forget a favour.

'Please ask her to be careful,' Daniel said quickly. 'I don't know how important he is . . .'

35

'Of course,' Blackwell answered him. 'And he may be innocent!'

Daniel did not bother to argue with him. Just at this moment he did not care about Sidney's innocence so much as Patrick's. He liked Patrick, but he cared deeply about Jemima, and he was afraid for her. 'Thank you,' he said quietly.

Chapter Four

Three days went by and Daniel heard nothing from Roman Blackwell. The only time he saw or heard from Patrick was on the third day, when he went to dinner at Keppel Street, arriving a little before seven.

He was greeted in the hall by his mother, holding the hand of Cassie, who stared at him with great interest.

'You remember your uncle Daniel, don't you?' Charlotte asked the little girl.

She hesitated only a moment. 'Yes,' she said solemnly. 'He said his daddy's a policeman, like mine. Are you, too?'

'No. I'm a lawyer,' he replied.

'But what do you do?' she persisted.

'I argue with people . . . in a big room called a court. When people say someone has done something bad, I argue and say that he hasn't!'

She stared at him in amazement, turning into awe. She looked up at Charlotte. 'Grandma, when I grow up, that's what I'm going to do. I love arguing!'

Charlotte smothered her laughter with great difficulty. 'I already know that, sweetheart. Just like your mother, who could argue the leg off an iron pot!'

That had Cassie totally confused. She looked at Daniel. 'Do you argue legs off . . .?' She had forgotten the rest.

'No. That's Grandmama being silly. I argue so they don't punish people, if they haven't done anything wrong. Or sometimes, if they have, they make the punishment less.'

'Like not having any pudding? Or going up to bed early?'

'Pretty much,' he agreed.

'Oh. Would you do that for me?'

'Of course, I would!' He wasn't going to argue that one.

She smiled at him and then became shy, and hid her face in Charlotte's skirt.

'You've acquired another client,' Charlotte told him, holding her laughter in with difficulty. 'You had better come in, or we shall be late for dinner. I'm going to take her up to bed. I think you've sown enough future trouble for one night. Come on, Cassie.'

Jemima came out of the sitting room and saw them. 'I'll take her up, Mama, and check on Sophie. You don't need to. Go and talk to Daniel.'

'You'd better be careful,' Charlotte warned. 'Cassie has just acquired a lawyer!'

'What?'

'She has just acquired a lawyer to argue for her, if she should need it,' Charlotte repeated.

'She is perfectly capable of arguing for herself!' Jemima replied. Then she turned to Daniel. 'I'm sorry, but we are going to need your skills for someone less able. Patrick will tell you . . . after dinner.' She turned away and took Cassie's hand, talking to her all the way up the stairs and round the corner on to the landing.

Daniel stared at Charlotte, trying to gather how much she knew. It was a skill he had attempted all his life, and never really achieved. He had never grown out of the feeling that she knew everything he did, and more. Did she still read him with such ease? Or was it just the comfort of memory?

'Be careful,' she said very quietly. 'Jemima is a little . . . romantic.' He was about to ask her more, but she turned and led the way into the drawing room, where Pitt and Patrick were standing, staring at the last of the sun on the poplar trees, whose leaves were flickering and turning. Pitt and Patrick were talking of the boats that took them past all the historic places, from Westminster Bridge, past the Tower of London, with Traitors' Gate opening on to the water, Execution Dock where pirates had been drowned in olden times, the beautiful Queen Anne architecture of the Greenwich Naval College, and on down south towards the estuary, Gravesend, and ultimately the sea.

They greeted each other and Daniel continued listening to the account of their day. Then Jemima returned. They all went to the dining room and dinner was served.

The conversation about the day out on the river continued. Daniel was interested and amused by Jemima's patriotic pride in the city of her birth, and her showing through her attempts to smother it to be sensitive to Patrick's very clearly mixed emotions. Daniel was pleased to catch his eye more than once and see the amusement in it. After all, Jemima had lived in America for four years, quite a bit of it in Washington, and Daniel profoundly hoped she had kept her comments about the merits of London to herself. She was gentler now than she had been in the past. Was that marriage? Or perhaps it was also living in a new place where she was not well known, and a culture with which she was unfamiliar. She was more discreet now, and definitely not critical. Daniel liked that, but it was still a difference from the Jemima he knew, and was so comfortable with.

Daniel, whose mind had not been far from Philip Sidney and the Thorwoods since Patrick had first told him, realised he was holding his knife and fork so tightly, his knuckles were white. He caught his father's eye, and wondered what he was thinking, even if he knew anything about Philip Sidney, and the assault on Rebecca Thorwood. He held the gaze for several moments, and still did not know. He felt oddly isolated at the table, even though they were his family.

After dinner, Patrick excused himself to take a short walk in the garden. He glanced at Daniel, almost said something, then changed his mind.

There was an awkward moment. Jemima looked at Patrick, then at Daniel.

No one spoke.

Then Jemima seemed to make up her mind. She turned to Charlotte. 'Mama, let me tell you about my house. I so much want you to be able to see it in your mind's eye.' She smiled, as if it were important to her. Then included Pitt almost nervously: 'Papa? Would you be interested?'

Pitt saw her eagerness. 'Of course I would. Before we visit one day.'

Daniel saw Jemima's shoulders relax as she slipped her arm through her father's. Was that really about the house? Or to leave Daniel alone with Patrick? And did Charlotte and Pitt know that, which was why they had agreed so easily?

Patrick opened the French doors and stepped into the evening garden. Daniel went out after him, closing the doors firmly. He caught up with Patrick on the grass. The earth

40

smelled rich from a sudden shower of rain earlier. Above them, a flock of starlings flew up from the hedge next door and scattered into the air.

Patrick watched them, the light in his face showing his pleasure at the beauty of it. Daniel wondered how often Jemima had told him about it, or about the climbing roses, now twelve or fourteen feet over the pergola.

It was a moment before he spoke, and Daniel waited.

'We've done it,' Patrick said simply. His voice was tight, emotional, but it was difficult to tell whether it was entirely triumphant. There was a strong note of anxiety as well.

Daniel noted that he had said 'we' and not 'I'. 'Done it?' he asked.

'The police have arrested Sidney for embezzlement.'

Daniel could see in the half-light that Patrick was staring at him, waiting. 'Embezzlement?' he asked with surprise. 'From whom? He's only been back for a couple of weeks! Embezzlement takes ages.'

'From the British Embassy in Washington,' Patrick replied. 'That's British territory . . .'

'Embezzlement,' Daniel repeated. 'Then he must have been doing that when he was there! And somebody's just discovered it now? A bit . . . convenient, isn't it?'

'Not for Sidney,' Patrick replied wryly. 'But if he was guilty all the time, it's not so surprising if, when you discover one thing, and look at it carefully, it leads to another, and maybe another after that!'

Daniel studied what he could see of Patrick's face in the soft, almost diffused light of the setting sun, which was still well above the horizon and staining the air with colour. Patrick was not elated, but there was hope in his face.

'You believe it?' Daniel asked. 'Really? I know you want

41

to have him tried over here, where he's got no diplomatic immunity, and certainly nowhere to run to – I understand that. Most of me wants it, too . . .'

'Most?'

'Part of me wishes you could find Thorwood was wrong and it wasn't Sidney at all.'

'Then why did he run, instead of staying in Washington and challenging the accusation?'

'Come on! What chance would he have had, in a foreign country, and with a victim like Rebecca? With Tobias Thorwood swearing it was him?'

Patrick stiffened. It was almost indefinable, just an angle of his shoulders. 'Are you saying American law is unjust? Unfair? What . . .?'

This could rapidly descend into a quarrel.

'Would you want to face a French court on such a charge, if a French girl and her father accused you?' Daniel asked quickly.

'I don't know French law,' Patrick began.

'Nor do I,' Daniel agreed. 'But I know French emotions!'

'What's different about them?' Patrick was puzzled, and indignant.

'Nothing! That's the point. We're all stacked a little against foreigners, and for our own. Don't you cheer your own side at an international game? Whether you know the players or not? And for that matter, even if you do, and you don't like them?'

'I don't cheer men who attack women, whoever they are!' Patrick said sharply.

'Of course, you don't. None of us does. We just don't believe, if they are ours, that they are attempted rapists, or thieves or anything else. Which is my point. He might have

42

run because he was scared, or he might even have been told to.'

'By whom? The British Ambassador? Bad advice . . . and unbelievably arrogant.'

'And whoever heard of an arrogant ambassador?' Daniel said sarcastically. 'Especially a British one!'

Patrick gave a slightly jerky laugh, in spite of himself. 'All right. Running doesn't prove him guilty. Don't ask where the evidence came from, but there is evidence on paper. And it's not stolen or forged. Or obtained dishonestly. It is enough to prove him guilty of embezzlement. It's not a fortune, but it's still stealing.' His voice grew more urgent. 'We can make him answer for it. But even if he was found not guilty, or if they couldn't come to a verdict at all, they'd still try him and all sorts of evidence would come out.'

'Not about assaulting Rebecca Thorwood.'

'He took the pendant, for heaven's sake! Apart from it having belonged to Rebecca's godmother, May Trelawny, and so means a great deal to her, it's valuable. It's a theft. In fact, even if it weren't real, it's still a miserable, violent, mean-hearted crime. Would you want to have anything to do with a man who would do such a thing?'

'No,' Daniel said without hesitation. 'Look, I'm not saying any of it is excusable. If he's guilty, he's a complete rotter! But he can be tried only for the embezzlement. How much was it for, by the way?'

'I don't know. I don't think they've got to the bottom of it yet. It could have been going on for years.'

'It can't have been going on any longer than Sidney's been there, or it can't be him.'

'If we can just get him into court, we can expose him!' Patrick insisted. 'That's all we need!'

43

'We?'

Patrick was losing patience. 'Yes, *we*. I thought you were in on it, too, but it's definitely Tobias Thorwood, and it's me!'

'Rebecca?'

'She will be, when she realises she can win.' There was certainty in Patrick's voice.

'She can also lose,' Daniel pointed out.

'Are you always this passionate for justice?' Patrick said with more than a touch of sarcasm. 'I thought Jem was argumentative, but you take the prize.'

Perhaps that was a compliment. 'Does *she* think this is a good idea?' he asked.

'Sometimes she does, and sometimes she doesn't.'

'Then she takes the prize,' Daniel said, deliberately laughing. 'She can argue even with herself.'

Reluctantly, Patrick smiled as well, then instantly he was serious again. 'Daniel, will you take the case? You know the law, but you know justice, too. Jem says you're good. More to the point, so does your father.'

Daniel was horrified. 'You discussed this with him?' The thought appalled him. He loved and admired his father, but there was a part of Pitt that was different and always would be, a self-control he had tried to instil in Daniel, not often successfully. Daniel wore his heart very much on his sleeve and he wasn't too sure his father would understand why he had allowed himself even to think this might be a case he could take up and pursue to any satisfactory conclusion.

'No! No, of course not. He'd have to defend Sidney. He's part of . . .'

'The government?' Daniel finished for him. 'And you think the government always agree with each other? I knew the

American government was different from ours, but I didn't know it was that different! It takes half an hour for them to agree on what day it is, according to him! And diplomats are the worst. By the time they've finished being polite, you've forgotten what you were talking about in the first place.'

Patrick was smiling. 'Well, I haven't forgotten what I'm talking about, and you must have forgotten that I'm Irish if you think I can't talk around in circles with the best of them. Those diplomats might have learned it, but it's in my blood! Are you going to help or not?'

'Very circular,' Daniel said drily, to give himself time to think. Before committing to a promise he would have to keep, he needed to be certain what he could do, and what he believed. 'Do you want me to help prosecute?'

'Yes. To be certain they don't wrap it up before the whole story is told. You might learn why he stole the diamond. Perhaps he needed it to sell to replace the money he embezzled. Of course, he wouldn't say so, but it might be provable.'

'Have they found the diamond?' Daniel did not have to feign surprise, he was astounded. 'Anyone could prosecute that! You could tell them what you suspected, even if they did not ask you.'

'No,' Patrick said flatly. 'He's probably sold it already.'

'"Probably" isn't going to cut it with anyone.'

'I know! That's why we need a clever prosecutor, and one who knows about the attack on Rebecca and the theft,' Patrick said reasonably.

Daniel opened his mouth to say 'has heard about it', but knew from the look on Patrick's face that this was not the time. Had Pitt really told Patrick that Daniel was a good lawyer? Did he really think so, or was he just standing up for Daniel a bit? 'It's an important case, because of the people involved,' he said instead. 'And because it's international, if it ever gets the assault of Rebecca into it. The Embassy will want it handled very carefully, even settled out of court, if possible.'

'Can they?' Patrick's voice was bitter now. 'If it's embezzlement? What will they do? Sweep it under the carpet so no one knows? Get his father, or whoever, to put the money back, and perhaps a little extra?'

Daniel felt all the muscles tighten in his jaw so hard he heard his teeth grind. 'Why, is that what they do in America?'

Patrick's shoulder muscles bunched and he shifted his weight, then relaxed. 'Sorry,' he said.

Daniel was not sure if he meant he was sorry for the offence, or only that he had said it aloud, because it was bad judgement. 'No,' he said. 'It isn't how they do it here. At least not very often. If they're caught, they'll go down for it.'

Patrick was silent for a few moments, then apparently decided to behave graciously. 'I thought you were pretty good. I trusted you couldn't be bought.'

'I am pretty good,' Daniel said tartly. 'They'll want very good. And no, I cannot be bought. But then I hope I can't be threatened or persuaded, either. But before you lose your temper again, I can't act for the prosecution because I'm not senior enough, or for the defence either—'

'Defence?' Patrick interrupted.

'There's got to be a defence. You don't want him to plead guilty or there'd be no trial! Or nothing at all will come out!' Daniel reasoned.

'Yes. Yes, I can see that. Defend him of the charge of embezzlement but work towards exposing the assault and the theft. You'd have to be damned good to bring that about.'

'My senior colleague Kitteridge is. He'll let me sit second chair, I think. I already told him something of the case.' Daniel was not sure if he should have mentioned that, but it was past the time of playing games. The big question, though, was whether Kitteridge would have anything to do with so dubious an idea as to defend a man on one charge in order to have him tried for another.

'Good!' Patrick decided immediately. 'How do I get in touch with this Kitteridge? And even more to the point, how do we get Sidney to choose him for the defence? That could be a flaw in your idea, rather a big one.'

'fford Croft and Gibson is one of the best firms in London,' Daniel said with some pride. 'If Kitteridge offers, Sidney will take him if he has any sense. We're not only good, we're discreet. I don't think people will be lining up to defend Sidney in this.'

'Is Kitteridge really that good?'

'Yes, and I'll help him.'

'Thank you. And . . . Daniel?'

'Yes?'

'The Thorwoods are our friends, Jem's and mine. Particularly Rebecca. They are . . . they've been good to us. They had a son who would have been about my age. Lost him in an accident. It's got nothing to do with guilt or innocence, but it's got a lot to do with friendship, with debt, if you like.'

'I understand,' Daniel said quietly, understanding loyalty while a small part of his mind wondered if Patrick wasn't taking his loyalty to the Thorwoods a little too far. 'Just that it's absolutely straight, understand? I don't want to be wondering how far I can trust the evidence. If he's guilty, we'll get him. It's not as if we were looking for someone and

47

didn't know who it was, or what he did, and how.' As soon as he said it, he wondered if he had gone too far. Not in provoking Patrick – that was fair enough – but in making a promise he might not be able to keep.

'Of course!' Patrick said more gently. 'Apart from the fact that I would not put you in any danger, if it couldn't be within the law, it wouldn't stick. He'd appeal against it, and win. We'd lose more than the case. I wouldn't do that to you, or to myself.'

Daniel was glad it was nearly dark now. The sun had sunk into the scarlet bank of cloud on the horizon and the garden was rapidly filling with shadows. He was not certain that Patrick had not lost sight of the smaller wrong in his fury at the greater one. 'Let's go inside,' he suggested. 'It's going to get cold soon.'

The next morning, before going in to fford Croft and Gibson, Daniel went to see Roman Blackwell. He was a man who enjoyed his food, and for him breakfast was the prince of meals. Daniel found him still at home, at the kitchen table, surrounded by the smells of kippers broiling, fresh toast, and the fragrance of newly brewed tea, which was more delicate, but still pervasive. It was a maid who had opened the door.

Blackwell waved a hand towards the other chair. 'Kipper?' he offered. And before Daniel could answer, he raised his voice. 'Mercy! Any more kippers?'

She appeared out of the larder doorway. 'Don't shout! I can hear you perfectly well. I knew it had to be Daniel at this hour. Good morning, Daniel. A kipper?' she offered. 'It says on the label they're Craster, but that's as maybe.'

Craster kippers, from the coast of Northumberland, were considered the best, and Daniel knew it. They were probably

48

also the most expensive. They would have been sent down to London on the night train, and Mercy would have gone out very early indeed to get them before they sold out.

'I've already had breakfast,' he replied. 'But thank you.' And then he paused, indicating discreetly that perhaps he would be persuaded.

'Then I'll cook this one for you. You'll need it, for what he's going to tell you.' She gestured towards Roman.

Daniel turned, waiting with a sense of chill for what Blackwell would say. Was Patrick's information false, and Blackwell knew it already?

Blackwell looked at the stove, with the kipper simmering on it. 'I looked for your fellow, Philip Sidney,' he said. 'For heaven's sake, sit down! Your kipper will take a while to cook. Have some toast. And marmalade. Or blackcurrant jam. Mercy made it.'

Daniel forced himself to accept, if only for the sake of good manners. If it was homemade, he would eat it. 'What about Sidney?' he asked. 'I found out only yesterday evening that he's been arrested for embezzlement.'

'Ah.' Blackwell let out his breath slowly. 'I have heard that, too. And learned quite a bit more as well. Philip Sidney – born twenty-nine years ago. Father Wallace Sidney. Got a bit of money, nothing special. Self-righteous man. Not very pleasant. Best thing he did was die young. Left a widow and one son, Philip. So named by his mother, a gentle creature, idealistic. Lover of history, and named her son after the Elizabethan hero Sir Philip Sidney. You probably know about him?' Blackwell eyed him curiously.

'Yes,' Daniel agreed. 'Presumably she told him all the stories?'

'Yes. She had great dreams for him.' Blackwell's face was

49

twisted with pity, and resentment from having to tell Daniel something he would clearly very much rather not know. 'She married again. Case of necessity, really. The new husband was a miserable beggar. Not literally, of course. Rather well-to-do. No style or grace, though; considerable sacrifice on her part, I should think. But he educated the boy well, along with his own sons. Young Philip came off second-best in most things, it would appear, except cards. Very good at that. Could thrash them at that. He was a damn sight better-looking than his stepbrothers, and cleverer. Forced to hide his light under a bushel, so to speak, for the sake of his mother's survival. Caught in a cleft stick! Justify her faith in him, and outshine his stepbrothers, and lose the stepfather's goodwill! Or dim his light a bit and stay in the family fold.'

'I see . . .' Daniel said quietly.

'No, you don't!' Blackwell contradicted him immediately. 'You've never had to protect your mother from anything. I've met her. Formidable lady. You can only imagine what it would be like to have to hide your light so your father doesn't humiliate her. And your imagination hasn't been stretched to that – anything like.'

'Does that have any bearing on the case?' Daniel asked.

'Can't see any,' Blackwell admitted. 'Except that Sidney is a good-looking, intelligent man who has had to watch his step pretty much all his life. He had an idealistic mother who was prepared to sacrifice her own happiness to give him the best start she could. Thank God, she's gone now, and whatever happens with this, she won't see it.' His face reflected his emotions completely. 'Stepfather's gone. Good riddance. Sidney doesn't keep up with the stepbrothers. They're not in the diplomatic service. Trade. Money. Something like that. Three of them. Sidney's well liked. Worked particularly with a fellow called Armitage at the British Embassy in Washington. Apparently Armitage speaks well of him. It was he who got Sidney out before the scandal in Washington could reach really high proportions.'

'What about the embezzlement?' Daniel asked. 'Sidney must have had limited means. Don't suppose his stepfather was generous to him?'

'No, he wasn't. Mean as dirt. Nor to the stepbrothers either, as far as I can tell. But Sidney's used to living within moderate means, and I found no trace of debt to anyone. Still good at the cards, drinks only in moderation. I'll look further. How much longer have we got before the embezzlement trial?'

'I don't know,' Daniel admitted. 'But very little time, I think. The Thorwoods are in Britain settling up the aunt's estate, but that won't take long. I dare say they'll push with all their diplomatic power to get it heard soon. And I believe they have both money and reputation.'

'And this brother-in-law of yours?'

'Four weeks altogether, unless there's a reason why the Washington police will let him stay longer . . .'

The kippers were ready, but Daniel found that he had lost his taste for them. He did not want any part of this case, either to prosecute Sidney or to defend him. It was painful to see the pattern of someone's life and the collapse of it, whoever's fault it was. Sometimes it was a fight for justice. Sometimes it was just a plain tragedy. This looked like being the latter. But he couldn't let Patrick down now – or, more truthfully, Jemima, who would take Patrick's side in everything, and who was a friend of Rebecca's.

'Thank you,' he said for the kipper, wondering how he would be able to eat it.

Chapter Five

Asking Kitteridge to defend Philip Sidney of embezzlement was one of the most difficult things Daniel had to do. But he had promised Patrick that he would, so there was no alternative.

Anyway, if Daniel avoided doing it then Patrick would probably ask Kitteridge himself, which would make matters worse in every way, and whether Sidney was guilty or innocent, to step aside was no answer at all. All that proved was that Daniel had the choice between an awkward situation and possibly coming out on the wrong side, and being a coward and running away from it altogether. Rather than being disliked by some, he would be despised by all, and that 'all' would include himself.

He knocked on Kitteridge's door. It was answered so he went in and closed it quietly behind him.

Kitteridge looked up from his desk. 'What happened?' he asked, looking at Daniel's expression with misgiving.

Daniel sat down in the visitor's chair. There was no point in trying to be subtle or evasive. 'The police have arrested Sidney for embezzlement while at the British Embassy in Washington. He's being charged, and Patrick asked me to appear for his defence. Which is pointless. I'm not competent to . . . yet . . . and Sidney would know it. He'll get somebody of his own, if he hasn't already, and we will lose control of matters altogether.'

Kitteridge's eyebrows rose. 'We have control of something in this wretched affair? I must have missed that bit.'

'No, but we can have.' Daniel was aware of making assumptions, but they would be implicit whether he spoke them or not. 'If we defend him, we have as much control as anyone ever has . . .'

'You have control if you know all the evidence, and it indicates your client's innocence,' Kitteridge said coolly. 'And better yet, someone else's guilt! We don't even know what the evidence is. We've seen none of it, and we have no idea if our client is guilty or not. And we believe he is guilty of a much worse crime, which he is only charged with by word of mouth, of the victim's family, and far from defending him for that, we actually want to expose him for it. A beautiful case, Pitt! Is there anything else you've omitted, that could make it even worse? Oh, yes, I forgot to mention that the accusers are foreigners, due to stay here only a month or so, and half your family is involved – who are also due to be here only for a month or so! And we don't know if our client – and by that, I presume you really mean *my* client – even wants our services. You have exceeded yourself.'

'There is . . . there is something else . . .'

'Rubbish! Even I can't imagine anything else!'

'I asked Roman Blackwell to look into Sidney a bit – background, reputation, et cetera . . .'

Kitteridge shut his eyes. 'What?' he asked with excessive patience. He was used to Daniel's passion for understanding every point of view, however little it seemed to be relevant. He did not pretend to agree, but he knew that it mattered to Daniel. Kitteridge thought it was something he had learned from his father.

'He seems to be an exemplary young man. Honest, likeable, good humour, even quite fun . . .'

'Oh God!' Kitteridge groaned. 'How did we ever get into this . . . this . . . fiasco? I suppose Patrick isn't some kind of practical joker?'

Daniel thought of Patrick's anger, but far more persuasive was Jemima's belief in him. 'No,' he said unhappily.

'You've only just met him!' Kitteridge pointed out.

'But I've known Jemima all my life. Do you think I haven't looked for a way out?'

'No, of course you have. About three days too late! You should have found it the day he mentioned the whole miserable mess. You are not only soft hearted, you are thoroughly soft headed as well. You do realise that if we – if I – take this case – and, please God, Sidney has his people and will refuse us – but if not, I will have no choice but to look very thoroughly into the evidence against him?'

'Of course,' Daniel said stiffly.

'I'll ask you now, are you sure Patrick didn't create it, or help it along?'

Daniel was angry and, above all, afraid. He did not really know Patrick Flannery. All he knew for certain was that Jemima loved him. He was her husband, and her children's father. Would loyalty demand she believe him, whatever the evidence suggested?

'Pitt!' Kitteridge demanded.

'No, of course I don't know. Although I don't see how he could. The information about the embezzlement came from

54

inside the British Embassy in Washington. He has no access to that.'

'Then how did he come by it?'

'He didn't! For heaven's sake, the police arrested Sidney. The London police.'

'Heard about the long arm of the law, but London to Washington is a bit of a stretch, isn't it?' Kitteridge asked, the sarcastic edge to his voice getting even sharper.

'Thorwood!' Daniel said quickly. 'He's the only one who has come to London from Washington. He could have had friends there powerful enough to have had a hand in this.'

'True,' Kitteridge said thoughtfully. 'Would he?'

'I don't know! But the evidence exists, or the London police wouldn't have it.'

'Well, then, I had better make enquiries, I suppose.' Kitteridge stood up. 'I imagine you are going to work on this, too? We'd better ask Marcus for permission. Perhaps I am being mean-spirited and unimaginative, but if Sidney even accepts me, has he any money? Or did you not think to ask such a pedestrian question?'

'I don't know.' Daniel stood as well. 'But if he hasn't enough to pay us, then he hasn't enough to pay anyone else either, so he'd be very grateful to accept us.'

'Pitt, sometimes I think you are a complete ass!'

Daniel had no answer to that. He tried to think of a rationalisation and failed.

'Well, come on!' Kitteridge said, standing in the doorway. 'Ass or not, you can't imagine I'm going to Marcus with this by myself!'

Daniel realised he had been imagining exactly that. His mind was preoccupied with the thought that he needed Kitteridge, not only because he was an extremely good trial barrister, but he was honest, completely so. He had no wish to lie, and no imagination to think of one, or a series of them, on his feet. That had annoyed Daniel, because at times he was tedious. And occasionally Kitteridge missed the truth when it seemed back to front, or absurd. But he also had the ability to accept it, and when it was against him, even when he had to backtrack and eat his own words. That was a quality Daniel admired without reservation. He feared he had yet to acquire it, with any grace. 'No, no, of course not!' he exclaimed.

'That took you a while,' Kitteridge said with a twisted smile. All the same, he gave Daniel time to hesitate.

Three minutes later, they were outside Marcus fford Croft's office door. He was the founder and head of the firm, and his office reflected that. Kitteridge knocked, not giving either of them time to think any longer and lose courage.

It was answered immediately and they were invited in to sit in the client armchairs. Kitteridge obeyed; Daniel remained on his feet. Marcus was of an indeterminate age, somewhere between fifty-eight and seventy. He was portly and not very tall. His hair was white, thick, and at the moment, looked like a haystack in the middle of a good tossing. He wore a velvet waistcoat over his mauve shirt, and a bow tie that might have been straight when he dressed in front of a mirror, but was very much turned in an anti-clockwise direction.

'Well?' he said with interest. 'What have you? Not another will or contested land boundary, I hope. I was so bored with bequests, I could paper the Sahara with them! The case!' he added. 'Speak up, Kitteridge! What have you brought Pitt for? Moral support?'

Kitteridge sat up perfectly straight. 'No, sir. This is his

affair, and he has asked me to take part in it, as . . . as a more experienced trial barrister.'

'Hard to be less,' Marcus said drily. 'Well, are you going to tell me about it? Or did you just come to hold the door for him?'

Daniel could see Kitteridge's muscles tighten all the way up to his scalp as he spoke.

'I will tell you myself, sir, but you may well wish to question him, as to further details.'

'No doubt. Details of what, exactly?'

'Of a case that began in Washington, in America, and has travelled across the Atlantic, for us to clean up.' Kitteridge went on too quickly for Marcus to interrupt, although from the look on his face he had clearly intended to. 'A theft and assault occurred in the home of a distinguished American family. The daughter was robbed in her bedroom, in the middle of the night. The father says he saw and recognised the intruder. It was a young diplomat, Philip Sidney, stationed at the British Embassy in Washington.'

Marcus was clearly fascinated, and furious, but he did not interrupt.

Kitteridge swallowed. After five years in these chambers, he had earned his place, but Marcus still overawed him. Possibly, he always would. Kitteridge was clever, and he worked hard, but he was a scholarship boy, socially awkward and unable to forget it.

Daniel wondered whether to say anything himself. If he did, he would be obviously rescuing Kitteridge. He did not want to acknowledge that that was necessary.

'He invoked diplomatic immunity,' Kitteridge went on after a moment. 'And fled back here.'

'Guilty,' Marcus said in such a tone that Daniel did not know if it was a question or an answer.

'It would all be irrelevant, at least to the law,' Kitteridge continued, 'if he had not now been charged with embezzlement from the embassy while on his tour of duty in America.'

Marcus sat bolt upright. 'And arrested? They're going to try him? Why, for God's sake? Take the money back and keep their mouths shut! Do they want the whole world to know we employ such . . . wastrels . . . to represent us abroad?'

'I'm afraid Tobias Thorwood will not permit that,' Kitteridge went on. 'And more than that, neither will the American policeman who wanted to charge him with robbery and assaulting Miss Thorwood—'

'What? Who did you say? What the devil has he to do with it?'

'He's over here in London, visiting with his English wife's family . . .'

'Kitteridge, is this your idea of an elaborate joke?' He turned to Daniel. 'Pitt! Why are you standing there like a bloody footman?'

'The American policeman concerned is my sister's husband, sir. That is how I come to know about it. Patrick, my brother-in-law, wants to see the robbery and assault come out during the course of the embezzlement trial.'

Marcus looked at him narrowly. 'Are you skirting around what I think you are, Pitt?'

Daniel breathed in deeply. 'Yes, sir.'

'Is he reliable, this brother-in-law of yours? And don't play around with sophistry. I knew more about that than you do, before you were born!'

'Yes, sir, I don't know. I've made a few enquiries about Sidney, and his reputation is excellent . . .'

'From whom? No! Don't answer that! I don't want to know your sources, especially if they are named Blackwell. So, you are sitting between a sharp rock of family loyalty and the very hard place indeed of the truth? You know your sister, but I'm guessing you don't know this brother-in-law of yours all that well. And since he is American, you are not likely to. Have I got that right?' Marcus's white eyebrows rose. 'And may I go so far as to presume you have had the good sense not to bring your father into this? Has your sister as much sense?'

'Yes, sir. And as far as I know, Jemima hasn't spoken to Papa, and I don't think she will.'

'That is the only good thing I can see about this. Why are you doing this? To protect your sister?'

Daniel knew there was no benefit in anything but the truth. More, or less, than that would come back to bite him, probably very hard, even fatally. 'To begin with, I wanted to help Patrick,' he answered. 'And I was furious and ashamed that an Englishman had behaved like that abroad. I wanted to fix it.'

'You put it in the past tense. What now?'

'I wish to hell I didn't know anything about it.'

The flicker of a smile crossed Marcus's face. 'That I believe to be the unvarnished truth, even if it is useless now. What do you propose to do about it?'

'Defend Sidney, if he'll accept us.'

'By *us*, do you mean Kitteridge, with your assistance?'

'Yes, sir.'

'To do what? What possible use is such a dubious case to fford Croft and Gibson? Sidney may be innocent of the embezzlement and it's that case that is being brought to trial.'

'To discover the truth. Either that he did do what

Thorwood accuses him of, or that he didn't. And, of course, defend him of the embezzlement charge, sir.'

'God help us! We're barristers, not crusaders, Pitt. I suppose the best we can hope for is that Sidney won't have you! Slim chance. This is the best firm in London for hopeless cases. You've seen to that with your last foray. Well, don't just stand there! Get on with it then! I imagine you'll be no use for anything else, until you've finished.'

'Yes, sir.'

'You mean no, sir?'

Daniel stared at him.

Suddenly, Marcus beamed. 'Another Gordian knot! You are never a bore, Pitt, I'll say that for you. Now get out!'

'Yes, sir!'

Chapter Six

Jemima enjoyed her days with her family very much. They explored some of the old squares in London, reading the plaques to commemorate once-famous people, both men and women. Charlotte had researched them, and explained who they were to Patrick, and incidentally to anyone else. Sophie went out in a pram Charlotte had borrowed for her granddaughter, while Pitt insisted on carrying Cassie on his shoulders, and she loved the attention paid to her, repeating much of what Charlotte said, but in simpler language. Patrick watched and, with an effort, did not reclaim his daughter. Jemima smiled at him and silently praised him.

They also played simple games that Cassie could join in, and laughed a lot. They prepared lunch that could be packed up as a picnic and took it out on to the lawn.

Patrick spent almost all his time with them. Charlotte was utterly charmed with her grandchildren, and interested in hearing everything about Jemima's life in America. Pitt worked only as hard as his conscience drove him. He had no urgent cases at the moment, and could happily delegate most of what there was to his juniors. Therefore, it was after a late supper, for which Daniel joined them, when they finally went up to bed, that Patrick had the opportunity to speak to Jemima alone.

'I've been waiting for the chance to tell you,' he said, drawing the bedroom curtains across the night sky.

'Tell me what?' she asked. She had not caught any urgency in his voice. She looked at him now, and realised that she had missed a tension in him that might have been there all day. Had she unintentionally paid too much attention to catching up on family he did not know, and ignored him? She was annoyed with herself. She convinced herself that she had no wish to remain in London, but the familiarity of it was easy and comfortable, and there were some good things she had missed. They were trivial: chocolate biscuits, meat pies, the sight of policemen's helmets characteristic only of London. Red postboxes; crossing the road without having to think whether the traffic was travelling from the left or the right.

It was the first time Patrick had been out of America. He must feel as strange as she had done there at first. She had been unmindful of that, and she regretted it now. She smiled at him and gave him her full attention.

'Thank you for being so patient while I catch up on the news of Aunt Emily, and all the other people I talk about, but that you've not met.'

He relaxed a little. 'I guess they're my family too, now. Just like Aunt Bridget is yours!' He smiled widely. 'And Uncle Cormac.'

'Who's Uncle Cormac?' she asked puzzled. Aunt Bridget she could never forget, try as she might.

'A treat in store.' His smile twisted and became rueful. 'But I wanted to tell you today that Sidney has been arrested for embezzlement, from the British Embassy in Washington. That's British soil, technically, and he can be tried here.'

'Embezzlement? Are you sure?'

'Of course, I'm sure!'

'How do you know?'

'You think he wouldn't stoop to such a thing?' There was a definite shadow in his face.

'No, of course not!' She heard a sharpness in her voice that she had not intended, at least not intended it to show. 'I didn't think he'd be so stupid as to do such a thing in the embassy and get caught!'

'Perhaps he meant to tidy it up, so it was invisible, and he didn't have time,' Patrick suggested. 'He left pretty quickly. He had no choice. He didn't expect to get caught, obviously,' he added with a degree of contempt. 'Arrogant bastard. People don't hide things if they really think they'll never have to pay. A lot of them aren't anything like as clever as they think.'

'That's a circular argument,' she said, then immediately wished she hadn't, but it was too late to take it back.

'What does that mean?' he demanded.

'It means that the ones you catch aren't very clever. If they were, you wouldn't have caught them.'

'And the British police would?'

'No one would. Nobody knows about them!'

'Then how is it you do?'

'I don't! You're trying to . . .' She stopped. This was only going to get worse. 'What are you going to do about Sidney?'

'I asked Daniel to defend him.' He ignored her startled look and the beginning of a protest. 'He says he's not experienced enough yet, and I have to accept that, but he said he'd get Kitteridge to, and Kitteridge is very good indeed.'

Jemima drew breath to argue, and say that so was Daniel,

then realised how childish she was being, how very defensive, Patrick was right. It just hurt her that an Englishman, with the same name as one of her childhood heroes, was letting them all down so badly. How simple-minded she was. How territorial. How much she missed belonging! It was so much easier not to have to think about everything, and above all, not to be different.

'Jem?'

'Good.' She forced a smile. 'Will Daniel help to get the result you want? You need someone to do everything they can to bring the assault and the theft of the necklace into it so that Sidney's reputation is ruined, even though he is answering another charge. It won't be easy.'

'Daniel cares,' Patrick answered her. 'He thinks it's as terrible as I do. And you! Don't you?' That was a challenge again.

'Of course, I do! I . . . am just not sure this is going to work the way we want it to.' Suddenly, she was frightened, even chilled, by the thought of all the ways it could go wrong, which could end by hurting Patrick in particular, more than any sense of justice or vengeance would be worth. 'Patrick, above all, I want you to be safe.'

The anger vanished from his face, as if washed away by a tide. 'Jem, I'm not going to do anything wrong, or stupid. I care about you and the girls more than anything else! But I'm no use to you, or even to myself, if I let an injustice go by and don't do all I can within the law to put it right.' He touched her hair gently. 'If that had been you, instead of Rebecca, would you expect me to stand by and do nothing? If it was Cassie or Sophie, I'd want to kill him, and so would you! Don't tell me you wouldn't.'

'I'd want you to do whatever was best for her.' Jemima

was furious to hear her voice waver. She controlled it savagely, swallowing her feelings. 'It isn't always the obvious thing that works out best in the end. You want revenge, but you have to think further than tomorrow, or even next week, or next month.'

'You sound like my mother.'

'I like your mother!'

'So do I, but I don't always agree with her. And this isn't revenge, it's justice, and it's about stopping it from happening again, and maybe it being far worse next time. What if Tobias hadn't heard her scream? What would Sidney have done if he hadn't been prevented? Have you weighed that in?'

She hadn't, but it wasn't the whole argument. 'Maybe nothing.'

'Oh, really, you can do better than that!' he said with disgust.

'You can't condemn a man for what you think he might have been going to do.' She sounded very reasonable, and colder than she meant to. She was not thinking of some future possible victim, she was thinking of Rebecca, and the looks and sniggers she would get. The thinly veiled suggestions. The conversations that suddenly stopped when she appeared. And the young man she might fall in love with who would always wonder if it had been a tryst and she had changed her mind. She would not be the first woman to make a false accusation to end an affair that had been consensual to begin with.

Jemima believed her, but she knew that not everyone would. Rebecca was very charming to look at. She was young, intelligent, fun to be with, and heiress to a great deal of both power and wealth. No matter how good she was, she would never be free of enemies. Didn't Patrick know that? Perhaps not. He didn't belong to a stratum of society that had possessed time and money for such considerations. The devil makes work for idle minds, even more than for idle hands.

'I just think we shouldn't make all the decisions for her, as if she hadn't the wits or the courage to do it herself,' she said at last. 'Now please, don't let us talk about it any more. What are you going to do tomorrow?'

'I know what I'm going to do tonight!' He pulled her a little closer.

'Oh, yes?'

'Oh, yes!'

She went to him, laughing and willingly, suddenly immensely relieved.

Jemima got up deliberately early the next morning, before Patrick awoke and, with any luck, before Cassie and Sophie awoke either. She slipped on a robe, borrowed from her mother, and went quietly down the stairs to find Daniel sitting at the dining-room table. They had stayed up late. He had been easily persuaded to use his old room for the night.

He looked up when she came in, surprised to see her. 'Good morning, going somewhere?'

'No, at least not yet. Is that tea still hot?'

'You want a cup?'

'Please.' She picked up one of the cups and saucers set out at the end of the table and passed them to him to pour.

He had finished the cooked part of his meal and started on toast and marmalade. He poured the milk, and then tea. He did it without asking her. He knew how she liked it, and assumed that had not changed. It had, but she did not mention it.

'Thank you. I came down because I wanted to see you before you went.'

He froze halfway through buttering a slice of toast. 'Oh?'

She smiled. 'Not that bad. Patrick told me about the embezzlement charge against Sidney, and that you and Kitteridge are going to defend him?' It was not really a question, but she made it one.

'Yes . . .' Daniel said cautiously. She saw the apprehension in his face. She could read him so easily. He had no idea how swiftly his emotions reflected in his face, especially his eyes.

'All I want you to do is go and see Sidney as well. I mean, don't let Kitteridge be the only one. You have to be sure of the justice of this case, that you're doing the right thing . . .' She stopped. What she meant was, don't let Patrick's emotions run away with you, but she was not prepared to put it in such blunt words. How could she be sure that he understood?

He looked at her and shook his head. 'Stop it. I'll always be younger than you are, but it gets to mean less and less with every year that goes by. Of course I'll go and see Sidney. I promise.' He took a deep breath. 'Jem, is there something you know that you're not telling me?'

'No!' She looked at him and saw the seriousness in his eyes, in the tense fine lines in his face. To her, he still looked so young. She could see the boy in him without even looking for it, especially at the crown of his head where his hair curled and would not lie flat. 'I'm just not as sure as Patrick is that public disclosure of what happened would be good for Rebecca. I don't know what she wants, but I mean to ask her.'

'Do you know something that I don't?' he said suspiciously.

She burst into laughter. 'Sweetheart! Of course I do! I

know hundreds of things you don't, and probably never will! I'm a woman . . .'

'Yes. I noticed that about twenty years ago,' he said drily. 'It doesn't mean that much!'

'Yes, it does! You tempt me to use language that would curl Mother's hair! Men can order things, people, events. Women have to persuade, understand, even manipulate a bit . . .'

'Never!' he said immediately, stifling his laughter with difficulty. 'Not you, surely? Manipulate? Mother would be appalled!'

She threw the toast at him and hit him, because he ducked the wrong way. Thank heaven he only burst into laughter.

'Very subtle!' he said when he had stopped laughing and wiped the butter off his cheek. 'And manipulative.' He picked up the toast from the floor, where it had landed. 'You're the only person I know who can do that: throw toast and have it land butter-side up.' He said it as if it were an achievement. Then suddenly, he was serious. 'Jem, of course I'm going to look into it seriously, very seriously indeed. I've got some idea of what's at stake. Justice for Philip Sidney, whatever that turns out to be. It is possible he's innocent. Either way, it needs to be proved. And as much justice as possible for Rebecca, but only if she understands what that entails. Legal justice isn't the same as public judgement. I want to make sure she knows that. Sidney has to be tried for the embezzlement now, but it isn't too late to decide not to disclose anything about the assault. But once that becomes public, you can't ever take it back. We have to make sure she understands that. And probably the most important to us – you and me – is that Patrick didn't do something that looks like private vengeance, and using police influence in the courts to exact a price he couldn't get in Washington, where the crime that matters took place. I know all that, and I'll see that he knows it, too. I like to win, but not at my client's expense, and certainly not at my sister's expense.'

Jemima's eyes filled with tears and she was furious with herself. 'I know,' she said huskily. 'I'm sorry. I'm . . . scared.'

He smiled ruefully. 'Good. That means you'll think before you act, except with the toast. Or maybe you're cleverer than I thought? Have I just been thoroughly manipulated?'

She was horrified. 'No! Of course not! How can you—' She stopped because he was genuinely laughing. 'Oh . . .' She looked at him with a little awe, and the realisation that while she was away in America he had grown up so much. She smiled back at him.

Chapter Seven

Later that morning, Jemima left to visit Rebecca. It was an hour when it was acceptable to call on people with whom you were friends, but not close. In such engagements, a certain formality had to be observed. Not if she were to meet with Rebecca, but most certainly with Bernadette and Tobias Thorwood, should they be in.

She chose a dress carefully from among the few she had brought with her. It was soft blues and greens. The colours suited her very well, but more than that, the cut, which was elegant, very fashionable, very flattering, especially to the slender. She found herself walking with grace, and a smile.

As it transpired, Tobias was not in, and Bernadette was preparing to pay a visit to an old friend herself. They were staying for a month at one of the best hotels in London, one in which it would be beyond Jemima's means to spend even one night, but since she had no desire to, she could look at it without even minor envy.

She was shown up to the Thorwoods' suite, where Bernadette welcomed her, but with some awkwardness. Jemima could not tell from the almost enamel-smooth face what her feelings were. She was in her early forties, having married young, and had her only child at the end of the first year. She was very slender, delicately so, and wore her fashionable heavy silk dress and flowing jacket with great flair. Her thick hair was an ordinary shade of brown, but her eyes were green, clear and startling, almost mesmerising.

Rebecca, slight and pale, stood beside her. Only her eyes reflected her pleasure at seeing Jemima.

'How kind of you to call, Mrs Flannery,' Bernadette said with a cool smile, immediately taking control of the situation. 'Of course! You were born here, weren't you! Is your family well?'

'Yes, thank you,' Jemima replied. This was a ridiculous conversation, considering what they both knew. 'Are you finding London pleasant?'

'As much as can be expected,' Bernadette replied. 'Considering what brings us here.' A tightness filled her face for a moment, and then she forced it away. 'I'm sure we shall come another time and it will be very nice.'

'I'm sorry . . .' Jemima felt compelled to apologise, and then resented it.

'Hardly your fault, my dear,' Bernadette replied. 'She was well over seventy.'

Jemima's complete incomprehension must have been clear.

'Rebecca's godmother, May Trelawny,' Bernadette said patiently. 'She died. Rebecca is her goddaughter; she has no children. It is our sad duty to settle her affairs.'

Jemima glanced at Rebecca and saw not only a deep grief in her face, but something else: an indecisiveness, a sense of trouble. She saw no way to rescue the situation. She refused to make herself ridiculous by trying, and making it worse by drawing attention to it, which she was certain Rebecca did not want.

'I'm sorry,' she said. 'I was so concerned with Rebecca's general spirits, I forgot for a moment all about Miss Trelawny. I came to visit Rebecca. I have never forgotten how kind you all were to me when I first came to Washington. I would like to take her to some of the quieter, more charming places in London and show her the same friendship. A walk in one of the parks, perhaps. We do not need to meet anyone . . .'

'I doubt she will wish to, but it was generous to offer,' Bernadette replied. It was clearly a dismissal, even though Rebecca herself was standing beside her.

Jemima's mind was racing, trying to decide whether she should mention the arrest of Philip Sidney. Did Bernadette know? She was sure Tobias must, but he might not have told her. That probably meant he had not discussed it with Rebecca either. That was deeply troubling. Were they going to conduct an investigation without asking her opinion at all? Then that meant it was going to happen in England. She would leave as soon as any evidence she had to give was over. Did she even have to give any? Would it all be done around her, about her, but never seeing or hearing her, as if she were a small child? Was that really the best for her?

Everything in Jemima rebelled, but it was not her life.

Rebecca would not be able to tell her experience, or deny anything said about her that was not true! And if Sidney were the sort of man who would break into her room at night, then rip her necklace from around her throat, and all but assault her, he certainly would not hesitate to lie.

'Are you sure . . .?' Jemima began.

Bernadette raised her eyebrows, wrinkling her otherwise perfect brow. She was unused to having her wishes or judgement questioned.

Jemima responded, perhaps the more fiercely with relief. She turned immediately and smiled directly to Rebecca. 'Are you sure you're well enough to go for a walk? You still look so tired. But I promise we will not go far . . .'

'It's the perfect time to take a walk, and I would love to get some fresh air,' Rebecca said. 'Your parks are so beautiful. I shall get dressed immediately. Ten minutes and I'll be ready. Perhaps we will find somewhere for luncheon. It's a little late for breakfast, but I haven't eaten for ages.' And without waiting for Jemima's reply, or giving her mother a chance to argue, she turned to her bedroom and disappeared behind the closed door.

Bernadette gave in with a certain amount of grace, and commanded that Jemima look after her daughter. She then excused herself to prepare for her own calls.

Jemima and Rebecca walked together towards Hyde Park, about a quarter-mile from the hotel. The sun was hot and bright, the roses were in their second flush. The neatly planted flowerbeds were dazzling with blooms, reds and dark blues, towering delphiniums, salvias in reds and blues, wide-eyed pansies in every colour possible. The grass on the other side had been recently mown and smelled wonderful.

The breeze was light, and as they moved along the path, they were one moment in the sun, the next the shade, and then in the sun again. There was the sound of distant laughter, shouts of children playing, and the crunch of gravel under their feet.

Jemima glanced sideways at Rebecca. She was very pale – far more so than her mother. That was partly her fairer hair, and her lighter, aqua-coloured eyes, but mostly her almost bloodless skin, bruised-looking around her eyes from sleeplessness. Jemima hated raising the issue, but it would not be mercy that stopped her, it would be cowardice. 'Rebecca . . .'

'What?' There was apprehension in her face.

Jemima hesitated. Was this necessary? Yes, it was. 'Did anyone tell you that Philip Sidney has been arrested for embezzlement?'

Rebecca stopped, her face paler still.

Jemima tightened her grip on Rebecca's arm. 'The embezzlement took place, apparently, when he was at the British Embassy in Washington.'

'Are you sure?' Rebecca sounded startled.

Jemima's mind raced, her imagination all over the place. She realised she had thought that Tobias Thorwood might be behind the charges: either it was real or created to force Sidney into a courtroom, and she knew now that she had thought the latter possible. She worried about Patrick – how far he would go to help Rebecca! How exactly did he know about the embezzlement? Was it a trumped-up charge and Tobias behind it? Had they asked Rebecca at all exactly what had happened, if she was sure it was Sidney who had broken into her room? How far beyond revenge had the Thorwoods thought about it, beyond a verdict? Had they thought about Rebecca afterwards at all?

'Didn't your father tell you?'

'No! How do you know?' Rebecca was shivering, although they were in the sun.

'Patrick told us that the police had arrested him. He asked my brother if he could defend him.'

'Defend him!' Rebecca's voice rose in the beginnings of hysteria. She was shaking, standing in the middle of the footpath, on the edge of losing control altogether. There was no hunger for revenge in her, no anger, just outrage and terror, and now, Jemima knew, grief for May Trelawny.

Jemima seized hold of Rebecca by the shoulders. 'No!' she said loudly. 'Only to defend him of the charge of embezzlement and see that there is a proper trial, with all sorts of questions asked. But let's start now with the most important: do you want to do this?'

'What?' Rebecca's voice steadied, but she still looked trapped. 'Do what? I don't . . . I don't even know anything about it!'

'Your father wants . . .' Jemima began, then realised she knew that only because Patrick had told her. 'I think your father wants,' she began again, 'to have Sidney charged with a crime here in England, or at least for which he can be tried in England, so that the fact of the theft of the pendant and the assault on you can be mentioned and Sidney's part in it be made public.'

'But it has nothing to do with the embezzlement. If that even happened!' Rebecca protested.

'I know, but you can bring all sorts of other things in, if you're clever enough, and it doesn't have to be proved. If everyone knows, because it is an open court, that will ruin him anyway. And . . . and you might get May Trelawny's pendant back.'

Rebecca was silent for a long time. Then she turned and began to walk along the path again, gazing at the gravel at her feet.

Jemima caught up and walked beside her, falling into step. 'I'm sorry, but I thought you needed to know about the trial. It should be your decision, whether you want to accuse him of the theft or not.'

'Father says it will make me feel better if I make it public . . .'

'Maybe it will, but you will have to live with people knowing about it, ever after that. Is that really what you want?'

'No,' Rebecca said quietly. 'I was frightened. He was so . . . so . . . rough! It was as if he hated me . . . and despised me . . . I felt isolated, because I'd liked him.'

'Had you rebuffed him?' Jemima tried to think of a reason for Sidney's sudden change of attitude. It was a ridiculous and horrible thing to have done. 'Or could he have acted only for money? The pendant – was it worth a great deal?'

'Only to me. I loved Aunt May, and I would never have told anyone, for her sake, that it wasn't even a real diamond. It was made out of crystal.'

Jemima reflected that had Sidney known this he may never have acted so rashly at all.

'Did Sidney say anything to you? Did you rebuff him? You didn't really answer me.'

'No. I . . . liked him. He was quite shy underneath the humour. I . . .' Now her eyes filled with tears and she was obliged to stop and find a handkerchief. She blew her nose, as much as was ladylike in a public place, and put the handkerchief away. 'That's another thing. It made me feel such a fool! I so badly misjudged him. If I can't tell a man who's violent – breaks into my bedroom at night, and steals what he thinks is a diamond, tears it off my neck so roughly it cuts my skin – from a man I thought I would like, and trust . . . even fall in love with . . . what kind of a complete fool am I?'

'Only the same as the rest of us,' Jemima said gently. 'Is it possible he knew you liked him and misunderstood?' There was no way to finish this decently.

Rebecca was amused, and Jemima liked her intensely for

it. She could so easily have taken refuge in anger. 'You mean did I lead him on? No, I didn't. I liked him. That's all. I'm not as sophisticated as some, but I'm not completely naïve.'

'I'm sorry. I—'

'I know,' Rebecca said quickly, putting her hand on Jemima's arm again. 'Please don't try to explain. You'll only make it worse. You should stop playing when you are winning. Nobody tells you to stop playing when you are losing. But you should, even so.'

'I should remember that,' Jemima admitted ruefully. 'And you're sure it was Philip Sidney?'

'No, I had no idea who it was, except it was his height and build, and his hair colour. But my father saw him in the corridor outside, in the light, just for a moment. It is difficult to remember and describe a stranger, but you know them quite easily if it's someone you've seen quite often.' Rebecca hesitated, uncertainty plain in her face.

Jemima felt sure that something deeper than that troubled her. Was it simply guilt that she had been so foolish, and had cared for someone who had so appallingly used her, or had she perhaps led him on, trusting him? There could be so much more to this, delicate, tenuous, but acutely painful. 'Never mind,' Jemima said quickly. 'I just thought you should know so you are not caught unprepared. If it ever gets that far, you may be called to the stand.'

'Who would call me?' Rebecca was astounded.

'The defence, I suppose, if . . . I don't know.'

'But that's your brother!'

'I don't know what will happen. If it comes up, if your father says anything about the assault, you may have no choice but to stand witness.'

'He wouldn't do that! I will . . .'

'Refuse? And leave your father out there, sounding as if he made it up? And if you do refuse, it would look like the same thing as saying it didn't happen,' Jemima pointed out.

'But it did! Look!' Rebecca pulled the collar of her dress away from her neck and showed the scar, still pink and a little inflamed in places.

'I don't doubt you,' Jemima said sincerely. 'I just want you to have the chance of following it up or not, with the correct information to make up your own mind. If I were in your place, I can only imagine what I would feel. I don't know, but I think I might prefer not to tell the whole world about it.'

Rebecca stared straight ahead of her. 'I'll have to think,' was all she could manage. 'Now let us please talk of other things. Tell me about Cassie. How is she?'

When they got back to the hotel, they found Bernadette already waiting for them. She was polite to Jemima, but clearly concerned for Rebecca.

'I'm fine, thank you, Mama. Please don't treat me like an invalid, or I shall begin to feel like one.'

'Was it pleasant?' Bernadette asked. She glanced at Jemima, then back at her daughter. 'I hope Jemima didn't . . .' She was looking for a courteous way of phrasing something without being openly unpleasant.

Jemima smiled. 'Rebecca was kind enough to ask me about Cassie . . . my daughter,' she added, in case Bernadette should have forgotten her name. 'What mother is not delighted to answer every such question?'

Bernadette relaxed, even smiling. It altered her face, giving life to its almost ceramic-like perfection. 'Of course. How is she?'

'Saying more every day. "No" was a big discovery a little while ago. Now it is "why?"'

Bernadette actually smiled; the subject was safe.

Ten minutes later, as Jemima was preparing to excuse herself and leave, Tobias Thorwood arrived, accompanied by another man, lean but elegant, at least two inches taller than Tobias, who was more than average height himself. This man was not handsome, but he was definitely distinguished, and his clothes were beautifully tailored. He had an air of confidence about him that was surprisingly comfortable, as if he knew in some personal way that everything was under control. Nothing could ever make him panic. He followed Tobias, whom Jemima had met many times. He was, as always, perfectly dressed, pleasant-looking in his own way, thick curly hair, a wide smile and very open face, in comparison with his friend, and they were clearly friends.

'Ah, Jemima,' Tobias said quickly. 'Come to see Rebecca? How kind of you. I'm sure your company will raise her spirits. May I introduce you to Sir John Armitage, from the British Embassy in Washington. John, this is the English wife of young Flannery I was mentioning to you.'

'How do you do, Mrs Flannery?' Armitage said pleasantly. 'Are you back in London for a while?'

'A few weeks,' Jemima replied. She wanted to avoid the subject of Sidney, and anything to do with the embassy in Washington, or the police, for that matter. 'It is the first time I have been back since my marriage.'

'And your family has not been out?' Armitage asked. 'Sometimes I forget just how far it is.'

'My parents have, but not my brother,' Jemima replied, and then wished immediately she had not. Either her father's occupation, or Daniel's, would strike far too closely to the subject she wanted to avoid. She did not look at Rebecca, because she could imagine her stiffening already, prepared to find a way of leaving them that would not seem churlish and embarrass her parents in front of this man. She must fill the silence. Armitage was staring at her expectantly. She felt like an intruder who must explain her presence. 'Rebecca was so kind to me when I was first in Washington,' she said too quickly. 'I want to show her some of my city, and it is a lovely day for a walk.'

Tobias was watching her. He seemed remarkably tense. His shoulders were hunched inside his jacket.

Armitage broke the silence. 'Mrs Thorwood,' he said to Bernadette. 'If you recall, you mentioned certain music you enjoyed the other evening. I bought a programme for the Promenade concerts at the Queens Hall and I thought you might find something there that you like. You're in London for so short a time, it would be a shame if you were not able to spend one evening with the timelessly beautiful.'

Bernadette looked at him with relief. 'How kind of you, Sir John. If you wouldn't mind waiting just a moment, I shall get my diary and see what engagements we have already.'

'Of course.' He made a small gesture, almost a bow. And when she turned to leave the room, he followed a pace or two behind her, as if she had expected him to.

Rebecca thanked Jemima again and excused herself to her room, apparently without feeling she had to offer an explanation.

As soon as she was gone, Tobias faced Jemima, speaking in a low voice. 'I hope you are here merely to see Rebecca, and not to try to persuade her not to proceed with her accusation against Philip Sidney, now that the police have charged him with another crime? Forgive me, but I do not entirely trust your . . . kindness.'

Jemima felt the heat burn up her cheeks. It was out of anger, but also guilt. That was exactly what she had done. How did he know? 'It was my husband, if you remember, who was doing everything he could to prosecute Sidney. I would not go against his wishes, even if I felt differently.'

'I'm sorry, but I do not entirely believe you . . .'

She stiffened. 'I beg your pardon?'

He looked uncomfortable. 'I apologise. That was discourteous. I am worried about Rebecca, as I know you understand. And Sidney is English.' He took a deep breath. 'You must feel—'

She cut him off. 'Why on earth would I? I've never even met Sidney! That is a very unjust thing of you to say!' It was an accusation, and she meant it. She had liked Tobias before, even trusted him, but he was not the one who would have to face other people, hear the whispers, see the half-smiles, and wonder what gossip his daughter had not quite heard. 'I do not know Mr Sidney, nor care what happens to him, and there is nothing to give you cause to think otherwise!'

'Except that you are English, and so is he. It is natural for you to think the best of your own, and wish to defend them. I saw him!' Tobias's face was flushed. 'Are you questioning me? Or does it not matter to you that he is guilty?'

Jemima could feel her temper flare until she was shaking and almost choked for words. She would soon return to Washington, where Tobias Thorwood was a force she would have to reckon with. More importantly, Patrick would, yet she would not be silent. 'No, Mr Thorwood, you are a guest in my country now, and you have just insulted me profoundly, and without cause. The fact that your daughter was the

81

victim of an assault does not give you the right to blame anybody and everybody for it. You are far more eager for revenge upon Philip Sidney than I am, because I am more concerned for Rebecca, and how she will feel long after this is over, how she will face a society in front of whom she has not a shred of privacy left! When she finds a good man, and falls in love, all he will see is the victim of an assault, a woman guilty of having misjudged a man, trusted him, and perhaps let him into her bedroom at night.'

'How dare you!' he shouted so loudly that even Rebecca, through the closed door of her bedroom, must have heard him. 'It is you she should be afraid of, and the other women like you, who are jealous of her position, her prospects.'

Jemima was really angry. 'I don't want her place in society! If I did, I would have stayed in England and not gone to America and married an Irish immigrant policeman! If you can't see that, you are far blinder than I took you for! I want Rebecca to have the choice of what she does, not you. I would have to know what is likely to happen, what people will say! Sidney will never go to America again. She will be perfectly safe, and no one need ever know. Maybe that is what she wants. It is her life; it should be her choice!'

Tobias's face was flushed red. 'So, we let Sidney go? She should stay silent and put up with it? What about justice? What about making him pay for having—'

'What? Ruined her reputation? He hasn't! No one else knows. But of course, they all will after you bring it up at his trial for embezzlement.'

His voice was like ice. 'Does your husband know you are going against everything he is fighting for, Mrs Flannery?'

That cut deeply. She felt the blood rush up her face.

Tobias grunted. 'I thought not! You have strange loyalties.'

'So have you,' she snapped back. 'You want revenge more than safety, more than giving Rebecca the right to decide,' she retorted.

'And these other things, important things, you appear to have overlooked,' he went on. 'Or perhaps not bothered to think of? Your thought is shallow, intuitive rather than intelligent.'

For a moment, he robbed her of words. She would have said exactly the same of him! He was acting with the self-righteous protective rage of a father, treating Rebecca as his property, damaged, lessened in value. But she dared not say that, even though it was on the tip of her tongue.

'Do you imagine this is an isolated instance, entirely out of character for him? Did you think at all?' he accused.

'You have found other cases, in the past?' she said incredulously. 'Did the British Embassy know of them? Why was he there, where such things could do international damage?' Another even worse thought suddenly burst into her mind, drowning out all else. 'You think they knew! Don't you? The embassy staff. Or you think they should have? That it is their fault? You'll make a big incident of this, even bigger than it is. You want damages? Money? No, not money, you want the British to be disgraced.' Her mind raced. 'An excuse for . . .' She gasped. 'You'll turn Rebecca's embarrassment into an international incident. How awful for her! She'll—'

'Silence!' he bellowed. 'You . . . you stupid, wicked woman! Of course I don't want any such thing! It isn't the past I'm thinking about at all, you fool! It's the future. Do you imagine he'll never do it again? Either because he can't help himself, or from sheer damned arrogance because he can get away with it? If we know what he is, and we do nothing, we will be at least in part responsible for the next victim, and the

83

next . . . Never mind that I would suffer, what about Rebecca?' He jabbed his hand towards her. 'You profess to be her friend, and yet you don't know her well enough to imagine her guilt . . . when it is too late. It may be embarrassing to come forward and accuse him now, but what will it be when there is a second victim, or a third?'

Jemima stood frozen to the spot. What he was saying was true, all true. She had not even thought that far. And worse than that was what Tobias had not said: if there were an attack anywhere that Sidney could have committed, never mind had done, Rebecca would not know! She would blame herself anyway. Her silence would hang around her neck like lead crushing her.

'I think you had better leave, Mrs Flannery, and do not come back again. If you do, Rebecca will not see you. I shall explain to my wife that you had another urgent appointment. Sir John Armitage will not care either way. I dare say he will not even notice. If he does, he will understand that I am doing what is hard, but what I am quite certain is in Rebecca's best interests in the end.'

Armitage's voice broke in before Jemima could reply. He had come in behind her without her hearing. 'Silence may be construed by many to be an admission of guilt, Mrs Flannery. Miss Thorwood will never have to lie, or conceal the event, if she faces it now. You may or not choose to understand Tobias's fear for her, her love of honesty and justice, or his trust in his daughter's courage, but I ask you to trust it anyway.' His voice was smooth, and clipped, very English, eminently reasonable. 'His desire is to protect her, not merely now, when she might well find it easier to be silent than to face her attacker. But in the future also, because there might be a dark shadow she is afraid of because she did not deny it when she had the chance. In brief, your defence of her privacy is short-sighted, if well meant.' He turned to Tobias. 'But your charge of defending an Englishman, right or wrong, is unfair. I think you owe the young lady an apology, and I would think the more of you if you offered it.'

Tobias's face flared red, but he offered it none the less. 'I apologise, Mrs Flannery,' he said stiffly. 'Now would you please take your leave before my wife comes back into the room and is distressed? She has already suffered enough.'

'No,' Jemima said quietly. 'It is I who should apologise. You raised a side of this that I had not considered. It is far deeper than I thought, and we cannot erase the past. But as you say, we will affect the future, whatever we do. I'm sorry.' She turned to Armitage. 'Good day, Sir John.' She took a step towards the door.

'Mrs Flannery,' Tobias said huskily.

She stopped and then turned back, waiting for him to speak.

'I spoke out of turn also, please do come back. Rebecca is very fond of you, and you seem to be able to pick up her spirits better than we can.'

'Thank you,' she said, 'I will.' She left without speaking to Armitage again.

Chapter Eight

'Yes, sir.' Daniel stood in front of Marcus fford Croft's desk.

Marcus stared at him benignly, his white hair surrounding his head like a halo, but there was no smile on his face. In fact, he looked increasingly grave as Daniel waited for him to speak.

'Doing well,' Marcus said. 'Ever since the Graves case. Proved your worth. Lot of good decisions . . .'

He seemed to be waiting for a response, so Daniel gave him one. 'Thank you, sir.'

'Don't thank me! Did it yourself. Now I want to see if you can keep it up. Not certain . . .'

Daniel was struck with a sudden chill. He drew breath to speak and changed his mind. This was a time when it would be wise to keep silent.

'Family loyalty,' Marcus went on. 'Very important. Scylla and Charybdis, and all that. Don't look so mystified, boy! The screaming monster in the rock called Scylla, and the ever-devouring vortex called Charybdis. Didn't they teach you classics at Cambridge? What is the world coming to?'

Daniel knew the reference, but it didn't help in the least.

'Loyalty to family!' Marcus said tartly. 'Loyalty to friends, even when they make mistakes. And, God help us, we all do. Loyalty to your country, which makes even more mistakes. Loyalty to your belief, right or wrong. Which, if you have a brain, and the courage to use it, will also be subject to radical review. If it isn't, it is probably totally ossified. Turn to bone, in case your Latin didn't go that far!'

'It does, sir!'

'Good. Then you will be equal to the test you're about to face . . .'

Daniel felt his stomach sink. He was good at tests, usually, but he still hated them. And why now? It was not exactly an idle time.

'A matter of necessity,' Marcus went on. 'Case may turn out to be more important than it looks. Of course, it also may not, but it is important for you . . .'

This time, Daniel did interrupt. 'I'm on a case with Mr Kitteridge, sir.'

'No, you're not!'

'Sir, it is . . .' Daniel's voice died away. Marcus was staring at him with a fixed look.

'I believe we can expect no fee for this work,' Marcus continued. 'Mr Kitteridge is taking on another, serious case for the Foreign Office. One for which he will be paid. Handsomely. You will take the defence of Philip Sidney yourself. I can give you a part-time clerk, if you feel you need assistance. But you are quite capable of conducting it by yourself. You may not think so, which is immaterial. I am head of chambers, and I do think so.'

'Sir . . .' Daniel protested, and then changed his mind.

'What? Not ready for it? Nonsense. Follow my advice and you'll be fine!'

'Sir?' This time, Daniel did protest.

Marcus ignored him. 'Don't follow it, go against it, and it will be the ruin of you . . . I promise!'

Daniel could not have been more surprised than if Marcus had risen from his seat and slapped him.

Marcus grunted. 'You will defend young Philip Sidney as if your career depended on it, because it does! It is your job to defend him for the crime with which he is charged, and to do it to the best of your ability, no matter what you think him guilty of. You owe loyalty to your family, your country, but you serve the law! That is your part in the scheme of things. And you will do it at this time, or you will cease to have the opportunity to do it in the future! Do you understand me?'

Daniel was too appalled to find an answer.

Marcus pursed his lips. 'You managed to do that in the Graves case, when it was your father's peril. Why? Did you think your father would disown you if you appeared to be against him? Don't tell me you did not think he could be wrong – you did! I saw it in your eyes. Do you think your brother-in-law could be wrong, and your sister will not forgive you for making her see that?'

Daniel clenched his jaw so tightly the pain went right through his head. Marcus had struck a raw nerve. It was exactly what he feared. That it was not his fault would make no difference at all. It would be he who was exposing it, making it impossible to deny.

This time Marcus's voice was soft, as if he understood, maybe more than Daniel would ever appreciate. 'You can't please other people, Daniel. All you can do is be careful how you uncover the truth. Now go and defend Philip Sidney. For the duration of this trial, that is where your loyalties lie.'

'Yes, sir.'

'Go on, then!'

'Yes, sir.' Daniel turned away and walked out of the door, and into his own small room. He should have seen this coming. He should have refused Patrick . . . and Jemima. It was too late now. Marcus was right.

Daniel began by going to visit Philip Sidney in prison. Kitteridge had been already so Daniel would have to explain that to Sidney as well as possible without making him feel as if he had been downgraded, fobbed off with a junior.

He had no idea what to expect. Whatever he felt, he must try to see the whole miserable exercise from Sidney's point of view. Whatever struggle it cost him, Daniel must see the good in him, the humanity, if there was any to find. How had he got himself into this mess? God knew, Daniel could empathise with him! How had he got into such a mess himself?

Of course, he had been to various prisons around London before, and police cells, and sometimes, when the crime was not serious or violent, to accused people's homes. It was seldom a pleasant experience. The accused person was almost always afraid, however they exhibited it. Sometimes they were pathetic, sometimes aggressive, sometimes completely and utterly bewildered.

This was a very ordinary police cell. Sidney was incarcerated only because he had the means to flee, and it had been suggested that he might do, rather than face the charge levelled against him, and the consequent disgrace of conviction. The offence was entirely non-violent, and the actual amount of money not very great, considering the embezzlement had taken place over an extensive period.

Daniel told the guard that he was Sidney's lawyer, and

showed him his credentials. Reluctantly, the guard took him into a small stone-floored room with one table and two chairs and told him to wait. Daniel had been in such rooms to visit men who were afraid and all too often filled with despair. He was used to the struggle to convince them that this was not yet the end, there was still something worth fighting for, even if it was only a lesser sentence.

When Sidney came a few minutes later, there was nothing about his manner that Daniel had expected. His physical appearance he already knew. It was in Tobias Thorwood's description of the man he had seen coming out of Rebecca's bedroom after she had screamed for help. It was very general: tall, slender, fair brownish hair, and an air of arrogance, of entitlement.

There was no arrogance in this man that the guard showed in, and slammed the door on as he went out. Sidney's hands were loosely manacled in front of him. Perhaps that was for Daniel's safety?

Philip Sidney said quietly, 'I'm sorry, I don't know you.'

Daniel stood up. 'Daniel Pitt. I work with Kitteridge.'

'Has something else happened?' He was trying to hide it, but there was an edge of fear in his voice.

Daniel decided it was best to be open. The situation was far too complicated as it was. Prevarications and attempted lies would make it totally incomprehensible. 'Yes, I'm afraid Mr Kitteridge has been assigned to another case, one with a far more serious charge. I have been given your case. I knew only this morning. So, I have come to learn as much as I can directly from you.' He indicated the other chair. 'Sit down . . .'

Sidney obeyed, and in watching him move, Daniel realised that he was emotionally exhausted and rigid with a fear he was trying very hard to hide. He looked stunned, rather than angry.

'I haven't been able to speak to Kitteridge since he came to see you,' Daniel began, 'so I don't know what he asked you. How much are you supposed to have embezzled, and from whom . . . precisely? I know it took place in the British Embassy in Washington.'

'About a hundred pounds,' Sidney replied. 'Not a fortune, but certainly a lot of money. Several weeks of my salary.'

'All at one time?'

'No, little by little. Five or ten pounds at a time.' He pushed his hair off his forehead. It seemed to be a nervous gesture. The manacles rattled with each move.

'How did they find out?'

Sidney looked miserable. He avoided Daniel's eyes. 'It showed up on my bank account, and disappeared again, as if I'd spent it.'

'Exactly how did you do that?'

'I didn't!'

'How did they say you did it?'

'Signed transfers for payments to people and companies that don't exist. All legitimate things for the embassy to have bought, except that they didn't.'

'But it's your name on the receipts, or whatever they are?'

'Yes, and it looks like my signature, it just isn't.'

'Going on for how long?' Daniel asked.

'Several months. But I didn't do it, Mr Pitt! I don't have a lot of money. I may have a name reminiscent of a hero from history but I'm from a very ordinary family. My father died a long time ago. He was a good man, but not exceptional.' His voice cracked a little, and he mastered it with difficulty, pretending it was a cough rather than emotion.

'Thank God my mother has gone, too. She . . .' Whatever he had been going to say, he changed his mind. 'I have enough money, but not a lot,' he repeated, and then he shrugged very slightly. 'It doesn't matter. I can't account for one hundred pounds. I play cards for pleasure, but I don't gamble. It always seemed like a waste of time. I can't afford to lose, and I can't win unless someone else loses. I would say look at my purchases, but I don't know what they will show. There must be something there that I don't know about, and can't explain.'

Daniel was struggling for something to say. Either Sidney was telling the truth, or he was an extraordinarily good liar. Was he a good diplomat? Was he practised at saying things he didn't mean, being polite to people he disliked, or even despised? Making excuses? Representing his country, whether he thought it was right or wrong? Who had said patriotism was the last refuge of a scoundrel? Patriotic lies were honourable, the loyal thing to say, over and over again, until you believed them.

Wasn't that what lawyers did? Defend the client until the bitter end, as long as he didn't actually admit it to you, and then lie on the witness stand?

'You didn't do it?' he said.

'No, I didn't,' Sidney replied.

'Have you any idea who did?'

'No. Do you think I haven't racked my brain?'

'Or why?'

'That either. Is this against me, or did I just happen to be standing in the wrong place? Was it really a matter of "anyone will do"?'

Daniel frowned. One hundred pounds didn't seem enough money over which to blame someone else and ruin them. 'Wouldn't buy you a house . . . well, not much of one.'

'It might be a way out of debt, if that's what you owed,' Sidney suggested.

Daniel hesitated. This seemed the ideal time to bring in Rebecca Thorwood. There would never be a better. 'Or is it really about something else altogether?' he said quietly.

Sidney drew in his breath as if to ask what, then there was a sudden understanding in his face. 'How do you know about that? You mean the Thorwood accusation in Washington? I didn't do it! But you think someone is trying to get revenge on me for that? Won't work. This money was taken while I was in Washington, but before that event happened.'

'If it was taken,' Daniel said, watching Sidney's face, his eyes, the tiny muscles in his jaw. He did not see guilt, or an actor planning the reaction, the next line to say.

'I don't understand,' Sidney replied. 'If somebody thought I did that, and it seems as if the whole of Washington does, how would they backdate the embezzlement to imprison me now?'

'I don't know.' Daniel was honest. 'But how could they do it anyway? Make it look as if you had taken the money?'

The little colour there was drained out of Sidney's face. He pushed his hair back again, as if the manacles were not there. 'I don't know what to do. It's coming at me from all sides. I wouldn't believe me, if I were you. Tobias Thorwood swears he saw me coming out of his daughter's bedroom after assaulting her and stealing a diamond pendant. He couldn't have, because I wasn't there. I didn't attack Rebecca. Actually, I rather liked her. I thought she was . . . different. Individual. A bit young, perhaps, but . . .' He stopped. 'I wasn't there!' he repeated hopelessly. 'I didn't take the diamond. I don't have it, and I didn't sell it or give it away

93

or lose it. I dare say all that happened – I don't know – but half of Washington was baying for my blood because Thorwood swore I did it. He's an important man. Very wealthy, from an old family, as Washington goes. Ridiculous, isn't it? The Sidneys go back long before Queen Elizabeth. It's a hell of a name to live up to. I've done just about the worst job possible. I'm glad my mother's dead. I never thought I'd say that . . .' He choked to a stop.

There were a few moments of silence.

In spite of his confusion and his loyalty to Patrick and Jemima, Daniel felt a surge of pity for this man, only a little more than his own age. 'I've got a father who has done brilliantly,' he said, assured that it was true, and following what Sidney had said about his name. 'They tease me at the office and call me Pitt the Younger, who, in case you have forgotten, was British Prime Minister before he was my age. Went up to Cambridge at fourteen, entered Parliament at twenty-two, was Prime Minister by twenty-four! And I'm twenty-five already, and what have I done?'

Sidney smiled. It was crooked and rueful, but it held a brief moment of understanding.

'Why did you use diplomatic immunity to run away?' Daniel went back to the subject. 'That makes you look guilty. Wouldn't the Embassy stand behind you and get a decent lawyer? If you didn't do it, they might even find proof of that.'

Sidney looked down at the scarred table. 'I can see that now. But "might have" isn't much assurance when they are howling for you to be flogged. The thing grew legs. It started out that I thought the best thing I could do for myself and for the Embassy was to get out and hope the whole story died down. Tobias Thorwood might change his mind about the identification and maybe even Rebecca would finally say that she was mistaken, and it wasn't me.'

'Did she say it was you?'

'They say she did, but maybe it was only her father. Hardly matters now: I did run away. My career is ruined. The Foreign Office wouldn't even look at me to sweep the floors now. I don't expect any government office would.'

'Even if you were found not guilty?' Daniel asked.

'Not guilty of what? Embezzlement? That's possible. But I still ran away from Washington, instead of facing the charge of assault like a man.'

'Did you think you'd get a fair trial?'

'No, not with Thorwood saying he'd seen me. His recognition would stand because we were acquainted. Anyway, that's not an excuse. Half the villains on earth say it's not fair! It's the oldest complaint in the world.' He said this with a bitter disgust on his face.

It would not be fair if Sidney did not have the best possible defence. Apparently, he had no one who would support him, no family, and the Embassy certainly would not. Where would he find the means for a good lawyer? And yet Daniel heard pain in his voice, and fear, but not self-pity.

Nothing was turning out as Daniel had expected it. Sidney was not the opinionated, arrogant man he had expected.

'We'll do everything we can about the embezzlement.' He'd made a rash promise; even while he was saying the words he had no idea how to fulfil them. Worse than that, he was putting himself in the position of opposing both Patrick and Jemima. How had what seemed at first a simple crusade turned into a many-tentacled disaster?

'Thank you,' Sidney said quietly. 'Please . . . please come back and tell me if you can find anything?' He was attempting to put hope in his voice, and trust, and it was painful to watch.

'I will,' Daniel promised.

Chapter Nine

Daniel and Kitteridge sat in Kitteridge's office and looked at the pile of papers in front of them.

'Is the clerk waiting for them?' Daniel asked dubiously.

'You could wager your life's salary he is,' Kitteridge said, pulling his face into an expression of disgust.

Daniel grunted. 'At this moment, that may not be very much. Marcus will not be pleased with me. Beneath his nonsense talk and his eccentricity, he's very patriotic, you know. He expects me to get Sidney off!'

Kitteridge looked up from the paper he was studying. He gave a slightly sideways smile. 'Of course he does. We are taking on the desperate case of a fellow countryman, not to mention the reputation of all British diplomats in Washington by association.'

'And losing?' Daniel said. 'Because it looks as though we may. Do you suppose Marcus would ever admit that Sidney is guilty even if it is proven in the end? Or even if he does, that his firm will go down as the one that couldn't get him off?'

'He wouldn't want us to "get him off", as you obliquely put it. Such delicacy isn't clever, it's disgusting! And if he is guilty, I don't want you to get him off. Neither do you. It was your blasted brother-in-law who brought this case here in the first place! Otherwise, we would never have known about it, unless we'd seen it in the newspapers. It would all be someone else's problem.'

'And if wishes were horses, beggars would ride!' Daniel added.

'What?'

'It's all completely irrelevant now.'

'Yes,' Kitteridge said firmly. 'The prosecution's clerk is waiting in the front office, guzzling tea and biscuits. And he'll stay there until you return these papers to him. He'll count them all and see you haven't given any changelings! He's put his mark on all of them!'

'You make him sound illiterate!'

'He has to make sure you don't put in any ringers!' Kitteridge explained.

'He takes me for a complete idiot!'

Kitteridge raised one eyebrow. 'Do you think that could possibly have anything to do with you taking on this case . . . perhaps?'

'They are all over the place,' Daniel said, looking hopelessly at the receipts, IOUs, papers of transfer. 'All sorts of things: paper, ink, postage stamps, biscuits, hiring cars, there's one here for hiring a chauffeur to drive to the Hamptons. Very expensive. Theatre. What some people will pay to see! Absolute—'

'Are all the signatures genuine?' Kitteridge interrupted him.

'Slight variation,' Daniel replied. 'Not much. But I don't suppose anybody writes the same all the time. I know I don't.'

'You only have to write "Pitt" on this. Be glad you don't

have to write "Kitteridge". Keep on looking through them,' Kitteridge said. 'We haven't much else. So far, they're pretty damning. He seems to have signed away a hell of a lot of money for goods no one else ever saw. Did you look up the Hamptons? Who are they? Are they British or American? Looks a bit like brokers.'

'They are a place,' Daniel answered. 'Very rich and very exclusive.' He touched several receipts. 'These look to be car trips there at weekends, and so on.'

'That could be what he spent the money on. You'll have to follow it up. Ask Sidney.' Kitteridge bent back to his papers and continued reading, his eyebrows brought together as he tried to see some pattern in them.

'How did we get them?' Daniel asked, ignoring his own pile. 'I mean, how are they in England at all?'

Kitteridge stared at him. 'The prosecution brought them. You know that.'

'Yes, but how did they get them?' Daniel persisted. 'Who went through and compiled this enormous pile of evidence, I wonder, searching out Sidney's signature?'

Kitteridge blinked. 'That is a very good question. I assume someone at the Embassy discovered the money missing, and when they looked harder, they concluded it was Sidney who took it.'

'Or it wasn't, and they blamed him for it because he's in enough trouble. It's an excellent time to get rid of a little more trouble and put it on to his plate?' Daniel suggested.

Kitteridge bit his lip. 'Are you hoping someone else is responsible for attacking Rebecca Thorwood as well? Someone that Tobias mistook for Sidney? Or are you suggesting Tobias is shielding this person, for some reason of his own?'

Daniel was startled. 'No. That makes no sense. Who, for

example? And why? Why would he protect the man who attacked his own daughter?'

'The papers?' Kitteridge repeated.

'They were handed over by a young man at the British Embassy called Morley Cross. They had to tell us that in order to validate them,' Daniel pointed out.

'When?' Kitteridge asked pointedly.

'What?'

'When did this young man from the embassy get these papers? How? How did they get over here so quickly? After Sidney came, and before Patrick?'

Daniel shook his head. 'I don't know. But I'm going to find out. If you'd just help me find the exceptions . . .'

'Oh, I don't mind clerking for you,' Kitteridge said sarcastically. 'I've got nothing else to do . . . except my own case! I forgot to mention that.'

'If I'm in doubt, I'll ask Impney to take a look,' Daniel went on, as if Kitteridge had not spoken.

'Exactly when did these papers get to England, and how?' Kitteridge persisted. 'You've got to get a time line on these, that's the real validation.' His face looked bleak. 'And I'm afraid it's possible your brother-in-law is somehow involved . . .'

'With the British Embassy, to set up Sidney for embezzlement to bring about a resolution of the theft and assault accusation?' Daniel said incredulously. 'He's Irish-American, for heaven's sake. Everything that's ever been wrong with Ireland is England's fault.'

'And everything that's right, which is a lot,' Kitteridge finished for him. 'I know, I've got a couple of Anglo-Irish cousins. Don't know how that happened! Actually, I do. Their father is Irish, and you couldn't meet a more delightful

100

chap.' For a moment, Kitteridge's smile was unalloyed pleasure.

Daniel was fascinated. It was the first time in the year that Daniel had known him that Kitteridge had mentioned any family. He had had the impression that they were all rather grim, sort of Evangelical churchmen out to save everybody's soul, whether they wanted it or not. All for their own good, of course. Then he went back to the original subject. 'They have to have come from the British Embassy, directly or indirectly, since they are their records. So, this embassy man, Morley Cross, must have brought them himself or given them to someone to bring here. And since it takes a week to get from Washington to New York and then cross the Atlantic to London, it is someone who left at least a week before the London police got them and could be persuaded to bring a case. And that's another thing! The police here recognised what they were, and acted on them?' The more he thought about it, the worse it became.

'Then you'd better start looking,' Kitteridge frowned. 'It's really the prosecution's job to validate them. They need to show how they got here, who brought them, and why. But if you don't know the truth, you can't put them on the spot in court and show the jury they're wrong. Just saying they're wrong won't help you. You've got to prove they can't be right.'

'Or that there is somebody lying in order to get Sidney into trouble,' Daniel said reasonably.

Kitteridge met his eyes. 'That, too. Sorry. But whatever the truth is, whether the papers are real or not – and so far they look real – you've got to find out for certain where they came from, who brought them to London, and why. It may be that Sidney did steal a hundred pounds from the embassy.

101

Or someone else did. But remember, you'll be talking to ordinary people, not bankers or financiers.'

'They'll be—' Daniel started out.

'The jury!' Kitteridge interrupted. 'Never forget that you are talking to the jury. If you don't understand it, then they won't, and there's damn-all chance they will acquit. You do not have to rely on the prosecution tying himself in knots.'

Daniel knew Kitteridge was right.

'And before you can even think of the assault and the damned necklace, and anything else, you've got to get this straight,' Kitteridge went on. 'They've got to think you know what you're talking about, and right at this moment, you clearly don't! This Morley Cross, the young man from the embassy who gave the papers to the police . . .'

'I don't know if he actually brought them over himself. They're being very tight-lipped about it. The earliest date I saw on any of the papers was three years ago.' Daniel thought back. 'Why did it take them so long to spot it? Why did this Cross fellow bring it forward now? It looks a bit like waiting till a man's down, then kicking him again. The jury won't like that.'

'You're going to bring that up?' Kitteridge said with a very twisted smile. 'Clever! You're going to tell him he was down because he had taken diplomatic immunity to run away from a charge of theft and assaulting a young woman in her bedroom?' he said sarcastically. 'Not exactly a standard defence. But it would get the point Patrick Flannery wants you to make across very well. Judge won't like it! And I dare say neither will the defendant. And what you will hate the most is how much Marcus will hate it. You could find yourself in a lot of legal trouble.' Kitteridge's expression said very

102

plainly what he thought of that. 'It would be the end of your promising career!'

Daniel realised how very thoroughly he had tripped himself up, and felt heat wash up his face. 'Cart before the horse,' he admitted. 'We'd have to use it as a last ditch . . .'

'Get back to the law, and leave the farming analogies, unless you've got something constructive to say. Find out who Cross gave those papers to, and why. Who knew about the embezzlement, when they found out, and how long they've known. That should keep you busy for a while.'

Daniel hesitated only a moment. 'Right. I'll report. Maybe tomorrow.'

The first thing he had to do was probably going to be the worst, but there was no avoiding it. And the less he knew, the more likely he was to make a mistake. He felt very much that he would rather not know, but running away from it would only make it worse. At least, if he had knowledge, he had some degree of choice.

He arrived at Keppel Street a little after eleven in the morning, feeling that if Patrick and Jemima had gone out somewhere, it would be the perfect excuse for him to avoid facing it. Was he looking for an excuse? It was irrelevant – Jemima was in and pleased to see him.

Cassie came over to him immediately. 'Hello, Uncle Daniel. Are you arguing?' She was fascinated with the idea of someone arguing, a thing she was so often forbidden to do, and being paid for it! He was proud of it . . . and Mummy was proud of him.

He looked at her eager face. Her concentration was total. She did not deserve a trivial answer. 'Hello, Cassie,' he replied. 'Not yet, but I'm working on it.'

She frowned. 'Why?'

'Before you can make a really important argument, one you need to win because something that matters depends on it, you have to make sure you know as much as you can about it, and that what you think you know is actually right.'

'Oh. How do you do that?'

He thought for a moment. 'Did you take the jam tarts from the pantry?'

She looked puzzled. 'No . . .'

'But you've got jam on your face.'

'I had jam on my toast.'

Daniel looked up at Jemima, who nodded to him. 'There, you see?' he said to Cassie. 'If I argued that you did take the tarts, I would lose. Because I didn't check that I was right!'

She smiled widely. It was as if she had won.

'And there aren't any jam tarts in the pantry, anyhow,' Jemima added.

'We ate them yesterday,' Cassie said. 'I had two.'

'You had three,' Jemima corrected her, choking back her laughter.

'But you've got the idea,' Daniel straightened up. 'If you don't check your facts, you can lose the argument.' He touched her head lightly. Her hair was unbelievably soft. 'I need to speak to Patrick,' he told Jemima. 'Is he still here?'

The amusement vanished from her face. 'I assume at this hour of the morning, you've come about the case? Checking facts?'

'Yes. Do you know where the papers about Sidney's embezzlement came from? I don't mean originally. Of course, they came from the British Embassy in Washington. But how did they get to London, and who gave them to the police?'

'Why? Aren't they real?' she asked.

'I don't know. They look real, as far as I can tell.'

'Then what does it matter? If they prove he embezzled money? I don't understand?' It was clear in her eyes that she didn't.

'I've got to put on a defence, Jem. And Marcus has put Kitteridge on to another case. I've got to do it all myself. The first thing to do is find out who brought the papers over to England, and who gave them to the police to prosecute Sidney. Any competent defence would do that. So far, it's the only weakness in the case. And Sidney says he didn't do it. It's my job to believe him, for as long as I can.'

She stared at him for several seconds. Cassie moved even closer to her, sensing in the air some sudden tension, a change in the tone of voices. 'Are you asking me if Patrick brought them?'

'Did he?'

'No! Of course, he didn't!' There was anger and disgust in her face. 'If we had them at the time we came over, he would simply have given them to the police! He wouldn't have involved you at all. He doesn't know any more about them than you do!'

Daniel believed her, and the answer made sense. 'He knew about them,' he continued, 'because he was the one who told me the police had arrested Sidney, and asked me to defend him. So that we could somehow raise the issue of the attack on Rebecca, and the diamond pendant.'

'That doesn't mean he caused it to happen! Where would he get them from? How would he even know they existed? You're not making any sense.'

'How did anybody know they existed?' Daniel continued. 'And took a ship leaving New York for Southampton so soon after Sidney, and came straight to the police here? Do you really believe that was all a matter of chance?' His disbelief was strong and bitter.

'No, that would be ridiculous,' she agreed. For the first time, there was real doubt in her.

Cassie gripped her mother's hand more tightly.

Daniel saw it. He spoke more gently. 'It's something I've got to answer, Jem. They didn't get here on their own, and they weren't posted. Somebody brought them over. The post would take longer than a courier, especially for as many pages as there are. They go back about three years.'

She looked totally confused. 'I'll ask Patrick. Please, let me do it. He'll think . . .'

'What?'

She faced him very squarely. 'That it's the English trying to protect their own, and that's reasonable. They protected Sidney from the charge of assaulting Rebecca, and that's much worse.'

'Which English?' he asked. 'Me? It has to be an Englishman who got the papers out of the embassy in the first place. What was he doing?'

'Maybe he was the embezzler and he was afraid they'd catch him,' said Jemima. 'So he took the chance to blame Sidney for the theft, and everything else. Everybody knew that Sidney had fled here to escape the other charges,' she said reasonably.

'Half of Washington knew that, at least half!' Daniel pointed out.

'Then that's your answer!' Jemima said. 'A motive, a necessity, an opportunity, and the means!'

Cassie looked at Daniel. 'Did Mummy win?'

Daniel was about to deny it, then he looked at Cassie's

anxious face. The answer was easy. 'I rather think she did,' he replied. 'She's good at it. And actually, it helped me get that straight.'

Cassie smiled directly at him, then turned away, overtaken by a sudden self-consciousness.

Jemima smiled at him, too. 'Thank you,' she mouthed the words.

Daniel left with his mind struggling with the question as to whether Patrick had somehow known about the embezzlement before he left Washington. That led inevitably to the question as to how he could have known of it, if he had no part in seeing that the evidence followed Sidney to England. Daniel believed Patrick when he said he wanted justice, no more. But do you press so hard, and take risks with your own future, if it is merely a case, one in which you have no personal investment? Daniel had had many cases, and fought them all to the best of his ability. But ability was stumped, and lack of it kept you awake at night, and invaded all the rest of your life. In some cases, not in all.

Why was Daniel defending Sidney? Was he also defending the British Embassy from the accusation of foreigners? It shouldn't make any difference, should it? It was the uncovering of the truth that mattered.

So why was he striding down Keppel Street with his fists clenched, trying to avoid facing Patrick, hurting Jemima, and confusing that little girl whom he had met only three times and already cared about so much?

He caught a bus on the Tottenham Court Road and made his way to Blackwell's house. If either Blackwell or Mercy were at home, it would be lunchtime. They would offer him some, they always did. He would accept, and then explain himself.

It was an excellent meal.

Lamb chops, the first of this year's peas, as mild and delicate as possible, with a little mint and plenty of butter, and boiled potatoes. Daniel would far rather eat than talk, and he did, putting the discussion off as long as possible.

'Come on!' Blackwell said at last, when there were no more potatoes or peas left.

'Tea?' Mercy said, rising to her feet. 'Cake?' She did not bother to wait for his answer – it was always the same.

Daniel was going to offer to clear away the dishes, but Blackwell gripped his arm, and he sank back in the chair.

'What's happened?' Blackwell demanded. 'Don't lie! It's bad, isn't it?'

'I don't know,' Daniel replied, more or less honestly. 'But I do know that if I don't mount the very best legal defence possible; Marcus will fire me. And when I look at it honestly, so he should. It's . . . it's so easy to be partisan.'

Blackwell looked straight at him. 'Philip Sidney didn't do it, did he?'

'I don't know. I really don't know.' This time he was totally honest. 'And that goes for either assaulting Rebecca Thorwood, or embezzling money from the British Embassy in Washington. And it's not because I like him, or because I don't want an Englishman to have done that, but because the whole thing doesn't make any sense . . . yet.'

'And you like your sister's husband, and you love her. She's been your sister all your life,' Blackwell went on. 'And you can't make sense of it.'

'Yes.'

108

'What does Sidney say?'

'That he didn't do any of it, which is what most people accused say, to begin with. Either that, or they insist they were justified. The blame is always somebody else's. But Sidney's no help, because he has no idea who has done these things, or why,' Daniel admitted. 'And you're right. It doesn't seem to fit with his past behaviour, or his reputation. Not that that means a whole lot.'

'What else?' Blackwell asked.

'The papers showing the embezzlement come from the British Embassy in Washington. A man called Morley Cross compiled the evidence. It's all personal expenses and book-keeping. It's only a hundred pounds that's gone, over a period of time.'

'Not exactly ambitious,' Blackwell observed.

'That's probably why he wasn't caught for three years.'

'Or because he wasn't doing it!' Blackwell said.

'Yes.'

'Did the real thief forge Sidney's name?'

'Probably, yes. But it's a mighty coincidence if the em-bezzlement just happened to come to light the same week that Sidney ran away from the accusation by Thorwood,' Daniel pointed out.

'Not if the real thief was looking for somebody else to blame. Then the timing is perfect. He'd stopped taking the little bits of money, and no one would go on looking for him,' Blackwell answered.

Daniel thought hard. 'Or it's not really about the money. It's only ever been about blaming Sidney for something he didn't do, to get rid of him, out of the embassy? Or to blame him for this to achieve something else? A position, possibly. A promotion several people are up for?' He realised with surprise how easily he had moved into defending Sidney, as if he really believed him innocent.

'Precisely,' Blackwell agreed. 'I have a feeling, Daniel, that there is possibly something bigger here than we have realised: bigger, and a great deal uglier behind this. What are you going to do next? Get it in order.' He held up one broad hand, and counted finger by finger. 'Find out exactly where those receipts and invoices came from, what department of the embassy? When were they last seen there? Who had worked there then? How did Morley Cross get hold of them? And has anyone questioned him? And then, who brought them from Washington to London, via New York, and when? Very important, that! When did that person leave Washington? When did he leave New York? When he got to London, who did he see? Lawyers? Police?'

Daniel sat still. 'I know.'

'What?' Blackwell asked. 'Do you really?'

'Yes. It's what Patrick has to do with this,' Daniel said unhappily. 'He knew of the embezzlement as soon as Sidney was charged. I want to know how, I probably do . . .'

'The Thorwoods,' Blackwell said quietly.

'Yes.'

'And Patrick is acting for them?'

'I suppose so. I've got to find out a lot more about how they know each other. Not exactly the same social circles. Jemima said they became acquainted over a job Patrick did for them previously.'

'Tread softly. Or let me do it. I don't have ways yet, but Mercy does.'

'For getting information from Washington?' Daniel said doubtfully.

'Not up to date,' Blackwell admitted. 'But up to the

beginning of this year, at least. America is not that far away, not to certain classes of person: the rich, the political, those in trade, especially certain kinds of trade. And people don't often change suddenly. Or have pasts beyond digging out. The source of all things almost certainly lies in the past, if you just know where to look. You find out how those documents got from the British Embassy in Washington to the police in London. That's the first thing to unravel.'

Daniel rose to his feet reluctantly, his smile a bit less twisted. 'Thank you, Roman.'

'You have a better idea?'

'No,' Daniel replied. 'If I had, I'd be following it.'

Blackwell walked with him to the door. 'Do your best, Daniel – for your own sake. It's too early to make big decisions. You don't know the half of it yet.'

Chapter Ten

Daniel did not want to do any of the things Roman Blackwell had advised, but he knew they were all unavoidable. First, he must face the one he dreaded the most. If he did it badly, repercussions could last indefinitely. Even the idea of it hurt. During her four years away, he had forgotten how big a part of his life his friendship with Jemima had been. It was safe, funny, honest. It had survived all kinds of quarrels, hard times growing up, facing dilemmas, struggles to understand and accept adulthood, separation, responsibility. She would be affected deeply by how this turned out – what it exposed that would change the things she loved.

Daniel had known Cassie a matter of days, but he was already enchanted. To have her think of him as an enemy, someone who had hurt her mother and father, would be acutely painful. He had already seen that shadow in her eyes when she thought he was distressing her mother.

Charlotte and Thomas would understand, but they would still be hurt.

Being brave was so easily put into words. The reality offered only pain.

No use thinking about it. Do it!

He found Patrick at Keppel Street in the afternoon sun in the garden, casually pulling weeds and enjoying the sun. Cassie was lying on a rug, sound asleep, arms and legs spread, a stuffed toy dog beside her. Daniel glanced at her as he stood at the open French doors. He walked out and on to the path, then across the grass. He passed the sand pit, dim memories of playing in it slipping him through time for an instant. He knew every inch of this garden.

Patrick saw him and rubbed his hands on the grass before standing up. 'Sorry. Still too dirty to shake.' He smiled.

Daniel wanted to stop and pull weeds with him. He even entertained the idea for a split second. He smiled back, a little twistedly. 'I need to talk to you – get a bit of advice.'

'Come this way.' Patrick moved a dozen yards to the other end of the lawn and sat down, adjusting his position so he was still looking at Cassie. 'About the case, I guess.'

'Wish it wasn't,' Daniel said, sitting facing him. 'But we must do it well, for all sorts of reasons. Practically, it won't work if we don't, and morally we'll neither of us be happy if we cut corners or tell half-truths. And it could get appealed! And dishonesty—'

Patrick held up his hands. 'Did nobody teach you one argument of proof is good, ten makes you suspect them all?'

'Yes. Frequently,' Daniel admitted. 'But a chain of evidence is as strong as its weakest link.'

Patrick shook his head. 'Get to it, man! What is it?'

'It's about these documents relating to the missing money, which Sidney signed,' Daniel replied. 'It certainly seems to be his signature. That isn't a problem. Thing is, we know who handed them over, but who compiled them at the British Embassy in Washington, and who brought them across the

113

Atlantic and gave them to the British police, and why? Why now?'

Patrick stared at him.

'I care, because I need to question him,' Daniel explained. 'That's about the only defence Sidney's got. And we have to defend him. Apart from the fact that every man deserves a defence, if we don't make a good job of it, it'll look connived at, and grounds for appeal—'

'Of course,' Patrick interrupted. 'I'm not trying to ruin your career!' He looked surprised, even hurt. 'I don't even know if he's guilty of the embezzlement. But if he could assault Rebecca and steal the pendant, that's probably not the only rotten thing he's done and got away with. Jem doesn't want to raise the assault at all. She thinks it will only hurt Rebecca more in the future. Maybe it would be enough to convict him of the embezzlement.' He frowned. 'Tobias wants it all brought in . . . but I'm not sure. If it were my daughter, I think I'd . . .' He looked over at where Cassie was still asleep on the rug in the grass.

'You'd kill him,' Daniel said, only half-joking.

'Probably,' Patrick agreed. 'If Jem didn't get there first.'

Daniel waited a moment or two. 'Turn her over,' he suggested. 'She could get a little burned. Sun is hot today.'

Patrick got to his feet and did as Daniel had suggested, moving Cassie very gently, and without waking her. He came back and sat down. 'I don't know the answer to any of these questions,' he said. 'But I'm pretty sure the truth lies with a man in the embassy in Washington named Morley Cross. He may well be able to tell you something of what happened to the papers after they left him.' He hesitated a moment. 'I am still in touch with people in the Washington Police Department by wire. There can't be many ships docked from

114

America in the right time period. It has to be after Sidney left, or the papers wouldn't have come here after him. And before the police arrested him, because that gave them cause. How will that help?'

'Not sure. But Kitteridge wired the Washington police to check into this Morley Cross. When we find out who he passed those papers to, to bring them to London, and why, we could learn a lot more. At least we'll look as if we're really trying. Good idea in court to know the answers before you ask the questions.'

'Do you think you can defend Sidney . . . I mean, get him off?'

'If the prosecutor is halfway competent, I will not be able to get him off if he's guilty.' Daniel met Patrick's eyes squarely and saw him wince, but there was no evasion in them. Some of his fear melted away, but then a different part of him knotted up. He liked Patrick. It would hurt very much if, somehow, he had rigged this.

Daniel next reported to Marcus fford Croft and told him all the progress he had made so far.

'Humph,' Marcus said, looking at him narrowly. 'I'm not watching you that closely, Pitt. Why are you explaining all this to me now, to be precise?'

Daniel had the strong feeling that Marcus knew exactly why he was doing it, he just wanted to see if Daniel had the nerve to tell him.

'Well?' Marcus demanded.

'Because I need to see someone high enough up in the diplomatic service to take the next step in finding out about those documents,' he replied. 'Whether they're real or forged, they came out of the embassy in Washington and landed in

115

London at exactly the right time to convict Sidney. It may all be coincidence, but I don't believe it. And if the prosecution is going to succeed, they need to prove it.'

'You really are trying to defend him, aren't you!' Marcus raised his eyebrows. 'Good! I was not looking forward to having to tell your father I couldn't keep you any more.'

Daniel felt a wave of shame engulf him that that had ever been in question, above all, in his own mind.

'Don't look so surprised!' Marcus said sharply. 'I meant what I said. No empty threats. In my place, would you keep a man who professed to be defending a client, while actually sitting as judge, jury, and executioner of the poor bastard, without telling him?'

Daniel could feel the flush washing up his cheeks. 'No, sir . . .'

'Good. Because you haven't a snowflake's chance in hell of ever sitting in my chair if you would. Your first duty is to the law! Family, friends, anybody else comes after that! I hope you really mean that?'

'Yes, sir. I need to know the truth before I can defend Sidney. For that, I need to know who Cross gave the papers to, and how they got them out of the embassy and to London. And if possible, why. For themselves, or because someone else asked them to? And if so, I want the name of that someone.'

Marcus's face softened into a seraphic smile. 'Excellent. You want to see Sir John Armitage. High office in the British Embassy in Washington. In London for a few weeks. Or maybe it's a few days. Comes this way regularly. I'll arrange. Don't let me down by being in awe of him. He's a clever man, but he's got two arms and two legs, just like you. Now go and make yourself useful. I'll let you know what I've arranged. And straighten yourself up a bit! You look like you've been crawling around the floor, searching for something you've dropped. Remind me of your father – in his early days!'

'The lawn, sir.'

'What?'

'Crawling around the lawn. I was speaking to Flannery.'

'Well . . . I suppose you know what you're doing! Can't imagine it myself.'

'He has a three-year-old daughter, sir.'

Marcus sighed. 'Ah! That explains everything.'

For an instant, Daniel remembered Miriam fford Croft, Marcus's daughter. She was thirty-nine now, fourteen years older than Daniel, brilliant, irrepressible, eccentric and, underneath it, Daniel had glimpsed, vulnerable as well. He had not seen her since the Graves case, three months ago. Perhaps Marcus did know about little girls?

'Thank you, sir,' he said quietly, and escaped to see what he and Kitteridge could do between them.

It was two long and unproductive hours later when Impney came into the library with Kitteridge's tea and excused himself to speak to Daniel. 'I have a taxicab waiting for you, sir. It has instructions to take you to the Foreign Office, where Sir John Armitage will see you. If you don't mind my saying so, sir, you had best hurry. You don't want to make a bad impression by being late, and . . . er . . . you might tidy yourself up a bit?' He flushed slightly at his own temerity.

'Thank you, Impney. Indeed, I don't!' Daniel smiled. 'And yes, I'll find a comb, and even a mirror.'

He left Kitteridge sending a wire to the Washington police, asking them to track down Morley Cross and learn more

117

about those receipts and invoices. Who was this Cross fellow, and why had he waited so long before exposing Philip Sidney's embezzlement?

Daniel spent the whole ride, although it was not so very long, forming and re-forming in his mind exactly what he was going to say. He could not forgive himself if he spoiled this one chance to speak to Armitage in a non-adversarial setting. Never mind what Marcus would think of him!

He arrived at the Foreign Office, climbed out, paid the driver, then stood on the pavement in the wind, wishing he were almost anywhere else. He would be late if he didn't go now. He must ignore his hair across his face, and his heart beating as if he were going into the lion's den.

He was a trifle more composed when he was shown to Sir John Armitage's door, and a moment later, was in a luxurious suite. It was no doubt meant to impress, and it succeeded. The room was full of sunlight, which streamed through the huge windows open to the sky and a few lush green treetops, leaves twisting and turning in the wind.

There was no time to appreciate the paintings or the polished mahogany furniture, the Aubusson carpets. Armitage stood in the centre of the room, a tall and rather handsome man with thick hair swept back from keen features, almost arrogant, but for a courteous smile on his face now. Or to be more correct, on his mouth. It did not reach his eyes. How much of his agreeing to see Daniel was due to Marcus fford Croft, and how much to Sir Thomas Pitt? To resent it was stupid. Better to use it wisely.

'Daniel Pitt,' Daniel introduced himself. 'Thank you for sparing me time at such short notice.' He made it courteous, not too grateful. He watched Armitage's face. He could read nothing in it.

'Not at all.' Armitage turned and indicated one of the armchairs. 'I understand from fford Croft that it is urgent. And that it has to do with the miserable business of Philip Sidney.' It was not a question. He already knew the answer.

'Yes, sir. My firm has been engaged to present his defence.'

Armitage's eyebrows rose and a slight smile touched his lips. 'And do you believe he's innocent?'

Daniel smiled back. It was good manners, without humour. 'Of course, sir. Until proved otherwise, beyond reasonable doubt.'

'Do you always do exactly what you are hired for?' Armitage asked curiously.

'If I'm going to make a mistake, it will be more interesting, and less fundamental than that.'

'I think you will go far. I am not yet prepared to say in which direction,' Armitage replied. 'What exactly do you want of me? Remembering that my first duty is to my country, and incidentally yours also, not to the defence of your client, if they should prove to be incompatible.'

'The first thing I need to do is get to as much of the truth as I can.'

'It will always be only partial.'

'Sometimes you can tell a beast by only the shape of his head, sir. Of course, if it is one you've never seen before, the rest of it could be anything.' Before Armitage could reply, Daniel went on. 'The signatures on the papers appear to be genuine, but we have not had an expert look at them.'

'The papers are not in your custody, for heaven's sake?' For a moment, Armitage sounded alarmed.

'No, sir. But we do have limited access to them. I want to establish who realised they were not for genuine expenses, and why they were looking at old letters of transfer anyway.

And why the money was not missed earlier. Who brought them over to England? It must have been after the incident at the Thorwood house, but not long after. I believe you were instrumental in assisting Philip Sidney to avoid prosecution in that matter?' He kept his voice soft, with hardly any emotion at all in it.

A shadow crossed Armitage's face. 'Yes. I thought it best. Public opinion was outraged, and he had . . . an unfortunate manner. Some people thought him arrogant. He gave the impression sometimes of thinking he had a right to things that were, in fact, privileges for which he should have been grateful. In the diplomatic service, you learn quite quickly how important it is to placate, to compliment, to evade unpleasantness always, even if the other person is unreliable or belligerent. Sidney didn't . . . didn't always control his impulses.' He did not move his gaze from Daniel's. 'I care very much how our country is perceived abroad. We can afford mistakes now and then. Everyone makes them. But not many! Not many at all! Sidney may well have had to go, but it was dreadful that it should be this way.'

Daniel did not interrupt.

'I had no idea about the money, though,' Armitage went on. 'I gather it was not even a large amount? Possibly he was bored, and did it just to see if he could get away with it.'

Daniel looked down and noticed Armitage's hands in his lap, knuckles shining white where the skin was stretched across the bones. The subject disturbed him. Perhaps he was embarrassed? After all, he was Sidney's superior, and responsible for him.

'We will argue the case the best we can,' Daniel promised. 'And the money has to have been taken by someone in the embassy. I assume no outsider would have had access?'

'No. And even if they did, we are hardly going to create a diplomatic incident by blaming some gardener or housemaid!' Armitage's face was pulled tight with distaste. 'I wish I could make the whole miserable episode go away, but it is far too late to do that.' He was now watching Daniel intently. 'Have you noticed how often it is not the crime or the disaster of a scandal that brings down an otherwise great man, but the lies he tells to avoid admitting it?'

Daniel was not sure whether the question was rhetorical, or if Armitage wanted him to answer. He decided to answer anyway. 'That is a profound observation, sir. I think many people might agree with you, if you put it to them—'

'And you don't?' Armitage's eyes were wide and angry.

'I wasn't going to say that, sir. I was going to remark that would be an excellent thing for a lawyer to remember at all times. It is not what the witness or the accused has done, it is what he will lie about. And that is useful in different ways, depending on whether he is for you or against you.'

Armitage drew in a long breath and let it out slowly. 'I apologise. I interrupted you far too soon. I hope I am never on a witness stand with you against me. You are much sharper than I thought. A bad error, that, to underestimate your opponent.'

Daniel smiled. 'Then perhaps you should not have warned me, sir.'

'Hmm . . .' There was a surprising flash of humour in Armitage's eyes.

'I thank you for your wisdom,' Daniel said, holding his breath for a moment. 'But I cannot afford to waste the valuable time you have given me. I need to find out all I can about these letters and, most importantly, how they

121

attracted the attention of Morley Cross, and then got to England. Mr fford Croft told me that if anyone at all could help me, it would be you. He also said that you would be the most likely person to help because you would find it deeply hurtful to see a man of Sidney's . . . possible standing, of his name . . . convicted of two miserable crimes in America. The embezzlement is petty and wretched. The assault upon Miss Thorwood is disgusting.'

Armitage sat up a little straighter. 'My God, he's not being charged with that?' He closed his eyes. 'Damnation! I should have seen it. How blind I am. Of course! That's what this is all about! The embezzlement's a set-up job so the assault can be brought in, if not as a charge, at the very least as a slur on his character. The jury will convict him just to see him punished for the assault! I wonder who the hell is behind it?' He leaned forward a little, his face now in the sunlight that shone through the window. 'Pitt, do you know? If you are sitting there in that chair and you know who's behind it, and you don't tell me, I'll—' He stopped suddenly. 'I apologise. You would not commit such an act of betrayal against your country.'

Daniel found himself gripping the chair arms and shaking very slightly.

Armitage waited for him to speak.

Daniel's mind raced. 'I don't know the truth, Sir John. But I need to before I stand up in court and start asking questions. I've heard about the Thorwood incident, but it's all hearsay. It sounds very ugly, but cannot be pursued legally here. So it was you who helped Sidney to leave America . . .?'

'Who told you that?' Armitage demanded.

'Mr Sidney, sir.'

Armitage relaxed. 'Yes. Of course. I forgot that you would naturally have been to visit him. How is he?'

'Frightened, of course. He risks being convicted for something he swears he did not do.'

'But you will defend him? And see that this other damned business does not come out. Thorwood swore it was Sidney he saw, you know?'

'So I believe. If you could help me trace whose hands those letters passed through? And if possible, why the actual money was not missed before? It raises questions, at least. Was Morley Cross involved . . . or someone else? Maybe someone who is even entirely responsible for the crime. If there was an audit done, or something of that nature, then the thief may have taken the chance to make it seem as if Sidney were responsible. Hanged for a sheep as a lamb, so to speak.'

Armitage stared steadily at Daniel for several seconds. 'Indeed,' he said at last. 'I see you want to clear Sidney's name as much as I do, because it's indirectly England's name. Damn it! In the Washington embassy, of all places! Yes. Yes, I'll certainly get as much of that information as I can, and let you know as soon as I do. I'll keep in touch with fford Croft.' He rose to his feet. 'Good luck. God knows you're going to need it!'

'Yes, sir. Thank you.' Daniel rose and, with a brief inclination of his head, walked out of the magnificent sunny room and into the corridor, feeling definitely encouraged.

'You've got to get these looked at by an expert while you've still got them,' Kitteridge said urgently. He had offered Daniel his help to search the letters. He was still sitting at his desk, his bow tie crooked, his jacket on the chair behind him, and his shirt rumpled. He looked exhausted. 'The prosecution's clerk has gone, but he'll be back in the morning, and he'll expect to collect them then.'

'Thank you,' Daniel looked at the scattered papers. 'I really appreciate it. But where am I going to find an expert at this time of day?' He flopped down in the chair opposite Kitteridge's desk. 'It's after five now!'

Kitteridge ran his fingers through his hair, making it look even worse. His eyes were red-rimmed from straining over untidy, hand-written notes. 'Only one place I know, good enough to have any idea what they're doing, discreet enough to trust, and willing to work all night.'

'In your dreams?' Daniel asked sarcastically.

'Yours, perhaps,' Kitteridge said with a wry smile, oddly not unkind, considering all the edge to his words.

Daniel stared at him.

'Miriam, of course,' Kitteridge said sharply. 'Don't sit there blinking at me like an owl. We might like to think we solved the Graves case, but we wouldn't have done so without her. You know that as well as I do. Have a cup of tea and think what you're going to say, then you'd better go and get her.'

'What if she's not there?'

'Then you go and find where she is, for heaven's sake! And bring with you any equipment she needs. We can't take the letters out of the office. I've signed a promise to that effect. Otherwise, the clerk would have taken them. I said I'd work on them all night, if necessary.'

'So, you will!' Daniel said, standing up again wearily. His tiredness was inside. It was only five in the afternoon, still broad daylight. He did not want to go and see Miriam fford Croft again because she made him feel both comfortable and uncomfortable, often at the same time. During the months between the end of the Graves case and now, he had thought of visiting her on several occasions, but had always changed his mind.

'Get on with it!' Kitteridge said impatiently.

'I'll be back as soon as I find her,' Daniel promised. 'If Impney is going to be here, you should send him out to get some sandwiches or something.'

'I'll get them myself,' Kitteridge said, standing up slowly, unbending from the position he had been in too long. 'And some ale. If you pricked me, I'd bleed tea.' He knocked himself on the corner of the desk and swore mildly.

Daniel found himself smiling. Kitteridge was such an odd mixture of emotions, control, obedience and vulnerability. It showed far more than he knew.

They went out together, telling Impney when they expected to be back.

'Yes, sir,' Impney said, without the slightest change of expression.

They parted at the corner of the street, Kitteridge to the left to the best public house to buy supper, Daniel to the right to find a cab to take him to the fford Croft home, where Miriam lived and had her laboratory.

He arrived more rapidly than he was prepared for. He told the cabby to wait. If she was home, he would try to persuade her as quickly as possible to come back to the office with him. If she was out, he would have to start looking for her. Of course, even the servants might not know where she had gone, or be willing to tell Daniel, even though, since she was Marcus's daughter, of course they knew him.

It was three months since he had been here. It seemed

like only days. The path down to the separate cellar entrance was familiar. He knew where the cracked step was, and the paving stone that wobbled. He rang the bell and heard it jangle on the inside.

There was no answer. He felt a rush of emotion. Relief? Disappointment? Now what? Try the main house. He took a step backwards.

The door opened and Miriam stood in the entrance. She looked just the same as the last time he remembered her: high cheekbones, fair skin, too strong a nose, too wide a mouth, and the bright auburn hair pinned back whenever she thought of it, one long strand having fallen out of its original knot.

'Mr Pitt?' she said in some surprise. She had called him 'Daniel' when they had worked together, but that was three months ago.

On the ride here he had considered several different ways of approaching her to ask for her help immediately, this evening, without anything to offer her but an intellectual problem, and gratitude if she helped. It looked extraordinarily graceless, even manipulative. How could he even begin, without sounding ridiculous? How on earth had it once seemed so natural? He knew all sorts of things about her: what made her laugh, what angered her, what she read, her ambitions, both the ones she had achieved and those that were denied her because women did not do such things, like becoming recognised forensic pathologists. And that her birthday was in October, and this year she would be forty! She must look at him as if he were a boy.

'You are not looking for my father or you would have gone to the front door, not the cellar,' she remarked. 'So, you are looking for me. You want some information? You

126

don't appear to have anything with you, so you have nothing you want tested. Not another corpse to dig up, I trust? You are a little early. We don't do that sort of thing until midnight. It tends to disturb the locals.'

Daniel felt himself blush. She was making fun of him, quite gently, but unmistakably. He deserved it. 'You are right. I do have something upon which I need your opinion. I haven't brought it because I can't take it out of the office. I . . . need you to come. We have to give it back to the prosecution tomorrow.'

Her eyes widened. 'Do you have it legally? Or would I rather not know that?'

'Yes! It's perfectly legal. It's just that Kitteridge swore he would not take it anywhere else. It's . . . only paper.'

'What do you need to know about it? I ask so that I can bring the appropriate instruments with me.'

'Documents. We need to know if they're forged or genuine.'

'And presumably you need to give them all back? And in the state you received them?'

'Yes. Is that a problem?'

She looked at him a little more closely. 'Are you sure that you have them legally?'

'Yes! I wouldn't ask you to be involved if it weren't legal!'

'Stuff and nonsense! Of course you would, if you believed it was to bring about justice. Is that the cab I see waiting at the kerb?' She looked over his shoulder.

'Yes.'

'Then you had better come in and help me carry my good microscope. And don't drop it! Don't tell me about the case yet. I want to make an unbiased judgement.'

He followed her in and pushed the door closed behind him. He knew the taxi driver would wait because he had not paid him yet.

Miriam walked ahead of him, stiff-backed, straight-shouldered. He had forgotten how slender she was, the certainty with which she moved.

The huge cellar at first looked vast and full of shadows, but his eyes became accustomed to the lack of light quickly and he recognised the outlines of cupboards, tables, sinks where there was running water, drains, others where there were burners and retorts. Shelves were filled with glass jars full of chemicals. Here, the mystery substance, charge, action and reaction, the laws of matter, were explicit.

'Daniel!'

He brought his attention back to the moment. She was holding out a large case for him to take.

'Be careful of it,' she warned. 'Please take it to the cab and look after it. I shall follow in a moment.'

'Do you want me to come back and—'

'No! Don't leave that. It's about the most expensive thing I own.' Her eyes flared with pride, and challenge that he should even think such a thing.

Perhaps it was meant to warn him, even make him nervous. It had the opposite effect. He remembered with a surge of pleasure the elation of discovering patterns, making sense out of chaos, human passions flaming up out of inanimate objects.

As if she could read his thoughts, she suddenly blushed. Or perhaps it was because her own memories were just as sharp.

He turned and went out of the door, while she held it open for him. He carried the box up to the cab and set it down gently on the seat. 'The lady will be coming in a moment,' he told the driver.

'Yes, sir,' the man answered patiently. Little surprised him in human behaviour.

They arrived back at the chambers a little after six, and by half-past Kitteridge was watching with interest as Daniel passed Miriam sheet after sheet of paper: letters, pages of ledger and pages loose from account books, notes kept on meetings, and reminders to do this or that.

Each page she looked at under her microscope, looking carefully at the signature for a few seconds. Then she made brief comment, and passed it to Daniel to put in one pile or another. Two piles? No, three.

Daniel was aching to ask what she saw, but held his tongue with difficulty. He knew she would tell him nothing until she was finished. His mouth was dry and he felt hollow with hunger. But the pile to be done was growing shallow, as the other three piles grew larger.

Behind him, Kitteridge fidgeted restlessly.

Finally, Miriam was finished. She looked very carefully at the last one, and put it on the nearest pile. She turned to face them. 'These are genuine. The middle pile is questionable, but not provably forgeries. This pile here is forged.'

'You sure?' Kitteridge interrupted her eagerly. 'They would stand up in court? There's something anyone else could see? I—' He stopped abruptly. 'I'm sorry. We need to have something.'

'To do what?' she asked. 'Prove your client guilty? Or someone else guilty?'

Kitteridge let out a sigh. 'I'm not sure. To have anything

to say, to cling on to as truth. And no, a forgery would mean he's innocent.'

'You mean he had the right to some of the money, but not all of it?' She caught the meaning of it right away. 'They're all from the British Embassy in Washington.' Her face tightened. She directed the question to Daniel. 'Is this the Philip Sidney case? My father mentioned it. It's not much money for such an issue.'

Daniel knew what she meant. Perhaps she had gone to the heart of it. 'I don't think that's really what it's about,' Daniel said quietly. 'It's a smaller case to carry a bigger one, a lot darker.'

She looked at Daniel. 'What are you trying to do? Open up the darker one behind? Or protect him from it?' She searched his face and remained puzzled.

He should have known she would see it clearly and press him to answer. 'I'm not sure.' He could not lie to her. He would never get away with it anyhow, nor did he really want to. He would lose something. He was not sure what, but it mattered. 'I want to know what the truth is. I thought I was sure when I started. The case behind this is despicable. This one, I'm not sure. And it matters rather a lot. Because if the accusation is false, who's doing it? And of course – why?'

'Well, some of these signatures are forged, but I think most of them are genuine.'

'How do you know?' Kitteridge asked.

'I'll show you under the microscope, so you can be prepared to ask the right questions.' She frowned. 'Although I'm not sure how it will help you. Except . . .'

'What?' Daniel asked immediately.

'It's not terribly well done. When we sign our name, it's

130

not the same every time. Close, but hardly ever exactly the same.'

'They aren't all the same,' Daniel argued.

'No. Whoever it was, he was clever enough for that. But several are. Or there may be two or three that are identical. And then another two or three. But if you are making it exactly the same as one you copied, you move slowly to be sure to follow the lines. When you write your own signature, you move swiftly, with certainty; you touch the pen to the paper differently. Here, I'll show you.'

She turned and put one of the letters under the microscope, then adjusted the paper so that the lens was directly above the actual signature. 'Look,' she told him.

Daniel leaned close to the eyepiece and focused it. He saw the ink on the paper in something he hardly recognised. The lines were thick and, in places, almost as if they had scales, tiny little spikes, all pointing the same way. It was extraordinarily clear where the pen had lifted off the paper, and where it had touched down again. He stared at it for several seconds.

Miriam stood close behind him and moved the paper away, then replaced it with another. It was completely different. The line was smoother, the place where the pen lifted off the paper was clean, as if it had landed with a light pressure, and taken off again easily. It would be impossible to confuse one with the other.

He turned away from it to look at her. 'Are those the forgeries, with all the little spatters?'

'Yes, you can't help it, however careful you are, if you write slowly. The best forgeries may not be as close to the originals as a really good copy, but they are done swiftly, with assurance, so they look natural. Whoever did these was

131

very careful, but not clever enough to do away with the signs you can see with a microscope.'

'Would you be willing to swear that in court?' Kitteridge asked.

'Of course,' Miriam replied. 'But you'd need a lot more than that to prove anything.' She turned to Daniel. 'What are you trying to prove, anyway? That he did embezzle, or that he didn't?'

'We're for the defence,' he answered. 'That he didn't.'

She looked at him very candidly. 'And what about the other crime you said was worse? Are you trying to bring that up? Or make sure it doesn't arise, even tangentially in character reference? Or as explanation as to why he left Washington so hastily? Because if you want to protect him altogether, you should have him plead guilty to the embezzlement, pay the money back, and get the Embassy to withdraw the charges. Case closed. Nobody would have any cause to raise the other issue, whatever it is, never mind give evidence of it in court.'

Suddenly Daniel's mind was whirling. He thought of her as a forensic doctor, a pathologist who read evidence as another person might read a book. He had forgotten she was a lawyer's daughter. Of course, if they really wanted to protect Sidney, they would at least point out that option to him. Whether he took it or not was his choice. Whether they proved that some of the letters of authorisation of payment were forgeries or not had nothing to do with using the trial to revisit the question of the attack on Rebecca and make it hideously public.

What would Sidney choose, if he really were innocent of the embezzlement? And of the assault?

Or innocent of the embezzlement, but guilty of the assault?

Miriam must have seen these thoughts written in his face. Daniel felt totally transparent and, for a moment, terribly young.

'Damn!' Kitteridge swore. 'What a thundering mess! Thank you very much, Miss fford Croft. You have clarified half of it for us and made the other half much worse.'

'I haven't changed what it is, Mr Kitteridge,' she replied. 'Just shone a bit of light on it. If you have any other evidence, I would be happy to look at it for you.'

'Not yet, and probably not ever,' he said ruefully. 'Before we tidy this up, and preferably so that we haven't done the prosecution's work for them, would you like to have supper? I've got some pretty decent pork pies. And cider.'

'Thank you very much. I would,' she accepted. She looked at Daniel and gave a half-smile. 'It doesn't help, does it?'

He forced himself to smile back. 'Not yet.'

Chapter Eleven

The case against Philip Sidney opened in a minor court several miles from the Central Criminal Court at the Old Bailey, and thus also from Lincoln's Inn, where most of the lawyers' chambers were situated, including those of fford Croft and Gibson.

Daniel went by underground train. Later, if things got more urgent, he might hire a taxi.

The train was crowded and noisy as it rattled from station to station under the city. He did not want to read papers relevant to the trial in public, so he sat in silence and considered what he could do. There were very few possible arguments. He knew them by heart and did not feel sanguine about any of them. The only good thing was that the prosecution had produced a far longer list of witnesses than he had expected, which indicated a very thorough case, but which also allowed him far more time to work for, and hope for; some break in Sidney's favour.

Having been given the list, at somewhat short notice, he had spent the intervening time learning as much as he could about the witnesses whose names appeared on it.

'All character witnesses,' Kitteridge had remarked sourly

when the list arrived, and Daniel had shown it to him. 'As we supposed. They're not going to ship half the Washington Embassy over here. Still, you might be able to make something of it. Better find out what you can about this lot. Got to have something to argue about – with luck, trip them up over. Get to it, Pitt!' And he had handed the list back to Daniel.

That had been three days ago. Four, if you counted Sunday, when nobody's office was open. Kitteridge had not yet heard back from the Washington police about Morley Cross's whereabouts. Was the man afraid of being questioned?

The train arrived at the nearest station to the court. Daniel walked the three blocks through the hot, dusty street to the courthouse and went in. The halls were already buzzing with people. Someone had seen to it that word got around, Daniel thought grimly. This case was going to be about a lot of different things, least among them the possible embezzlement of one hundred pounds from a British embassy thousands of miles away.

Philip Sidney looked cornered when he was brought in and led to the dock. He glanced anxiously at Daniel, almost as if he were awaiting execution: brave and desperate, but determined to show it as little as possible. Was he a superb actor, or was there something essentially brave in him, something like the hero whose name he bore?

Daniel could not ally that with Rebecca Thorwood's account of the assault, essentially the act of a cowardly man. And yet Tobias Thorwood had sworn to it. They had done a certain amount of digging into Tobias's character and found only a decent and honourable man, with a deep love of his wife and his only living child. No one had caught him in any dishonesty, verbal or financial.

135

The judge was a clean-shaven, middle-aged man of unremarkable features, but the more Daniel looked at him, the more he saw a scholar within the robes, rather than a man here to exercise power or further his career with a controversial decision. Or perhaps Daniel was just being hopeful. Heaven knew, there was little enough to cling to.

The jury was sworn, twelve ordinary citizens, all of good standing, all men, of course. Women were not considered serious and emotionally stable enough to make an important judgement that might affect the rest of a person's life. They might too easily become frightened or confused. Daniel had grown up with a mother and sister who had dispelled any such idea very quickly. In his earliest years, he had known the Pitts' maid, Gracie, all five-foot-nothing of her, and she was the most down-to-earth judge of character he had ever met. And Great-Grandmother Mariah was not impressed by anyone at all, probably not even the old Queen, if she had ever met her!

And he could remember very clearly Great-Aunt Vespasia. Kings had admired her, for courage as well as beauty, never mind high court judges.

But you dealt with what was, not what you would like to have had, and Daniel was here trying to defend a man he was deeply afraid might be guilty, if not of the lesser crime, then of the greater.

His Honour Judge Ullswater brought the court to order and Mr James Hillyer opened for the prosecution. 'Your Honour, gentlemen of the jury,' he began easily. He was a man of about forty, unremarkable except for his most beautiful hair, and the deep lines in his face of a considerable sense of humour. 'I am going to show you a man accused of a trivial, and so far as we are aware, completely unneces-

136

sary crime. It is a series of comparatively petty thefts. A few pounds here and, days later, another few pounds there. A steady bleeding away, if you like, of his employer's funds, amounting altogether to one hundred pounds. And this concerns you deeply, because the employer concerned is His Majesty's Government, your government. Specifically, the British Embassy in Washington, the capital of the United States of America. The disgrace and embarrassment to this country is vast, compared with the amount stolen. Of course, he could pay back the money within a little while. It is not a serious loss to the government. It would be ridiculous to portray it as such.'

He smiled ruefully and gave a tiny shrug of his shoulders. It was an elegant gesture. 'But it is a devastating loss to our honour, our national pride. I even considered whether to plead with my superiors not to prosecute the case and draw attention to it. Let it die in ignominy. But others know of it. Are we a people who hide our sins away from others, and so let them breed, and let others see that we are willing victims, afraid of the truth, favouring a lie? A fit subject for mockery. As it is said, you can pull the lion's tail with impunity, in fact he has no teeth!'

There was a stir of anger in the gallery, a nervous giggle towards the back. Daniel saw several jurors stiffen in their seats. One even shook his head sharply.

'I perceive you see that as I do,' Hillyer said softly. 'Justice is not partial, and is not in fear of any man, or people, or nation. I will show you the accused as a well-bred young man, carrying a name that used to be honoured in the noble tales of our history. But a man who also carries with him a sense of entitlement, to do as he pleases without answering to the law, as lesser men do.'

137

What on earth was Daniel going to say that could undo that picture drawn in the jury's mind? He wished that Kitteridge were doing this, and not him. It was his turn at last, and he stood up reluctantly. He cleared his throat and began.

'Good morning, Your Honour, gentlemen.' He smiled very slightly, only a patch of light crossing his face. 'My learned friend may succeed in showing some of these things, but you will see for yourself, and judge for yourself. It is your duty, and I trust your nature, not to prejudge a man because of the way he speaks, or dresses, or what name his mother chooses to give him.'

He felt ridiculous. Was anybody listening to him? He cleared his throat again. 'I could bring you any number of witnesses to tell you Philip Sidney is an honourable man, that he is not extravagant, nor does he live beyond his means. They can show you no proof that he has debts, honourable or otherwise, because there are none. But there are papers, financial documents, showing the transfer of a few pounds in payments for expenses, some of them highly questionable. Some of them we will prove to you are forgeries.'

Now the jurors were all upright, their faces alert. In the gallery there was rustling and shifting of feet.

Daniel continued, 'You will find it fascinating how that can be demonstrated with a microscope. That, at least, shows that there was someone else involved, with dishonourable intent.'

Though Daniel had spoken for only a few moments, when he sat down, his heart was beating hard in his chest, almost choking his breath.

The first witness Hillyer called was a quiet, nervous-appearing young man with soft, fair hair that kept flopping over his brow. He identified several pieces of paper, which were solemnly passed around the jury for them to look at. They were letters of authorisation to pay small sums of money to certain tradesmen, restaurants, hotels and so forth. The total amount was approximately one hundred pounds.

'And do these letters of authorisation to pay all carry the same signature, sir?' Hillyer asked with interest.

'Yes, sir, they do.' He sounded very certain. 'Mr Philip Sidney.'

This looked as if it were going to be solid and tedious presentation of the case against Sidney. Surely Hillyer, whose reputation was high, was going to do something more than this? Daniel began to feel far less comfortable. He had no idea what to expect. Of course, he had studied several of Hillyer's recent cases. All they obviously had in common were surprises, sudden and unforeseen turns in the line of evidence, entirely different conclusions suggested, and then supported. It made it impossible to know what to expect or prepare for.

He looked at Sidney in the dock, and saw the same intense concentration on his face, as if he were not aware of what to expect. If he really did not know, how frightening for him! No wonder he looked so white. Would the jury take that for guilt?

The next witness was a clerk from the Foreign Office in London who had once held the office that Sidney had held in Washington.

'Mr Partington,' Hillyer began pleasantly, 'please describe, briefly, the position you held in our embassy in Washington, just sufficiently for us to understand Mr Sidney's duties, his responsibilities. Especially, we would like to know what trust he enjoyed from his superiors.'

'Yes, sir.' Partington relished his importance in explaining the workings of the office to the jury. He was simple, lucid, and just before the cliff edge of being an utter bore. It was exactly what anyone who had ever worked in an office would have expected.

Hillyer held up his hand and stopped him at the perfect moment. He turned to Daniel. 'Your witness, sir,' he invited. He sat down with a pleasant, slightly satisfied smile. He knew the jury had heard everything they wished from this witness. Anything more would be lost in confusion and boredom.

Clever bastard, Daniel thought. If the jury heard much more of this, they would fall asleep. He stood up and spoke to both Hillyer and the judge. And then turned to the court. 'Thank you, but I think that is as clear as anyone could be.' And then he turned to the witness. 'Just one thing, Mr Partington. Did you know Mr Sidney? Personally, I mean?'

'No, sir, I have never met him.'

'I thought not. You are merely telling us what his job was. I think the gentlemen of the jury will already understand that, in so far as it is necessary at all. I assume that you never wrote a letter of authorisation for payment that was . . . erroneous?'

'No, sir!' Partington said stiffly. 'I never took anything that was not mine!'

'We have not yet established that anyone has,' Daniel said, and then before Hillyer could object, he sat down.

Hillyer called his next witness, another clerk who kept similar ledgers in some British embassy somewhere else.

Daniel sat silent, only half listening. It was difficult to concentrate on anything so infinitely tedious. But he knew that the one thing that might matter, if he caught it, could change the course of the trial, and he could miss it through a slip in attention.

Then he became aware of someone standing in the aisle beside him. For one bright moment, he thought it might be Kitteridge. But it was not. It was someone darker, and more naturally co-ordinated.

The judge was staring at them.

The man kneeled down in the aisle, next to Daniel, to appear at the same level as if he were sitting. It was Patrick.

Daniel tried to look as if he had been expecting him. 'What are you doing here?' he whispered sharply. 'What's happened?' He was terrified there had been some disaster that would be far worse than anything that could happen here.

Patrick looked at his face. 'We need to talk . . . now . . . about the case.'

'Can you be brief? Or shall I ask for an adjournment? For how long?'

'Fifteen minutes? I don't know how much it matters, but you ought to judge.'

Patrick was intensely serious, and Daniel could see that there was something far more grave than anything he had yet said.

'Mr Pitt?' the judge enquired patiently. 'Is this interruption relevant?'

'Yes, Your Honour. If I could ask you for a fifteen-minute adjournment?' Daniel requested.

'Very well, fifteen minutes,' the judge agreed wearily, but there was a flicker of amusement in his face, there and then gone again, as if he could use a break from the tedium of the evidence so far.

Daniel left the courtroom as quickly as possible, with

Patrick on his heels. He had no office here, and nowhere in the building was private enough for whatever this might be. He stopped on the steps outside.

Patrick stood in front of him. He knew time was short. 'I've been in touch with the police department back home in Washington by wire. Actually, it's pretty good, if you can be brief.'

'What did they tell you?' Daniel had no patience to wait until Patrick worked around to it.

'That Morley Cross, the young man who worked at the British Embassy and who we believe found the false expenses papers, went missing, and now his body has turned up in the Potomac. That's a river in Washington.'

'You mean he has drowned?' said Daniel, thinking he must have misunderstood.

'He was murdered,' Patrick said.

'Not . . . an accident? You said in the river?'

'Yes. But he didn't drown. He was shot.' Patrick looked at Daniel steadily. 'It's probably connected. He worked in the same department in the embassy as Sidney. He handled the same accounts and money. I'm sorry. It looks much worse than we thought – than I thought, anyway.'

Daniel was stunned. His mind raced to accommodate this new information and fit it into any story that made sense.

'When did he die?' he asked Patrick.

'Not sure, exactly.' Patrick looked grim. 'Been dead a while, and in the water. There's not a lot to go on. But it looks like a while. Lucky they could identify him. But it seems to be long enough ago that it could be before Sidney left Washington.'

'You're saying Sidney killed him?' Daniel's stomach sank as he asked. This was worse than anything he had imagined.

Then another thought occurred to him. Could Hillyer possibly know this, and be waiting for some further detail before he called witnesses, who would drop it on Daniel? He would be taken totally by surprise and have no possible answer for it.

'I'm saying he could have,' Patrick answered. 'I'm sorry. But you have to be prepared for this coming up now. Somebody did it. He was shot in the back of the head. He couldn't have done it himself. Not at that angle.' He hesitated. 'Can I do anything at all to help? Find out anything? I . . . I didn't mean to lumber you with this. I didn't know Morley Cross was even missing.'

'But you keep up . . .?'

'I care about this. I want it to come out right. I think Sidney's arrogant, takes things that are not his, regardless of who gets hurt. He terrified Rebecca. She's still scared stiff to sleep at night. She has nightmares. And he took a pendant, which Jemima has learned wasn't worth a lot of money after all, but was precious to her, because it was given to her by someone she loved, and who is now gone.'

'I understand,' Daniel said quietly. 'If he's guilty, then he is mean-spirited, cruel . . .' He forced himself to go on. 'And if he's not guilty, this could mean the complete destruction of the man's character, of his whole life that he's had in the past, or will have in the future.'

'I know. I wish to hell I knew what the truth was!'

'So do I,' Daniel said with profound feeling. 'Tell me anything else you hear, please. Now I've got to go back and sit through this tedium, because Hillyer could be hiding something important in all this!'

Patrick smiled. 'Good luck.'

*

143

Death by boredom, Daniel thought to himself as the court resumed. Why was Hillyer stringing this out? Was he playing for time? The answer was painful and clear. Daniel was almost certain Patrick was right: Hillyer was delaying until he had enough proof of Morley Cross's murder to introduce it, and charge Sidney with that as well.

That's why he had to listen. Hillyer could go on like this for days! Even weeks!

Daniel felt every muscle in his body tighten as the thought struck him: was there another witness who knew something about the murder of Morley Cross? An old enemy? Rival? Sidney's job in the embassy was hardly worth all this effort, was it? Was there something about it he didn't know? Someone had murdered Morley Cross. That was undeniable. It would be absurd to hope it was nothing to do with Sidney, and the embassy. But what? No witness Hillyer called made it any plainer.

Daniel left the court at the end of the day without speaking again to Sidney. He had no idea what to ask him. He needed to speak to Kitteridge.

He found him in chambers, having just come back from a different court himself.

'Hell, Pitt! You look awful! What happened? And sit down, before you fall over.'

Daniel obeyed. 'Most of the actual evidence was just time wasting,' he answered. 'Hillyer called one character witness after another. I had to listen, in case he is burying something.'

'Was he?' Kitteridge interrupted.

'Not that I could see. But . . .'

'Well, what is it, for heaven's sake?'

Daniel took a long breath. 'Morley Cross, the man who

handed over the financial papers? His body was found floating in the Potomac River. He'd been shot.' He saw Kitteridge's face turn pale, his eyes widen, but he did not speak. 'And it might have happened before Sidney left the States,' Daniel added.

Again, Kitteridge remained silent.

'Hillyer has said nothing,' Daniel went on. 'Perhaps he doesn't know . . . yet. So, witnesses are giving details. But after what we've learned, it's all waffle. He's taking up time, and boring the jury half to death.'

'Then he's hiding something,' Kitteridge concluded. 'But what? News of Morley Cross? Why?'

'Not enough information? So, he'll move on to focus on the assault on Rebecca? Unless . . .' He stopped, the words choking him.

'Unless . . . what?'

There was no point in biting it back. 'Unless one of the character witnesses is going to announce the murder.'

'And if not?'

Daniel thought for a moment. 'That he assaulted some other young woman, which ties into the Rebecca story.' Then another thought occurred to him, worse than the first. For a moment, it robbed him of speech. The jeopardy to Sidney had suddenly doubled, tripled, in size and threatened everything. His mind was racing ahead.

'What is it?' Kitteridge demanded. 'Pitt! I'm not a mind reader. What are you thinking? That Sidney is guilty? What if he is? I know you quite like him, or at least have a sympathy for him. But if he's guilty, then he is. I'd far rather Hillyer proved it on his own than we had to engineer some way of introducing the whole beastly business.' He hesitated a moment.

Daniel said nothing. His mouth was as dry as sawdust.

'Pitt! Don't look like that. We've had guilty clients before. And if this is a pattern, then he has to be put away. We have to bite the bullet, and admit he's charming, and rotten!'

'That isn't what I was thinking,' Daniel answered at last. 'If Thorwood were to be called as a witness his identification of Sidney would be very easily believable. And give him a painful motive everyone would understand, for wanting to take Sidney down, to pay for his assaulting Rebecca.' He stared at Kitteridge. 'But . . . the murder?'

Slowly, Kitteridge turned pale. 'You mean if Thorwood got it wrong, and somehow framed Sidney for the embezzlement, to get revenge?'

'Isn't that the obvious defence? That the identification was wrong? But Thorwood believes it, perhaps because he has to, for whatever reason. Perhaps Sidney and Rebecca were having an affair? Thorwood wants to get rid of Sidney. Disgrace is the obvious answer. Ruin him. Return him to England in disgrace. Then he can't marry Rebecca, and the Thorwood money. But what if Thorwood knows nothing about Morley Cross? The murder must be part of the whole business but if Thorwood framed Sidney, and he's innocent of the assault and the embezzlement, how does the murder of Morley Cross fit in with that?'

'God! You've got a devious mind, and you want to understand everyone!' Kitteridge said, but it was awe he expressed, not denial. 'I see why you're going all shades of pale,' he went on. 'What is Patrick Flannery's part in this? Or what would Thorwood say it was, regardless?' He took a deep breath and was about to go on, when Daniel cut across him.

'Patrick came to the court today.'

'What? Why?' Kitteridge looked startled.

'He came to tell me about Cross.'

'Cross . . .' Kitteridge repeated, and then fell silent.

Daniel said nothing. Clearly, the man was formulating some idea.

'Could Morley Cross have attacked Rebecca?' Kitteridge said with disbelief. 'Then he set up Sidney with the embezzlement charge?'

'I hadn't even thought of that,' Daniel admitted, a wave of nausea coming over him. How had he not considered that?

'Oh, great heaven!' Kitteridge said slowly, the colour draining out of his face. 'And they are thinking Cross's murder happened before Sidney left Washington?'

'That's just it,' Daniel said wretchedly. 'It's too close to say . . . yet.'

Chapter Twelve

The trial continued. On the second day Jemima sat in the gallery beside Patrick and watched Hillyer proceed to call his witnesses, each describing Philip Sidney as they had known him. It was all boringly predictable, but Jemima could not drag her attention from it because, surely the moment she did, it would be that time when something interesting would be said, something on which the whole case might turn.

Was it going to turn? Which way? She and Patrick had spoken about it little, and not at all since yesterday. He did not seem to want to, and she realised she was actually afraid. Why? Frightened that justice would not be done? That Sidney would escape? What? Whatever was the sentence for embezzlement, that was not what this was really about, for any of them. She felt confused about her feelings when a man was being tried for a crime he probably didn't commit to expose one that he probably had, but which she wasn't even sure she wanted to be made public.

She looked sideways to her right, across the aisle, where Bernadette Thorwood was sitting, pale-faced, next to Rebecca. Tobias was not present.

Bernadette had her hands folded in her lap. They looked relaxed, except that every now and then she would twist her ring. The large diamond would catch the light, and then disappear again.

Why had they brought Rebecca to this? Did they fear that perhaps this was all the justice she was going to see? Jemima had not spoken to Rebecca alone since the angry words they had said after their meeting in the park. Jemima had called again, but both times either Bernadette or Tobias had been present and the meetings had been awkward.

Jemima tried to think what it would be like to waken in the night and find a man in her bedroom, perhaps sifting through her belongings looking for money, or more likely, jewellery. Had she sat up? Called out to him, perhaps? Why had he not run while he still could? That seemed stupid to Jemima. Had the light caught the pendant at her throat, and he had gone after it, as a magpie after all that glitters? Regardless of losing his chance to escape?

Or had she herself been the object of his breaking in, theft not the motive at all? Was Rebecca telling the truth about how well she really knew Philip Sidney?

Jemima hated herself for that thought. She owed her friend more loyalty than that. How hurt she would be were it the other way around, and Rebecca has disbelieved her! And yet she did doubt. Something was missing from the account. It might be something perfectly innocent, just private, but left out of all this. She sensed that Patrick knew more than he was revealing, but had chosen to say nothing. Why? To protect her from knowing something bad about Rebecca?

Jemima had learned that long ago: any crime that is investigated means that all sorts of aspects of your life are opened up, not just to the police, but to your friends, acquaintances, servants if you have them. To other members of your family. Perhaps most telling of all, sometimes, to yourself. What will you elaborate, or tell just a little lie, to protect? Usually it is less out of dishonesty than embarrassment, foolishness, above all vulnerability.

Who will you lie to protect? But then you have to lie again and again to keep up the whole story you have created, one tiny thread at a time. It would be like building a cocoon, woven by single stitches, until you could not move inside it, much less escape.

She looked across at Philip Sidney. What was he guilty of? A series of errors? Or something darker? He was nice-looking, in a mild, semi-humorous sort of way. As if he could see the joke, even when it was so much against him. But he was frightened. She could see that after a moment or two. He was breathing too deeply. He kept looking at Daniel, as if aching to find reassurance, and then turning away again just as quickly, before he could see that there was none.

Daniel, of course, she knew much better. Although in the four years she had been in America, he had changed in so many indefinite ways. He was certainly far more sure of his opinions, and less compelled to defend them. That was part of growing up, and she admired it. He seemed more than four years older. The air of innocence he always had was still there. Maybe it always would be. But now she saw beneath it. He had known victory and defeat. Much less could take him by surprise.

And the spell away from home, away from his parents, had allowed a whole set of ideas and characteristics to grow. He had opinions she had never seen in him before, but she had caught a glimpse of the need to understand everyone that he had always had; she could remember him as a little boy asking over and over, 'Why? Why did he do that?'

Hillyer finished questioning the witness, someone who had known Sidney before he had gone to America, and disliked him. He had attempted to hide it, to seem so scrupulously fair, that the whole account sounded artificial. Would Daniel pick that up? It wasn't the facts, it was the emotions. Would he see that?

Daniel began to question the witness, a man by the name of Edgeley.

Jemima's fingernails were digging into her palms. How could anything so boring also make her so tense? It was like a firing squad! Why wouldn't someone just shoot and get it over with?

'You say that Sidney was careless at times, Mr Edgeley. He made mistakes and allowed you to take the blame for them?' Daniel asked calmly, as if he were only checking the facts.

'Yes, that's right.'

'A nasty habit.' Daniel pulled his mouth into an expression of distaste. 'In fact, I would call it a mixture of cowardice and dishonesty.'

'Yes, I suppose so,' Edgeley agreed.

Jemima thought he was insufferably smug. She glanced at Sidney and saw the distress in him, but of course he could not speak. It was the ultimate horror of the mind, to have to sit there and listen to people say things about you, and not be able to protest, or explain, not defend yourself at all! Like being tied up while people hit you, unable to move, let alone strike back. They would even be watching your face to see if it hurt enough, and perhaps judge you on that, too. You could not even deal with your pain privately.

She looked at the jurors and saw them staring one minute at Edgeley, the next at Sidney. A decent man would want to turn away, as you would if you had accidentally intruded on someone naked. But it was their job to judge him. They were obliged to look!

'It must have upset you,' Daniel was continuing. 'Did you ever suffer actual punishment on any of these occasions, Mr Edgeley, such as the loss of an opportunity? A promotion, perhaps? Or the handling of a particular visit?'

'Hard to tell,' Edgeley replied with the slightest shrug. 'People don't give reasons for things.'

'I am beginning to appreciate what a difficult profession it is,' Daniel said sympathetically. 'Whom do you trust? Not Sidney, apparently.'

Edgeley snapped, 'Not if you've any sense!'

'And yet they didn't dismiss him? Curious, don't you think? He has no wealth, no connections, no family influence. Perhaps you can explain that, so the jury understands. I admit, I don't.'

Jemima held her breath. She was only dimly aware of Patrick stiffening beside her.

'Mr Edgeley?' Daniel prompted.

'I don't know!' Edgeley snapped.

'You did tell them, I take it?' Daniel affected innocence. 'Perhaps they are corrupt also?'

'I didn't say they were corrupt!' Edgeley was now very clearly upset.

'No. I believe you still work at the Foreign Office. Or am I mistaken?'

'Yes, I do.'

'And you are about to see Mr Sidney get his just deserts. Even to make something of a contribution to that? You must be very . . . satisfied?'

'Leave it alone,' Jemima said under her breath. Patrick turned to look at her, puzzled. He could barely have heard her, surely? Then with a flood of horror, she realised why he was staring at her. She wanted Daniel to win! She was cheering him on! It couldn't be Sidney she was supporting. She would have to explain that, perhaps when they got home. Certainly not now.

Hillyer knew enough to leave the testimony well alone. He called his next witness, another pleasant enough man, older than Edgeley. Hillyer wouldn't be caught out the same way again. Mr Stains gave his evidence with a kinder manner. It added little to the picture. It bored Jemima. Hillyer was wasting time, as Daniel said. Why? What was he waiting for?

Luncheon was agony. It was unavoidable that Jemima and Patrick should accept Tobias Thorwood's invitation to dine with them. A table had already been reserved at a very nice restaurant not far away, and the meal requested in advance so they would not have to wait for service.

Jemima dreaded it.

'We have to,' Patrick murmured when they had a moment alone, the Thorwoods, united outside the courtroom, having gone ahead. 'For heaven's sake, say as little as you can without being rude. No opinion, please, Jem?'

'I promise. Really!' She meant it far more than he might believe. She was aware of just how deeply she loved him by how much this whole case hurt. She did not want even to question him, let alone consider that he might be wrong about

Sidney. Or even if it was absolutely right, that he had engineered the evidence so the assault would emerge, even though Sidney might not actually have embezzled anything. It wouldn't matter. If he couldn't even be tried for the assault, let alone convicted, it would still ruin him. There would be nothing left for him in England. No employment. No friends. No acceptance anywhere. Society would punish him indirectly for what it could not get the law to exact. There would be no reprieve. No payment, therefore no freedom from the debt, ever.

Was that really what Patrick wanted? Was there something big, and very important, very dark, that she did not know about?

Could she ask him, so it did not lie between them?

Not now. They were walking out of the courthouse and into the street. There were five of them. Two motor cars were waiting by the kerb.

Jemima sat beside Patrick. Three times she started to ask him just what he knew, then lost the nerve to continue. She could not find the right words. It all sounded accusing. How do you ask someone you love every day, every night, whose triumphs, dreams, and losses you share, if he is framing a man for a crime he did not commit, so that they would punish him for one you were sure he did?

They arrived at the hotel and were taken straight to the dining room. It was decorated in a comfortable, time-dulled sort of Persian red, deep and rich. The furniture was heavy, carved oak, and looked as if it had never been moved since it was first put there, perhaps a century ago. The linen was all crisp white, the crystal sparkling, and plenty of staff to attend to every wish. Bottles of white wine nestled in buckets of ice, and a bottle of red wine stood open on the next table to breathe.

The meal began immediately. It was delicious, and served on the best porcelain. At another time, Jemima would have relished it. Now, she was hardly even aware of its taste.

'I don't know what he is driving at,' Bernadette said suddenly, putting her napkin down completely. She seemed to be speaking to Tobias. 'What is he achieving? What's he waiting for? These people are boring the jury as much as they're boring the rest of us. I suppose he's building the tension, so that Sir John will be a complete contrast, and they will remember everything he says.'

Jemima thought that made excellent sense, but she did not want to join the conversation. Bernadette must be referring to Sir John Armitage.

Tobias looked slightly surprised. 'Is he up this afternoon? I didn't know that. I'm sure he didn't mention it when I saw him this morning.' That sounded like an accusation.

'I dare say he thought you already knew,' Bernadette dismissed the oversight.

'Will they ask him why he got Mr Sidney out of America, so he didn't have to face charges for breaking into our house?' Rebecca said suddenly. She had been pushing her food around the plate in a pretence of eating. Now she stopped altogether.

Tobias's hand tightened on his fork, until he unintentionally scraped it across the porcelain with a loud squeak.

Jemima drew in her breath to reassure him, then realised she should not interrupt.

'No, of course not,' Tobias said without looking at her. 'Armitage would only answer the questions he's asked. But if he is asked anything that would lead to that answer, then I am sure he would not be less than honest. I know how you feel, but nothing is your fault. We have already been over this.'

155

'I know,' Rebecca kept her eyes on her plate. 'I . . . I just hate it!'

Bernadette put her hand over her daughter's, quite gently, stopping the nervous fidgeting of which Rebecca seemed unaware. 'You will not be required to say anything. Patrick has promised you that, haven't you, Patrick?'

Patrick was obviously caught off guard. He hesitated a moment.

Jemima wondered then how much Patrick really knew about what was going on, what Tobias planned, and with whom. She looked at him now and saw the shadow in his expression, the second's silence before he answered.

'You don't know anything,' he said to Rebecca with a slight smile. 'You woke in the night and found a stranger in your room. You screamed. He tore the pendant from your neck, then ran away. It was your father who came immediately to your aid, and saw him in the hallway. He recognised him. You can add nothing. They know that.'

He was explaining too much, Jemima knew that. If he had been sure, he would simply have said 'no'.

Rebecca relaxed, smiling back. She believed him.

It was Tobias who would not let it go. 'Why is Armitage prepared to testify this afternoon? He can hardly say he knew Sidney was embezzling. If he had, he'd have dismissed the man whenever he first found out. Saying that he was in charge, yet didn't know he was being systematically robbed, makes him appear incompetent. He's far too proud to do that! Has he no sense of patriotism?'

'Obviously Sidney has none,' Bernadette cut across him. 'Perhaps that is why Sir John sent him back to England, so he would not disgrace the embassy in Washington, but still answer the crime in London. After all, it is essentially an English crime.'

Jemima stiffened. 'Embezzlement?' she said very coolly, taking exception to Bernadette's wording. 'Really?'

Bernadette's eyes were like stones as she stared across the table. 'One Englishman steals from his own embassy and is got out of the country by a man high in that embassy, who then accuses him when they are over here, back in England, and gives evidence against him in an English court. I don't see what you are questioning. It seems to be both an honourable and a just way of dealing with it. In all respects.'

Jemima was furious at Bernadette's tone and her objecting to Jemima defending her countrymen from what could be taken to be a racial slur, and yet she could think of nothing to say. And certainly nothing she ought to say in the circumstances. She was the Thorwoods' guest and she disliked it intensely, but it could not be helped.

She felt Patrick's hand on hers, where the tablecloth hid it, and closed her fingers over his. Did he understand? Perhaps he hated it too, but he was better at hiding it? Or more used to having to.

Bernadette bent to her meal again.

'I doubt I will be called,' Tobias added. 'I can add nothing about the embezzlement. How could I possibly know what goes on inside the British Embassy?'

'But you know Philip Sidney,' Jemima said suddenly. She wanted to disconcert him. 'You could be called as a character witness.'

Tobias looked stunned. 'You think I'm going to . . . to stand up there and say that I think well of the man? After he . . . assaulted my daughter . . . in her bedroom? And tore the pendant from her neck? Are you . . .?' He bit back what he'd been about to say.

It was Patrick who explained what Jemima had meant.

'Not for the defence,' he said quietly. 'For the prosecution.'

For seconds, no one spoke.

'Are you?' Bernadette said at last, staring at her husband with an expression that was unreadable. 'Are you going to do that?'

'The man's a . . . a total swine!' Tobias almost choked on his own words. 'I cannot stand by and let him get away with it! Is that what you expect of me?'

Bernadette stared down at her plate and the delicate fishbones on it, the flesh taken away. 'No, my dear,' she said very quietly. 'It will be very difficult for you, for all of us, but you have to do what is right. Rebecca will understand that. And if it is done here, that will be so much easier for us. I . . . I thank you for your courage and foresight.'

Tobias flushed deep pink, but it was impossible to tell what mixture of emotions caused it.

Jemima considered saying something normal, unconnected with the case at all, but nothing came to her mind that was not ridiculous.

The afternoon evidence began with Hillyer calling Sir John Armitage to the witness stand. Now, at last, the attention was complete. The jurors sat up straight, eyes wide open.

Armitage swore to his name, and his occupation, then faced Hillyer with grace and intense seriousness.

'Good afternoon, Sir John,' Hillyer said gravely, his face almost without expression. 'I believe you have known Philip Sidney for many years. Indeed, it was on your recommendation that he gained his position at the British Embassy in Washington.'

'Indeed,' Armitage shook his head ruefully. 'It was perhaps

the worst mistake I have ever made in a man. I knew his mother. A very fine woman. She — I suppose like many women do — saw only the best in her son. I did not see it as such. I accepted that she was basically correct in her judgement of him. I now regret that.'

'He did not live up to his mother's words?' Hillyer asked.

Jemima looked across at Sidney and saw such pain in his eyes, his mouth, that it was as if she had felt it herself. She thought of how she would have felt, had her father recommended her for something, and been bitterly disappointed in her. She could not bear it. She could not bear it for Sidney, and she hardly knew him! She had unwittingly seen what should have been private. Was it true, and she was just being a coward, complicit because she was not brave enough to face the truth?

Armitage was talking about Sidney's earliest years in the embassy. He seemed to have been excellent.

'You saw no fault in him?' Hillyer pressed.

'No, none at all, at that time,' Armitage admitted. 'I even imagined he had an outstanding career ahead of him. Indeed, I thought so until—' He stopped suddenly, as if he had unintentionally let slip more than he had intended. There was a moment's silence.

'Until what?' Hillyer prompted.

'It is not relevant to this case,' Armitage replied.

'We should judge that,' Hillyer told him. 'I—'

Daniel shot to his feet for the first time in the trial. 'Your Honour, if it is irrelevant, it should not be offered. Once the jury has heard it, it will affect their view, and thus their judgment. Even with the best intentions, we do not forget our feelings, just because we no longer remember what prompted them.'

159

'Indeed,' the judge said, shaking his head. 'Mr Hillyer, you know better than that. Fly fishing, sir? I cannot allow you to plunge in with a net!'

Hillyer sighed. 'Yes, Your Honour. I apologise. I will come at it a little later, more directly.'

The judge gave him a sour smile and nodded. 'Indeed.'

Jemima let her breath out very slowly. She dared not look at Patrick. She did glance at Daniel, but he was staring straight ahead of him. Surely Armitage had been about to refer, perhaps obliquely, perhaps quite openly, to the attack on Rebecca. At the very least, it would have been a thread someone would follow. The jury had heard this, and had to be wondering what it was that could not be said.

Daniel must have known what he was doing, mustn't he? Did he intend to defend Sidney, *really* defend him? And as the question came clearly in her mind, Jemima knew that yes, he did.

What had changed?

She turned her attention back to Armitage's testimony.

Patrick was almost silent on the way home, and even later over dinner. When he did speak he did not mention the trial. Jemima felt her mother watching, and twice Charlotte was on the edge of asking him something, her face filled with concern. But Jemima smiled and spoke of something else. It was not until the bedroom door was closed that he spoke before she could. He stood in the centre of the room, stiff with pent-up tension.

'Did you know he was going to do that?' he asked, his voice brittle and sharp.

'No! Of course, I didn't,' she said straight away. 'Armitage was the prosecution's witness. We took it for granted he was going to say that Sidney seemed to be all right, but underneath he was bad. And he did! But he must have intended to drop the assault in—'

'Not Armitage,' Patrick cut across her. 'Daniel! If he'd waited a couple of seconds later, Armitage would've said it. Then it would all have come out eventually. You couldn't keep it in, no matter how you tried.'

'Don't keep saying "you"!' she interrupted. 'It's not me . . .'

'Not you, Jemima Pitt – you are the English, the society, the people Sidney belongs to. People sticking by their own, no matter what.'

She felt her heart cramp with an overwhelming sense of loss. 'I thought I was Jemima Flannery! Am I suddenly "them" and not "us"? Is that what it's about? Not whether Sidney is guilty or innocent of either crime, but whether he's English or American?'

'Isn't it?' Patrick flashed back. 'Loyalty. None of us, except Sidney himself, knows exactly what he did . . . or why. We take the word of the people we know against those we don't. We trust the people who are like us, and who trust us. It's natural.'

'It's tribalism,' she replied. 'We should be beyond that.'

'Beyond loyalty, patriotism, trusting and being worthy of trust? What is beyond that? Every man for himself?'

'You're using words—'

'Well, what the hell else?'

'No! I mean you're using them, making them mean what you want, emotion, not thinking.'

'About what? It's a big thing to be trusted, Jem. Look at Cassie and Sophie. They trust you in everything. Would you give that up? Betray it?'

'That's not fair! They are my children! That's not tribalism, it's . . . family.'

'Which is the beginning of the tribe. Do you want to walk through life alone?'

'Of course not! But that's different. Sophie's a baby; Cassie's only three!'

'When are you planning to stop? When she's six? Twelve? Eighteen?'

'When she marries!' she flashed back. 'But that's not the point, Patrick, and you know it! There comes a time when you can't give loyalty without thinking.'

'Questions of loyalty don't often give you time to debate.'

'Then you need to know what matters most, before you have to make a decision,' she replied. It sounded smug, and she knew it, even as the words were on her tongue.

He shook his head. 'And you know it all, Jem?'

'No, I don't! Of course, I don't. But I know I don't decide the Thorwoods are right because I know them, and Sidney is wrong, because I don't.'

'And Daniel is your brother? That means nothing? Don't expect me to believe that you don't trust him, because you've known him all his life.' He smiled reluctantly. 'I've seen that same look on your face when you watch him that you have for Cassie. Just for an instant.'

'All right! So, he's my little brother.'

'I like it. And actually, I like him. And I had to tell him yesterday that it's highly possible the man he's defending for petty embezzlement is also guilty of murder. The body of some other man who worked at the embassy just washed up on the shore of the Potomac. He took it well . . . considering.'

She let out a gasp, then a sigh of sorrow. 'I'm so sorry.'

'Yes. It's bad,' Patrick agreed. 'And I see that you've got to be on his side, a bit.' After a moment, he added, 'You

162

know when you look at someone you love, you're beautiful, really beautiful.'

She looked at him and found her eyes full of tears. 'That's because I love you. It doesn't mean I agree with you over everything!'

He doubled up with sudden laughter.

'I don't!' she shouted.

'I'm a detective, sweetheart. I had that worked out the second time I met you!'

'That doesn't mean Sidney's guilty, or innocent . . . or right, or wrong.'

'Nobody's always right, or always wrong.'

'Nonsense,' she returned. 'You're always right – aren't you?'

Chapter Thirteen

'What in hell was that about?' Kitteridge demanded as he caught up with Daniel and walked down the steps of the courthouse into the warm August air of the street. They both turned automatically towards the underground station.

Kitteridge's case had finished early and he'd come along to observe the puzzling case of Philip Sidney, on which he had spent so much time helping out Daniel.

For a moment or two, Daniel did not answer.

Kitteridge grasped his arm and pulled him to a stop in the middle of the pavement.

'I don't know,' Daniel answered before Kitteridge could ask again. 'It seemed wrong. It could have been wrong. Do you want him to get off on appeal because he had an incompetent defence?' At the moment it was a very real fear. 'I don't know if I want him condemned at all, but certainly not because I made a mess of it. For his sake, and mine.'

'You don't think he's guilty! Do you?' Kitteridge said, as if making a suddenly discovery. That was not so much a question as much as a challenge. 'If he's innocent, is someone else guilty? Someone at the embassy, for example?'

'Guilty of what?' Daniel asked. The body of Morley Cross,

dragged out of the Potomac, haunted his mind. 'Let go of my arm!' He snatched it away. 'Stop standing here in the street and come and get a beer, or something. We've got to get this sorted out. This trial isn't going on for ever. Even a snail arrives somewhere in the end.'

'Stop talking rot!' Kitteridge said tartly. 'You're avoiding the question. Did Flannery arrange this somehow, to avenge Rebecca Thorwood? Isn't that what he and your sister are really over here for?'

'I'm not going to believe that unless I have to,' Daniel said more quietly. 'That would be . . .' He had been going to say 'awful', but then he wondered what he would have done in their place. He had been angry, hurt, confused enough to be sorely tempted to step outside the law in the Graves case. Would he, if things had been different? If he had felt sure enough? He was certainly not sure enough now! Of anything. Not of Thorwood, certainly. And less and less of the truth about Sidney and the assault of Rebecca. But with growing certainty he believed Patrick in that the events were tied in with the murder of Morley Cross.

They came to a decent-looking public house and went inside. They ordered ale and cold mutton sandwiches with horseradish sauce.

'I would feel better if I knew what Hillyer wanted,' Kitteridge said while they waited for their food to arrive. 'How did the case get brought at all? Did the Foreign Office bring it? Is there any way of finding out?'

'You mean like asking my father?' Daniel raised his eyebrows. 'I agree, it's very unlike the Foreign Office to wash its dirty linen in public.'

'I asked somebody I know in government.' Kitteridge fiddled with his napkin, turning it over, his knuckles white.

'He said he'd have expected them to throw Sidney out, without notice or pay, and then shut up about it. It's his reputation, as well as theirs. In fact, if I were the Foreign Secretary, I'd want to know why in hell they let it go this far. Wouldn't you? Pitt, there's more here than a piece of rather clumsy embezzlement.'

'Some of it forged,' Daniel added, evading the real subject.

'Well, we'd better be damned quick about finding out what!' Kitteridge said.

The waitress brought their food and the ale. They thanked her and waited until she was out of earshot.

'Politics?' Kitteridge suggested, before taking a mouthful of his sandwich.

'Embassy politics? Or do you mean international ones?' Daniel said. He bit into his sandwich. It was really good, fresh, coarse bread, crusts crumbling, thick-cut mutton, and just enough horseradish to give it a tingle. 'Or British? I don't see what issue could be involved, or how removing Sidney could affect it anyway. I looked into the stuff he was handling, as far as they would let me. Somebody else took it all over anyway. Nothing really changed.'

'So, it was personal about Sidney?'

'Or Thorwood?' Daniel suggested.

'What does he have to do with the embassy?'

'Nothing that I know of. I was thinking revenge for Sidney having assaulted Rebecca, and taken the pendant. But then he'd have had to have some influence at the embassy to bring about his revenge with the charge of embezzlement.'

'Is the pendant worth a lot?' Kitteridge asked.

'Jemima told me it was made of crystal, not diamond, so it wasn't worth anything, except sentimentally, because it was May Trelawny's.'

'Whom Sidney has never heard of, I imagine?'

'Don't know. But if he has, it would have been from Rebecca. I can't think of anyone else who would mention Miss Trelawny to him,' Daniel said.

Kitteridge ate another mouthful of his sandwich, then looked up intensely seriously. 'So, you think Sidney did it.'

'Which, the assault or the embezzlement?' Daniel was playing for time to think, and he saw in Kitteridge's face that he knew that.

'Well, the embezzlement came first,' Kitteridge pointed out. 'They are going to say he stole the pendant in the hope of selling it and putting the money back before anyone knew it.'

'What?' Daniel said incredulously. 'I hope they do! It's nonsense. Is Hillyer half-witted? He didn't look like that to me. Anyway, why is Hillyer doing this?'

'Presumably, his firm is appearing for the Crown. What else? The . . .'

'The what?'

'The Foreign Office will have employed him. He's very reputable.'

'Then he must owe somebody a favour. Or he's bucking for silk! Maybe Sir James Hillyer, King's Counsel? Has a ring to it.'

'Do you think so?' Kitteridge said doubtfully.

'No, I don't,' Daniel replied. 'I'd want ermine, never mind silk, to argue that!'

'Seat in the House of Lords? You're an ass, Pitt!'

'Not a big enough ass to argue that Sidney steadily embezzled five or ten pounds here and there for a year, then decided to put it back by breaking into Thorwood's house and assaulting his daughter before pinching a glass pendant by ripping it off her neck. Then escaping, allowing himself to be seen by someone who knew him well enough to recognise him by sight. In the hope of . . . what? Recovering all the individual papers that prove his embezzlement, and replacing them with five-pound notes! Then fleeing the country? What defence did he intend to plead – insanity? We could always make that stick!'

Kitteridge stared at him. 'Well, what is it then?'

'I don't know! But there's something we've been missing, because this doesn't make sense.'

Kitteridge rolled his eyes. 'For heaven's sake, Pitt, half the cases we get don't make sense. Where the hell did you ever get the idea that they did? Didn't your father teach you anything? Haven't I taught you anything?'

'The law doesn't always make sense,' Daniel agreed. 'But there is a kind of cumulative structure to it. There will be to this case, when we have it all. There's something missing. Hillyer is not a fool, however much we might like to think that he is. He knows something that makes sense, at least to him. We've got to find out what it is.'

'Someone in the Foreign Office wants to get rid of Sidney? Or . . . is it tied into Morley Cross's murder?' Kitteridge suggested. 'I can't see how. Perhaps Sidney knows something? An indiscretion? Only a fool would try blackmail at that level, but perhaps he is a fool? Or someone thinks he is?'

'I think you're right,' Daniel said. 'And it will come out soon. I think proof of it is what Hillyer is stringing this all out for . . .'

'And Cross was working in the same department of the Embassy in Washington as Sidney!' Kitteridge exclaimed.

Daniel watched Kitteridge's face and saw the play of

emotions on it, from horror to pity, and pity to understanding of what it meant.

'And that points to Sidney?' Kitteridge went on, his voice catching in his throat.

'I've no idea. But it could be,' Daniel replied. 'They haven't fixed the time of death yet, and maybe they won't be able to, exactly. Could be just before Sidney left Washington . . . or just after.'

Kitteridge was, for once, lost for words.

'It will be a capital case as soon as they get the information organised,' said Daniel. 'That completely explains why Hillyer is boring the jury half to death. Anything to keep them there while he awaits a positive identification, and time of death, if at all possible.'

'Why would Sidney kill Cross?' Kitteridge asked.

'Because he knew Sidney was guilty of embezzling. In fact, they very possibly did it together. Perhaps they quarrelled over the money . . .'

'A hundred pounds? Don't be idiotic. Anyway, by that time there was probably nothing left of it. You said it was only a few pounds at a time.'

'They'll find a motive,' Daniel said miserably. 'Maybe we've missed something.'

'No,' Kitteridge interrupted. 'Next thing is, Sidney and Morley Cross fight over the pendant, diamond or not, and Sidney kills Cross. Perhaps he gets it back, or perhaps it is in the Potomac and so we'll never know.'

'All right,' Daniel agreed. 'But why? Sidney is very glad to accept Armitage's help to get back to England without being charged for the assault on Rebecca.'

'Does Armitage know about the murder of Cross?' Kitteridge asked.

169

'I don't think so, but he knows that Sidney's accused of taking a pendant from Rebecca, in particularly unfortunate circumstances . . . according to the Thorwoods. But that would be some passionate motive . . . so maybe we've got the thing all wrong? There's no big political stake. Sidney's not that important. He might have been, someday, but he's nobody now. And he's connected to nobody that I can trace. And believe me, I've tried. Marcus even looked into it and asked around. Sidney's not even courting anybody interesting. Or anybody at all! I looked into that, too, in case some parents wanted to make sure their precious daughter didn't marry beneath her. I tried money, title, influence. Nothing!'

'I suppose Rebecca couldn't be it?' Kitteridge said, but even as he framed the words, he lost belief in that possibility. 'No, you'd have known about it by now,' he answered for himself. 'From Flannery or your sister, if no one else. Sidney's not connected to anyone, poor devil. It's something else. And I think Sidney knows what it is, and it's nothing he can afford to admit. He's facing ruin, if they find him guilty, and we don't have a real defence. We're playing at it. Hitting each ball as it comes. But you haven't got a plan. You know, and I know it. We aren't really hacking it for him. Look at his face!'

Daniel thought for a moment. 'Does he look like a man who's taken the blame for somebody else?'

'No.'

'I don't think so either. I think he's even more lost than we are,' Daniel agreed, noticing with a wave of relief that Kitteridge had said 'we' and not 'you'. 'But we'd better find something soon. We've got to do more than discredit one witness. Are the embezzlement letters or receipts forged and we can prove it or not? Some of them are, according to Miriam, but not all of them. And the assault on Rebecca. Did it happen? Did it happen the way Rebecca says, and her father says? For that matter, was May Trelawny's pendant a diamond or really just glass? Or both?'

'It can't be both,' Kitteridge pointed out meticulously.

'Yes, it can. A diamond that was sold, given away, stolen or whatever, and replaced by glass. Or maybe it never existed at all.'

'Don't, you're making it even worse than it is already.'

Daniel leaned forward. 'I'm trying to work out what we really know, and what we are assuming.'

'All right. In order. There's the money missing from the embassy,' Kitteridge began.

'No! In order. And we don't know that Sidney took it anyway.'

'The money had to be stolen before the assault,' Kitteridge corrected him. 'After the assault, Sidney had no chance . . .'

'Good point,' Daniel agreed.

'Go on.'

'The first thing we know of it is that Tobias reports an assault on his daughter, substantiated by her, except for the identification of Sidney. But he was sure she was too upset to say anything. And by now, Morley Cross, if he is involved, has the diamond – let us say it was a diamond – or he thought it was. For the purpose of motive, that's as good. Next thing is that Sidney leaves America for England to escape prosecution. That could be us protecting our own. I'm not sure if that's really a good thing to do, but I suppose it's understandable. Patriotism – misguided – or the wish to prosecute him for the embezzlement, but that . . .'

'Makes no sense,' Kitteridge finished for him. 'An enemy

in the embassy does. But we can't find one. He was generally liked.'

'The next thing to happen is that the Thorwoods arrive in London,' Daniel went on.

'Next thing was your brother-in-law and your sister arrive in London. Sorry, but it's true.'

'Yes. Right. Then the Thorwoods arrive in London, and Sidney is arrested for embezzlement, and then tried, and the evidence emerges, forged or not,' Daniel summed up. 'And Hillyer is waiting to hear more about Cross: body, time of death, and so on, before he adds murder to the charge. What's missing?'

'A real motive,' Kitteridge replied. 'And a connection between the events. A purpose! If Sidney's not guilty, why is he being made to look it? Who hates him? Who is profiting? It has to be more than the hundred pounds. If it was even embezzled at all? There's no core to it, Pitt, no . . . centre. Men don't kill each other over five pounds!'

Daniel said thoughtfully, 'I was looking for a thread through it, something that ties it together. But what if it isn't all connected? I mean, not the way we can see . . .'

'The pendant is missing and Sidney appears not to have it. That is something to profit from and is worth over a few pounds if it's real. But if that is only of sentimental value, that doesn't make sense,' Kitteridge replied. 'What started it off? With a crime, there's something that makes it happen that day, that way.'

'You don't need to explain it. I understand,' Daniel responded. 'Circumstances change in a way that is intolerable to someone. Or an opportunity comes that someone can't resist. Who needed a bit of money, a few pounds in the beginning? And saw how easy it was and made it a habit? But what happened that caused the first theft?'

172

'We should be able to find that out, if we hunt hard enough. We've got notes of all the embezzlement letters. What happened in Sidney's life?'

'Or somebody else's.'

'What?' Kitteridge looked taken aback.

'It doesn't have to be in Sidney's life, if somebody else is behind it all.'

'Why would something in somebody else's life make Sidney assault Rebecca?'

'Aren't we starting from the beginning?' Daniel asked. 'What is this really about? What's the passion behind it? Is Sidney the heart of it, or is he only collateral damage along the way?'

Kitteridge winced. 'That sounds brutal. Collateral damage? Morley Cross as well? Shot in the back of the head.'

Daniel winced. 'A lot of us only see what we can afford to believe,' he said. 'What changed then? For anyone? We're missing something, Kitteridge. I don't even know what shape it is to begin to look for it. Who does know? Is it anyone we are looking at, or someone we haven't even thought of, not in the way we need to see them?'

Kitteridge shivered. 'Then we'd better hurry up and find it, or Sidney's going to pay the price. Do you really think he's innocent?'

'I'm not sure. Is that good enough for you?'

'No.' Kitteridge ate the last of his sandwich.

Daniel drank the rest of his ale and stood up. 'I'm going back to see Sidney . . .'

Kitteridge stared at him. 'Tonight?'

'Tomorrow's too late. He must know something. He's scared, but not scared enough.'

'Don't scare him so badly he can't think,' Kitteridge

173

warned. 'Most of us can't think clearly when we're really terrified. But you've got to tell him about Morley Cross.'

'I will,' Daniel said miserably. He knew there was no escape. 'But now your case is finished will you take over this case?'

'No. I'll second chair. I know I said I'd never do that again after the last case. But sometimes "never" is less time than you think.'

'Thank you,' Daniel said sincerely.

Chapter Fourteen

The prison authorities were not happy about letting Daniel in to see Sidney at that hour of the early evening, but it was not the first time, nor would it be the last, that a trial had turned on an issue that had to be dealt with immediately.

Daniel paced back and forth in the usual grey room and waited. These rooms all looked the same, and regardless of the weather, they always seemed to be cold. Even on an August evening, which was still warm and bathed in the last of the sun, the place had a dead air to it.

Sidney was still dressed in his own clothes from the courtroom. At any other time, it would have been casually elegant. As he came in, he glanced at Daniel's face and his whole body tightened with apprehension. He opened his mouth as if to speak, then changed his mind, and sat in the chair opposite where Daniel now sat. The guard left the room, but they both knew he was just outside the door.

'What is it?' Sidney spoke as if his mouth were dry and he could barely swallow. 'Has something happened?'

Daniel wished there were anything at all he could say to lighten this man's fear, but there was nothing. At the moment, he was accused of petty embezzlement. He would probably serve some time in prison, and it would be hard, but he would survive. It was the disgrace, the future suddenly torn away from him, the loss of friends, of reputation, of the trust and the hope that had driven him all his life. But behind, and dwarfing all the other entanglements, was the figure of Morley Cross, and the inevitability of his murder being introduced and added to the charge.

Daniel could see anticipation of more bad news in Sidney's eyes now, even though he tried to hide it, and to smile. Daniel knew he must get all of the other information he could, before he told him of Cross.

Daniel swallowed, wishing he were anywhere but here. 'Sidney, the more I think about the whole of this, the more I realise there is something important that we don't know.'

'I've told you everything . . .' Sidney's voice cracked. 'I . . .' He shook his head in desperation.

'You haven't,' Daniel said quietly. 'You may not know what it is, but there's something more. Something that makes sense of this whole thing: the embezzlement, and why it was in your name, why it was only discovered after you left, even though, I presume, the Embassy check their accounts regularly. Either it wasn't there earlier, or somebody else was covering it up. Why did it come to light at all? Why didn't they just cover it up and force you to pay it back? Why expose it to the whole world? Junior officer in the British Embassy embezzles money from the accounts! On trial for everybody to read about. Great diplomacy. If I were Foreign Secretary, I'd want the head on a plate of whoever handled it like that, wouldn't you?'

Sidney thought about it for only a moment. 'Yes,' he said. 'I didn't think about that.'

'I know you're stunned, and scared,' Daniel said more

gently. 'But you've got to think; help yourself. If you don't, you're tying my hands. You're doing their job for them!' He wanted to stop Sidney from being so passive. 'If you're innocent, then fight back!' He allowed all the anger he felt to come through in his voice. 'Stop being such a damn gentleman, and fight! You don't have to go like a lamb to the slaughter! It's not heroic, it's damn stupid! Drink the water and fight!'

'Water?' For a moment, Sidney was lost. Then he remembered the story of Sir Philip Sidney. 'Consider it drunk,' he said with something close to a real smile. 'About all those things you mentioned relating to the embezzlement, which I did not do, there's the assault on poor Rebecca Thorwood. I didn't do that either. I only met her two or three times, but I liked her, and I don't steal. I certainly don't break into bedrooms and assault people. Am I supposed to still have this diamond pendant, or did I sell it before I left Washington? I didn't have time! Even if I knew who to sell it to.' His face tightened. 'But I couldn't prove that in London. Lawton-Smith came with me to the dockside! But he's still in Washington. He was supposed to see I got safely on the ship.' He gave a tiny shrug. 'Maybe for my welfare. But more likely to make sure I really left. I was a considerable embarrassment to the ambassador.'

Daniel could see the shame in his face, but there was no time for sympathy now. 'We could send him a wire, I presume,' he said without much hope. 'I expect he'll say whatever he's told to. And the court will assume the same. The prosecution certainly will. I imagine his job will depend on it. Or they will presume it does, anyway. I still want to know why they made the whole thing public. *Why* did they? It hardly serves the Foreign Office's agenda.' He looked at

177

Sidney intently. 'Have you got some very powerful enemies that you haven't told me about? Come on, man, I need to know! I can't save you if you won't be honest with me.'

'Do you imagine I haven't been thinking?' For the first time, there was anger outweighing fear in Sidney's voice. 'I don't know of anybody. Of course, I've got friends, and there are also people who don't like or respect me, or think I'm a fool. But everybody knows such people. Nobody pleases everyone. That's not an enemy. They're decent enough, just—'

'This is no time for being fair, or saying they're all honest,' Daniel said tartly. 'Someone isn't. Your career now, or any other time in the future, depends on believing that and acting on it. Your original Sir Philip Sidney may have given his last drop of water to someone else, but I'll bet nobody walked over him, and he fought for what he believed in. He fell in battle, didn't he? He didn't just sit down and die?'

'Of course . . .' Sidney took a deep breath. 'Do I really seem such a spineless man as that? I don't shoot because I don't know where to aim. I haven't got any idea who did this, or why. If I lash out mindlessly, I might hit the only friend I have, as well as hurting innocent people, and looking like just the sort of self-obsessed dandy they're making me out to be.'

Daniel felt guilty for a moment. But he had to fire Sidney out of this lethargy, whatever it took. He smiled grimly. 'Well, don't hit me, and you're off to a good start. Maybe it's not an enemy in a personal sense? Perhaps you're in someone's way of achieving something. If you don't know what, we'll have to work it out.'

'Not a promotion anyone else is seeking,' Sidney said ruefully.

'So far as you know.'

'I'm not likely to be promoted to anything that's worth lying and stealing for,' he said with certainty. 'Could have been one day, maybe. But it's not in sight yet, or ever . . . now.'

'Do you know anything dangerous? And don't deny it without thinking. We're running out of options.'

Sidney hesitated, making a concentrated effort. 'I don't know anything damaging about anyone. The little things, like who keeps a bottle of brandy in his desk drawer, who visits a lady of the night now and again and isn't always discreet about it, or someone else's wife, who pads his expenses once in a while, nobody with any sense is going to "notice" things like that.'

Daniel thought for a while. 'Sounds dreary, and rather predictable,' he said after a moment.

Some of the light drained out of Sidney's face. 'I've thought about it. Believe me, I've turned over every stupid or thought-less thing I've done, and nothing matters a damn in the scheme of things. I've even thought whether I could have witnessed anything I shouldn't have. But I can't think what. I don't know of any thefts, or affairs.'

'Then it's two or three things added together,' Daniel said. 'You're a danger to somebody, and it could be a man or a woman.'

This time Sidney actually laughed. 'I'm not about to steal the affections of anybody's wife or daughter; I'm hardly a glowing prospect.'

'Not even Rebecca Thorwood?'

'No! I like her, but as I've said, I've only met her a few times, and all of those in public! And if I were courting her, why the hell would I ruin everything by breaking into her

179

bedroom and apparently ripping the pendant from her neck? That's just stupid.'

'Where did you meet? The first time?' Daniel asked.

'At a party at the embassy in Washington. I was there on duty, more or less. She came because we were showing a display of Waterford crystal, which she admires. We got into conversation. It seemed so . . . easy, and comfortable.'

'Was the diamond in her pendant worth a lot?'

Sidney was startled by the change in subject, but not disconcerted. 'I've never seen it, so I don't know. But I wouldn't expect to find her wearing it in bed, anyway. Look, I didn't break into the Thorwood house. I don't know anything of the plan of it. I wouldn't know which is her bedroom, and even if I knew all of that, I wouldn't go and break in. You can't have it both ways! Either I am courting the girl and hope to marry the Thorwood money – in that case, it would be an idiotic thing to do – or I were a petty thief and just happen to pick on her, and get lucky finding the right room, and very unlucky in running into her father on the landing, or wherever.'

'She screamed and he came running,' Daniel put in.

'So, I ran straight back to the embassy, drew everybody's attention to the account ledgers, and whatever I embezzled, for three years without anybody noticing, and then, when Armitage advised me to flee because Thorwood would see I'd never get a fair trial in America, I came home where they would find me. I should be locked up in a place for the feeble-minded!' There was real anger in him now. 'However did I qualify to get into the Foreign Office and the British Embassy abroad? Somebody should lose his stripes for that.'

Daniel felt a surge of hope. Sidney was galvanised at last. He was beginning to think, and to be angry enough to look for answers, even unpleasant ones. 'If you didn't do it . . .' he held up his hand to stop Sidney from interrupting him, '. . . and you hadn't seen anything you shouldn't, courted anyone you shouldn't, learned any dangerous facts about anyone, or edged anyone out of a promotion, there's only one thing left that I can think of: you don't realise it, but you know something you shouldn't. Not necessarily one thing, perhaps several, but if you put them together, they add up to something very ugly indeed.'

'Such as what?'

'I don't know,' Daniel said, hope leaking away as if he had only just thought of all this. 'But I think you know it all, if you can just bring it to the front of your mind. Someone needs you out of the way – silenced.' He looked directly into Sidney's eyes. 'Are you going to go willingly, like an animal led by the nose? Or are you going to find out where the pieces fit, and who's putting them there around you? We're doing our best to work out what shape this thing is, so we know which pieces are part of it, and which are not.'

'How can . . .?' Sidney bent his head and stared at the table top. Then suddenly he looked up. 'What do you want to know? I'll tell you anything. Maybe you can work out what has meaning. Who's behind this? Who can it be, and what do they want?'

'They want you not to put the pieces together and know who they are, and why they're doing this,' Daniel answered.

'I don't know what's connected and what isn't. Ask me. Ask me anything.' There was a note of desperation in his voice, but he was struggling to control it.

Daniel tried to catch hold of anything that was a place to begin. 'Who do you know in this whole mess? To do with any of it.'

181

Sidney thought for a moment. 'Mr and Mrs Thorwood, slightly—'

'How?' Daniel interrupted. 'How do you know them? Mr Thorwood recognised you, or said he did. He must have seen you several times.'

'He did. I met them maybe half a dozen times. At receptions and so on. I dined at their house. I escorted Rebecca to a dinner – once. He must have known something reassuring about me, because he wouldn't have let me take her if he didn't. He's very protective. I imagine that, as an only child, Rebecca would be heir to quite a lot. But she's actually very nice. She doesn't use it . . . if you know what I mean.'

'I assume you mean she doesn't trade on it. Except that Thorwood didn't recognise you. He couldn't, if you weren't there. So why is he lying?'

'No. I . . . I don't know whether that was an error or . . .'

'Deliberate?' Daniel said curiously.

'I don't know.'

'Well, go on with who you do know.'

'Armitage, of course. He helped me get out of America. He thought I wouldn't get a fair trial. That all sorts of things would be said that I wouldn't be able to prove were lies, or mistakes, or assumptions. I'm not sure now that he was right, but I thought so at the time. I went. I escaped. I still don't know what would have been better.'

'How long have you known him?'

'He knew my mother, only slightly. He has connections in the West Country, where I come from, and I believe they had acquaintances in common. He was kind to me when I started at the Foreign Office. I think that was a courtesy to her, but I might be mistaken.'

'He was a friend to you?'

182

'Not as much as that, just gracious.'

'Does he know the Thorwoods?'

'Most people at the top of Washington society know each other, more or less. The Thorwoods have a great deal of money. Armitage is a senior diplomat and a gentleman. They were gracious to him. I don't think it was any more than that. Mrs Thorwood participates in several charities, as most wives of wealthy men do, and they included Armitage in several formal events. Not very helpful, is it?'

'Not yet,' Daniel admitted. 'Keep on. We can't give up.'

Sidney started again patiently, going over everything he could think of, revealing a quiet sense of humour, a man of more acute judgement of other people than Daniel would have expected, a depth of emotion he concealed almost all the time.

Daniel learned nothing that he thought of use. But he had discovered one thing by the time the guard returned to show him out. He did not think Sidney capable of anything as shabby or self-serving, as ill thought out, as the crimes with which he was charged. He hoped it was a lawyer's judgement, and not just that he liked the man.

Chapter Fifteen

Jemima had achieved a minor domestic victory. She had been playing with Cassie in the sand pit in the back garden, and had tired her out. Cassie was not only willing to sleep, she couldn't help it. Jemima looked at the peaceful, happy face of her elder child, then closed the door silently and went downstairs. To her surprise, she found Daniel waiting for her in the hall.

'I didn't know you were here,' she said apologetically.

'I've only just arrived,' he answered. 'The maid offered me tea, but I said I'd wait for you.'

She looked closely at his face, trying to read it. He was concealing his emotions well. For anyone else it might have worked, but she had known him for a quarter of a century. Heavens, put like that, it meant they were both more than a quarter of a century old! She broke the spell. 'What is it? It's the trial. Sidney, the Thorwoods . . . Patrick . . .?'

'Actually, I would far rather have played in the sand with you and Cassie,' he gave a half-smile.

And she knew he meant it. Not so much for the pleasure of joining in, but to avoid the reality that had brought him here, away from the court, in the middle of the afternoon, when Pitt was at Special Branch and Charlotte had taken Patrick to see the Tower of London, which would be too tiring for Cassie. Had he finally asked Kitteridge to help him – even to take over the case? Or be tactless enough to ask. She could see the disappointment in him. It was subtle, a tightness in his shoulders, a hesitation before smiling.

'But you came here to see me,' she responded. 'I can see it in your face. It has to be the trial of Philip Sidney. It's not going well?' She led the way to the end of the sitting room, next to the French doors into the garden. The sand pit was just visible. She would tidy it up later. She sat down in one of the comfortable old chairs, full of cushions, and he took the one opposite her. Twenty years could have slipped away and taken them back to childhood. The same flowers were in bloom in the garden: snapdragons, marigolds, nasturtiums, pansies always out. The same flowering chestnut towered over the neighbour's garden in the parallel street, its flambeau cast, May long over for this year.

'It's incredibly busy,' he replied. 'Loads of unnecessary details and character witnesses who say exactly what you expect them to.' He smiled ruefully. 'I keep looking for the hidden bombshell to go off, after we have passed it by.'

'Morley Cross?' Jemima said quietly.

Patrick had told her! But he should have expected that.

'Hillyer hasn't mentioned him yet. He's probably waiting to see if it can be proved he died before Sidney left Washington, or at least that it wasn't after.' He leaned forward a little, resting his elbows on his knees. 'Jem, there has to be something else big that we don't know. Or it doesn't make sense. The root of this matter is certainly not over five or ten pounds, or even who knew about it. Or about the attack

185

on Rebecca. Morley Cross had nothing to do with that! Did he? Did he know something?'

'Do cases always make sense?' she asked, not trying to argue, but to find the truth. 'I do things that don't make sense sometimes, and then wonder how to get myself out of the mess I've made. Could Sidney just be someone who doesn't think ahead? Doesn't realise what the results of his behaviour will be, and then makes it worse by lying?'

'It could be, but even so . . . it doesn't help. When you argue a case to a jury, or anyone who is really listening to you, and is going to think about it, you have to answer all the reasonable questions they would ask. Like . . . why? How did he know that? Who else knew? What if he isn't lying? What does he want? Things like that. It really matters. You know the Thorwoods, particularly Rebecca. You know how long and how well Patrick knows them, don't you?' he asked.

'I think so.' Suddenly, just as quickly as that, he could pass from the general to the personal, which was full of doubt and perhaps pain. 'I know what he told me, and I have never had reason to doubt him, over anything at all.' She said that last phrase with emphasis he could not mistake. She was defensive already! Did she think Patrick was so very vulnerable?

'Nobody tells everything, Jem. Especially if they haven't been asked.'

'Clever,' she said, trying to keep the sharpness out of her voice. 'But isn't that what you're asking?' She had no doubt that it was. It was the question he did not want to approach, and the one she was afraid of. Why? What did she think Patrick had done? The answer was too easy. Somehow, he had created a net and slipped it over Philip Sidney to convict him for the crime he really had committed. It did not matter if he was found guilty of embezzlement or not. It was Patrick's idea of justice. Or a favour to people he liked, or owed for their favours to him. The thought was repulsive! And dangerous. It was a crime against the law, and worse than that, it was supremely arrogant to appoint yourself judge and executioner.

Did she think Patrick would do such a thing? Or only fear it? She wanted to avoid the thought, but that was to admit there was something to be afraid of. 'He met the Thorwoods when we first went to Washington, about three and a half years ago.' She raised her chin a little. 'We didn't have a lot money. I was carrying Cassie. She was almost due.' Her hands clenched at the memory of it. It had been a hard, cold winter and she had felt it badly. She had not told anyone in England, not even her mother, how difficult it had been. She had felt very isolated. Patrick had worked so hard to give her extra luxuries, the best he could afford, and more. He seemed to be away so much. She had learned only later he was moonlighting to earn extra money. He dared not tell anyone. If he were caught, his superior would understand, but he might not be able to overlook it. And the extra had meant so much! More warmth! Better food. The things she would never ask for, like chocolate, apples, really good bacon. She found tears in her eyes as she remembered.

'Jem?' Daniel interrupted her thoughts.

'Sorry, I was just remembering . . . all the things Patrick did for me in those months. I was probably very difficult. You don't know what it's like, being with child. You really want to be able to talk to your own mother.'

'The Thorwoods, Jem . . .?'

'Oh, yes. Tobias Thorwood wanted extra security work.

He already knew Patrick – because they have an apartment in New York as well. I don't know exactly what it was, but he needed someone he could trust. He never mentioned it to anyone else. So as not to get Patrick into trouble with the police department.' She smiled in spite of herself, at the look on Daniel's face. 'Don't look like that, Daniel. Although moonlighting was frowned upon it was perfectly legal, or Patrick wouldn't have done it. If you don't believe in his morality, at least believe in his sense of survival!'

Daniel blushed. 'I would've done the same, I hope. So that is how he knows Thorwood. And Mrs Thorwood?'

'Less well. And Rebecca was just coming into society. She is only twenty-one now.' She remembered that more clearly. 'I think it may have been about finding out about some young man who was courting her – whether he was suitable or not. I presume he was not. I don't think it matters. Three and a half years ago, she was rather too young anyway. And very naïve. She still is!'

'Was it Philip Sidney?' Daniel asked. Had he been lied to about when Sidney first went to Washington? He had been at the embassy less time than that, but nothing said he had not visited Washington, or New York!

'No!' Jemima said immediately. 'Unless . . .'

'Unless what? Why couldn't he have visited before working at the embassy?'

'He could.'

'Doesn't take long to fall in love,' he pointed out.

She felt the heat rise up in her face. She had gone to America for a very short time, to accompany a friend to her wedding, and during those dramatic weeks . . . days . . . she had met Patrick and had fallen in love with him. It felt crazy, impulsive, even foolish at the time, and yet she was perfectly certain of it. The only question in her mind had been, was he? Yes . . . yes. Still . . . yes.

'Not like that,' she said with certainty. 'If I had waited this long, caring but not knowing, I'd be half crazy.' She saw the laughter in his eyes. 'All right! You wait! Your turn will come, I hope. But no. Rebecca's not a very good liar.'

'Or she's a very good one?' he suggested.

'Oh, really!' Jemima dismissed it out of hand. 'No, she isn't. She likes him.'

'Even after the assault?'

'She didn't know it was him. For that matter, she still doesn't.'

'Doesn't she?'

Jem looked down, then up at Daniel quickly. 'She doesn't want to,' she said very quietly. 'In her place, I wouldn't either. That's part of the reason I know she didn't know him before. She . . . she's only just on the edge of falling in love with him now.'

'And Thorwood wouldn't approve?'

'I know Sidney's an old name, an old family, even if he comes from a very junior branch, if any at all,' she explained. 'But there's no money. Even if he were higher up, he wouldn't be the first English aristocrat to marry a rich American for her money!'

'Or the first American to marry a man for his title!' he said.

'What title?' she dismissed it.

'Maybe this is when he ceases to be attractive?'

'You're miles away, Daniel. Tobias Thorwood would never have heard of Sir Philip Sidney, the hero of romantic Elizabethan poetry! Even to us, it's only a great story. No, no . . .' She waved away his interruption. 'Rebecca wouldn't

189

want to marry a man who wanted her money. The thought's revolting! Her father would be protecting her from that. If it's got anything at all to do with Sidney and Rebecca, which I don't think it has.'

'Don't think?'

'You may not be able to tell if a woman's in love with someone – although you ought to learn – but I can, usually even if it's someone I don't know, and I do know Rebecca.'

There was a moment's silence. The maid brought tea, and light, very thin sandwiches, which she knew Jemima loved. Jemima smiled and thanked her with feeling, not only for the sandwiches, for the moment of respite from the subject.

But as soon as she was gone, and the tea poured, Daniel returned to it. 'I can understand why Patrick is so loyal to Thorwood,' he said gently. 'He gave him an honourable way to earn money he badly wanted, to give you a little extra when it meant so much to you. You must remember it with warmth every time you look at Cassie.'

'I'm not blinded by it!' she said, almost choking on the words.

'But is Patrick?' Daniel could not leave it alone.

'I . . . I don't know. He's familiar with crime, Daniel. He's a policeman.'

'So is our father, but everyone is different. Our father is not half as intuitive as Victor Narraway! And neither of them was as subtle to the dimensions of the mind as Aunt Vespasia.' He winced. 'I still miss her.'

'You always will,' Jemima said gently. 'She's part of everything that was good when we were children, and after that. You never die in the memory of the people who loved you.'

'Don't change the subject,' he said.

She saw a momentary tremble of his lips and smiled. 'You changed it. You're looking for what it is you don't know about Sidney. And it's possible the assault was not at all what it seems. Or if Tobias was mistaken as to who it was that night? Or if he's lying? Anything to prove Sidney is not guilty?'

'Not . . . not really. I'm looking for a reason he would do such a crazy thing! Even with Morley Cross and his murder, the centre isn't there. Why kill him?' He looked totally puzzled. 'There's something a lot darker behind all this. Does Patrick know something even he doesn't realise fits in?'

'Such as what?' Jemima racked her mind, but she could think of nothing.

'I don't know,' Daniel answered. 'Does Patrick owe even more to the Thorwood family than he's told you? It doesn't have to be a debt of money. It could be anything. It could even be a secret he knows about them, and which has earned his pity.'

She did not answer him, her mind searching the past.

'Don't be slow, Jem. You know as well as I do, if someone has a deep vulnerability in something only you know about, a fear, or a failure, a secret they are ashamed of, you would never betray them. You can't. Pity and loyalty can be very heavy burdens . . . even crippling. An obligation . . .?'

'I don't know!' She wanted to, and yet she was also afraid to. Patrick had trusted her with his emotions. At least it seemed so. But everyone has to have a private area, somewhere even those closest to him did not go, at least not uninvited. It was part of becoming adult, to be able to keep secrets. It did not matter what they were, only that they would be exposed, or healed in private. It was part of knowing someone that you did not intrude, or even want to. 'I don't know,' she repeated. 'But I have no sense of it. I'm almost certain Patrick really believes Thorwood saw Sidney in the corridor. Which means he was there. And even if Rebecca invited him, he should have known better than to take advantage of her.'

'I don't think that's it,' Daniel said, shaking his head. 'That's bad behaviour, but not something to ruin his career over. And why take the pendant?'

'Perhaps . . .' she struggled for an answer. 'It was only rock crystal, not a diamond.'

'That's no answer!' Daniel's disbelief was clear in his face. 'Come on, Jem. He tore it off her neck. It must have hurt. And why did she scream? If she invited him there, the last thing she would do is scream and wake the household! It has to make sense – at least to someone.'

'I know. To the someone who did it!' She gulped. 'What you're really asking is, does Patrick believe it was Sidney, and want to make him look guilty of embezzlement to punish him for it?'

Daniel nodded minutely. 'Yes. It could be for a perfectly honourable reason that he wants to make sure Thorwood gets justice for Rebecca's assault. Perhaps Thorwood is a witness to some crime, and Patrick is afraid for him. Or Thorwood is involved in something dangerous and needs Patrick's protection. Or perhaps Patrick knows of Sidney's guilt in some way he can't reveal . . . to protect someone else? There are lots of answers that leave him innocent of any wrong, but unable to speak. Crime can get very complicated. Debt is difficult, and you cannot walk out of it when it gets expensive, or uncomfortable.'

Ideas poured through her mind, but the fear eased away. 'Do you think so? Please . . . please unravel it carefully.'

'I'm not sure I can unravel it at all,' Daniel replied. 'But I will be careful, I can promise you that!'

Jemima did not ask Patrick when he returned from his visit to the Tower with Charlotte. He was full of enthusiasm for exploring history with her. Part of it was courtesy to her, and the fact that he found her company enjoyable. She was too much like Jemima for him not to. But much of it was fascination with the relics of history he had seen, even touched, in one visit to the Tower of London, built by William the Conqueror shortly after 1066. She had told him how, ten years after his conquest, he had had an accounting made of his new kingdom. The Domesday Book named every house and holding, every hamlet and steading. And of course she included what she could remember of the Yeomen Warders – the Beefeaters, as they were known – who guarded the Tower in their traditional heraldic scarlet uniforms.

When they were upstairs changing for dinner, Jemima made herself take the opportunity to bring up the subject when Patrick spoke of what he had seen.

'Did you have a good day, too?' he asked, not casually as if in good manners, but watching her, as though he cared.

'Yes, Sophie was looking on while Cassie and I built sandcastles.'

'All day?' he smiled.

'No, not all day. Daniel came.'

He caught the difference in her tone immediately. 'In the middle of the afternoon? Why? It must be serious to take him away from the court. The trial isn't over . . . unless Sidney has changed his plea. Has he?'

'Do you think he might?' she asked. She did not explain

that Kitteridge was now defending him, too. Maybe she would be spared having to ask him about Tobias Thorwood.

'He would if he had any sense,' Patrick replied. 'In fact, he would have pleaded guilty in the first place, and avoided a trial at all. Then we would have had no chance at all of raising the assault. Daniel hasn't done it yet, has he? Jem, is that what you're looking so tense about?'

'No. At least not so far as I know. Not when he was here.'

'Then what? Come on! What's happened?' He spoke gently, but there was an edge of anxiety in his voice.

'Why would he do it, Patrick? It doesn't make sense! And kill Morley Cross? You think he did that too, don't you?'

'Most crimes don't make sense, when you think of them afterwards.'

'They make sense at the time to the person who commits them,' she answered. 'That's how you catch them. People steal things because they want them, or they want to sell them, or take them away from whomever has them. They attack people because they're angry and can't control their rage. Or they want to silence them because they know something, or will say something, or they're jealous or greedy. Or they hate someone for any number of reasons. Or they need to—'

'All right!' he cut her off. 'I don't know why Sidney did it. I don't know why he took the money. It's little enough over a time, but if someone knew about it, I can see why he would want to make sure they didn't tell on him. And Morley Cross was in a perfect position to know. He worked in the same department. Perhaps he even blackmailed Sidney over it. But that wouldn't explain about Rebecca. I don't know. But that doesn't mean there wasn't a reason. Tobias saw him! There isn't any doubt about it. Even if it makes no sense at all. Maybe he was drunk? Or it was a stupid . . . someone dared him to! Or he had some grudge against Tobias that we don't know about. It doesn't matter. He was there!'

She did not look at him. 'Unless Tobias was mistaken.'

He looked exasperated. 'He wasn't guessing. He knew. He wouldn't swear to it in court and ruin a man's career on a guess.'

She did not answer.

'Is that what you think of him?' he said, his voice lower, carrying hurt as well as anger. 'What did Daniel say to you?'

What could she say, without betraying one or the other? 'That it doesn't make any sense. That there's something bigger that we don't yet know.'

'Such as what?'

'I don't know.'

'Daniel has to think that! He's defending Sidney. He has to look for anything he can! What would you do in his place?'

'The same,' she said softly. 'I'd look for an explanation that made sense. I'd ask someone who knew anything about it. I'd . . . I'd try to break Tobias's identification, but I hope I'd do it honestly.' She stepped away from him and looked up at his face. 'I'd have told Sidney to plead guilty to the embezzlement, even if he was innocent, and so prevent anyone raising the whole issue of the assault. He would then offer to pay the money back, and expect dismissal from the service. And before you say it, I know Daniel didn't do that because at first he believed that Sidney assaulted Rebecca, and deserved to pay for it, even indirectly. I don't know what Sidney thought! Maybe that he'd get away with it all.' She looked directly into his eyes. 'Did he embezzle the money, Patrick?'

195

He winced. 'Do you mean did I make it look that way?'

'No, not you. But do you suspect that Tobias Thorwood did?'

He was silent for a long time.

She did not move away from him.

'I don't know,' he said to her. 'I didn't. I really didn't. And I would stake a lot – maybe not everything; some things I wouldn't stake at all, not on the sun rising tomorrow morning, like you . . . and Cassie and Sophie . . . but short of that, everything – that he really believes he saw Sidney in his house that evening.'

Jemima did not have to say that she believed him. He would see that in her eyes, feel it in the way she touched his face, gently, with her fingertips, before she kissed him.

Chapter Sixteen

Thomas Pitt had a study at home, as well as his office, and it too was lined with books. It was the one place where he was allowed to be untidy. No one commented; even the maid was not allowed in. In spite of appearances, he knew where everything was. Now he stood by the window and thought about missing Jemima when she married the man she loved, and of course, went to live with him in America. He was realising it far more deeply since she was home – no, he should say back again in England. Her home was wherever Patrick was. He would have expected Charlotte to have followed him, had his work taken him elsewhere, and he never doubted that she would have. Nevertheless, Jemima had been missed by both of them. And now that Cassie and Sophie were in the world, in their world, not merely spoken of, photographs sent, letting Jemima go and realising it might be a year, even two years before they saw her again, it was difficult.

Pitt liked Patrick. He even trusted him. And it was obvious that he made Jemima happy. He clearly loved her, and more surprisingly, he stood up to her! It remained to be seen how long he would stand up to his daughters! Cassie reminded

Pitt of Jemima when she had been at that age. It seemed a past too distant to recognise, except that Cassie had many of the same characteristics, the same curiosity, and the same absolute trust that he would never hurt her. That was what reached him the most deeply with a wave of sudden emotion that caught him unawares.

He had made it a point of honour not to enquire into Daniel's cases. It would look like interference, as if he believed that Daniel was not man enough to solve them himself. But this case troubled him in a different way from others, because although he did not know how – and he had very carefully refrained from asking – it clearly affected Jemima very closely.

He closed the study door and went into the drawing room. He knew Cassie and Sophie were in bed. Patrick was talking to Charlotte. They seemed to get along very well. Maybe they were both working at it, for Jemima's sake, but it looked from the outside to be perfectly natural. Jemima was standing by the French doors at the end of the room, not closed yet from the warm August darkness. She was perfectly still, and there was a tension in her face, in the way she held her shoulders. He ached to do something about it. She was afraid. He knew that in a way more clearly than if she had actually said so. Looking at her stiff shoulders, and the grace of her head, he could see Charlotte in her, and Cassie, too.

'Like to go for a walk?' The words were out before he thought about them. 'Only to the end of the garden.'

She hesitated quite a few long seconds. Did she fear he was going to ask her what was troubling her? She was right: he was, wasn't he?

'Yes,' she said at last, turning towards him. 'Let's go. I always took my troubles to the end of the garden. Do you remember the time you had me write them down on a piece of paper, and then bury it there?' Her expression was filled with too many mixed emotions for him to read.

He offered her his arm. It was an oddly old-fashioned gesture for these modern times, and yet it felt right. She took it and they walked out on to the grass and along the lawn. There was no sound, except the after-sunset breeze whispering in the poplars.

'I don't want to interfere in Daniel's case,' he said when they were halfway to the far end of the grass. 'It's an agreement between us that I don't.'

'I know,' she agreed. 'He told me.'

'But I'm worried,' he continued. 'It's a delicate balance. If I offer advice, he'll refuse. If I do so without his asking, he'll resent it, even if it actually helps.'

There was gentle amusement in her voice. 'It's not difficult to imagine how you feel. Cassie's only three, and she gets cross if I do something to help her when she thinks she can do it by herself. Funnily enough, she'll let Patrick help, usually.'

'Yes, you were the same,' Pitt observed.

'Was I?' She was surprised. 'I don't remember. At least, not many things. I remember pulling weeds . . .'

'You were helping me,' he pointed out.

She said nothing, but he could tell she was smiling, even though he could see only the outline of her face, the line of her cheek. He knew to say nothing.

'Can I collect on that now?' she asked.

'Any time,' he replied.

There was another silence for several moments. The air smelled of the warm earth and something sweet. Perhaps it was the late roses covering the wall.

He was tempted to say something, but managed not to.

'Just afraid Patrick's loyalty is preventing him from seeing something that's going to hurt him in the end,' she started.

'It's to do with this Philip Sidney case?'

'Yes. Or Daniel?'

'Loyalty to Daniel?'

'No, that's not what I mean. I'm afraid Daniel is going to get hurt.'

'Sweetheart, if you take sides, you're bound to get hurt sometimes, the only thing worse is not to take sides in anything, and stand apart from life, always on the edge, never part of it.'

'Is that supposed to make me feel better?' It was not asked with anger, but rather ruefully.

'What are you really afraid of? That they are on different sides, and one of them is going to get badly hurt? You want somehow to stand between them?'

'In part,' she admitted.

'Then what else?'

'That there's something else behind it that's really bad, and they can't find it – maybe that it will never be found – and they'll know they missed it for all the wrong reasons: too busy trying not to hurt each other . . . or not to be right, without it costing,' she hesitated. 'Or to be right, without it costing . . . I don't know what.'

'It's going to happen sometime,' her father pointed out. 'Maybe not between them, but with someone. Cases that can wound people you know, perhaps badly, are always going to be hard. And one way or another, you're going to know a lot of people. If you don't see it at the beginning of the case, you will by the end.'

'Did you get a lot of cases like that?' she asked gently.

He looked away, his face towards the slight breeze. 'A fair few.'

'Did any of your friends make bad mistakes? I'm not asking who.'

'We all make mistakes, Jem. It's how we live with them afterwards that matters. And how we forgive them in others, or never really forgive. Accept that it really was wrong; don't make excuses or blame anyone else. The moment you say "I was wrong" you can begin to move on.'

'Do you think Patrick's wrong?'

'I have no idea. I know little about the Philip Sidney case. Do you want me to find out?'

She waited a long time before she replied. 'Yes, please. I think so. Daniel asked the same questions Patrick did. Why did the Foreign Office charge Sidney with the embezzlement? Why not just demand he pay the money back and get rid of him? This is going to be a horrible embarrassment to the government. And, of course, if they drag out the assault—'

'What assault?' he interrupted her. 'Sidney's only charged with minor embezzlement.'

She told him the story of Rebecca Thorwood.

'Ah,' he said softly. At last, it made sense to him. She heard it in the change in his voice at least as to why they were so engaged in it. 'That is much uglier. And even more reason for the Foreign Office not to make a case of it. You're right, there's far more behind it than we can see at the moment. Does Patrick intend somehow to bring the assault out?' He did not ask the question he really meant: did he engineer the embezzlement evidence so that Sidney would come to trial and the assault would come out at that trial? Would she know he meant that?

'He can't,' she said quietly. 'He's not a witness to anything.'

'But he wants Daniel to?'

'It's a terrible thing for someone to break into the one

201

place you believe you are safe – and where you are so vulnerable. Without even your clothes. Wouldn't you want to see somebody punished if they did that to me? Or the girls?'

He heard the note of anger, and more than that, of fear in her voice. 'Is that how you got so much leave to come here? Over a month altogether, with both voyages?'

'What?'

'Don't play with me, sweetheart. I simply thought Tobias . . . I mean, through Tobias Thorwood's influence.'

'I . . . I don't know. I hadn't thought about it. Maybe. But he doesn't have any influence in the British Embassy! Or, more importantly, in the Foreign Office!'

'I hope not. But not as much is impossible as we would like to think,' he replied. He put his hand out and touched hers very gently. 'I'm going to find out, for my own sake, as well as for yours.'

'And Daniel's,' she added.

'And Daniel's,' he agreed.

Pitt debated whether to ask Daniel or not. It kept him awake for more of the night than he allowed Charlotte to know. He turned the matter over and over in his mind, and by morning he had come to a conclusion. Whether it was the right one or not remained to be seen.

He said nothing of it to Charlotte. She was busy preparing to take the whole family to see her sister, Emily Radley, and enjoy the little time they had before Jemima should have to return to America.

By ten o'clock, Pitt was in the Foreign Office. As head of Special Branch, and with the delicate state of so many international relationships, especially in Europe, he gained almost immediate access.

'Good morning, Sir Thomas,' the Foreign Secretary greeted him. 'What can I do for you? Not more bad news about that Balkan business, I hope?'

'Not at all,' Pitt replied. 'Another thing altogether. I'll be brief. I know you have a ten-thirty meeting. So do I. It's about this wretched embezzlement in our own embassy in Washington. I'm sure you know about it?'

'Yes.' The Foreign Secretary shook his head. 'Damnable. Don't know the details. Embarrassing, but nothing I can do now. If that's what you want, I don't think I can help. Is it tied up to something of yours? Damn. Stupid question. Fellow defending him is called Pitt. Your son, I presume?'

This was exactly what Pitt had dreaded. He knew Daniel would hate it even more. And blame him! 'Yes, he is,' he conceded. 'It seems against our interest in every way to make a public case of it, and there's worse than that that could come out.'

The Foreign Secretary's face was bleak. 'What?'

'Apparently Philip Sidney also broke into the Thorwoods' house.'

'Tobias Thorwood?'

'Yes. Sidney denies it.'

'God damn!'

'He assaulted the daughter in her bed and tore a pendant off her neck.' Pitt thought he might as well get it all out at once. 'She screamed. Her father came running and caught up with Sidney in the corridor. He escaped, but not before Thorwood saw him clearly enough to identify him.'

'Is that what this is all about?'

'I think so. Apparently, Sir John Armitage got him out of the country on diplomatic immunity, but Thorwood still wants blood.'

The Foreign Secretary grimaced. 'Can't blame him.'

'No, but we would have done a lot better to bury it quietly all the same. Pay damages, whatever. The girl wasn't hurt, and the necklace has mainly a sentimental value.'

'Did they get it back?'

'No.'

'So, a pretty good bloody mess all around?'

'Yes. But Thorwood's daughter is better than they said in the newspapers. Not really hurt and not indecently attacked.'

'There's not much point in telling me that now! The cat's well and truly out of the bag.'

'That's not the point,' Pitt began.

'There's more?' the Foreign Secretary asked with disbelief.

'I think so. If it's just that, why did Armitage get Sidney out of Washington, then let him get prosecuted here, over the theft of just a hundred pounds? He could have asked you to let it slip, made Sidney pay it back, and then thrown him out? Thorwood couldn't pursue the other matter because Sidney cannot be tried for the assault over here.'

The Foreign Secretary frowned. 'I suppose Armitage must have thought of that.'

'If he didn't, he shouldn't hold the job he does!'

'You're right. He's still over here. Go and ask him. I'd like to know the answer myself. I'll give him a call.'

'Special Branch?' Armitage said with surprise when Pitt found him in a discreet meeting room half an hour later. They had met before, but only briefly. Armitage stood and indicated the other chair for Pitt to sit, then followed suit. 'Drink?' he enquired. 'Pot of tea? Something stronger?'

'No, thank you,' Pitt declined. 'I won't take up much of your time.'

Armitage smiled. It altered his face, making it lighter, easier. 'I have half an hour.'

'So have I.' Pitt deliberately relaxed, as if this did not matter to him deeply. 'So, I'll come to the point. The case of Philip Sidney . . .'

'Of interest to you, or to Special Branch?' Armitage said with surprise. Then the puzzlement vanished from his face. 'Of course! Pitt! Young Daniel Pitt is presenting the defence case. Your son, I presume?' The inflection of his voice made the question something of a challenge.

Pitt had not intended to deny it, but he was caught slightly by surprise that Armitage should have made the connection so quickly. It suggested that it had been at the top of his mind. Interesting. 'Yes,' he agreed with the faintest smile. 'I see it concerns you also.' That was a statement, not a question. Armitage could make of it what he wished.

Pitt was even more experienced at the game than Armitage was.

There was a flash of recognition in Armitage's eyes, then gone again almost too rapidly to know what it had been. Was this going to be a battle?

'I haven't spoken to Daniel about it.' Pitt took the next step immediately. 'I am concerned to know why you prosecuted Sidney at all.'

'Ah!' Armitage let out his breath slowly. 'I suppose I should have realised you would get to that, if you were on the case at all. Has Daniel told you why he's defending Sidney?'

'No. Nor have I asked. I gather you know.'

'I . . . uh . . .' Armitage looked up, his expression serious, and yet rueful, as if there was some faint humour in it. 'I had no intention of telling you, but now I see that I have to. I don't want Special Branch in it. No slight on your abilities. Rather the opposite. But the more delicately it is handled, the better.'

'But since I know enough to be aware that there's a problem, you are going to tell me,' Pitt said.

'I see no alternative. You asked why we are prosecuting. The answer is simple. We cannot have Sidney free to continue what he is doing. He is not the innocent that he affects to be. Far from it. He is very skilled indeed. And he has killed at least one wretched young man who got in his way.'

'Really?' Pitt kept his voice expressionless, but with difficulty. Neither Daniel nor Jemima had mentioned a murder to him. It must have been in America. 'Then he appears to be extraordinarily clumsy. If the charges are true? He embezzled small amounts from the embassy accounts in a discreet way, but it was not a clever thing to do. He was bound to be caught one day. They look like the petty thefts of a young man who cannot manage his own finances and is regularly in debt for small amounts. He never seems to get control of it. Not clever, or honest, but not unique either.'

'Yes,' Armitage agreed. 'That is what it looks like.'

'But it is not? He is telling the truth, and someone else has made it appear that he isn't?'

'I prefer not to comment on that. I don't know the details.' Armitage smiled apologetically. 'Enough to say that young Morley Cross worked in the same department, and was found shot dead in the Potomac River. The embezzlement we can prove, and it is a crime. It is a cause for which Sidney can be dismissed from the Service, and for a small time at least, imprisoned.'

'And that serves your purpose?' Pitt allowed his surprise to ring in his voice.

'I imagine between young Pitt and Tobias Thorwood, they

206

will also manage to raise the assault upon Thorwood's daughter,' Armitage answered. 'A far more serious matter, even if it cannot be prosecuted in England. If mention of it came before the judge, he would be certain to imprison Sidney, and his word will be taken for nothing from then on.'

'And that is what matters to you? That his word should be dismissed?'

Armitage flushed and there was a darkness of real anger in his face for a moment, then gone again.

'For God's sake, Pitt! I'm not doing this lightly . . . or should I say "allowing it to be done"! This is only the part you can see. Sidney is a traitor to England. Not just ideologically, but in a very practical way. The truth beneath all this trivial but ugly rubbish is that he is telling the Germans all he can about our harbours, their depths, their navigation details, what defence we have in certain places. Cornwall and Devon, the north coast of Scotland. God knows, we are weak enough as it is! We live in the past, militarily speaking. And more important, our navy is bloody useless, compared with what the Kaiser is planning. Submarines! The Germans have a huge advantage over us in underwater vessels. We are an island nation, Pitt. We can be invaded from all sides, and now from under the sea, too. Worse than that, we can be starved, not only of weapons, supplies, but of food to survive with the use of these machines!'

He did not wait for Pitt to respond, but went straight on. 'I don't know whether the damn fool assaulted Rebecca Thorwood, and since she is unhurt, frankly, I don't care. Far bigger things are at stake. Treason, and I now know, also murder.' His face was tense, almost pinched, as if the strain was almost more than he could bear. 'I can't tell you more than that, Pitt. Leave the bloody thing alone! If Sidney goes down for some petty, stupid theft, and they manage to ruin him with the charge of assault, so much the better. I trust Tobias Thorwood. He's a good man. If he says he saw Sidney in his house, let it stand. Far better that people don't know Philip Sidney is a traitor, prepared to kill if it suits his purpose. Let young Daniel do his job. Just pray he succeeds!'

Pitt said nothing. There really was no answer that expressed what he felt, or would answer Armitage's fear. He would already know that Pitt would do as he asked. There was no honourable alternative.

Pitt took his leave quietly, and went out into the sunny street, cold inside.

But what could he tell Daniel? As the head of Special Branch . . . nothing.

Chapter Seventeen

The same morning that Pitt went to see Armitage, Daniel spoke early to Kitteridge on the courtroom steps, before they went inside, catching him by the sleeve. He realised how tense he had been, in case something had prevented Kitteridge from coming here this morning. It was at the back of his mind that Marcus might still view the case as entirely Daniel's problem, and forbid Kitteridge to help him.

'What is it?' Kitteridge stopped. It was the first thing in the morning and already he looked hot and short tempered. 'Can't it wait until we get inside?'

'I'm not coming in,' Daniel said bluntly. 'With your permission, that is. We haven't got a defence.'

'Well, goodness me! How did I miss that?' Kitteridge asked sarcastically. 'That does not excuse you bunking off and leaving me to fry alone!'

Daniel kept his temper. He felt just as panicky inside as Kitteridge possibly could. 'One of us has to stay. Do you think I can do better than you at stringing out these endless character witnesses? Not to mention the judge's temper.'

Kitteridge did not hesitate. 'No.'

'I've got to find something tangible to fight with. I'm

going to see Miriam again. She might find some holes in this. If Sidney really didn't do it, then someone else did.'

'There might have been no embezzlement at all,' Kitteridge said grimly. 'I'm beginning to wonder if it's a put-up job from the start. But I can't work out why and by whom. Sorry, but I suspect your brother-in-law, for Thorwood to get justice for the attack on Rebecca. But how did he do it? How did either of them get into the embassy at all, let alone get into the account books to fudge them?'

'I don't know,' Daniel replied. 'It . . . it could have something to do with Morley Cross. He worked in the same department as Sidney. But his death could be coincidence. There's far too much we don't know, because it doesn't hang together as it is.'

'Do you think I don't know that?' Kitteridge snapped. 'We're fighting blind! I don't even know whether I believe Sidney is innocent or guilty – and I don't mean just of embezzlement. You know, I know, and more importantly, Hillyer knows that any hour now we'll get news of when Morley Cross died, and if it was before Sidney left Washington, they'll charge him with it. And they could possibly be right!'

Daniel could feel Kitteridge's mounting desperation, as if he were touching him and it was transferable, like fear. He let go. 'We aren't getting anywhere,' he said. 'And I'm not doing any good in court, except moral support, whatever that's worth. Miriam might see something we've missed. If you've got a better place to look, I'll do that.'

'No,' Kitteridge said a little more graciously. 'See if she can at least tell us what shape it is, this thing we're looking for. Do we even have all the pieces?'

'I don't know. You know I don't! But perhaps we have them upside down? Trying to fit them in the wrong way?'

Kitteridge finally smiled. 'At least you're good entertainment, Pitt. I'll say that for you. You're never boring for long! Now please get out of my way, before I change my mind. I've still got to work out what I'm going to say that's any use. Hillyer's going to guess that we know about Morley Cross, no matter what I say, and that I'm here because of an escalation of the case. And I'm not going to lie openly to the court.'

Daniel took the underground train to the nearest station to the fford Croft house, and walked the rest of the way. By the time he had arrived, he had almost worked out in his mind what he was going to say. All of which, of course, depended upon whether Miriam was at home.

The butler welcomed him without surprise, although Daniel wondered whether, after having worked for the fford Crofts for years, anything would surprise him.

'Good morning, Mr Pitt,' he said, opening the door. 'Miss fford Croft has gone to the post office, but I expect her back within about ten or fifteen minutes. If you would care to wait for her in the morning room, sir, I will inform her when she returns. I expect you have had breakfast. Is it too early for a pot of tea for mid-morning? And perhaps a piece of shortbread? Cook is very skilled at baking, if I may say so.'

Daniel smiled. 'I remember,' he said with some enthusiasm.

'Very good, sir.' He bowed and withdrew.

Daniel was enjoying his third piece of shortbread and wondering if he should eat the last piece, or if good manners suggested he should leave it, indicating that he had been given more than sufficient, when he heard footsteps across the parquet of the hall floor, which were definitely not the butler's. Did he recognise Miriam's step?

The next moment there was a brief knock on the door, then without waiting for an answer, she came in.

He stood immediately.

She glanced at the teapot and the plate full of crumbs and then closed the door behind her and walked across the Turkish carpet. 'I see you have been taken care of. I am sorry to have kept you waiting. Is it the Sidney case again?'

All his articulate arguments vanished, as if he had not formulated them. 'Yes. It doesn't make sense. Something new has come to light, and there's something missing. In fact, quite a lot. I thought if I told you all we have, you might . . . put a different shape to it.' He was gabbling.

She sat down in the chair opposite the one he had risen from. 'Do you mind if I stop you if not everything is clear?'

'No, I . . . I hope I'm not wasting your time,' he apologised.

For a moment she, too, was awkward. 'I . . . have nothing urgent. I know you are several days into the trial.'

'You've been following it?' He was surprised. There was nothing forensically interesting in it. And yet he was pleased.

'There isn't much to follow,' she replied. She was looking at her hands, not at his face.

'Not yet,' he admitted. 'I'm afraid it's going to end without having ever really begun. It doesn't make sense. The core of it is missing. I thought you'd help me see what shape it is . . .' He stopped. He was embarrassing himself. He sounded so young, and really foolish.

She looked perfectly serious. 'What's missing? And you haven't told me what it is now!'

He did not reply immediately.

He saw her face shadow.

'When the news reaches London, I mean the last piece of

212

it, they'll be changing the charge to murder,' he answered.

She stiffened. 'What? Who's dead? When did that happen?'

'A young man called Morley Cross,' he replied. 'He worked with Sidney in the same department of the British Embassy in Washington. He was just pulled out of the river there, and they haven't proved when he died yet. It all hangs on whether it was before Sidney left Washington, or while he was still there.'

'How was he killed?'

'Shot in the back of the head. That can't have been an accident.'

'I see.' It was clear from her face that she understood completely. 'The timing would be hard to prove. Water can do a lot of damage. And the longer the body was in it, obviously the harder it is to prove a time. What else? I mean, to make sense of it.'

'A thread that ties it all together,' he said immediately, 'so that we can see a plan, a motive strong enough to make whoever is behind this follow it all the way from Washington to here, and drive it through the courts.'

'And what are the real reasons for any of it?' she asked.

He looked at her greenish-blue eyes, searching for a moment, and saw no mockery in them. 'It could be anything: love, hate, money, revenge,' he started. 'Even ambition if someone felt Sidney was standing in his way for promotion.'

'What about fear?'

'Yes. That, too, I suppose.'

'You named hate,' she pointed out with a smile. 'And wounded pride?'

'These would lead to the motive of revenge, so that, too.'

Her eyes widened. 'Rebecca Thorwood rebuffed Philip Sidney and he broke in and attacked her, stealing the pendant

213

in revenge? Does he seem like a man who would do that? If he is, then he will have done it before. She can't be the first one who ever turned him down. And is the embezzlement somehow to be connected with this?' She did not say that she did not believe it, but it was plain in her face.

'Doesn't work, does it?' Daniel said with a grimace.

Miriam relaxed just a little bit. He saw it in a sudden ease in her fingers, where they rested in her lap. 'Not even a little bit. I'm assuming you have traced her behaviour in the past, and asked if Miss Thorwood ever rebuffed him?'

'Of course,' he agreed.

'Then it is something else. Daniel, do you like him?'

He was about to argue that that was irrelevant. Then he realised she was asking for a reason. Did it affect his judgement? Was he looking for a way out of admitting Sidney was guilty. No! He was looking for a way out of finding that Patrick was guilty of framing a man he believed had committed a particularly intricate and spiteful crime. He felt he owed it to a family that had befriended him.

'Yes,' he said quietly. 'But that isn't my biggest problem.' He told her about his dilemma, and why it mattered so much.

She listened to him without interrupting.

'But even if he is guilty,' he finished, 'I want to convict him genuinely, not . . .'

'I know,' she nodded. 'But let us look at it from another direction, at least for a moment. The worst thing for you would be if Sidney really is not guilty, and Patrick helped in constructing a case to find him guilty. If Tobias Thorwood saw Sidney in his house, then at least he is telling the truth, or part of it.'

'All of it!' Daniel said. 'That's all he said!'

214

'That's not all he implied,' she corrected him. 'Thorwood came because Rebecca screamed. That was what he said. And Sidney was running out of the bedroom on to the landing. Did he go down the stairs? Or into another upstairs room and out of a window? Is that even possible? How high up would that be? For that matter, did Thorwood try to stop him? Did he call the police that night? Immediately? Or perhaps after he made sure that Rebecca was all right? And in his place, I would have asked for the account of how Sidney got in. And how *did* he get in? Did he break in?'

Daniel realised he had not asked Patrick any of these things. It had not seemed to matter at the time. Thorwood had seen Sidney in the house. He certainly knew him well enough to recognise him. Rebecca had sworn she had not invited him, or let him in. It probably made no difference, but Miriam was right to ask. 'I don't know, to all of those things,' he said. 'But Sidney ran away. He claimed diplomatic immunity and left the country. That's at the core of it.'

'No, it isn't.' Miriam shook her head. 'It's one fact that's unarguable. That's all. At the core of it is the thing you are looking for. The emotion. The reason for it all. Somebody who cares so deeply they are following through with all this. Why did Sidney break in, if he did? If he didn't, did anyone? Is Thorwood lying about any part of it? Could he be protecting someone, and he has sworn the intruder was Sidney, so he can't go back on that. But if that is so, then why not let it all blow over? Why on earth follow Sidney to London and keep up the pursuit? I assume you must have asked Sidney if he knew?'

'Yes. And he says he doesn't.'

'You believe him? Apart from the fact that you like him, do you believe him?'

Daniel thought for only a moment. 'Yes, I do. About this, anyway.'

'Then if we take that as truth, Thorwood is lying, or mistaken. Who is he covering for, and why? Does Rebecca know the truth?'

'She says not, according to Jemima. And the pendant was glass, anyway, although Sidney, or anyone else outside the family, would not know that,' he reasoned.

'What about Tobias Thorwood himself?'

'Why? What has he to gain?' He was puzzled.

'I have no idea. But he seems, from what you say, to be the one who's keeping the whole case alive.' She hesitated a moment. 'What is really troubling you? Is it the Morley Cross murder? Or Patrick's part in the whole thing?'

How had she read him so easily? Was it all written in his face? It was uncomfortable to be so obvious to anyone. And yet it would be ridiculous to lie, even to evade. 'I suppose it is,' he admitted. 'This is the first time I've met Patrick, although Jemima has been married to him for four years. But they lived in New York, and then Washington. I was more than fully occupied with exams . . . I couldn't go to the wedding.'

She smiled, although there was pain in it. 'I understand. You can't take that time out, three weeks at least with travelling, and to pass law or medicine . . .'

He remembered that she had sat and passed all the exams with honours to quality her as a forensic pathologist, but they would not take her seriously, because she was a woman. He had been thoughtless in his own vulnerability to a sacrifice of many things, perhaps relationships, and she was still denied the fruits of her qualifications, even the right to practise.

216

'I like Patrick.' He sat back. 'But the real thing is I don't want Jemima to be hurt. She probably knows him very well, but how well do we ever know anyone? Especially if we are in love with them?'

Immediately after he had said it, he wished he had not. He had taken all protection off the wound. That was what he was really afraid of. And of losing his own compass in all the mixed loyalties. Was there a real core at the heart of this? More than a minor, grubby theft perhaps? And a young man, whoever he was, attempting a burglary with more violence than necessary? The only evidence of that was the fine red scar on Rebecca's neck. Yes, now there was the violence of a young man.

He said as much to Miriam, suddenly finding the words with ease.

She was silent for several moments after he finished. He knew she would speak when she was ready.

'We haven't got it yet,' she said at last. 'But I think that is the right place to look. When we know what happened in the Thorwoods' house that night, and why, we will have at least the beginning of the thread, and perhaps an idea why Cross was shot.'

He smiled in the moment of self-understanding. 'We need to be in the middle, or beyond! And what is the emotion?' he asked. 'What is it that matters so much? It's got to be more than anyone's hurt pride.'

She smiled. It was more than self-mockery now. It was gentle, completely honest. 'I haven't the faintest idea.'

Chapter Eighteen

'Who, exactly, is Miriam again?' Jemima asked Daniel.

They were once more standing in the garden in Keppel Street, the August sun beginning to lose its heat in the late afternoon. Sophie was having her nap and Cassie was also upstairs asleep, a smile on her face. She had been difficult to settle, she was so pleased because she had beaten Daniel at a game with sticks and a sand bucket. He had made up the rules as they went along, and made absolutely certain he had lost in the end, but only just. It had been an exciting victory, with squeals of delight and lots of laughter.

Now, Daniel and Jemima were alone and had time to speak on the first occasion since he had arrived a couple of hours ago, leaving both Hillyer and Kitteridge to keep stringing out the testimony in court as long as possible. Jemima had told him Charlotte and Patrick were at the trial, but in another hour and a half, at the latest, they would be home. They had to be, Jemima told Daniel; she and Patrick were going to dine with the Thorwoods.

'She is Marcus fford Croft's daughter,' he answered. He had said that before, but she was not sure what that meant.

'How do you know her? And why?' She watched his face

in the light. There was now emotion in his eyes, in his mouth, more than she would have expected.

'She has done all the studying and taken all the exams to be a doctor, or a forensic pathologist, but no one will grant that she knows what she's doing, because she is a woman,' he replied.

She heard the edge to his voice. There was anger, as well as pity, that burned in him as if he not only shared it but felt it. Why? Because he did not like her? Or because it hurt? Or because he respected her, and in any kind of fairness there should have been nothing to pity?

'How do you know her?' Jemima repeated, skirting around the painful place, like a cliff edge that might crumble.

'Marcus suggested we ask her help in a very difficult case. She found the fact on which it all turned. I thought she might help in this.'

'Can she?'

'I don't know. She framed the questions we need to answer. She's very logical. I was going to say you would like her, but I'm not sure.'

She started to say, 'You do . . .' but changed her mind. Perhaps it did not matter now. Miriam fford Croft sounded interesting and different, and courageous. Jemima stayed with the subject of the trial. 'What do you need to find? I presume I can help, which is why you came to see me.'

He drew his breath in sharply, as if to speak.

'I'm not being petty,' she said quickly. 'Time is too short for you to spend it on a social visit. What is it? It's Rebecca, isn't it? You need to push further on the attack, and you want me to do it?'

'Not quite,' he answered, this time with an apologetic smile. 'But I think Tobias Thorwood might be the key.'

'You mean Miriam does?'

Daniel coloured very slightly. 'If I didn't agree, I wouldn't have come. Tobias is at the centre of it, in a way.'

'You mean his identification of Sidney is,' she corrected him. 'Or are you working around saying that he had to protect Rebecca? Why? Do you mean it was an assignation? That Tobias found her in bed with Sidney and threw him out? Framing him for robbery and assault so he can't blacken her name?' It was a very painful thought, for the dishonesty of it, but she couldn't deny it was possible . . . on the facts, anyway. Was Rebecca so feeble she would let a man she loved be ruined because her father disapproved of him? Was that what really haunted her – shame, and guilt?

Daniel was watching her. 'Don't think of yourself, Jem, think of what people do to protect their children, especially if they think they are vulnerable. Rebecca is not you. You would be horrified, but would she? Maybe she feels over-protected, or that she wants to escape.'

'She screamed!' Jemima pointed out. 'Fiercely enough to waken him and bring him running. In the middle of the night. That's some scream.'

'Sidney said he wasn't there,' Daniel pointed out. 'What if that were the truth, and the rest is lies?'

'Are you saying she tore that necklace off herself? That would be difficult. I've lost my patience with a necklace I couldn't undo before, but I've never torn it off. Actually, I tried once, and stopped pretty smartly long before it made a mark like that on me. If someone is lying, isn't it more likely that it's Sidney? He has everything to lie for.'

'Except it doesn't make sense. Just think for a moment. If it isn't the truth,' he argued, 'then what is?'

'Then Rebecca and her father are lying.'

'Didn't she say she didn't know who it was in the bedroom?'

'Yes.' Jemima thought for a moment. 'But if it wasn't Sidney, then who was it? And why did Tobias say it was Sidney?'

'And also, how did he get in, whoever it was? Did she leave a key somewhere? Or even actually let him in herself? Scullery door, or garden door, if they have one?'

'And lie to get Sidney into trouble? Or to keep somebody else out of trouble?' She thought of that with distaste, even revulsion. But she had never been attacked. How much did it change everything inside you? Would she want it to be Sidney rather than some ruffian she did not know? Perhaps in some twisted way, she wanted it to be someone she could blame, and keep locked up. Then she would feel safe. He could not ever do it again. But that made no sense, for if it were not Sidney, then whoever it was, he was still free. He could come back again! She would wake in the night at any noise, afraid, see shadows move and be terrified! Feel the hand on her throat, and her heart stop . . . 'I don't know,' she said. 'I can understand. If someone hurt Cassie or Sophie, I would want to think that we had him! But then if it were someone else's child hurt, and they said Patrick or you had done it, I'd fight them to the death to prove it wasn't.'

Daniel sat perfectly still for a moment, his face full of conflicting emotions.

'And Thorwood?' he asked. 'Why would he lie?'

'What do you want to know about him, apart from did he really see Sidney in the house? Or thinks he did? Does Miriam have anything concrete to suggest?'

'Yes.' He was looking at her very directly. 'Miriam said one thing for which I have no answer, and I think it could be at the core of it . . .'

'Not Patrick!' Her voice choked. It was the thought at the back of her mind. She knew how angry he had been. Was it over something about Rebecca that he knew would hurt Jemima?

'No!' he said quickly. 'Come on, Jem! I wouldn't go sideways at it like that! It's Thorwood again. Once he got Sidney out of America and out of the embassy in disgrace, why didn't he let it be?'

'He wants . . .' She stopped, uncertain.

'Yes? What does he want? In hot blood, he wanted revenge for the assault. But in cooler blood, he wants the whole world to believe that Rebecca was actually attacked. This is a lot of revenge for the theft of a glass pendant. Is she persuading him to do it?'

'No. I think she would rather he didn't.' Her mind went back to a conversation with Rebecca. 'He is saying she will feel better if she gets him locked up, where he can't hurt another young woman. She'll be to blame if anyone else is hurt, and perhaps far worse than she was.'

'He must be very sure it was Sidney in the corridor,' Daniel said quietly, very seriously. 'Miriam told me that the first time people come to swear to something, they are remembering what happened. The second time, they are remembering what they said the first time. And each time after that becomes more what they said than what they can actually relive in memory. In time, they come to use exactly the same words.'

She started to argue, then thought back a moment and realised how that might be true. She was sure of what she had said, but after a little while the actual memory was constructed by the words, not by the vision or the hearing of what had happened. 'I'll see what I can get,' she promised. 'You can go back and tell Miriam I shall do my best.'

'It's not for Miriam! It's for . . .' He saw in her face that she was teasing him, and he blushed.

Later in the evening, however, other things drove Daniel and Miriam out of Jemima's mind. She had had no opportunity to speak alone with Patrick until they had to dress for dinner with the Thorwoods. She had not time to consider it before, but watching Patrick straightening his tie for the fifth time before the looking-glass, she remembered how high his regard for the Thorwoods was. She admired gratitude; a sense of appreciation was a generous thing. A sense of debt for a gift fairly given, or as in his case, for a chance to be of service to someone else, did not warrant permanent obligation, unless there was more to it than she knew?

He caught her eye in the looking-glass. Suddenly all pretence fell away and he turned and spoke. 'You're going to ask what part I played in certain events in Washington, aren't you?'

'Yes. Is it to do with Tobias?' When he did not respond, she insisted. 'Tell me!' she said simply. 'Stop . . .'

'Morley Cross, who worked with Sidney at the Embassy, you remember I told you they found his body in the river about the time Sidney left Washington? I'm waiting to hear whether it was before or after Sidney left. I'm not sure I believe Sidney really did that.'

'Why would he?'

'I don't know, but I'm doing everything I can to find out. Come on, or we'll be late . . . and you hate being late.'

This was not the time to discharge old obligations. She needed to understand Thorwood better. What Miriam had apparently said made sense. Jemima watched Patrick now, and then the moment he turned to face her, she looked away.

He would see in her face that she was anxious. It would not take him more than seconds to guess why. She pretended to be concerned with her appearance. The gown was new, a gift from her mother. Jemima had no idea what it had cost and she did not ask. It was a gorgeous, rich dark blue, falling to just above the ankle, the most fashionable length. It was made of silk, and cut as low at the neck as she dared wear. Patrick's eyes had widened when he saw it, but he had said nothing. Perhaps fashions in London were a little more avant garde than those in Washington. Certainly, London was closer to Paris!

It was a short journey from Keppel Street to the hotel where the Thorwoods were staying. No time for serious conversation, which was a relief. Jemima occupied the time relating memories of visiting them in their home in Washington, and saying how much they must miss it.

They arrived about five minutes late. As far as she was concerned, it was perfect timing. For the hosts to wait a short while for people was excellent; to be caught not quite ready was not.

The Thorwoods were all waiting in the sitting room of their suite when Patrick and Jemima arrived. The usual greetings were made, as if the threat of unpleasantness did not exist. Tobias was in a dark suit, very formal, without quite being evening dress. Bernadette was extremely elegant in soft, plum-toned pinks. With the delicate way the fabric moved with her when she walked, it can only have been silk. She came forward as they entered and greeted Jemima warmly, although it was Patrick whose eyes she met first, before glancing at Jemima's gown, drawing in breath, and deciding that whatever comment she was going to make was inadequate.

224

'What a charming colour,' was all she said. 'It is most flattering.'

'Thank you,' Jemima replied, as if it had been an unqualified compliment. 'It is one of my favourites.' She hid the smile that came to her lips, and turned to Rebecca, who was dressed in green. It was too dark for her, and made her look as if she were cold. She was a little thin, and at the moment too pale to carry so heavy a shade. 'I'm so happy to see you,' Jemima said warmly. 'Every time I think of Washington, I remember how kind you were in showing your favourite places to me. I would never have seen the dogwood in bloom had it not been for you. Everyone speaks of the azaleas, and they were gorgeous, but the dogwoods are magical.'

Rebecca's face lit at the memory. 'Oh, yes! I've always thought so.'

'We must go out again,' Jemima said.

Tobias drew breath as if to say something, then changed his mind. He glanced at Bernadette, who shook her head minutely and said to Jemima, 'Shall we go into dinner?' It was a directive, not really a question.

Jemima noticed as they went into the dining room that Tobias offered his arm to Rebecca, rather than to his wife. Otherwise, Rebecca, as the unescorted one, would have gone in alone. Patrick had remained close to Jemima, perhaps thinking of her as the odd one, the only one not American, not in on some of the references in conversation, the one without a common heritage. She did feel it at times: the sense of being a stranger, not sharing the idealism of a relatively new nation burning with pride for its uniquely noble beginnings. There had been one or two conversations in the past on the superiority of being a republic. Jemima felt far too vulnerable to argue. Anyway, it was ill-mannered and pointless.

The issue of loneliness in such company was sometimes very deep. She must make sure Patrick did not feel that in the Pitt family. Without thinking, did they do that sometimes? Perhaps everybody felt separate in some way or other, at times?

Her father came sharply to mind. Knighted by the Queen. One of the last things she had done at the end of a reign that had lasted most of the century! And now he was confidant of the King, for some service he would never speak of; head of Special Branch, and keeping the secrets of any number of people, the great and the small, public and private. And yet, with his humble background he was never one of the establishment by right.

Jemima thought about how alone we all are, behind the smooth manners or the awkwardness.

She was suddenly aware of the Thorwoods. They were talking to her and around her when she did not answer, and she had not been aware of it until Patrick touched her arm and repeated the question Tobias had asked.

'Oh, yes, thank you,' she answered a little awkwardly. She took the seat he was indicating for her. Everyone else took his or her place as Tobias directed.

Dinner was ordered. Patrick had ordered for her, and she did not mind in the least. He knew exactly what she liked.

Conversation was casual, not exactly awkward, but not flowing. It was as if each person were intending to say something else, but wound up evading it. It was Bernadette who finally leaned forward, and the stillness in her, the tight muscles of her neck conveyed such tension that everyone else stopped speaking. She seemed to be talking mainly to Patrick, but every so often she included Jemima. 'I'm going to speak over our dessert, but this cannot be avoided all

226

evening. It hangs over everything, and we are so busy avoiding it, it has finally become central. Tobias will be called to testify at Philip Sidney's trail. If not tomorrow, then very soon. Perhaps the next day.'

'They seem to want me for tomorrow,' Tobias cut in. 'For several days now, it has been almost meaningless . . .'

'Why?' Rebecca interrupted. 'You aren't for the prosecution! You know nothing about the embezzlement, do you?' She looked completely puzzled.

'No, I don't.' Tobias looked miserable, as if he had been cornered and faced enemies in every direction. 'I'm . . . sorry . . .' It was unclear whom he was addressing: Jemima, Rebecca, or even Patrick.

'Has the prosecution called you, sir?' Patrick asked. Under the table, he reached for Jemima's hand.

'Yes,' Tobias said quietly.

Jemima looked at Bernadette. She was smiling, very slightly.

'Papa?' Rebecca began. 'You said—'

Her mother silenced her with a glance. It was of such finality, it would have silenced Jemima. 'I have no choice,' Tobias said quietly. 'Something has happened that has taken from me the choice of remaining silent.' He stopped for a moment.

Jemima looked at Patrick, but his eyes were concentrated on Tobias. Jemima was sure he did not know what Tobias was going to say.

Tobias looked at Rebecca. 'I'm sorry, my dear, but your godmother's pendant has turned up.'

'How can you know?' Rebecca demanded.

'The police in Washington found it, and sent a wire to the embassy here. I was notified this afternoon.'

'Where did they find it?' Rebecca asked.

'In a pawn shop. The owner was an honest man, and he reported it.'

'But it's weeks later now,' Patrick pointed out. 'His honesty works rather slowly.'

'Yes, that needs a little explaining,' Tobias replied. 'Apparently it was brought in by a man who took it in a gambling debt, the evening after it was stolen.'

Patrick frowned. 'But apparently Sidney didn't leave the British Embassy after you reported the assault. This can't be true . . . or at least it can't be entirely true.'

Tobias bit his lip. 'That's the point, I'm afraid. This young man worked at the British Embassy. He took it in payment from Philip Sidney, then finally had to pawn it for cash. I'm afraid it seals the question as to Sidney's guilt. Not that any of us doubted it.'

Patrick leaned forward, his face creased with anxiety. 'So, what are you going to testify to? It still has nothing to do with the embezzlement. All this man at the embassy could swear to is that Sidney gave him a pendant in payment of a gambling debt.'

Jemima looked at Patrick. She tried to read his expression. Was it this young man, Morley Cross, who had been shot? In which case they had only the pawnbroker's word for any of this. Patrick did not look vindicated at all; rather he looked even further troubled. Was he pleased? Was he sorry for Sidney? It was not fully a moment of triumph, to judge by his expression. It was not a victory at all.

Patrick's frown deepened. 'How are you going to bring that in? In fact, why is the prosecution calling you at all? If Hillyer bends the rules, which, watching him, I can't see him doing—'

'Character witness,' Tobias said simply. 'And if by some chance he doesn't, your fellow Kitteridge can do. That might be better.'

'Difficult,' Patrick said. 'That would make him look like an idiot. Seem as if he were deliberately sabotaging his own client.'

'That's why Tobias wants it to be Hillyer,' Bernadette said patiently. She turned to Patrick after a quick glance at Jemima, and then away again. 'I'm afraid we will take Kitteridge by surprise, but if Hillyer asks, we must answer.' She smiled with deep satisfaction.

Somehow, Jemima found it chilling. She tried to put herself in Bernadette's place; imagined it had been Cassie hurt. Would she then have felt that throb of triumph? Why didn't she? The pendant turning up, traceable through a gambling debt directly to Sidney, was just what they needed. Maybe the pawnbroker had already identified the man who brought it in as Morley Cross from a photograph of him. Daniel would not doubt Sidney's guilt after that! Would they then bring in Morley Cross's part in handing over the embezzled expenses? Was that what they were waiting for? It would tie it all together.

'What will you do?' Jemima asked. 'Appear for Hillyer, and very reluctantly admit that you are now in a position to condemn Sidney's character utterly? And since the pendant was to pay gambling debts, you find it not difficult to believe he also stole . . . and . . . killed?'

Under the table, Patrick's fingers tightened over hers. He knew she did not want Sidney to be guilty – possibly because he was Daniel's client.

Tobias was staring at her. 'Killed! What on earth are you talking about?'

The colour burned up her face. There was no escaping it. She had totally trapped herself. They were all staring at her. 'I'm sorry,' she murmured to Patrick, then she looked up at Tobias. 'The man who you believe pawned the pendant. He was found dead, in the Potomac. That surely has to be connected, doesn't it?'

Bernadette looked suddenly pale.

'I'm afraid it does,' Tobias agreed. He sounded relieved.

'You will have to tell the whole story,' Jemima began, looking across at Rebecca.

Rebecca winced. She turned to her father. 'Do you have to, Papa? Can't you just say it was stolen?'

'If he is even competent, never mind clever, Hillyer will ask details,' Patrick warned. 'He won't just accept it.'

'Can't Daniel stop him from pressing it?' Rebecca asked, looking at Jemima.

'I'll tell him,' she replied. 'But if Hillyer is going to raise the subject, Daniel and Kitteridge have to challenge it if they can.'

'Do they?' Bernadette said sharply. 'Won't they only be making it worse for their client? It will be, you know. This was a very serious charge. Not some petty theft!' Her face was full of emotion. Jemima could see she was breathing rapidly and a little shakily, and she felt a wave of compassion sweep over her.

'I can point out to Daniel the damage that will do. Or to Kitteridge, if he is handling it. Damage not just to Rebecca, but to Sidney, who is, after all, his client. People will hate Sidney for it. He might get a far heavier sentence. I believe judges have some latitude but he might choose the heaviest sentence he can.'

She was surprised to see Tobias look troubled. He glanced at his wife, then his daughter.

Patrick was watching him, then he turned to Jemima.

'For goodness' sake,' Jemima said impatiently, 'no harm has been done yet. If you're uncertain about it, it will make people doubt you.' She was looking at Tobias.

He flushed a dull, painful colour and looked away.

Bernadette turned to Patrick. 'It was actually I who heard Rebecca scream,' she stated firmly. 'I am a lighter sleeper than Tobias is. I gathered my robe from the hook on the door and went out into the passage. I saw a man coming out of Rebecca's room. I screamed to waken Tobias. The man turned and ran. I admit . . .' She gulped.

Tobias put his hand on her arm gently.

'I was very shaken,' she continued. 'I ran to Rebecca's room, terrified of what I might find. I imagined all sorts of things. But she was all right. I mean, she wasn't injured . . . or worse. Only shocked and very frightened. And there was a red ring around her throat where Aunt May's pendant had been savagely ripped off her neck.'

Rebecca was white-faced. She was clearly reliving the whole thing, awakening in the night to find a man right there in her bedroom. She had screamed, and he had lunged at her for the necklace. Then fearing she had roused the household, he darted out of the room and fled.

'I saw quite plainly that it was Philip Sidney. I was only a few yards away from him. He hesitated and stared at me. I thought for a moment he was going to attack me. How misled we can be by people,' she said quietly. 'He seemed—'

'We were all misled,' Tobias agreed. 'I feel guilty that I ever allowed him into the house.'

'He worked at the British Embassy, Tobias,' Bernadette said gently. 'If they didn't know what sort of a man he was, how could you?'

231

Jemima felt all her muscles knot. And she also felt Patrick's hand tighten on hers under the table. She looked at Tobias. 'Why did you say it was you who saw him? Someone will ask you. It seems an unnecessary lie.'

Tobias's lips tightened. 'I was trying to protect Bernadette from having to relive that night again in front of strangers,' he said curtly. He clearly resented being obliged to answer her.

But no one challenged him, certainly not Jemima. She thought Bernadette was quite capable of seeing off a pack of dogs, let alone a gentle police questioning, respectful of her position in society and the crime that had taken place in her house. But she did not say so. There was nothing to be gained. And now that the pendant had been recovered and traced back through another member of the British Embassy, making the possible link to Philip Sidney, it seemed that it was all over. Sidney would be far wiser not to fight the inevitable any longer.

Why did she feel so defeated? Was it because Daniel was going to lose the case? That was absurd! He had accepted it originally in order to see justice brought about for another crime in what seemed impossible circumstances. And there was now the terrible weight of Morley Cross's murder hanging over everything. Did Sidney even know of that? Was he responsible?

She had better put on a more appropriate face than one of gloom, as if she had lost something. Daniel was wrong. There was no darker secret hanging over them at all, only a man who loved his family, and was defending them with a lie that was natural in instinct, but unwise on deeper thought.

And, of course, the people at the British Embassy behaving

232

like fools. Or perhaps not? Perhaps they were getting rid of Philip Sidney in a rather heavy-handed fashion.

She felt Patrick's hand grip hers a moment longer, then release it.

Poor Daniel. He was going to lose the case, badly. But he had to!

Chapter Nineteen

Early the following morning, Jemima dressed in a plain, dark grey costume and white lace blouse. She loved the stark contrast of colours, and the way the silky fabric moved with her. It almost felt like silk. She told everyone at the breakfast table that she had an important appointment, and hastened out before anyone could ask her what it was.

Patrick followed her to the front door. 'What are you going to do?' He made no attempt to be tactful.

'Nothing dangerous,' she began.

'Are you going to see Rebecca? You can't. She may know the truth, but she won't tell it to you, or anyone else, and certainly not in court, if it hurts her family.'

'Do you think it will?' she asked directly.

'Don't play games!' he said tartly. 'Of course, it might. The answer she is giving, is it believable? She'll stay with it, whatever it costs, because anything different will betray her family. Wouldn't you if it were your father? I've seen how close you are . . .' There was a break in his voice. He had several brothers and sisters, too many to pick favourites, and no deep companionship with either of his parents.

Jemima was instantly sorry. 'I'm not going to see any of

the Thorwoods. I'm going to see Daniel's friend Miriam ff.ord Croft, if she's in.'

'Why? Who is she, and what does she know?' He was genuinely taken by surprise. It was an answer he had not even considered.

'She's the one who knows there's something missing.'

'How can she help?' He was not satisfied. The anxiety was keen in his face.

'I need to see if she thinks this is it. Daniel thinks very highly of her.'

'In what way? Who is she? And don't give me an empty answer!'

'She studied as a doctor, then as a forensic pathologist, but she can't practise and hold any official post . . . because she's a woman.' She saw the startled expression on his face. She was not looking for a quarrel. 'She helped him before, with a very difficult case, about three months ago. I'm only going to ask her.'

'Medicine and pathology?' He raised his eyebrows. 'No one is dead over here, Jem. And the only injury is a scratch mark on Rebecca's neck. What can she tell you?'

'I don't know. Perhaps whatever it is we're looking at and can't see.'

'What do you mean, "we"? Jem, you're not meddling in Daniel's affairs, are you?' he asked suspiciously.

'Don't be ridiculous!' The idea hurt, because it could so easily have been true. 'Apart from the fact that I wouldn't, any more than I'd let him meddle in mine, Miriam ff ord Croft is the daughter of the head of chambers, and she's at least ten or twelve years older than Daniel is. She's just . . . clever.'

Patrick relaxed at last. 'I suppose if I come, I'll be in the way.'

'Yes, you will! It will look as if I've come with force! I want to—'

'I know. You want to help. You can't stop yourself.' His smile was wry, and gentle.

'I'm not trying to help myself! Oh. I see what you mean. I just—'

'Can't help meddling,' he finished for her. 'Apparently, just like your mother!' He leaned forward and kissed her cheek.

For a second, she kissed him back, then slipped away and walked briskly along the pavement. She had no idea what to expect. She would have asked Daniel more about Miriam, even a description of her. But she did not want him to know she intended to visit her. He would be quick to understand her motives, if she pursued it.

When Jemima knocked, a woman opened the door. She had bright auburn hair tied in a tight, untidy knot on her neck, and she wore a floor-length apron. Jemima was uncertain who she was. Her hands were wet, as if she had been scrubbing something, and her sleeves were rolled up to the elbows. She could easily have been a maid. Her greenish-blue eyes were bold and curious at first, then amused.

Jemima made a rash guess. 'Dr fford Croft?'

There was a moment's hesitation, then the woman laughed. 'You must be Daniel's sister. You have to be. You look quite a lot like him, and no one else would call me "Doctor".'

Jemima was surprised. 'Do you think I look like Daniel? I suppose I must do a bit. But yes, that is who I am.'

Miriam smiled. 'Please come in. You want to discuss the case of Philip Sidney, I expect.' She pulled the door wide open and stepped back.

'I'm interrupting you. I'm sorry,' Jemima began.

'Chores,' Miriam answered. 'Only too happy to have a good excuse to leave them. Come in.'

Jemima was startled. Surely the daughter of the house did not do the heavy scrubbing?

Miriam saw her confusion. She laughed cheerfully. 'Not the kitchen floor,' she explained. 'The table in my laboratory. I won't let the servants in there.'

'Thank you.' Jemima followed her into the hall, and then into a small study whose floor was partially covered with piles of books and papers. However, there was still plenty of room to sit down, and at least half the dark, plain Adam mahogany table was clear of clutter.

Miriam insisted Jemima sit down, and sat opposite her at the table. 'Something is new?' Miriam asked. It was only just a question. She clearly perceived that Jemima had come to tell her something that Daniel had not known.

'We dined with the Thorwoods yesterday evening,' Jemima replied. 'In the course of the conversation, Mr Thorwood admitted that it was not he who had seen Sidney in the corridor outside of Rebecca's bedroom. It was his wife, Bernadette Thorwood. She was disturbed, at first fearing that Rebecca had been attacked, even raped. Mr Thorwood said it was he who had seen Sidney . . . to protect her from having to be questioned.'

Miriam looked interested, but not yet drawn in. Jemima knew that she was waiting for the fact that made a difference, the detail as to who had seen Sidney would probably not matter.

Jemima swallowed hard. 'And Mr Thorwood said that the pendant has been recovered by a pawnbroker at his shop in Washington. The person who pawned it worked in the British Embassy there, and the pawnbroker was told he got it from another man at the embassy in payment of a gambling debt . . . the day before Sidney left America. That . . . that sort of . . . seals it.' She had no idea why she was telling Miriam this. What did she expect Miriam to say or do? Why was Jemima refusing to accept Sidney's guilt? Had she identified with Daniel because he still believed in Sidney? Would he still, when he knew about the pendant?

Miriam was still waiting. 'What else?' she asked.

'I'm not sure. I hope you can put all these things in their proper order, and relationship to each other, and see some sense in it. Rebecca told me the pendant was crystal. It only mattered to her because it belonged to her godmother, May Trelawny, who died very recently.'

'Is all her godmother's estate left to Rebecca?' Miriam looked suddenly far more interested.

'I don't know. I think so.'

'But the pendant was crystal, or so it was said?'

Jemima was sitting forward now. 'You think it could have been a real diamond? Does that make a difference? I suppose the point is, who knew it was real?'

'Yes. If it was. Or if they thought it was. It is one fact that seems to tie into a lot of things. I think we should look into May Trelawny's estate. The will must have been probated, if they are here to settle it. I have friends I can ask. It would certainly be interesting to learn.' She shook her head. 'I wish I could think it matters.' She stood up from the table. 'I will change my clothes and we shall go and visit one or two people. I shall make some telephone calls.' She did not wait for Jemima's acceptance; she had already taken it for granted.

Jemima remained at the table, almost oblivious of her surroundings. Why had she come here? What did she expect this woman could do, however skilled she was? The case against Sidney seemed unarguable.

If there were any single fact to uncover that would make a difference, possibly Patrick could find it through the connections he kept wiring in Washington. It was police work, not something a doctor would find over here!

She watched the seconds tick by on the clock, and felt more and more foolish. Why was it taking Miriam so long to get ready?

It was nearly half an hour later when Miriam reappeared, smartly dressed in a navy-blue costume, and her hair tidy, temporarily at least.

'I am sorry to have kept you waiting,' she said. 'I made a telephone call to my father, so he could begin enquiries.'

Jemima felt a wave of guilt run through her. 'I didn't mean to cause trouble,' she started.

Miriam smiled. 'Of course, you did! Nothing short of trouble is going to get the truth out of this! And even if it turns out the wrong way, and Sidney is guilty, at least you will know it, and it will not have gone by default. Is that not what you want?' Her stare was very direct.

'Yes, it is,' Jemima acknowledged. 'Thank you.' She stood up, and they went out of the door together and found a taxi almost immediately.

Thirty-five minutes later they were in Marcus fford Croft's chambers in Lincoln's Inn, accepting tea from Impney and waiting for Marcus himself.

He came in a few moments later. He was not very tall, overweight, but full of energy, white hair flying, hands gesticulating with energy and delicacy. 'Mrs Flannery, good morning. How do you do? Young Daniel's sister, heh? Married

239

an American. Live there, do you? Bring us this apparently hopeless case of young Sidney? Pity.' He smiled, a singularly charming gesture. Immediately he turned to Miriam. They did not resemble each other at all, and yet there was something alike in the intensity of their manner, their attention, even the gestures with their hands. Hers were so much more restrained, even delicate, but they were the same as his in meaning.

'Abigail May Trelawny,' he went on. 'Sit down.' He indicated the chairs and then continued. He had several pieces of paper in his hand. 'Born in Cornwall. As she ought to be, with a name like Trelawny. Good family. Old. Grandfather had a lot of land. The father was his second son. Not got a lot of it, but made his own fortune. Did well. She bought a place in Alderney. Do you know that?' He looked at Jemima with his eyebrows raised.

'Yes,' Jemima said immediately. 'One of the smaller Channel Islands and—'

'Yes,' Marcus cut her off. 'Right. Jersey and Guernsey are the big ones. Fewer live on Alderney. Very few on Sark. Lovely place. She had a large house on Alderney. Lived there. Loved it. Left the house and land to Rebecca Thorwood. Not a lot of money.'

'What is a lot, Father?' Miriam asked. 'That's very relative.'

'Relative to the Thorwood fortune, almost nothing at all,' he replied.

'Why to Rebecca?' Jemima asked. 'Was there a family connection? I thought all Rebecca's family were American? Her father's family has been respected in Washington for generations.'

'Possibly,' Marcus agreed. 'But her mother's family isn't American. She was a debutante in London. Quite lovely,

240

according to all accounts. I can recall reading about a love affair that went badly. Can't remember the name of the fellow but it was all a bit of a drama, and then she married well. Nice fellow, but a bit of a bore. Change from the one she fell for, who was apparently a bad lot; but had charm.' Marcus said it sadly, as if it were a pattern he had seen too often. 'I wonder what appeals to women in such men.'

'We don't want something that's too easily available,' Miriam answered immediately. 'And some of us are daft enough to think we can change them . . . redeem them, if you like.'

'I don't think, from what I hear, that Tobias Thorwood needed redeeming,' Marcus observed. 'Anyway, May Trelawny was a delightful woman who never married, wisely, or in any other way, and she was happy to be Rebecca's godmother, and leave her whatever she possessed. Can't see what this has to do with Philip Sidney. Except that he was born in Cornwall and his mother was a friend and relation of Miss Trelawny. Not such a big place, when you come to think of it in terms of society so it may be entirely a coincidence.'

'They could have met,' Miriam answered. 'Or they might never have heard of each other. Didn't you say Bernadette met Thorwood in London?'

'Yes,' Marcus agreed.

'Something else we need to know,' Jemima said. 'Is the pendant diamond or crystal?'

'Did you see it?' Miriam asked with sudden intensity.

'Yes.'

'Describe it. How big is it? How is it faceted? Colour . . . I mean shading, shadows, lights, flaws? Does the light move in it? Glitter? How is it set? Gold? Silver? Platinum?'

Jemima tried to picture it in her mind. Exactly how big

had it been? A half-inch across? Almost. Colour? Plain white, but it glittered, it shone. The setting? White, not gold. Was it silver? She tried to describe.

'The cut?' Miriam said.

'I don't know much about cuts, but it had a large, flat front.'

'Rock crystal,' Miriam said. 'Very pretty. Not of great value, but something you could wear every day without being ostentatious.'

'Rebecca said she loved it because it had been her godmother's, and it was pretty.'

'They were close?' Miriam pressed. 'How? Where did they meet? It's a long way from Cornwall, or Alderney, to Washington.'

'Rebecca told me her godmother used to write the most wonderful letters. Sometimes they were descriptions of Alderney during the seasons. She loved to say how the light changed over the sea. No two sunsets were the same, or twilights, and even the dawn. "The coming of the Light", she called it.' Jemima remembered the pleasure in Rebecca's face as she recounted May's words. 'Other times, the letters would be about her animals, especially the horses. And about the wild birds, too. And, of course, the people. She was never unkind, but was often funny. Rebecca said it was almost as good as living there herself.'

'And did Rebecca write long letters back?' Miriam said quickly.

Jemima smiled. 'Oh, yes. Accounts of things in Washington, but often hopes and dreams as well.' After a moment, she added, 'You mean, might she have told her secrets? I doubt it. Rebecca lives a very sheltered life. Her father particularly is very protective. It would drive me demented!'

'But they knew each other through letters?'

'Yes, Rebecca . . . liked that. And May never told her what to do, and what not to. Actually, I think May Trelawny was quite a character in her own way, and always had been. Rebecca really loved her.'

Miriam gave a soft laugh. 'The perfect friend. Every young woman should have one. A friend who shares your adventures with you, perhaps slightly shaded? Full of good humour, even wit. Stories of other times and places. No criticism.'

Jemima felt a wave of sorrow that Aunt Vespasia was gone, too. She missed her wisdom, her laughter, above all her spirit. 'Poor Rebecca,' she said softly. 'She's going to miss her godmother terribly. There won't be anyone to fill her place. No wonder she wants the pendant back. I'm so glad they found it and she'll have it again.'

'The house,' Miriam looked at her father. 'Is it up for sale? Or is it part of Rebecca's inheritance?'

'It's part of her inheritance,' Marcus said. 'She may choose to sell it – or to keep it and visit. Why not? It's beautiful, different, an escape from what she is accustomed to. But I imagine she will sell it, when the legal side is settled.'

'Yes,' Miriam said thoughtfully. 'Thank you, Papa.'

Jemima looked at Miriam, and knew that she had an idea, even a plan.

Chapter Twenty

The trial was continuing at a lumbering pace, one character witness after another. Daniel seemed to be dragging it out even more, cross-questioning people to no possible purpose. Kitteridge thought he sounded desperate to put off the inevitable. He had no defence, and the jury must know that.

It was Friday afternoon, surely everyone was ready for a weekend? Did Hillyer imagine the answers regarding Morley Cross's murder were going to come forward over the next two days? Daniel tried to force his mind into a sort of clarity. Any answer would do to build on. Just waiting was not good enough. What could change, and be for the better, or worse? He felt a nudge at his elbow and ignored it. The second time he turned, irritated at being distracted, and found the court usher standing deferentially beside him. He was holding an envelope.

'For you, sir. The young lady said it was important.' He inclined his head, an acknowledgement more than a bow, then turned and took himself back down the aisle, towards the door. He seemed to assume no answer was expected.

Daniel tore it open. There was a single page inside. He unfolded it and read.

Dear Daniel,

I have given much thought to the matter, and I believe May Trelawny's house in Alderney may be at the root of some of this.

I was looking for how this could have started off, if Sidney were not guilty, and we must presume that. Perhaps it is May's death that is central to events? I think we need to go to Alderney this weekend, before it is too late. I have arranged for a car to the coast, and will then catch the ferry across the Channel. I realise this is a liberty, and if you are not able or willing to accompany me, I shall go alone and return by Monday, to show you what I have found.

I plan to leave London this afternoon by four, so we may reach Alderney before dark, or shortly after. If you choose to come, I shall meet you at my house at four.

Sincerely, Miriam

It was about three o'clock. If he raced, he could just call by his room and pack a case, leaving the taxi waiting, and make it to Miriam's house by four.

'Kitteridge!' Daniel hissed.

'What?' Kitteridge did not turn to look at him. He was trying to concentrate his mind on tedious listening, feeling that there must be something in it, if only he could think what, in all the mass of detail that surrounded the facts. He had already agreed with Daniel's suggestion that Hillyer was keeping it going only because he was waiting for a final witness, or a piece of evidence yet to show up that would settle the case for him. Presumably, a damning one. He knew that Daniel had no defence to mount. His only recourse would be reasonable doubt. And with this weight of fact, was the jury even listening any more?

'I'm going to Alderney,' Daniel committed himself.

For a second, Kitteridge froze, and then he turned around in his seat. 'You are . . . what?' he said incredulously.

'I'm going to Alderney,' Daniel repeated.

'When? And what on earth for?'

'Now. And I don't know . . . not yet.' He stood up, felt the judge's eyes on him, and bowed slightly. 'Excuse me, Your Honour. I'll find you when I get back,' he said to Kitteridge. 'Keep on going. It could matter.'

'Pitt!' Kitteridge scrambled to his feet. But Daniel was already striding up the aisle through the gallery, towards the door and then out.

He arrived at the fford Crofts' and his heart sank. There was no taxi in sight and he felt ridiculously disappointed. Then he realised it must be somebody's idea of a practical joke. Of course Miriam was not going to Alderney. How incredibly foolish he had been!

There was a very elegant-looking motor car parked further along the kerb. It was clear red, like a pillar box, and had long, sweeping lines he loved on sight. It must be capable of amazing speed. It must mean she had visitors. He would go very quietly and never tell her about this. He would have to think of something to say to Kitteridge to explain it. Not that Kitteridge would ever let him forget it!

The front door of the house opened, and the butler came outside, on to the path. He looked around and saw Daniel. 'Good afternoon, Mr Pitt. Good of you to come, sir. Miss fford Croft will be out in just a moment. She had a late telephone call that is rather important. May I put your case in the car, sir?'

Wordlessly, Daniel gave it to him. Where was the driver? He hoped Miriam did not imagine he was going to drive it. He felt as if he had let her down. He had intended to learn, but somehow other matters had always taken precedence. He had played around at it a little in Cambridge. A friend had a car and was keen to show it off, but it was nothing like this! And driving on the country roads in Cambridgeshire was another world from driving in London! There were few other cars on the road, but there were horses, wagons, drays, omnibuses, and who knew what else?

The front door opened again and Miriam came striding out. She was dressed in a shirt and what looked like a riding skirt, and she carried a tailored jacket in one hand. Her face lit when she saw Daniel, and she increased her pace before stopping beside him. 'You could come! I'm so pleased.' She took a breath. 'It is always so much better to have another view of something. Binocular vision, so to speak. Are we ready to go?'

'Yes . . .' What else could he say? Not whether he was relieved, or terrified, or both.

'Excellent.' She indicated the passenger seat and climbed into the driver's seat. She thanked the butler, who wished them both a successful journey.

'I have learned a little bit more about May Trelawny,' Miriam said, as soon as the butler had cranked the car, returned the handle into the place it was stored, and wished her *bon voyage*. She moved the car on to the road with ease, as if she enjoyed it, and Daniel kept his eyes straight ahead. He was determined not to let her guess that the thought of speeding along the open road towards the sea, with her at the wheel of this car, driving at over thirty miles an hour, was the second to the last thing he wanted. The very last was for her to know he was afraid.

'Have you?' he said, his mouth dry.

'She was quite a rebel, in her own quiet way,' she answered. 'She had a sister who was the obedient one, who was forced to marry "well" and was very unhappy. She died in childbirth, poor soul, and I believe the child died soon after. May was terribly grieved. She never really put it behind her. Somebody who knew her has said it was as if she were living for her sister, too.'

Daniel had never known them, and yet he felt the loss of that young woman and her child. 'I'm sorry,' he said softly. He looked sideways at Miriam and saw tears glistening on her cheek.

'That was when May decided to break from her family and go her own way,' Miriam went on. She steered around a horse and a two-wheeled carriage going at about half their speed. 'It was a rift never really mended,' she continued. 'But she was a clever woman. She learned a lot about stones.' She stopped, perhaps obliged to look more carefully at the road ahead. The traffic was increasing, but Daniel thought it was more likely that she averted her eyes to compose herself from the emotion of that long-ago grief.

They drove in silence for several minutes at a steady speed. They seemed to be taking the road for the south coast, through Guildford, the village of Haslemere and then over the glorious sweep of the South Downs to Portsmouth.

'Stones?' he prompted her.

'Yes. All kinds, except the really precious ones. She had no interest in diamonds and rubies and such. She liked rock crystal, malachite, topaz, and other less well-known semi-precious stones. And river pearls. They come in different pale colours, you know. And dark ones sometimes, greys and purplish shades.'

'What did she do with them?' Daniel was interested, in spite of himself.

'She made jewellery and sold it. That was how she supported herself. She worked for a few famous jewellers. She just signed her name "Trelawny", and became quite famous. She probably made the rock crystal pendant she gave to Rebecca. If it were a Trelawny piece, it'll be worth more than if it were not.'

'Do you think that matters?'

'It might do. She did quite well, but she was never rich – at least, as far as anyone knows. She gave quite a lot away, so it was said. But to unusual characters, like those who cared for old and unwanted animals, such as horses that couldn't work any more.' She was picking up speed again along the road leading to the coast.

Daniel wanted to ask if she had booked tickets for them on the ferry, or if there was more than one, in case they missed the next one. But he was not sure he wanted the answer yet. Maybe there were several at this time of the year. But they would travel from Portsmouth to Cherbourg on the French coast, and from there by another ferry to Alderney, which was far closer to France than any of the other Channel Isles.

He realised that in some ways he knew Miriam so well from the Graves case. He knew her imagination, her logic, the strength of the anger and the pity that drove her to find the truth. He had felt the fierce gentleness of her compassion for the young man in the wheelchair, possibly for the rest of his life, and who painted such beautiful pictures of birds in flight, as if he had felt the exaltation of freedom, the soaring wings, the endlessness of it. He had felt the same emotion himself.

And yet he also knew her so little. He knew what she dreamed of, and could not have, because she was a woman. He had no idea what she wanted and could have, or at least aspire to, whether she had ever fallen in love, or wanted to marry. Had she wanted to have children, but left it too late? Or loved someone not free to marry her? Was it a pain too deep to share with anyone? So much of what he knew was in the head. The heart was only guessed at.

It was she who broke the silence. 'We may not learn anything.' She sounded as if it were going to be an apology at first. 'But I think Rebecca may be more at the centre of this than we supposed,' she continued. She seemed unaware of having included herself in the case. 'But she knew Sidney, and apparently liked him. If he took the pendant, then he must have been a pretty good rotter. But if he didn't – if he was telling the truth, as far as he knew it, in all other things – then there are big pieces of this that we don't know. And the person we know least about is the one whose death lies at the beginning of this.'

'May?' he asked, forcing his mind to pay attention. 'The Thorwoods already have very much more money than May Trelawny, and Rebecca is the only heir to both, or should I say all three of them,' he replied. 'Presumably, if her father dies first, her mother will be provided for. And I didn't have the impression from Jemima that Rebecca cares about money anyway. I suppose she has never had to.'

'Possibly it is something to do with this house in Alderney,' Miriam suggested. 'Or maybe something happened there that matters.' She did not offer any suggestion as to what that might be.

For another little while they drove in silence through Guildford, and then through the lush countryside towards

250

Haslemere. They spoke of other things: books, ideas, current politics. She supported the King, but without much enthusiasm. His odd mixture of personality did not please her, although she granted his talents. She was troubled by his travels so often to visit his cousin the Kaiser of Germany, and the increasingly difficult political situation there, and incidentally the rising power of the German navy. Daniel's father would have agreed with her on that.

'England is stuck in an historical time lock,' she said, with an edge of either fear or anger in her voice – he was not sure which. She was staring at the road along which they were still travelling at higher speed than when they had begun. The last thing he wanted was to distract her attention, and yet he wondered what she meant. He had to ask. 'If not in the present, where are we?'

'A hundred years ago,' she answered without hesitation, unknowingly echoing what Thomas Pitt had said. 'Only fifty militarily, with the Crimean War, perhaps. But as far as the navy is concerned, we still think we have mastery over the oceans of the world, as if Nelson were only just dead, as if unaware of the new developments such as the Germans are making with their submarines.'

'My father says the same thing,' Daniel replied, and then wondered if that were tactless, as if implying she was of the same generation. He wished he had not said it, but to retract it would make it worse. He avoided looking at her.

'I wish you had said he thought the opposite,' Miriam answered. 'Although I would not have believed it.'

In spite of himself, he looked at her. He did not need to ask. He was quite sure she meant it. If Pitt had believed otherwise, she would have been prepared to reconsider her view, and find one she liked far better. 'Do you?' he asked curiously.

'Yes. I wish he were right, and he is in a position where he knows far more than we do.'

He realised she was afraid. His instinct was to reach out and touch her, as he would have Jemima. He even began to, then saw that the gesture would be far too familiar. Even condescending, although he did not mean it to be. 'Do you think the growing naval strength of Germany has anything to do with this? With Sidney? Could he have known something?' The instant the words were out of his mouth, he regretted it. It was a silly idea, but he could not take it back.

She turned to look at him for a moment, then back at the road. She did not see his white knuckles as he held on to the dashboard while she swept over the crown of a hill and the great panorama of the land opened up before their eyes: rich harvest fields, clumps of trees, villages marked by towering church spires, and beyond them all the gleam of the light on far distant water.

'Perhaps,' she replied to the question. 'Whatever it is, we've missed it so far. That light over there, that's the sea.' She was smiling. She did not look at him, but kept her eyes straight ahead.

Daniel could not think of the right words to say anything, so he remained silent.

They came over the rise, and the deep blue of the sea filled the horizon, dotted here and there with little boats, white sails dazzling against the water. Already the sun was lower, the air tinted with colour.

She drove down into Portsmouth and towards the dockyard. The town of Portsmouth was a naval port, with the dockyard home to many classic ships from the great naval history of the nation. But it was also a busy working dock of the present with cargoes from every country in the world.

They parked the car in a secure place near to the terminal and went to the pier to purchase tickets for the ferry to Cherbourg. It turned out they had only twenty minutes to wait until boarding.

The wind was cooling a little, although the sea was calm and the gulls circling above them moved on the currents of the air, the low sun catching them white and gleaming. Miriam watched them, clearly fascinated. Daniel stood on the wooden pier, smelling the tide, hearing it lap against the stanchions below them, and wondered what she was thinking. Scientific thoughts about the dynamics of flight? Or dreams of a world of light and air? He did not ask, because he realised how much he hoped it were the latter.

It was quite a short journey, so there was no luxury on board the ferry, but it was pleasant enough. The seats were comfortable, and they sat side by side, facing forward.

They talked of many things during the sea crossing, but they sat silently also, confident to rest in their own thoughts. Daniel would have liked to let his mind wander, but time was too short. He rehearsed over and over again every step of the case, using alternative interpretations of facts.

If Sidney were not guilty, then who was? And what motive had they? Every step must fit the explanation. Was it very carefully planned, each move forming part of it from the outset, every alternative planned for? Or was it a series of accidents, new plans made even while changing course? Was the person behind it brilliantly clever, or just lucky, time and time again?

Was the motive idealistic, if misguided? Or was it greed? Or to save themselves, or someone they cared for, or someone necessary to them for . . . what?

How much was it going to hurt when they knew the

truth? If they ever did. He realised how much he was afraid for Jemima. Was Patrick's part in it going to stain her world irreparably? And would she hate Daniel for being the one to expose it? That tempted him to let it go. It would be easy not to find the answer. He might not be able to find it anyway. Yet how often had he condemned other people for doing exactly that? But who, apart from himself, would know if he had not looked? If Jemima ever found out, she would know it was because he was afraid of what he would find . . . which could only be that Patrick was guilty of playing some part in the involvement of the Thorwoods in Philip Sidney's downfall. Could it possibly be unwitting? He doubted it. Patrick appeared very direct, open, but then he would. He was with his wife's family. And he was very much in love with Jemima. Anyone could see that. But it did not mean there was not a complex and clever man behind the smile and the humour, the will to please.

And if Daniel willingly looked away, his father would know, and despise him. He would have betrayed his greater trust, the one Pitt had in him, and, if he were to succeed in anything, the trust he must have in himself.

They disembarked at Cherbourg and went straight to the Alderney ferry. There was little time to spare because they were timed to coincide.

The second journey was only a few miles.

The ferry docked and Daniel and Miriam disembarked, Daniel carrying their small bags, and walked in the summer darkness up the slight hill to the little town of St Anne. The whole isle of Alderney was only three miles long and one and a half miles wide.

They had come without contacting anyone in advance to make an accommodation booking. There had been no time.

They would have to trust their luck in finding a hotel. It was August, the best month for holidays. The hotels might well all be full.

'Well, May Trelawny's house will be empty,' Miriam said with a wry smile. She did not apologise for the oversight, and the assumption that he would not mind, but he thought from her slight hesitation that she had considered whether she should, and had deliberately not done so.

'She's been dead over a month,' he pointed out, smiling back, although she would see little of his face in the soft darkness. 'It would be warm enough, this time of year, but there won't be any food, and there may not be any sheets or blankets.' He deliberately avoided mentioning any of the other possible inconveniences, or the awkwardness of doing so much together, and yet in most ways, so far apart. 'And how do you intend we get in? It's breaking and entering.'

'Yes, I realise that,' Miriam admitted, 'and I'm not happy about it, but what else can we do? Daniel, we need to get into the house. I really believe the answer lies with May Trelawney's death.'

'I know,' he said gently, then smiled. 'Luckily, I can pick locks.'

'What?'

'I can pick locks without leaving a trace. Roman Blackwell taught me.'

'I should have known.' She laughed quietly.

'Don't worry, I won't break anything.'

'We'll eat in St Anne,' she suggested. 'And then walk there. Actually, I think there's no choice. I don't believe they have cars in Alderney.' She was looking straight ahead, as if

255

watching where she was going, but he thought she was also avoiding looking at him.

'Well, May Trelawny's house can't be more than a couple of miles,' he pointed out. 'Or we will be in the sea.'

They were in town already, but there was no one about.

'Fortunately I remembered to bring a lock pick,' he added.

'What? Oh! Yes.' She turned to look at him in the light of a streetlamp. 'I hadn't thought of that.'

'You! Hadn't thought?' He tried not to laugh as he said it.

For a moment, she seemed off balance, as if not sure if he was teasing her or not.

It was the first time he could recall her at a loss and suddenly he saw her vulnerable – not absolutely sure of herself – then it was gone.

'No. But we'll manage better with one, won't we?' There was less confusion in her voice now. It had been only a moment, but it stayed with him.

'Of course,' he said cheerfully. 'The hotel will give us a decent meal and, please heaven, they will know where Aunt May's house is!'

'Do you think I don't?' she asked. 'I did do at least that much. I was prepared for the possibility that you wouldn't come!' She shot a brief glance at him, and then looked away again.

They reached the hotel and went in the well-lit doorway into a warm reception room decorated with flowers.

They asked for accommodations, but were not surprised to be told that every room in the town was taken. The weather had been lovely, and the island was very popular in that the few people who knew it well returned again and again. But they were welcome to a hearty dinner.

'We'll start tomorrow,' Daniel said, when they had been found a table and looked at the surprisingly sophisticated menu. It was only then that he remembered they were on English territory, though actually geographically far closer to France. The French influence was so natural, so easily fitting in, that they barely noticed it.

'We haven't time to be subtle,' she agreed. She chose a simply cooked dish of fish and vegetables.

He decided to order the same. 'Have you any plans, specifically? We already know the disposition of the will. It all goes to Rebecca. The only thing we might learn is why it is important, if it is . . .' Suddenly, the adventure of it seemed pointless. They were pretending they could succeed, but the mirage needed only to be touched to disappear.

'We can find out who is interested in buying the house,' Miriam answered, suddenly very serious again. 'And I want to learn more of May's death. There may be nothing to find, but we came to look.'

With news of the murder of Morley Cross they had discovered the total darkness behind what had looked to be no more than shadows. They could not ignore that now that the victims in this whole case could be more numerous than they had ever envisaged.

'I wonder if Sidney ever came here,' he said. 'Or anyone else involved in the case did. Do they even have a policeman here?'

'They'll have a postmaster . . . or a postmistress would be even better,' she answered. 'I wager she knows everybody and much of their business better than any constable. It will be gossip, so leave it to me.'

He raised his eyebrows. 'Are you good at gossiping? I

would never have guessed it. It is so . . .' Then he was lost as to how to finish.

'More a woman's thing?' she asked quietly, but with a definite flicker of humour in her face.

He did not know how to interpret that. A compliment? Or an insult? But he had heard that hesitation again, the moment of hurt. 'An inexact thing for a scientist,' he answered with sudden assurance.

She smiled. 'Aren't lawyers exact, too?' She looked very directly at him.

'When it suits us,' he agreed, again with an edge of humour.

'And when it doesn't?'

'Then evasive and devious as an eel!' he replied.

She laughed outright, a rich, happy sound. 'I must remember that!'

'And we should see the doctor, too,' he added. 'They usually know much of the community. He won't be able to say a lot, but he can tell us who was here.'

'And how Miss Trelawny died,' she said, suddenly very solemn again.

He looked steadily at her. 'You really think that this may be far more than assault, and petty theft?'

She did not evade the answer. 'Don't you?' she challenged. 'And even if it is no more than a stupid, petty mess, we have to find out.'

'Yes. First thing in the morning. Now let's enjoy this hot dinner and then a walk to where you know Aunt May's house to be. On an island this size, we can't get lost for long, even in the dark, although I'd rather not have to wake up some farmer and ask him the way. He may not think we have any right to be there.'

'We haven't,' she agreed. There was the tiny pucker of a

frown on her brow. 'Are you worried? I know you have moral concerns that I don't, because nobody is trusting me.' She looked at him gravely. 'But you believe, as I do, that the very thing that lies at the heart of all this also caused the death of May Trelawny?'

She had used very gentle language, but there was a sudden ice-like chill over his skin, and he knew she meant *murder*. The murder of May Trelawny. 'Do you think so?' he asked gravely. 'Really?'

'Yes,' she answered. 'I think it would be big enough and dark enough to be the missing piece. Don't you?'

There was no purpose in hesitating, let alone denying it. 'Yes.'

Their dinner eaten and paid for, Daniel and Miriam walked through the summer night the mile and a half from the hotel in St Anne to the manor house perched on the coast above a quiet cove. Miriam seemed to have no doubt that it was the right place. They could see a flower garden at the front. In the summer evening the sky was scattered with a million stars, dusk-scented blossoms were sweet in the air, and in the stillness, their scent easily discernible above the salt wind from the sea. They glimpsed a vegetable garden at the back, the tall stands of beans unharvested, rows of lettuces and a glass cucumber frame. There was no one around, but Miriam still looked for a window away from the road, and a back door to break in.

Daniel nearly asked if Miriam was absolutely sure this was May's house, but he had already asked twice. To do so again would offend her, he had no doubt. It would have offended him, had she entrusted a task to him, and then kept checking and rechecking that he had done it.

He took the lock pick out of his pocket and practised the

art Roman Blackwell had taught him. Miriam watched without comment, but he could almost feel the questions on her lips. It took him several minutes. He decided he needed to do this more often to keep up his skills. It was more difficult than he had remembered. He could not make the tumblers turn.

She reached past him and put her fingers on the door handle. She turned it, and it opened.

She breathed out in relief and stepped inside. She turned on a single light, and he closed the back door. They were in a tidy kitchen that looked as if it had been left with every expectation of the owner returning.

Miriam ran her finger over one of the shelves and looked at it. There was a film of dust. Her face reflected a sudden, vivid sadness. She did not need to say anything for Daniel to know her thoughts, and share the moment of sorrow.

He reached out and touched her hand, gently, and made a very rash promise. 'We'll discover if she is a part of this,' he said softly. 'For now, let's find some blankets and places to sleep. There must be two good rooms upstairs. If there aren't, I'll sleep on the sofa. There's bound to be one. We have a lot to do, and less than two days in which to do it. The trial resumes on Monday, and it could end quickly.'

Miriam nodded, for a moment too moved to speak, or perhaps a little awkward faced with the reality of the situation. It was a little late for embarrassment. She had invited him, not the other way around.

'Yes,' she answered a second too late to have avoided the hesitation. 'Yes, of course.'

Chapter Twenty-One

In the morning, they rose early. It was a bright, sunlit day, and the sea breeze was gentle, no chill in it. They agreed to walk into St Anne and find a good breakfast, then begin to search for everything they could learn about May Trelawny and her house. It was a short walk with views of the sea, vivid blue water stretching to the horizon, or breaking white on the rocks close in to the shore.

'We must find out if anyone was seriously asking about buying,' Daniel said over bacon, eggs, sausages and mushrooms. And French coffee was available. To him, in the bright sunlight, sitting outside a café, at a table open to the breeze off the sea – no more than a breath in the air – was the best of all worlds.

Miriam was wearing a dress; it was the first time he had seen her in one. He might had expected her to wear something traditional for anyone with such bright auburn hair, like a gentle blue or green. He should have known better! She wore a subtle pink and wine-coloured floral, composed entirely of warm colours. Without giving a thought as to whether it was appropriate or not, he complimented her on it. He saw instantly that he had made her uncomfortable, but he was not going to apologise. He did like it, and it did suit her. In fact, he saw several other people in the café, and passing along the street, hesitate and look at her a moment longer.

'Yes, of course,' she agreed about the house. 'And find the doctor to question him. I'm a little apprehensive about how we should do that.' She looked at him earnestly. 'I have no authority at all. You have a little. You are acting for someone in court but we have no written authority. Perhaps we should ask about Miss Trelawny first? At least, how she died. We'll begin at the post office.' She saw him frown. 'Don't look like that! We have to ask someone. The doctor will be much more careful of what he says. We have only today and tomorrow, and tomorrow is Sunday so there may be no one available. What else can we do?'

'Tomorrow we can go to church,' he suggested.

'What?' She was startled.

'Go to church,' he repeated. 'A better place for gossip than even the post office. All said in the utmost solemnity, and only kindly meant, of course. I can see there are two of them. Look, the towers are clear to see above all the rooftops.'

Her eyes lit with amusement. 'Daniel!'

For a moment, he was afraid she was also offended. Was she laughing with him, or at him?

'How very practical of you! Indeed, we should! I didn't bring a hat! I shall have to buy one.'

'Do you mind?'

'Of course not. I shall call attention to myself if I don't wear one.'

'You will draw attention anyway . . .' Again, the words were out of his mouth before he considered them, or how she would feel.

'Then I had better choose one that you think would be discreet,' she said a little hotly.

'Why? Do you want to be discreet?'

She did not reply, uncertainty in her eyes. It was the first time he could remember seeing her disconcerted by another person, rather than circumstances or evidence. What an odd mixture she was of assertion and vulnerability.

'Sometimes being conspicuous is the best disguise.' Did that sound like a contradiction, and a possibly ambiguous reference to her appearance? What could he say that would not make it worse?

'You mean I will not look like a forensic pathologist?' she asked.

'Can you imagine Sir Bernard Spilsbury in that dress . . . and a hat?' He smiled.

She put her tea down before she spilled it and burst into laughter. 'That was wicked!' she said when she had regained control of herself. 'And very funny.'

'You don't like him,' he observed. They were referring to the most famous pathologist in Britain, perhaps in the world, and virtual father of the science in criminal trials.

'One doesn't like Sir Bernard,' she answered. 'One respects him, if one is in the right. And fears him, if wrong. To like or dislike him would be impertinent.' She was watching Daniel, reading his reaction closely. 'Suggests he's . . . human!'

'Then I shall be impertinent,' he replied. 'And probably dislike him. Another cup of tea?'

'No, thank you. It's time we began on what we can do today.'

They went first to the post office. It was a short walk along a sunlit street, cobbled and shaded here and there by enormous trees. Woodwork around windows was painted in blues and yellows, stone-faced buildings supported swathes of climbing flowers in rich bloom.

Early sun reflected off large shop windows, making everything bright.

They waited outside while two or three customers went in, then when the office was temporarily empty they took the opportunity. It was a little shop, with several books and postcards, writing paper for those visitors who did not think to bring sufficient, or found more to say than they had expected. Daniel went immediately to look through those, Miriam went to the counter. Pleasant greetings were exchanged, then Miriam asked for stamps.

'I imagine you have some unusually handsome ones?' she asked. 'I have friends to whom I would like to send something sort of out of the ordinary. It is, after all, a unique place.'

'Indeed,' the postmistress agreed. 'Your first time here?'

'Yes. Although I have friends who live here, and one in particular had a godmother who lived here. Or . . . she used to.'

'She left?' There was surprise in the postmistress's voice.

'No,' Miriam's tone was suddenly subdued. 'She died. I would like to visit the grave, or perhaps lay some flowers.'

'Oh dear, I'm so sorry.'

'You might have known her?' Miriam said hopefully.

Daniel knew the lift in her voice and could imagine her expression as clearly as if he could see it, although he had his back to them, and a fan of postcards in his hand.

'I know most people,' the postmistress agreed warmly. 'Oh dear, I hope you don't mean Miss Trelawny?'

'I do. Why?'

'I'm so sorry, my dear. A lovely lady. We all miss her. It's as if a little colour of the island had gone away. And . . .'

'And?' Miriam asked anxiously.

'Well . . . such a terrible way to die,' the postmistress said softly. 'Poor soul. The last person to whom I would have expected . . .' She tailed off, as if it were too dreadful to say.

Daniel felt his fingers gripping the cards. He was in danger of bending them.

There was silence. He knew Miriam was wondering what to say to draw the rest of the story, without sounding over-curious. The last thing she wanted would be to turn the postmistress against her.

'All they would tell me was that it was unexpected,' Miriam said at last. 'That doesn't mean anything, not really. I supposed I should have realised it was because they were hiding the truth. Now it makes me more . . . disturbed.' She took a breath and let it out in a sigh. 'People talk. They can be very unkind. All sorts of things are said by people who should . . . I expect you have heard such things. It is not unusual. But I believe she did not deserve it. I would very much like to tell them that I know the truth, and they are talking malicious nonsense. There is no scandal!'

'There certainly is not!' the postmistress said with rising anger. 'She had a sick horse and she rose to tend to it in the night. She went out to the stable and found it in some distress. No one knows exactly what happened, but she must have tripped on something, or lost her balance. The horse was frightened and lost its head. It kicked her, very badly. She must have fallen against it and that panicked it further. It plunged around and . . . and she was kicked to death.'

'Oh dear!' Miriam sounded really distressed. 'How very dreadful. Poor woman! I think . . . I think I will not say exactly that . . . should I be called upon to say anything at all.'

'Yes. Very wise. No use distressing people. You could always just say her death was quick.'

'Thank you. It must have been very dreadful, but you have put my mind at rest regarding people speaking ill of her now. She was . . .' Miriam hesitated, as if lost for adequate words.

'Indeed,' the postmistress agreed.

Daniel turned around slowly, until he could see the post-mistress's face. She was smiling, as if at a memory that pleased her.

'She was always collecting stones. Some of them were quite lovely, but all of them interested her. You know the expression "marching to a different tune"? Well, I would say Miss Trelawny danced to her own tune.'

'And such a sense of humour,' Miriam added. Daniel knew she was guessing, drawing a word picture of someone she would have liked.

'Oh, yes,' the postmistress agreed heartily, and proceeded to give several examples of it, and she and Miriam ended laughing together.

'And she loved the house,' Miriam went on. 'I heard there were people interested in buying it from her heir. Will they be taking the animals, too?'

'Oh, bless you, certainly not. The cats have found new homes nearby. The wild birds she fed will forage for themselves. They always could; she just liked it when they came. And the doctor took the horses.'

'That would be Dr . . .'

'Dr Mullane. They were good friends, you know. He was very upset by her death.'

266

'Of course. You have been very kind. I'm afraid I have taken up a lot of your time,' Miriam apologised.

'Not at all,' the postmistress assured her. 'But the house is not for sale, you know. Not at any price. She left it to her goddaughter. She was adamant about that.'

'Did the interested party offer a lot for it? Oh! I'm sorry. That is not any of my business.' Miriam sounded shocked that she could have said such a thing.

'Well, I did hear say it was more than twice what it was worth,' the postmistress replied. 'Very insistent he was. So I'm told.'

'Young man? Tall? Rather nice-looking, with fair hair?' Miriam asked, taking Daniel's description of Philip Sidney. 'In his late twenties, perhaps.'

'Bless you, no!' The postmistress was amused. 'This man must have been fifty, if he was a day.'

'Oh. Then it wasn't who I thought. Perhaps that's just as well. Thank you again for giving me the ammunition to silence some of the gossips. Good morning.' And Miriam turned and went out of the door.

Daniel made up his mind about the cards, bought a couple of sea views, and one of a bright, narrow street with garlands of wisteria up the walls, with a mind to give them to Cassie, then he followed Miriam into the street.

She was waiting for him about fifty yards away.

'Excellent,' he said, taking her arm and starting to move further away from the post office in case the postmistress should come to the door and see them conferring. 'Although it's pretty wretched that May Trelawny died so horribly. I hope Rebecca doesn't have to know. But . . .' He stopped. What he had been going to say sounded so cold-blooded.

'But what?' Miriam was not going to let it go.

'But it doesn't help Sidney,' he replied.

'That isn't what you were going to say.'

'Oh? What was I going to say?' He kept his voice soft, and his face almost entirely without expression.

She lifted her chin a little higher. 'It doesn't indicate a crime. Particularly, it doesn't sound as if she was killed by someone else. Although I can't see why anyone should kill her over the house. Can you? It's nice, but there are many others like it, and in better repair. Did we miss something?' She looked at him curiously.

'I don't know. I can't think what. It would need quite a lot of money spent on it to turn it into a really beautiful house. It's too small to be a hotel. The views are marvellous, and the garden is I think the most beautiful I've ever seen. But you don't kick someone to death over a lovely garden, quite small, but full of flowers, and with the most exquisite view.'

'It's very solitary,' she said. 'If you wanted to be left alone . . .'

'A hermit?' he said, half-jokingly.

'Possibly. Of interest as a religious retreat. Or to a painter or, even more likely, someone writing a book. A lot of peace.'

He had let go of her arm and they walked along the street slowly.

'Or a smuggler?' she suggested.

'Smuggling what? There aren't enough people here to buy much. Tobacco? Brandy? I thought they took that sort of thing into Cornwall.'

'They probably do. I don't know. It's halfway between France and England, but it's a lot shorter straight across the Channel from Dover to Calais. I want to see the doctor, Dr Mullane. See what he says.'

'You think she was murdered!'

'I won't be satisfied until I've proved to myself that she wasn't.'

'Then let's find him.' Daniel started forward determinedly. 'And after that, we can see if there is someone who deals with the sale of houses. Or who can at least tell us something about whoever was interested in buying May's house. From the postmistress's description, it certainly wasn't Sidney.'

It was two hours before Dr Mullane was free and could see them. This time they had decided that Daniel should begin the conversation, and Miriam ask the questions only if necessary, at least to start with.

Mullane was a man in his late forties, with a full head of untidy, sandy-coloured hair turning white at the sides, and a pleasant, wind-burned face. Daniel liked him immediately. He decided to be candid.

'No medical particulars,' he said to the enquiry as to what the doctor could do to help. 'At least not anything for which there is any treatment now.' Daniel had already introduced himself and Miriam, without of course mentioning Miriam's qualifications. 'I'm a lawyer representing a man on trial for a crime for which, if he is found guilty, he will lose his reputation and career, and at least for a while, his freedom. Quite apart from the fact that I must do my best to represent his interests, I believe he is innocent. Others have made him look guilty, to cover a far more serious crime.'

Mullane looked frankly confused. 'So how can I help? I can give you no medical opinion without seeing the patient.'

'Of course not,' Daniel agreed. 'I would not ask it of you. But you can tell me medical facts of a case that is already closed, and with which I think you are familiar.'

'Not without the permission of the patient.'

'She cannot give it. Unfortunately, she is dead.'

Mullane started to rise from his chair, his face dark with distaste.

'Miss May Trelawny,' Daniel finished. 'There seems to be a great deal at stake here, Dr Mullane. I think her death may not have been accidental.' Had he just committed himself to a collision course with failure?

Mullane froze. 'She was kicked to death by one of her own horses,' he said quietly. 'How can that be deliberate? And who on earth would wish that on an elderly lady of moderate means and great charm?'

'For the house?' Daniel suggested.

'What?' Mullane looked stunned. 'Don't be absurd. I'm sorry, that was rude. But it's a very ordinary house of quite modest proportions, and in need of major repair. I happen to know that the estate has not sufficient means to effect them. I believe it goes to a goddaughter. I think that is what May said.'

'May?' Miriam raised her eyebrows only slightly.

'May Trelawny,' Mullane said.

Miriam smiled. It was delicate, and a little shy. 'You called her May. That suggests you knew her quite well, even that you were friends?'

'We were. She was a woman of character, kindness, imagination and . . . and fun.' He said it warmly, and there was sweet memory in his eyes, and sorrow. 'I miss her deeply.'

'That's what Rebecca Thorwood said of her,' Daniel put in. 'That is her goddaughter. I don't think she knows exactly how Miss Trelawny died. I will not tell her, if it is not necessary. I think she believed Miss Trelawny was a good horsewoman.'

'She was,' Mullane agreed. 'It was a . . .' He stopped, raising his hands in the air, and then shrugging. He fell silent.

Daniel looked at Miriam. If they were ever to find out more about May Trelawny's death, it was now or not at all.

Miriam understood. She nodded so slightly it was almost imperceptible. 'Dr Mullane, what happens to the house?'

Daniel drew breath to remind them that the postmistress had said it was being looked into by someone, then realised that that was not the issue.

'What are you thinking, Miss fford Croft? Mr Pitt mentioned the death may not be accidental before. The horse was startled by something and lashed out. It appears to have panicked. Perhaps if it struck May and she fell over, perhaps fell against the horse to try and stay upright . . .? We will probably never know what happened. May's injuries were very violent, as if the animal that caused them were in great fear or pain, but there was nothing to account for that. And certainly there was no one else seen in or near the house. Nothing to account for the incident but terrible mischance. If you are thinking that the animal was drugged with something, we tested its blood and there was nothing discovered.'

'No injuries?' Miriam asked.

'Nothing but a few bruises. Poor May was trampled. Horses are very heavy animals. If you have ever been trodden on, you will remember it.' He looked palpably distressed.

'It matters very much,' Miriam said earnestly. 'May we see the animal? Please?'

'I don't know what good that will do, but of course you may.' He rose to his feet and gestured for them to follow. He led the way out of the side door of his house and into the yard to the stables and carriage house. It made sense that

271

he would keep horses and a trap. If he were needed urgently, he would not waste time walking, even though in no case would it be more than a couple of miles. The stable was quite a large building. He probably kept a store of both hay and grain there in the winter.

'I've two horses of my own as well,' Mullane told them as he opened the door and led them inside, showing them the three stalls. All the animals pricked their ears as they heard the steps. One of them whinnied. 'All right, Acorn,' he said gently. 'Nobody's going anywhere. Hello, Hazel.' He touched the next horse where it poked its head over the half-gate. 'We've come to see Rosie.' He stopped by the last stall where a beautiful bay mare was watching him, and then looking beyond him to Daniel and Miriam. She stepped backwards sharply. 'All right, Rosie,' Mullane soothed. 'Nobody's going to hurt you, girl.' He turned to Miriam. 'Perhaps you would talk to her, Miss fford Croft? She's been more used to a woman, though she'll have to get used to me now, I suppose.' He turned to Daniel. 'Sorry.'

Daniel stopped.

Miriam went ahead, very softly now, talking to the horse all the time. She opened the stable half-door and went in.

Daniel was holding his breath. He wanted to stop this. What if the animal really was damaged in some way, frightened or hurt, and she kicked whoever was there, as she had apparently done to May Trelawny? How would they stop it?

Miriam hesitated.

Daniel thought she was going to come back out again, but she stood where she was, beside the animal, still talking to it. It was a one-sided conversation, but quiet, and the horse's ears flicked. She was listening.

'What happened, eh?' Miriam said, reaching out and touching its neck.

The horse stood perfectly still.

'Did something frighten you?'

Daniel was hardly breathing.

Miriam slid her hand over the horse's neck, still talking quietly. 'What happened, eh? Was someone there, other than May? Someone you didn't like?' She moved her hand further down its back. 'Did they hurt you?' Her hand moved another six or seven inches down the horse's back.

No one moved.

She slid it a little further, and suddenly the horse threw its head back and lashed out, kicking violently behind it.

Miriam went white as a sheet and leaped away, but she did not cry out.

Mullane shot forward and grasped the horse's halter, pulling her forward. 'Quiet, Rosie! Quiet, girl. There now! Nobody's hurting you.'

Daniel started forward to help Miriam, and then realised a sudden movement might only make it worse. He froze.

Seconds ticked by.

The horse quietened. Slowly they all relaxed.

Miriam came out of the stall and moved over towards Daniel. Without thinking, he put his arm round her. She was shaking.

Mullane gradually settled the horse.

Miriam walked away from Daniel, but took him by one hand and pulled him along with her. She was going towards the saddle and harness and the general tack in what was almost a separate room. She ignored the two larger saddles and went to the graceful side saddle, a little dusty from weeks of disuse in an atmosphere where hay and corn were stored.

She went to pick it up, and Daniel reached across her and picked it up for her. She turned it over and stared at it, examining it closely, for something small.

Daniel watched her, and then looked at the saddle. He saw it first, perhaps because he was looking more closely and with more care than she. It was a small spot of blood, dried, smaller than a little fingernail.

Then Miriam saw it and turned to him, her eyes shining.

'What is it?' he asked.

'Rosie,' she replied. 'The horse. I found the corresponding wound on her back, hidden by her mane. It looks like something in this saddle spiked her. It's not there any more, but it left a sore on her back. It became infected and it's suppurating now. It must hurt like hell when any pressure is put on it. You can't see it, because it's partially healed over, with a splinter or something still there. That may be why she lashed out.'

Daniel stiffened. 'Mullane?'

'No. He would have taken it out and done something to heal the wound before it got worse. Then there'd be no trace of it. He doesn't know about it. I expect he touched her lightly – nothing more than a brush now and then. She's very skittish. I dare say May's death frightened her badly.'

Daniel saw Mullane walking towards them. 'Are you sure?' he said to Miriam.

'Please God, it wasn't him!' she said under her breath.

'Are you all right, Miss fford Croft?' Mullane asked anxiously.

'Yes, thank you.' She took a deep breath. 'But I've got a lot of questions to ask you. And I think Mr Pitt may need you in London.'

Mullane looked from one to the other of them. 'I don't understand. This . . . this rather proves that poor Rosie is to blame. I'd rather let her just go to breeding – or not be used at all. I'm not—'

Daniel took a risk, not a very carefully evaluated one. He knew it was rash even as he said the words. 'Somebody put something very sharp in her saddle. It hurt her. The wound is still there, partially healed over, but suppurating and infected. That's why she lashed out, when Miriam touched it.'

Mullane started to speak, then stopped.

Daniel smiled. 'You're a doctor. If you'd done it, you'd have had the sense to treat the wound, wouldn't you? It must be only a small piece of something sharp like a thorn still left.'

Mullane was pale. 'What son of a bitch would do that? To a woman like May Trelawny? Or to the horse?'

'I don't know,' Daniel replied. 'But I mean to find out.'

'I'll help you all I can,' Mullane said fervently. 'But you'll need more than my word for this. I'll take photographs. We'll get them developed in the post office. Miss Wescott does that, among all sorts of other things. We'll take them with us to London on tomorrow's boat. But be quick. I want to get that horse treated!'

'Yes,' Miriam agreed, surprisingly, not moving from Daniel, who still had his arm around her.

He did not move either.

Chapter Twenty-Two

'We've got a lot more to do before getting the last boat back to England tomorrow afternoon,' Daniel said to Miriam, when Mullane had taken photographs of Rosie's back, and of the blood mark on the saddle, and set out to deliver them to the postmistress for immediate developing.

'There's only one boat to Cherbourg, and then to Portsmouth,' Miriam replied. 'We should book a place on it, in case there are too many passengers going back after their holidays.'

'Yes, of course,' Daniel agreed. 'But we've got to get a much clearer picture of what happened to May before then. We know exactly what day Miss Trelawny died and we can find out who was on Alderney then, or at the least, who definitely was not. Did it happen in the stable, do you think, like the postmistress said?'

Miriam considered it for a moment. 'No. That spot was rubbed badly. The prongs of the thorn were quite small, but very sharp. But the saddle was on there for a while. Something must have increased the pressure.'

'Perhaps when she mounted?' he suggested.

'Longer than that. And she wouldn't mount in the stable.

The ceilings are too low. She'd have to duck right down to get out of the door. Maybe whoever did it had intended it to look as if she fell when she was out riding and was kicked and dragged when the horse panicked.' She winced. 'There must have been a lot of blood, from the injuries the doctor described. If we look, we'd find traces of it in the stable.'

'What will that prove?'

'I'm not sure.' For a moment she looked puzzled. 'There's something missing, because it doesn't make sense. The thorn in the saddle was to bring about a riding accident and yet May was supposedly kicked to death in the stable. . . .'

'Mullane must have seen the difference between an accident out riding and her having been kicked in the stable, and Miss Westcott said May was killed in the night.'

'Yes, of course. That's what I don't understand. And whoever did this had to get the burr, or what acted like a burr, in place. Maybe he meant to take it out again, but, anyway, nobody found it until we looked. And we found it only because we knew where it would be. Miss Trelawny's death would have been seen as an accident by everyone. Being killed in a riding accident is not unusual, especially for an older woman.'

'Then why didn't that work?' Daniel asked. 'Perhaps it did but she kept control of the animal? Or had regained control by the time she got home?'

'Possibly. And then when she took the saddle off, she unintentionally dug the thorn in deeper, not knowing it was there.' Miriam was thinking aloud. 'But, of course, that can't be entirely right as Miss Trelawny was killed in the night so she wouldn't have just been for a ride.'

'Of course, there's another alternative,' Daniel said quietly. 'What?'

'That the horse wasn't involved in May's death at all. May was beaten with something as hard as a horseshoe, and with great force, and left in the stable for the horse to get the blame.'

Miriam frowned. 'That's horrible, but much quicker and easier. No chance of it going wrong. Not dependent on an animal. But why use the horse, and a thorn in the saddle at all?'

'Because that would make it look like an accident, should anyone find the thorn. The last thing whoever did this wants is to have the police called in. It must all look ordinary, but very sad. Elderly woman has thorn in her saddle. Doesn't see it. Rides the horse and when the animal is hurt enough, it kicks her when in the stable. No investigation. No delay in putting the will through probate. Nothing to draw the attention, and certainly nothing to connect it in any way with . . . anyone.'

'Yes, but who?' Miriam said. 'And even more, why?'

'I thought you were going to say that. I don't know.'

'Then we will take the rest of the afternoon to find out,' she answered. 'One of us should search the house. Perhaps among the things there is something that would tell us. I hate going through the personal belongings of someone who died suddenly and did not hide or destroy what was private. It seems such an intrusion. But we must.'

'You should,' he said with a twisted smile that was meant as an apology. 'It's better that a woman does it. You would not just be less intrusive, but you might see things that I wouldn't understand. And I'll get the photographs from the postmistress, and make enquiries about who visited around that time, and interest in buying the house, who asked, if anybody knew what was offered, and anything else I can find.'

'Be careful!' she said quickly, then blushed. 'I mean . . . if the perpetrators really beat the old lady to death over it, they may feel so safe they are happy to let us poke around as much as we want, but they may not. We are getting a lot closer.'

'Then perhaps you shouldn't be alone here.'

'Shall we pack up and leave?'

'What?'

'Shall we—' she began.

'Yes, I heard you.' He searched her face, trying to find out if she meant it, if underneath the bravado, the anger at injustice, the violence, she was actually afraid, and would be grateful for the chance to leave and not look cowardly. There was nothing of that in her face. It was anger in her greenish-blue eyes, not fear. Or perhaps it was both. One thing he was certain of: she would not take kindly to being supposed a coward. Should he leave the question to her?

He replied instinctively, without thought. 'I thought not. Lock the doors when I go. I know! I know! Anyone could break in. But that would make a noise. Don't fight them. Hide.'

'For heaven's sake, Daniel! Nobody's coming. All the people involved in this are in London, waiting to see Philip Sidney convicted of all the crimes he is charged with, and put away before anyone believes anything he says. Go and get the photographs from the postmistress. There's still time to take more, if those aren't any good. And see what else you can learn. See if anybody saw a man like Sidney. Or Thorwood. Get several descriptions of the man trying to buy the house. That couldn't have been Sidney.'

He was about to argue, for argument's sake, but he realised it was emotion speaking, in both of them. They were afraid.

May Trelawny's death had been a violent and terrible one. Whoever had caused it was the dark centre of the whole elaborate web of accusations and lies, the unseen shape they had been looking for all the time. They could not run away from it without losing all the things that mattered to them both, but to try to say that would be clumsy, and he was afraid she might think he did not understand.

'I'll be back before dark,' he said.

Daniel spent a busy afternoon, hurrying to pick up the photographs, which were excellent. He then went to speak to the man who assisted in the few house sales that there were in so small a place. For a practising estate agent, with all the legal knowledge, one would have to go to the much larger island of Guernsey. He could only say that there had been a couple of people interested. Miss Thorwood would get an excellent price for the house, if she chose to sell. No, he could not describe the man who had been interested, except that he was at least forty-five years old, maybe fifty. Well spoken, and with no outstanding features he could recall. Yes, he had spoken to Miss Trelawny several times, but she had no wish to sell. She had taken against the man, it seemed, but she would give no reason.

Daniel also reserved three places on the boat back to Folkstone, for mid-afternoon on Sunday. He bought what he thought would be a nice dinner for them, and breakfast for the following day. He tried to remember what Miriam liked, or more specifically, what she did not like, and was annoyed with himself that he had very little idea. Careless of him: he had always been too intent on watching her, or listening to her words and their inflection, to notice her choice of dish.

So he settled for fresh bread, butter, cheese, sliced fresh

ham, a small jar of marmalade, and a packet of tea. He added fresh plums. It was too early in the season for apples.

He was walking the mile and a half back to May's house as the sun dropped towards the horizon and the sky deepened in colour. The sunset breeze smelled of salt, but softly, without chill to it. Gulls were circling high, light catching the gleaming undersides of their wings. He watched the water rippling like silk, an indefinable colour, not blue, not green, not grey, nor silver, but infinitely changing as it moved. His gaze shifted closer to the shore, where it was smoother, like satin under the shadow of the headland. There it was almost still, as if it were very deep.

Then something broke the surface. A fish? Very big for this far inshore. Then it was gone again. Perhaps it had only been a momentary change in the wind, a trick of the fading light. But the water was deep where the shadows lay. Deep enough for a big fish, like a huge shark. Did whales ever come into the English Channel? Bit out of their way to the great oceans. A seal? That was possible, even likely.

Or a ship? A submarine. Of course! Never mind smuggling brandy or tobacco, or anything of that sort. What an old-fashioned idea! It belonged to the last century, and before that. This was an ideal place for a submarine harbour. In the deep water, they need never be seen at all, except by whomever owned May's house. Suddenly everything fell into place. The house was wanted by the navy – not the British Navy, the German! That was why May had had to go.

Daniel quickened his step, striding out down the slope towards the house. If the solution to the murder was that big, he should never have left Miriam alone! He reached the front door and tried to open it. It was locked fast. Of course! He had told her to lock it.

281

He stepped back and looked up at the windows. He could see nothing through them from the outside. 'Miriam!' he shouted. 'Miriam!'

An upstairs window opened and she looked out. From the red of the sunset, her hair gleamed like fire. 'Daniel! Are you all right?' She sounded alarmed.

'Yes, let me in! I know what it's all about! Open the door!'

She disappeared from the window and several moments later he heard the bolt slide on the front door and it swung open.

He stepped inside quickly and then closed it. 'So, you did lock it!' he observed.

She ignored his remark. 'Tell me!' she demanded.

He put the shopping down on the hall table. 'Deep water!'

She was mystified. 'What?'

He pointed in the general direction of the sea. 'Deep water. Under the shadow of the headland. For submarines.'

Understanding filled her face. She breathed out slowly. 'Germans!'

'Yes. I'll bet it was they that wanted to buy this house. It has the only view of this bay. The rest is rocky, and you'd have a terrible job building on it. And anyway, since this house has the perfect view, you couldn't do anything in secret.'

'Yes. I see! I see! And May wouldn't sell. I wonder if she had any idea.' Then she dismissed it with a gesture. 'Doesn't matter why she wouldn't sell . . . she wouldn't. So, they got rid of her. But—'

'I know,' he said quickly. 'Why frame Philip Sidney for assault, and then for embezzlement? Are they going to try to tack murder on to it as well?'

'What a vile thought. We've got to stop them. Who is "them" anyway?'

282

'That is the big question, and we've got till tomorrow, midday, to find the answer. And, I suppose the voyage back.'

'And tomorrow evening,' she added. 'Although, if we haven't got a pretty good idea by then, it's a bit late.' She picked up the shopping and carried it through to the kitchen.

'I've got the photographs,' he told her, following behind. 'I debated whether to ask Mullane to write a statement, in case he didn't actually come.'

Miriam put the shopping down on the kitchen table and looked at him very gravely. 'And did you?'

'No. I thought he might be offended and change his mind. And to have him on the stand, where he can be cross-questioned, would be far stronger than a piece of paper, no matter who it is signed by. Do you think I was wrong?'

'No. No, I don't. Let's make dinner and consider all the possibilities.'

He was startled, until he saw she was smiling. 'Oh, yes, you make it, I'll watch, and tell you if you're doing anything wrong,' he agreed.

She threw the dish towel at him.

After they had eaten, they washed up the dishes together, Daniel doing his full share this time. Then the discussion could no longer be deferred.

'Look at the lies,' he said gravely. 'They're always more revealing than the truth.'

'Then let's take the truth we're sure of, and see what's left,' she responded. 'Tobias Thorwood said he saw—'

'No,' he interrupted. 'Didn't I tell you? Sorry. He lied, to defend his wife, heaven knows why. It was she who said she saw Sidney coming out of Rebecca's room. And if she is telling the truth, then Sidney was lying about being there.'

'And if he is telling the truth, then she is lying. Why?'

'To cover for who it really was. Or to get Sidney in very deep trouble.'

'Except that the Embassy got him away,' Miriam pointed out. 'Could she know what they wanted?'

'No idea. Possibly. But why not simply say she had no idea who it was? A stranger she wouldn't know if she saw him again?'

'So, she wanted to get Sidney into trouble. Or Tobias did. We are back to why.' She frowned. 'What threat was Sidney to them?'

'He said he liked Rebecca, but he wasn't courting her. She wouldn't marry anyone against their wishes, anyway. She probably can't yet. The insistence on following him to England, and raking up the embezzlement charge, suggests they aren't satisfied with ruining his reputation in America. They want more.'

'It seems like that,' she agreed.

'What is it he knows that he doesn't realise? What comes up if we put together all the pieces? At last we have the centre of it. If whoever is guilty is British, then it's murder and treason.'

She shivered, looking at him with shadowed eyes. 'Yes. And what is anyone's life, compared with that? And the heart of it is here,' she whispered.

'We are going to sleep in the attic tonight. No arguments. And pile a couple of old kitchen chairs on the steps, so if anyone comes, we'll have plenty of warning.'

She did not argue. In fact, she did not even try to.

'Church! I forgot to buy a hat!' Miriam said with chagrin.

'Does it matter?' Daniel asked. 'I mean—'

'I know what you mean,' she cut him off. 'Yes, it does.

It's disrespectful to turn up at someone else's church service without a hat! That's spiking my guns before I start!'

Part of him did understand what she meant, even sympathise, but her word picture was too much, and he found himself laughing.

A flush of temper rose up her cheeks, until she saw it too, and smiled reluctantly. 'You know what I mean!'

'Yes, I do. Can't you borrow one of May's? All her clothes are still here . . .' He stopped, realising that that was tactless in the extreme. Sixty-year-old May's hats would hardly be what Miriam would be seen in. She might think he saw her as a woman so much older. Now it was his turn to blush, painfully. How could he have been so clumsy? He feared anything he might say now would only make it worse.

She swung round and stalked out of the room, and he heard her feet on the stairs.

He waited, uncertain what to do, and feeling miserable out of all proportion to the situation. She had forgotten to buy a hat. He had suggested a solution that was tactless, insulting her in a way peculiarly painful to her, which he would have known had he given it a moment's thought.

The minutes ticked by. Should he go upstairs after her? Would she take his remaining in the sitting room as tact, or indifference? Or stupidity, not even understanding what he had done?

He heard her footsteps across the hall. He was so tense his neck ached.

She opened the door and came into the room. She was wearing one of May's hats. It was made of straw, and probably a gardening hat, totally plain, except that Miriam had put a silk scarf around it, very loosely around the brim and up to the crown. She had managed to tie it in a loose knot so that it flowed to one side. It was a deep rose pink, and against her red hair was startling, and perfectly lovely.

'I'll . . . I'll get you a rose from the garden to put on it,' he said. It was not an offer, it was a statement. 'Have you got some sort of pin to hold it? It will be the best hat in the place!'

'I'll find one,' she replied. 'I saw a hatpin on May's dressing table.' She turned and went out of the room again.

Daniel, overwhelmed with relief, went into the garden and picked the rose he had seen, and had in mind when he spoke. It was a deep apricot tipped with a blush of red.

He came back with the flower, trimmed the end of it, and removed the thorns. Then he took the hat from her and placed the rose to one side of the brim, on top of the scarf, and pinned it securely.

She placed it on her head, tilted a little.

He did not need to pretend his admiration. 'If you ever get tired of being a pathologist, you could always become a milliner,' he said.

The pleasure in her face told him that she took that in exactly the spirit he had intended.

'Thank you. I shall consider it.'

The towers of the church were easily visible above the rooftops of the surrounding houses, and they walked the mile and a half in the sun, discussing what sort of information they might seek from those in the congregation with whom they were able to talk. They decided to tell a slightly lopsided version of the truth as to who they were, why they had come to the island, but only if they were asked. What their relationship was, or where they were staying, they would leave to speculation. The truth would be too unlikely to be accepted, or perhaps to be understood, considering that they were both staying in May's house, without servants or anyone else. Only the seriousness of their reason for coming at all would justify that. And without even discussing it, they knew it should not be revealed. That would jeopardise the whole purpose of their mission. It was an ugly thought that somewhere, in this tiny, close-knit community, there might be one person at least who had had a part in May's death, and perhaps, unwittingly, taken a path towards treason.

Miriam had brought a small bunch of flowers from the garden to put on May's grave. Apart from it being an easily understood action to explain their visit, it was something she wished to do. 'I think I would have liked her,' she said simply. 'So would you.'

Daniel agreed with a smile. No words were needed.

The graveyard surrounded the church, as was common. They did not need to look to find the newest grave. The headstone was already carved and placed. Perhaps with a population so small, the stonemason did not have much call for such an art.

Miriam was just straightening from laying the flowers when a small boy of ten or eleven spoke from behind her.

'Why are you putting flowers for her? You knew her? You're not from around here.'

Miriam turned slowly to face him. 'Do you mind my laying flowers for her?' she asked curiously.

It was not what Daniel would have said, but it was a better opening to asking questions. He realised it as soon as the words were out, and he saw the boy's face.

'I s'pose not. As long as they're nice ones.'

'They're the best I have,' Miriam replied. 'Isn't that good enough? But even if I'd picked wild ones, wouldn't they do, if I put them there to remember her?'

The boy thought for a moment. 'You're not from here, but you're all right! She liked wildflowers, anyway. Did you know that?'

'Yes. Are you going to put wildflowers on there for her, every so often?'

'Yeah. Yeah, I think I will. You going to?'

'No. I have to go back to London later today. But I'd like to think you would. You liked her?'

'Yeah. She used to let us take apples from her trees. Just as many as we could eat, now and again. We pretended we were scrumping them – you know, pinching?'

'Yes, I know.'

'But it was a game. And we'd pick wild blackberries up the hill and leave them there on her doorstep. She knew it was us, but she pretended she didn't.'

'Sounds like a good game to me,' Miriam said with a smile.

The boy was silent for a few moments. He smiled, but there were tears in his eyes he did not want to admit.

Miriam waited, as if she sensed he had something more to say.

It was hot in the sun, sounds of conversation drifted across from the church entrance, where people were gathering.

'Rosie weren't sick,' the boy said. 'Miss May knew horses. If Rosie'd been sick, she'd've had my dad to see her.'

'She didn't?' Miriam asked. 'Your father is a vet?'

'Yes. He's real upset 'cause he knows her – Rosie, I mean. And, how'd Miss May know Rosie were sick in the night, unless she was sick the day before? You don't get up in the night, out of your bed, to go look just in case! Miss May must've gone to check on her before it got dark, like she usually did. Rosie's a good horse!'

'Well, Dr Mullane is looking after her now.'

'I know that. He's going to keep her. But Miss May is still dead!'

'She is,' Miriam agreed. 'And I'm very sorry.'

The boy sniffed hard. ''S all right,' he said. 'You left the flowers. And I'll put some another day. Wild ones.'

'But no one would mind if you took a few from her garden as well,' Miriam answered him.

'You think?'

'Yes,' Miriam said decisively. 'I'm quite sure.' She turned back to Daniel. 'We should go, or we'll be late.'

The three of them walked together towards the church entrance and joined the people going inside.

'So, it wasn't the middle of the night,' Daniel said quietly, when they had found seats near the back of the congregation. 'It was round about dusk. Did it happen in the stable or not? Did she go for a ride to meet someone?'

'You mean intending to? Why? Her house was private enough, she could have met half a dozen people there, and no one would ever have known.'

'No,' he said slowly. 'In fact, half a dozen people could have walked out from St Anne and visited her, or come by small boat and landed in the cove without even going through St Anne!'

Miriam turned to stare at him, her eyes wide. 'So, you're saying that anyone could come to May's house unseen, because her cove is only visible from her house. I wonder if it's the only one on the island quite so private, with access to deep water? We should take a look after this, and see if there's another house so isolated, and if anyone is making an effort to buy that.'

'If there is, there would have been no need to kill May . . . but we can ask,' he said.

289

'There will be no estate agents open today. It's Sunday . . .'

'That's why we're in church. Everybody who's anyone will be here. Small communities are like that. You said so yourself.' He smiled at her. 'They'll know everything.'

She opened her hymn book and appeared to pay attention as the service began.

Afterwards, they introduced themselves as two friends of May Trelawny who had come to pay their respects to her, and had run into each other on the ferry. They made polite conversation, admired the island, the town, the weather, and asked, quite incidentally, if there were any other houses in isolated coves, and with such lovely views of the sea. There were plenty of houses with views, but no, none in so solitary a place.

As they walked away, Miriam said, her voice strong and sad, 'That's the reason.'

Daniel linked his arm in hers, and they walked back to May's house and its garden facing the sea. He felt exactly the same.

In the afternoon, they ate lunch and then cleared away any trace of having been in May's house. Daniel left with a sharp pang of regret. He turned at the gate and looked back at the house sitting in the clear sunlight. Its garden was bright with unkempt flowers blazing with colour. Its climbing roses festooning a few gently crumbling walls with softness, yellows and pinks echoing the colours of the stone, deepening it. Beyond, the sea was a fathomless blue, all the way to the horizon.

Miriam stopped beside him. He glanced at her. She was wise enough to say nothing. The words were too many, and not big enough to encompass what could be said. And to pick out one thing was to exclude all the others.

They turned back again to the road to St Anne and the ferry, and walked in companionable silence, hearing only the calling of birds, and the sea murmuring against the shore.

Daniel wondered if Dr Mullane, whom they had not seen at church, would come. If he didn't, was there anything they could do to force him? He thought now that he should have obtained a statement, anything on paper that he could show the court. But he did have the photographs in his pocket. That was proof of something. And the postmistress had dated them.

But his anxiety proved groundless. Mullane was waiting for them, suitcase in his hand. The ferry was already in sight, over a mile away, just a dot on the bright water.

Chapter Twenty-Three

Patrick went out early on Saturday morning, and Jemima was certain he was going to the post office again, although he had not said so. He seemed to be sending wires to Washington every day now, sometimes even twice a day. And answers were delivered to him almost as often. She had asked him what it was about, afraid that it was some kind of trouble because he looked anxious, but he would not discuss it.

She knew that her mother had frequently 'meddled' in her father's cases, when he was in the regular police, before he joined Special Branch. At that point, he began dealing with political issues, and what was often against terrorists, anarchists, people who planned attacks on the public, or the government. That was almost always secret work, and he would not involve her. Not that he had ever intentionally involved her in ordinary police cases. But she had a knowledge of, not to mention access to, personal information from high society, which was completely denied to him back then.

Jemima had no such advantage over Patrick in America. That was his country, his people, and his skill. She was working hard not to be an outsider, and she had found people very kind, very open, not nearly as closed against strangers as she had known English people could be. But she was still an outsider, albeit in New York, a city of outsiders. Washington was different. It was a capital city, a diplomatic city, and outsiders were of a different sort. They lived in Washington temporarily. Most people in the diplomatic service were among the best their country or their culture had to offer. She was permanent. It was now her country as well as Patrick's, and of course Cassie and Sophie were United States citizens, born and belonging, without thought.

Jemima wanted to help Patrick, but she had no ability to, and at the moment, no time. Cassie and Sophie had to be her world. Jemima had no sister here to help, as her mother had had. And she felt she would be giving up her own identity, her nature that made Patrick love her, if she were to become just like his sisters. Not that there was anything wrong with them, but he loved that she was English, sophisticated, with her own special sense of humour.

When Patrick came back from the post office, she asked him outright, 'Are you wiring the police in Washington? About this case of Daniel's?'

He must have seen her anxiety. 'Yes. I've got to help if I can,' he answered immediately.

'To make sure Sidney pays for attacking Rebecca?'

He looked stunned. 'Is that what you think? You think I want to make sure he's convicted?'

What should she say? That was what he had told her. So much depended on how she answered now. 'Didn't he do it?'

'I don't know,' he admitted. 'I thought he did. In fact, I was certain of it. But now I'm not. It has nothing to do with Daniel. It's not about winning or losing. Or who comes from where. Did I really seem that prejudiced to you?'

How could she answer that? Truthfully. The wrong thing would hurt. But a lie would hurt for ever. 'I don't think either you or Daniel could see beyond loyalties what you wanted to believe. I don't think I could, either. But it's not about nationalities or loyalties to your own now. It's about murder. If Sidney is found guilty of assaulting Rebecca, it will ruin his career, and he deserves it. But if he is found guilty of killing Morley Cross, he will hang. And if they think he's guilty of the first, they have every reason to think he killed Morley Cross, to hide it and get away. It's got to be about truth.'

They were like two strangers looking across a room at each other, on the edge of an abyss.

Patrick was the one to reach across. 'I know that. I'm wiring to the police at home because I need them to find out when Morley Cross died, and they can't! It's too close to call . . . medically. So, I'm trying to get someone who saw him as close to the time of his death as possible. We only need one person who saw him alive after Sidney left on the boat, and it will clear him beyond question.' His eyes searched hers, as if needing to see an answer, a belief in him.

She knew that as well as if he had spoken. Perhaps she should have known it all along, but she hadn't, not for certain. 'That would be wonderful,' she said warmly. 'It would be beyond doubt then. There would be nothing Hillyer could do. And . . . and if Sidney didn't kill Cross, then someone else did! Maybe Cross was the one who embezzled the money? Could he have attacked Rebecca as well?'

'I asked that,' Patrick said quietly. 'He didn't look anything like Sidney. It would mean that Bernadette Thorwood lied when she said she recognised him.'

'I'm sorry.' She meant it as an apology. She had wanted it to be the answer, to get rid of the whole mystery. She was looking for a comfortable answer, and she knew better.

Patrick came over to stand in front of her. 'No easy answer, Jem. We both know better than that. And I have a feeling your family does, too. Daniel, I'm pretty sure, and your father . . . I'd stake my life on it.'

She stared at him in surprise. 'You've only known him a short while!' Yet she felt a surge of warmth rising up inside her. Patrick wanted to belong here, too. Not just because they were her family, but because he cared about the same things. It felt simple. He might have to make all sorts of accommodations for their tastes, some of them surface habits or beliefs, but underneath, the foundations were solid. The choice was not 'my country, right or wrong', but what was right, regardless of country.

She reached out and put her arms around him, holding him tightly, and kissed him.

Although it was a Saturday, Jemima was pretty sure Kitteridge would be in his chambers at Lincoln's Inn. He could not afford to take a day off at this critical stage, during such a desperate trial. It would be noon by the time she got there. Would he have gone out for lunch? She could hardly go trailing around the likely public houses looking for him. She got the cook to make up a tasty sandwich to take to him. She had decided not to tell Patrick in case he disapproved of the idea. She didn't like going behind his back, but in such a serious situation, it was necessary.

She arrived just before noon and found the clerk, Impney, who let her in and informed her that Mr Kitteridge was in the library, but he was certain he would be delighted to see her.

'Would you like me to serve the sandwiches with a pot of tea, ma'am?'

'Oh, yes, please,' she accepted gratefully. 'I would love that.' She gave him a dazzling smile.

Ten minutes later, she was sitting in the library, opposite a clearly uncomfortable and nervous Kitteridge. He had to be hungry, and home-made sandwiches filled with cold roast beef, with pickles and tomatoes on the side, and some slices of fruit cake, and Impney's hot tea made the difference.

'If you could hold out long enough,' Jemima said earnestly. 'It might be a few days, but Patrick's working as hard as he can. He only needs one person who saw Cross after Sidney left Washington. It would prove beyond any doubt at all, reasonable or not. I don't know what you can do . . .'

'It doesn't matter,' Kitteridge replied, with his mouth full. 'Hillyer strung it out for ages. I can do the same . . . I think. Do you know what Daniel went to Alderney for? That is where he went, isn't it?'

'Oh. Did he not tell you? I'm sorry. He went racing off because he had to get to Miriam fford Croft's house in time to meet her and catch the boat. He thinks there's some forensic evidence he could find on the island.' Even as she said it, she knew she was defending Daniel instinctively. Kitteridge deserved better than that. 'Apparently, Miriam is very good.'

Kitteridge smiled suddenly. It was wide, lopsided, and surprisingly attractive, because he was totally unaware of it. 'I know! I've seen her on the stand. She can make forensics seem interesting and understandable to jurors.' Then he was suddenly very serious again. 'I don't know what they'll find in Alderney, if anything at all. But he'll be back by Monday,' he added.

Jemima heard the edge to his voice. 'He has to be,' she replied. Was she making a promise she had no power to keep? 'He knows that. But if he's a little late, please . . . keep going without him. Anything, any witness you rake up . . .'

'I will,' Kitteridge replied, taking the last piece of cake. Then he looked at it, suddenly aware that he had eaten all three slices.

She laughed at him. 'I brought it for you! I'm glad you like it.'

'But . . .'

'There's more at home, if I want it,' she said easily. 'Please . . .'

Jemima spent the afternoon with the family, apart from Daniel. They had tea on the lawn, played with Cassie and baby Sophie, talking, laughing, sharing memories. Dinner was early, then the children went to bed and were asleep in minutes. Later, Jemima went out into the garden to look for a favourite toy that had been left behind. She heard footsteps on the stone, then lost in the grass. She looked up, expecting to see Patrick. Instead, it was her father.

'Find it?' he asked.

'Yes. It was where I expected,' she replied. She stared around the evening garden, the wind whispering gently in the poplars, a last starling circling toward the nest. Suddenly, she was overcome with a knowledge of how much she missed this place. There was no question that she would go home with Patrick. That was where she belonged, probably for the rest of her life. But almost all of her life had been here, all the memories tied to these people, in this house, oddly enough, this garden. Emotion filled her too much to allow her to speak.

Her father put his arm around her. Did he know what she was feeling?

She was tired, afraid for the outcome of the trial – for Patrick, for Daniel, and also for Rebecca Thorwood.

'I like your Patrick,' Pitt said quietly. 'And he's a good policeman.'

'How do you know?' she asked, her voice almost level.

'Because I'm a good policeman, too,' he said, and even in the dark she could imagine a smile on his face.

'I'm glad you think so,' she answered, uncertain why he had mentioned it now.

'I do. I've been thinking of what an excellent addition he would be to Special Branch . . . one day.'

She was stunned. It took her a moment to realise what he had said, and what it would mean.

He did not prompt her.

'You mean . . . here?' she said at last.

'Yes. Perhaps for a while, anyway. I haven't said anything to him. Think about it.'

'You want Cassie and Sophie here, don't you?' She was half joking, half needing it to be true.

'Of course,' he replied. 'And you.'

'I'd be happy with that . . . if Patrick would be.'

Chapter Twenty-Four

Daniel and Miriam were accompanied by Dr Mullane on the long drive back to London. Daniel felt ridiculous for resenting his presence. They needed him. In fact, Daniel hardly had a defence without him. Yet he would so much rather have been alone with Miriam, to talk of anything at all, as the mood took him, related to the case or not. Just to watch the light soften over the rolling countryside, the colours change in the sky and across the land, would have been perfect.

But of course, that was absurd, and a self-indulgent denial of the truth, one that Sidney would pay for, for the rest of his life. Tomorrow morning, either Daniel or Kitteridge would stand up to defend him, with only a dim idea of what had really happened, and nothing to prove it, only a collection of ideas that did not fit into a picture. And the spectre of Morley Cross's corpse found in the Potomac. Would Sidney be charged with that murder, too?

They dropped Dr Mullane off at a hotel he was familiar with, then Daniel felt free to discuss the case at last. 'Five charges,' he said.

Strangely enough, Miriam knew what he meant. The assault, the embezzlement, Morley Cross's murder, and the

299

two the court did not yet know of: the murder of May Trelawny and the treason that prompted it. That was what it was really about. All of it! One way or another.

'But why Sidney?' she asked. 'Maybe that is where we should begin? And whether you know or not, you want to make the jury think how it happened, and that it has to be connected. You must not look as if you are searching. They must believe that you are choosing the most dramatic way to show them.'

She looked sideways at him and he saw her smile. He was warmed by it, and yet he also wished she would keep her eyes on the road. He was too worried about the trial only hours away to have energy to be afraid of her driving. The road passed through a tunnel of trees, a shadowed pathway of light and darkness, then round a wide curve and into the sunlight again, the fields gold. Then he realised he actually wasn't afraid at all. In fact, it was fun.

'You mean the thread needs to be visible,' he answered finally. 'I'm pretty sure what the thread is: it's Sidney. If he puts all he knows together, it's enough to tie someone into May's house, its place and importance as a deep-water naval base . . . for the Germans, if they bought the house. It's perfectly placed, and from the landward side, totally private. They could bring submarines in and hide them there, invisible from anywhere else, if they came in deep, and only surfaced after dark. May wouldn't sell, so the only way forward was to kill her. Rebecca inherits, and might well be persuaded to sell, especially if her advisors, principally her father, push for it.'

'Tobias Thorwood's behind it?' Miriam asked, severe doubt in her voice. 'Why? He can't need the money. German sympathies? We'd have to know that beyond a doubt. You can't simply assume it.'

'Blackmail?' He turned over ideas. 'We'd have to know that, too. You can't just suggest blackmail unless you show a vulnerability, and a pretty deep one for a thing like that!'

'His wife?' she suggested. 'But lots of people have secrets no one would ever guess at, things in their past, very well covered now. Old love affairs, debts paid by someone else. All sorts of things. It might be more useful to think who blackmailed him . . . than why. Or someone else altogether, not Thorwood at all.'

'He is part of it,' Daniel insisted. 'He testified that he saw Sidney come out of Rebecca's bedroom.'

'Because Bernadette told him that she did. Perhaps she is being pressured by someone?'

'Or has a German lover,' he said with a half-smile.

'Are there any Germans in this at all, that you know of?'

'No. And the next step is the British Embassy in Washington. That's where the embezzlement was forged. And where Morley Cross worked. It seems he's the one who took the pendant to the pawnbroker, which he said he won as a gambling debt with a colleague, and we know Sidney is fond of card games. It ties pretty tightly into Sidney.'

'Yes,' she agreed. 'But Sidney didn't kill May, though they'll say he paid someone. You are going to have to be very careful, Daniel, that in trying to free Sidney from a charge of embezzlement, or even of assaulting Rebecca, you don't end up by getting him hanged for murder.'

'I know,' he said, as if all the gentle apricot light had drained from the sky. 'I do see that!'

Daniel spent a miserable night. He knew he needed to sleep, but every time he even got close to it, new ideas surged into his mind, jerking him awake. He knew the witnesses he needed to call: a few who had already testified, plus Dr Mullane and Miriam. It was the order in which to call them that troubled him. Usually, witnesses were not permitted in the courtroom until after they had testified, in case the other testimony given might affect what they were going to say. It had both advantages and disadvantages. The art was in how to use them! Several of the people he wanted had already been called by the prosecution anyway.

Did it matter what order he called people to the stand? Yes. He must make it work for him, build the story so there would be no time to create a lie that would defend them. They must trip themselves up, trip each other, weave the web so tightly that it caught the man behind the whole affair . . . and not Sidney or, even more, not Patrick. Daniel admitted at last . . . not Patrick.

It was complicated, a story changing shape all the time, but with a constant purpose, the secret use of the deep-water harbour in Alderney.

He lay awake staring at the ceiling. He must move a step at a time, making sure the jury always believed, and above all understood, and for that, he must understand it himself.

Should he go and see Jemima before it all started? What was there to say? Did it even matter? Yes. He knew with desperate certainty that it mattered that he paid her the courtesy, the love even, of telling her himself. And Patrick, too.

Was he going to have to call him as a witness? Possibly. Not if he could help it.

He turned over and, within half an hour, fell asleep.

Daniel called by Keppel Street at seven in the morning, partly because he wished to catch his father before he went into his office at Lisson Grove, the headquarters of Special Branch.

There was no one in the dining room, which surprised him.

'I think they're all going to go to the court, Mr Daniel,' the butler told him. 'Would you like some breakfast, sir? It would be very simple to serve you with bacon and eggs, within a few minutes.'

Daniel hesitated. It sounded good, but his stomach was churning. 'Just tea, please. But I would like to speak privately with Sir Thomas first.'

'Yes, sir. Of course. And may I take the opportunity to wish you well, sir.'

'Thank you.'

Pitt came downstairs within moments and led Daniel to his study. He looked far more worried than he probably meant to reveal.

Daniel felt vulnerable, and protected, belonging and alone, all at once.

Daniel shut the study door to the hall as soon as he was inside. 'I know what it's about,' he said immediately. 'I'm telling you not because I want you to help, but I think you need to know. I might even call you . . . I don't know.'

For a moment, Pitt look startled, then he composed himself, and waited for Daniel to continue.

'I went to Alderney,' Daniel told him. 'I looked at the house May Trelawny bequeathed to Rebecca Thorwood. Someone else was very keen to buy it, but she wouldn't sell. She died soon after that. I'm sure she was murdered, and I intend to prove it.'

Pitt stared at him levelly, his attention total now.

'I think they killed May to get the house,' Daniel went

on. 'It's nothing in itself, but it overlooks, and is the only access to, a perfect deep-water harbour.'

Pitt looked slightly surprised. 'Smuggling?'

'Would that interest you?' Daniel said dismissively.

Pitt relaxed a little. 'No.'

'How about a deep-water harbour, in British waters, for submarines?'

Pitt breathed out slowly, but his attention was even more acute. 'Yes, that would interest me very much indeed. Are you certain?'

'I expect to be, one way or the other, by the end of this trial,' Daniel told him. 'Will you . . . will you please come to court, in case I need to call you?'

'Yes. I was coming anyway.'

'Did you know about this?' Daniel did not know whether he was hurt or not. He was certainly wrong-footed.

'I was coming because it's your case,' Pitt replied. 'The first important one you've had, where you are definitely leading. Even if you've got Kitteridge to back you. You have, haven't you?'

'Yes. But that isn't an answer.' Daniel felt a warmth none the less. He wanted to believe his father would have come for that reason alone, whether it was important or not.

Pitt smiled. 'It's the only one you're going to get.' Then the smile vanished. 'Be careful what you ask Jemima . . . or Patrick. At least, be careful how you do it.'

'They're not witnesses, I think.'

Pitt started to ask something, then changed his mind.

For a moment their eyes met and they were equals. Then Daniel smiled and went out into the hall, and then into the dining room.

Jemima and Patrick were both there now.

'We are ready,' Jemima said, her expression a little uncertain.

Patrick simply gazed at Daniel.

'I'd like you to come,' Daniel said quietly. 'I don't think I shall need to call you . . . either of you.' He glanced for a moment at Patrick, and then back to Jemima. 'But Rebecca might be glad of your comfort. And before you do, don't ask me anything. It's all going to unravel but I'm not sure how. I think I know, but . . .'

He saw Patrick's arm go around Jemima, and she moved a little closer to him. It said everything Daniel needed to know, all about love, doubt, trust and pain.

For an instant, he even envied them. Then he thanked them, forgot about his tea, and turned to leave. He had a great deal still to prepare. In the hall, he met Cassie with one of the maids. She ran to him excitedly. 'Uncle Daniel! Are you going to argue? Are you going to make a big argue?'

'Yes, I am.' He hugged her quickly, then let her go.

'Are you going to win?' Her eyes were bright, and full of certainty. She could not imagine him losing, or what that would mean.

'I don't know, sweetheart, but I'm going to try very hard. Wish me luck.'

'Aren't you right?'

'I think so.' Should he say 'right' didn't always win? She was three! This was too soon.

'Grandmama says you're very clever,' Cassie went on.

'Nobody wins all the time. But I'll try very hard.'

She looked uncertain for a moment, and then she smiled. 'I wish you win.'

'Thank you.' He leaned again and kissed her cheek very gently. 'Now, whatever happens, it won't hurt too badly.'

She looked at him very seriously for an instant, and touched her cheek where he had kissed her, then turned and ran into the dining room, where Charlotte was holding the door open for her, Sophie in her arms. Daniel's eyes met his mother's for a moment and Charlotte blew him a kiss. Then Sophie turned her big blue eyes to look at him and smiled a beautiful baby smile full of love and trust so that Daniel thought it was all he needed to sustain him through this most difficult day.

He went out the front door and walked swiftly to the nearest main street, where he could catch a taxi to the court-house.

He found Kitteridge almost immediately. He looked as if he had been pacing back and forth waiting for Daniel, perhaps wondering if he would ever show up. His relief was palpable.

'At least you're here, for whatever that's worth!' he exclaimed. 'Did you find anything in Alderney?' If Kitteridge was trying to hide his tension, he was making a poor job of it. 'For God's sake, tell me! Your brother-in-law's been sending wires back and forth to his people in Washington, but they still can't say when Morley Cross was killed. Hillyer won't wait much longer. If he has to, he'll just think it is arguing, and we will have to be clever to persuade the jury that Cross was killed after Sidney left. I don't believe it myself!'

'There's plenty I found out on Alderney,' Daniel took him by the arm, primarily to keep him still. 'May Trelawny was murdered.'

'What? I thought she fell off a horse, or something.'

'She was kicked to death by it, or at least that was what it was made to look like. But the medical evidence doesn't

306

fit together. And she was killed over the house she wouldn't sell. I've brought the doctor over to testify.'

'Never mind that! Was it Sidney?' Kitteridge demanded.

'No. It was somebody considerably older.'

'Why? What is special about the house? I mean, to commit murder for. It'll have to be something pretty big.'

'It is. Trust me. I'll bring it out. It's murder . . . and treason!'

Kitteridge looked at him narrowly, suspicion, disbelief and hope struggling in his face.

'I'll bring it out! I promise!' Daniel knew the risk he was running, even as he said it, but he felt he had nowhere else to go. Caution now would lose him everything.

Kitteridge grasped him by the arm. 'Well, come on then, you'd better lead. And, please God, you know where you're going!'

Chapter Twenty-Five

Court resumed and, in agreement with Kitteridge, Daniel rose to his feet to open the case for the defence.

'Gentlemen of the jury, I'm going to show you a long and twisted story of a man accused of two crimes he did not commit, and that involves a far greater and more terrible crime that he did not yet know of. Two crimes that did not actually happen, or not as you see them, and one that did, and was so well hidden that you did not know of it. A triple jeopardy, if you like.'

He saw in their faces that he had their attention, if only because they did not understand.

The judge leaned forward. 'Mr Pitt, make this brief, to the point, and with proof of all of it. This is a petty embezzlement, not a great crime . . . foolishness, a little greed, a case of a young man acting stupidly and ruining a very promising career. A tragedy, but unfortunately not an uncommon one. It will not serve your client well for you to attempt to make a grand drama out of it.'

Daniel made himself stand very straight and face the judge squarely. 'Your Honour, with the court's permission, I shall be as brief as possible, but I shall need to call several witnesses to trace this story from the first crime to this point. I may need to call Sir Thomas Pitt, Head of Special Branch, and I have asked him to be available.' Was that too soon? The judge's face had darkened.

Kitteridge was squirming in his seat.

'I am aware of who your father is, Mr Pitt.' The judge's displeasure was clear. 'I do not admire your drawing my attention to it!'

Daniel felt the heat burn up his face. 'I mention it, Your Honour, so that the court may know that this appears to be a petty embezzlement, but it leads to the crimes of treason and murder. And I beg you to allow me to present the whole story, as I can now prove it.'

He glanced quickly towards Sidney, and for the first time he saw hope in the man's face.

'You had better prove it, young man!' the judge warned. 'Very well, proceed. And you, Mr Hillyer, don't bother to object to every seeming irrelevance. I will stop Mr Pitt if he wanders too far off the path, without your assistance.'

'Yes, Your Honour,' Hillyer acceded, looking displeased and thoroughly puzzled.

The judge nodded at Daniel. 'Proceed, Mr Pitt. Call your first witness.'

'I call Miss Rebecca Thorwood.'

Hillyer started to his feet again, but sat down before the judge could direct him.

The judge glared instead at Daniel.

Rebecca, looking confused and highly vulnerable, took the stand and was sworn in.

Daniel could feel Jemima's eyes on him, suspicious and already a little hostile.

'Miss Thorwood,' he began. 'I believe you were the

goddaughter of Miss May Trelawny, originally of Cornwall? Is that correct?'

'Yes.' Rebecca's voice was barely audible.

'She lived recently in the Channel Islands, I believe. On Alderney, to be precise?'

'Yes.'

'Have you ever been there?'

'No.'

The judge leaned forward. 'Mr Pitt, you had better prove the relevance of this very quickly. I am prepared to indulge you, but only to a certain degree. This trial has already taken far longer than it should have. We are dealing with a petty embezzlement, for heaven's sake! The matter of a few pounds. Hardly the theft of the century.'

'Yes, Your Honour.' Daniel was sorely tempted to tell him that he would get there a lot sooner if he were not needlessly interrupted, but it would serve him badly, and he knew it. He turned to Rebecca again. 'Miss Thorwood, Miss Trelawny died recently, nearly two months ago, and is it true you are her only heir?'

'Yes, I believe so.'

Now the jury at least were paying attention.

'And the estate includes a manor house, and its own private bay, on the island of Alderney?'

'Yes, so the solicitor told me.'

'And some jewellery. Miss Trelawny was interested in semi-precious stones, particularly one piece of carved rock crystal. Did she give that to you?'

Hillyer fidgeted in his seat, stretching his legs, turning round, but he did not actually stand up.

'Yes, she did, but . . .'

'But what?'

'It was stolen.'

'From Miss Trelawny, or from you?'

This time, Hillyer did rise, but the judge got there before him.

'Mr Pitt, if you have a point, please get to it now!'

'Yes, Your Honour. Was it stolen from you, Miss Thorwood?'

She looked very pale and very young. Daniel knew that if he bullied her he would lose the jury's sympathy entirely.

'Yes,' she stammered. 'It . . . a man broke into my bedroom, at home, in Washington, at night. He attacked me and took the pendant with the piece of crystal in it. He tore it off my neck and escaped into the hallway, outside my bedroom . . .' She was clearly distressed.

The jurors were concentrating entirely on her, sympathy on the faces of every one of them.

This time, the judge did not interrupt.

'Do you know who did this, Miss Thorwood?' Daniel asked.

Rebecca looked wretched. She sent a begging glance in the direction of her father, or to where he had sat on Friday, but he was no longer there.

'Did you recognise him, Miss Thorwood?' Daniel persisted.

'No.'

'Did you cry out?'

'Yes.'

'And did anyone come to your assistance?'

'Yes, my father . . . I mean . . . I mean my mother was first, then my father.' She was stumbling over her words now.

'Did either of them see this man fleeing from your room? After all, he went into the corridor, not out of the window.'

'Yes . . . my . . . my mother saw him.'

311

Hillyer shifted in his seat but he did not stand this time.

'And did she recognise him?' Daniel asked.

'Yes.' Rebecca's voice was little more than a whisper.

'And did she say who it was?'

Rebecca's voice was inaudible.

The judge looked towards her. 'You must answer so that we can hear you, Miss Thorwood. I realise this must be extremely unpleasant for you, but please try.'

Rebecca cleared her throat. 'She said it was Philip Sidney.'

There was a rustle of movement through the gallery, and several audible gasps. There was no doubt that she had everyone's attention now.

'Are you quite sure?' Daniel persisted. 'Did you see him yourself?'

Rebecca shut her eyes. 'I didn't see him myself, just a shadow. It could have been anyone. But mother swore it was Philip Sidney.'

'Did she swear to it? In court?'

'No, my father said he would to save her the distress of—'

'I see. Did he lay any complaints about this assault and robbery? As a gift from Miss Trelawny's while she was still alive, the pendant must have been of great sentimental value to you.'

'Yes, but I have got it back.'

'We shall get to that,' Daniel assured her, but he had no objection to her explaining. The jury would need to hear, and if Daniel were prevented from asking her, then Kitteridge surely would.

'Did your father accuse Philip Sidney of the robbery, and the assault on you?' he continued.

'Yes. But . . .'

'But what?' he asked gently.

'But Mr Sidney worked at the British Embassy, and he had diplomatic immunity if he wished to claim it. He did, and left America. He . . .' Studiously she did not look at where he sat in the dock. 'He came back to England.'

'Where he was accused of having embezzled money while still at the British Embassy in Washington?'

'Yes.'

'Miss Thorwood, were you acquainted with Mr Sidney, socially?'

'Yes . . . a little.'

'Did your parents approve of him?'

'I . . .' She looked embarrassed. That in itself was an answer.

'Never mind.' He smiled at her. 'Were you fond of Miss Trelawny? I have heard many things about her. I believe she was brave, eccentric, at times very funny.'

'Yes.' All the shadows passed out of Rebecca's face. For a brief moment it was filled with the joy of memory. 'We wrote to each other often. She would tell the most wonderful stories.'

'Will you sell her house in Alderney? Or will you live in it one day?'

The idea seemed to distress her. 'Oh, no! I wouldn't dream of selling it!'

'Thank you, Miss Thorwood. I would like you to tell us some of these stories from Miss Trelawny, but this is not the time, or the place. Will you wait there in case Mr Hillyer has some questions for you?'

Hillyer stood up, straightening his shoulders. For a moment, he seemed undecided what to say. He did not even glance at Daniel. 'Thank you, Miss Thorwood. My sympathies for the death of your godmother, but I cannot see how it is relevant to this miserable affair, except that Mr Pitt has felt it appropriate to draw the jury's attention to the other wretched crime Mr Sidney is accused of, for which he saw fit to evade all responsibility by fleeing Washington and using his diplomatic immunity to escape the country altogether. It paints an even blacker picture of him. It is for your legal advisor to deal with, as to whether Sidney has been . . . adequately represented.' Hillyer sat down, looking surprisingly wretched.

Daniel felt guilty for putting him through this, but to have told Hillyer of his plans would have been a far deeper betrayal of Sidney, and of the law. He had to advise him of additional witnesses, but that was all. Hillyer had to tell him as well, if he intended to call someone to advise him of Morley Cross's time of death.

Daniel dared not look at Sidney himself.

The judge addressed Daniel grimly. 'I hope this is not as ugly as it seems, Mr Pitt? I warn you, it is your duty to defend Mr Sidney, whatever may be your personal opinion of him. I cannot believe that you don't understand this. I hope you have no such misguided plan as to ask for a mistrial? The consequences for you would be very grave indeed.'

Daniel stood up. He was embarrassed that he was trembling. 'No, Your Honour. I believe Mr Sidney is innocent of all charges, but I have to show the whole story, or it will not make sense.'

'Then you are off to an excellent start,' the judge said drily. 'So far this makes no sense whatsoever! Call your next witness.'

Daniel's mind raced. Could he tell the story without either Tobias or Bernadette Thorwood testifying? He must keep it as simple as possible. The charge was theft by embezzlement.

314

The real crime was the murder of May Trelawny. And if they brought it up, as they were bound to do, of Morley Cross also. He must not make any claims he could not justify, but neither must he be so oblique that he lost the jurors' understanding. And he must make the decision quickly. The judge was already growing impatient. He must keep it together. Do something dramatic. 'I call Dr James Mullane.'

Hillyer looked utterly bewildered. He had been informed, of course, as was required, but he had no idea who Mullane was.

Mullane accordingly took the stand. He faced Daniel and waited.

'Where do you live, Dr Mullane?'

'On the island of Alderney. It is one of the smaller Channel Islands.'

'And you are a doctor of medicine?'

'Yes.'

'You were Miss May Trelawny's doctor?'

'Yes. It is a very small island.' Mullane looked patient, solid, comfortable with himself, but at the moment burdened by a sadness.

'You were called when the body of May Trelawny was found?' Daniel sensed the judge's growing impatience and asked the next question without waiting for Mullane to answer. 'What was the cause of her death, Doctor?'

'It seemed that she was kicked to death by one of her horses,' Mullane said quietly.

There was an indrawn breath of horror around the crowd in the gallery. Two of the jurors shook their heads.

'An accident?' Daniel asked. It all hung on this. He must not seem to prompt the doctor.

'I thought so at the time,' Mullane answered. 'But after

the evidence was appraised more closely by Dr fford Croft, I saw that it was in fact contrived. I imagine you will wish to see the evidence of that.'

No one in the court was moving, barely even breathing.

'Let me be clear, Dr Mullane. Are you saying that Miss Trelawny was murdered?'

'Yes, I am.'

The judge interrupted sharply. 'Are you going to tell us that this, too, is Philip Sidney's work, Mr Pitt?'

'No, Your Honour, I'm going to show that it is the cause of the framing of Philip Sidney. Because he knows the motive behind this death, and who committed it, only he does not realise it yet. He has all the pieces, he just has not put them together. The man behind it needs to discredit him, even destroy him, before he can do so.'

If someone had dropped a pin on the floor, Daniel believed it would have been heard. Not a juror moved. They could have been made of the same carved wood as the bench on which they sat.

'Then you had better do so, Mr Pitt,' the judge warned. 'And to my satisfaction. Proceed.'

'Yes, Your Honour.' Daniel turned back to the witness. 'Dr Mullane, that is a very big change of mind, from an accident to deliberate murder. Could you describe the original evidence, briefly, and then the new evidence that changed your mind? What caused it to come to your attention? And remember that we are not doctors, so in as plain a manner as you can, please.'

Mullane looked pale, and he was evidently distressed, but he chose his words carefully.

'Certainly. I admired May Trelawny very much. She was a woman of courage and high intelligence, good temper and considerable wit.' His voice cracked only for a moment, and he recovered. 'To the best of my knowledge, she had no enemies. Alderney is a small island. We know each other well. As the island doctor, I would say I know most people as my neighbours, and my friends, as well as from time to time as my patients. It had never occurred to me that anyone would wish her harm. I did not look further than what seemed to be obvious. She had severe injuries to her head and shoulders. As if she had tripped and fallen in the stable, behind the horse. It had become startled and lashed out. Perhaps she had screamed, maybe for help. Maybe simply in pain. That had further panicked the animal and . . . the tragedy had happened.' He stopped abruptly, his pain at the image of this was clear.

Daniel allowed him a few moments to collect himself, and for the jury to absorb the emotional impact, then asked him to continue.

'It was the questions of Dr fford Croft that made me look further,' Mullane went on. 'She had discovered a partially healed injury on the horse's back, still suppurating under the skin, and the thorn in the saddle. It was May's. She had the only side saddle on the island. The injury was concealed by the lower part of the horse's mane, and one would not find it without deliberately looking. And there was no bruised wood in the stable, no marks of blood on the wood, but signs of there having been a great deal of blood on the stable floor.

'It had been cleaned from the floor in the intervening time?' Daniel asked.

'Yes. It was cleaned a day or two after, but the stains remained. We couldn't let it . . . just stay there. It . . .' He floundered, for a moment overcome by emotion.

Daniel felt it too. He had seen the stains. He could all too clearly imagine the depth of wet, scarlet blood that had made them. He wanted the court, the jury, to imagine it too.

Daniel drew a deep breath. 'It seems a mixed message to me. The wound on the horse and the thorn embedded in the saddle imply either an accident, or a deliberate attempt to cause a bad fall, but she was found in the stables, as was all the blood. What do you deduce from that?'

Mullane shook his head. 'It does not lie within my skill, Mr Pitt, but I cannot imagine May mounting a horse inside the stable. She was a tall woman, too tall to ride out sitting side-saddle. There was a mounting block outside in the yard; she would have used that, as was her habit.'

'Did you observe Dr fford Croft taking samples of blood from the stable floor, and from the horse in question, Dr Mullane?'

'Yes, I did. And I have photographs of that and of the saddle, and the injury to the horse.'

'Have you photographs of Miss Trelawny's injuries also?'

Mullane winced and closed his eyes. 'Good God, no, man! Why on earth would I want such a thing! As if I could forget . . .'

'But they were consistent with being repeatedly kicked by a horse?'

'Yes.'

'Or having fallen from a horse, and been dragged, perhaps?'

'No,' Mullane answered sharply. 'No, they were not. Having fallen would have left bruises on the body, which there were not, being dragged would have left lacerations, abrasions, drag marks. Perhaps dirt or gravel. There were not.'

'Then what was there?'

Mullane stared at him. 'You know what there was, Mr Pitt. She was beaten to death, and then the horse was blamed, albeit because of a thorn caught under the saddle.'

'I'm sorry to distress you, Dr Mullane,' Daniel apologised. 'I know Miss Trelawny was your friend, and by every account a fine woman. But have you any idea, with hindsight, why anyone might kill her?'

'None at all,' Mullane replied. 'Unless it was for the house. There were people trying to buy it. She wouldn't sell. Can't think what the devil they would want it for. Was nice enough, but rather dilapidated. Too small to be a hotel. Isolated. And there were other houses in better condition coming up for sale.'

'In St Anne?'

'Yes. Nicely situated.'

'But not isolated, with its own bay, out of sight of others?'

'No, but . . .' Mullane tailed off.

'But?' Daniel prompted.

Mullane was dismissive. It was clear the subject was painful. 'If you're thinking of a good secret place to land a smuggling ship, there's not much of that going on now, and what there is could come ashore anywhere on the island. Or on other islands, for that matter. It's certainly not worth killing anyone for.'

'Actually, it wasn't smuggling I had in mind,' Daniel said with a twisted smile. He must not lose either the jury's sympathy, or above all, their interest. 'But it is a good, private, deep-water harbour none the less?'

One of the jurors craned forward. Another sat up straighter.

'I suppose so,' Mullane agreed.

319

'Dr Mullane, do you recognise Mr Sidney? Have you ever seen him before?'

Mullane looked towards the dock. 'No.'

'You haven't seen him on the island? Enquiring about buying Miss Trelawny's house, for example?' Daniel pressed.

'I haven't seen him at all.'

'Thank you. Please wait for Mr Hillyer to speak to you.' Daniel sat down, his mind racing to think if he had asked everything he could. A chance missed now was gone for ever. He glanced at Kitteridge. Did he want to add something? But Kitteridge gave a slight shake of his head and smiled. He was satisfied. Or at least he could think of nothing to add now.

Hillyer rose to his feet, hesitated for a moment. Perhaps he realised that Mullane was a sympathetic witness, and cross-questioning him would gain nothing. 'I have no questions for this witness, thank you,' he said quietly, and sat down.

Daniel called Miriam fford Croft to the stand. He had her recite her qualifications and the reason she did not have a medical practice, only an occasional consultation on pathology. He hated doing that, because his own anger on her behalf was difficult to hide, but he knew it would get in his way. If the jury sympathised, or thought it was unfair, unjust, that was enough. Perhaps they would remember that Mullane had called her 'doctor'.

Daniel cleared his throat. Hers was the evidence upon which it would all turn.

'Miss fford Croft, we have been discussing the death of Miss May Trelawny, even though the case that the prosecution is bringing is one of embezzlement of money from the British Embassy in Washington. Were you consulted on that, in your capacity as a specialist in the detection of forgery?'

'Yes. I was,' Miriam replied.

As rapidly as he could, Daniel had her explain again to the judge and jurors the details of particular interest in a forged signature, the drag marks in tracing a signature, the difference in little spikes of ink where a pen had been used carefully, rather than spontaneously, so that each member of the jury could see them for himself. They must understand, and believe that for themselves, not because Daniel said so, or that Miriam did.

'Do you draw any conclusions from these signatures, Miss fford Croft?' he asked at length.

'Yes. Some of these signatures are genuine, but at least half are forged. You cannot see it with the naked eye, and very few people even possess a microscope, still less are likely to put it to a signature on the transfer of a relatively small amount of money,' she replied.

Daniel did not need to look at the jury to know that he had their total attention. They liked Miriam's brevity, and that she had brought them pictures they could very clearly understand. Also, it was a relief to be talking of petty theft, rather than violence, and the death of someone they felt they would have liked, and for which, in due time, someone would have to pay with their own life. It was a welcome relief from the weight of responsibility of the previous evidence, and it was something they could unquestionably understand.

Daniel smiled at Miriam. 'Does this mean that wherever the money went, either to the correct place or some other, Mr Sidney did not sign it out?'

She had the papers in two piles in front of her. 'He signed

these ones,' she answered, pointing to one pile. 'He did not sign those.' She touched the other pile.

'Thank you, Miss fford Croft. Now to turn to the far grimmer matter of Miss Trelawny's death. Have—'

At last Hillyer stood up. 'Your Honour, Miss fford Croft can have no knowledge in this matter. I don't doubt her forensic skills, but we are not accusing Sidney of having had any part in Miss Trelawny's death. Miss fford Croft's speculation on the matter, however percipient, is completely irrelevant here.'

The judge looked at Daniel, his eyebrows raised.

Hillyer was right. Daniel felt as if a hole had opened up in the floor in front of him, and he had fallen straight into it. He should have guarded against this.

'Uh . . . if you please, Your Honour,' he began, aware of all eyes in the room upon him. 'The question arose of . . . Mr Sidney having been guilty of the assault on Miss Thorwood, and of stealing the pendant that had belonged to Miss Trelawny. It seems to be the beginning of—'

'Yes, yes.' The judge agreed impatiently. 'The theft of the piece of jewellery seems to be the beginning of whatever the point is that you are labouring to reach. You are leading us on a winding trail, Mr Pitt. Does it lead anywhere? Did Mr Sidney steal it or not?'

'No, Your Honour, he did not,' Daniel said firmly. 'Miss Trelawny was murdered, as Dr Mullane testified. Her possession of the house on Alderney was the key to it, and the fact that she bequeathed it to Miss Thorwood.'

'Well, tie it up, Mr Pitt. The court's patience is not endless.'

'Yes, Your Honour.' Daniel did not look towards Hillyer. 'Miss fford Croft, did you this last weekend go to Alderney and visit the house of the late Miss Trelawny?'

322

'Yes, I did. I will summarise for the court what I found relevant, if you wish?'

'I do . . . thank you,' Daniel agreed.

'Keep it relevant, Miss fford Croft,' the judge warned. 'And with minimum displays of your undisputed skills, if you please.'

'Yes, Your Honour,' Miriam said meekly. 'I believe Dr Mullane has told you how Miss Trelawny died. If his account is correct, then there's evidence to substantiate it: injuries such as he described would have left a great deal of blood. I searched the stable floor for the stains that would unavoidably have been left. I found the massive stains of much blood, and took samples.'

'But you said it had been washed out!' Daniel interrupted her. The jury had to follow this, and believe it.

'Yes,' Miriam agreed. 'But roughly washed out. It was a concrete floor, full of irregularities. Lots of places had been missed. And it was covered with straw. I also examined the horse and found on it, not yet healed, the wound of the thorn which came from the saddle.'

'And what do these things prove?' Daniel asked.

'A very elaborately set-up plot,' she replied.

There was silence in the room. Every eye was upon her.

'How?' Daniel prompted.

'The blood was that of a pig,' Miriam replied.

The judge leaned forward. 'What did you say, madam?'

'That the blood was that of a pig, Your Honour,' Miriam repeated.

'And how on earth would you know?' he asked. 'Blood is blood.'

'With respect, Your Honour, it is now possible to tell the source of blood, animal or human. This was pig's blood, and

323

most definitely not that of Miss Trelawny. And incidentally, the horse was uninjured, apart from the sore made by the thorn.'

'And how do you explain this?' the judge asked, his face puckered with concentration.

'I don't, Your Honour,' she replied. 'All I can say is that I do not believe that Miss Trelawny died in the stable, but somewhere else, probably close by. It is a small island. And the place would have been one out of sight of any dwelling. And it has rained several times since her death. We also looked for the weapon used, and did not find that either. My guess is that it is in the sea, probably in the deep water close to Miss Trelawny's own property. It would not be hard for a strong man to hurl it into the sea, only fifty or so yards from the house itself.'

'Thank you, Miss fford Croft,' the judge acknowledged. He looked at Daniel. 'Have you anything further to ask this witness?' There was both apprehension and curiosity in his expression.

'No, thank you, Your Honour.'

'Mr Hillyer?'

Hillyer rose to his feet. 'Thank you, Your Honour.' He turned to Miriam. 'Miss fford Croft, did your enquiries uncover anything at all to indicate who killed Miss Trelawny? I mean proof, not speculation.'

'No, sir . . . only how brutally, and for what reason.'

That was clearly not the answer that Hillyer had wanted, but he could not refuse it now. He had invited it himself. 'Why? And not guesses, please. I do not want anything for which you have not powerful evidence.'

Miriam smiled briefly. 'A buyer had been most persistent in his attempts to purchase the house. He had visited the island at least twice. He was present over the time of her death. I believe he is still trying, and now Miss Thorwood, who has inherited the property, is the focus of his attention.'

'Proof?' Hillyer repeated.

Miriam faced him without her expression changing at all.

Daniel knew the instant before she answered that she was going to say what they had concluded. If he had said it, it would have been dismissed, but Hillyer had asked her. He had walked into the snare set for him.

'I believe Mr Sidney has that,' Miriam replied, 'only he does not know it. He has not put the pieces together. It is imperative to the would-be buyer that he does not, that Mr Sidney's reputation be completely destroyed and he be imprisoned for whatever crime they can blame him, before he understands what those pieces are and how they complete the puzzle.'

Once again there was silence, except for indrawn breath, and somewhere at the back of the gallery, a man stifling nervous laughter, perhaps at Hillyer's discomfort.

The judge closed his eyes and took a very deep breath.

Hillyer shot Daniel a look of exasperation.

'Mr Pitt!' the judge said loudly. 'I will not have my court-room made into a theatre of the fantastic. Bring me some tangible proof of this . . . this pile of supposition, fancy stories and horror! Or give me your closing argument and we will let the jury decide if Mr Sidney is provably guilty of anything, apart from almost unbelievable clumsiness and misfortune.'

'Yes, Your Honour,' Daniel replied. 'Thank you, Miss fford Croft. I call Sir Thomas Pitt.'

'What?' Hillyer demanded. 'What are you . . .?'

Daniel did not answer.

Thomas Pitt came to the stand, climbing the steps easily and facing the court. He was immaculate in black, even elegant. He swore to his name, and the fact that he was head of Special Branch.

Daniel could feel the sweat break out on his body as he faced his father, and drew in his breath to question him on the stand.

'Sir Thomas . . .' His voice almost choked in his throat. In his mind he had tried a dozen ways of beginning this. All of them seemed inadequate now: too direct, not direct enough, giving away information that should be secret. He began again. 'Sir Thomas, England has always been highly dependent on its navy for its defence.' He must come quickly to the point, or either Hillyer or the judge would stop him. 'It was founded by King Alfred well over a thousand years ago, and has saved us often since then. But is it vulnerable to submarines? Modern ships that move and survive totally beneath the surface of the sea, and come in for supplies in very deep-water harbours, such as the one lying close in to the island of Alderney, just by the land owned by the late May Trelawny. And now, by Miss Rebecca Thorwood.'

There were gasps of alarm and sudden understanding around the room, even the jurors looked pale. They all stared at Thomas Pitt on the witness stand.

'Yes,' Pitt answered. 'Submarines, carrying torpedoes that can sink even a battleship, or any cargo ship carrying food or other supplies, are the greatest invention in naval warfare, certainly in my lifetime. I would guess since the time of Admiral Lord Nelson and the Battle of Trafalgar. I would judge that they might be an even greater threat to our lives than the invention of ironside ships, or the power of steam.'

'Then the neglect of deep-water harbours, where these

things can hide, on our own outlying islands, must be avoided, almost at any cost?' Daniel asked.

'Or the use of them could be obtained by our potential enemies, at the cost of treason and murder,' Pitt replied.

'Thank you, Sir Thomas, that is all I have to ask. The ruin of one young man at the British Embassy in Washington is a price hardly worth mentioning.' Daniel said it deliberately, knowing how his father would reply.

'The fairness of the law is always worth mentioning,' Pitt said.

'Yes, sir.' Daniel turned to Hillyer.

Hillyer rose to his feet and looked at Thomas Pitt for several seconds, then declined to ask him anything.

The judge glanced at the clock, then at Daniel. 'How many more witnesses do you have, Mr Pitt?'

Daniel had to make his decision immediately. He had two more witnesses to call, although one of them might be enough, if he chose the right one. He knew what had happened, at least he thought he did. Proving it was another thing. If he misjudged it and failed now, there would not be another chance. Sidney was here in the courtroom and had heard everything. Did he at last understand? He must be allowed his chance to speak for himself.

On the other hand, Armitage was waiting outside to be called, if it all fell into place . . .

'Mr Pitt!' the judge repeated.

'Yes, Your Honour. I call Sir John Armitage to the stand.' The decision was made. Please heaven, it was the right one!

The judge looked exasperated. 'Mr Pitt, my patience is not endless, and you have tried it further than most. I hope you know what you are doing!'

'Yes, sir,' Daniel replied. He hoped more than anyone else

that, indeed, he did. They all seemed to be here. His parents, Patrick and Jemima, Miriam, all those he cared about. This was going to be a triumph . . . or a disaster. He could feel his heart beating, as if it were trying to break out of his chest.

Chapter Twenty-Six

Sir John Armitage was called and took the stand, swearing to his name, and his position in the British Embassy in Washington.

Daniel knew he had to be quick. If he did not prove his case, and the judge adjourned for the evening, tomorrow would be too late. If it were forced upon him, he must at least leave it at the point where Armitage could not escape without damning himself!

Now the courtroom was full of people who were involved, but it was a one-to-one battle, and too late for anyone else to help.

Daniel cleared his throat. He must keep Armitage on the wrong foot – always the wrong foot. 'I believe you know the defendant, Philip Sidney,' he began. 'You were the one who gave him his opportunity to work in the British Embassy in Washington. Was that because you were acquainted with his mother?' He was deliberately handing him an opportunity to rake up the petty weaknesses or offences Sidney might have committed in his youth. Please God he took it! It was bait, to prove he knew Sidney, and had done for years. And, therefore, possibly May Trelawny and the island.

The jury looked puzzled, the judge impatient. He was about to speak, but Daniel refused to look at him. 'Sir John?' he persisted.

'Yes, I knew her,' Armitage replied. 'Mrs Sidney was a delightful woman, and devoted to her son. I imagined I was doing her a favour. I had no idea of his . . . weakness.'

'Do you have a specific weakness in mind, sir?'

'Gambling,' Armitage answered. 'I know that is at the root of it all. It is, in itself, not a sin, if it is kept in check. But he would not be the first young man, far from home, and in an exciting world capital, who loses his sense of proportion.'

'I suppose not.' As soon as Daniel said the words, the last piece of the puzzle fell into place in his mind. 'It would make a man extremely vulnerable to blackmail, I imagine – that is, if he lost consistently . . . and badly?'

'I'm afraid so,' Armitage agreed.

'And you have seen this?'

Armitage looked grave, a wise man observing the weakness of his inferiors.

'Yes, I tried to intervene, but I have only so much power. And my own . . . very important job to do.'

'Of course. And you can only advise,' Daniel said sympathetically.

Hillyer shifted in his seat.

Kitteridge was sitting silently beside Daniel, but he was watching him with increasing concern.

'And had you any reason to believe that Philip Sidney was being blackmailed by anyone?' Daniel went on. 'An increased anxiety, perhaps? An appeal for an advance in salary? Borrowing from other colleagues? Borrowing from funds, and then resorting to more desperate means when he could not repay?'

'I see you understand the path downwards very well,' Armitage replied. 'You have seen it before, perhaps?'

'The end is predictable,' Daniel agreed.

There was a slight movement as Patrick Flannery came into the court, held up a piece of paper in his hand and nodded at Daniel.

Daniel nodded back, and turned again to Armitage. He said almost casually, 'By the way, since you know Philip Sidney's mother, perhaps you know May Trelawny as well? They were related, I understand, and quite close friends.' He smiled. 'Sidney mentioned it to me.' He was waiting for an objection, but no one made it.

Armitage sat absolutely still. 'We met once or twice,' he conceded.

'And you would, of course, know the Thorwoods,' Daniel continued. 'I believe they are quite close friends of yours in Washington. Is it part of your position to know the people of influence in that city?'

'Yes, of course I know them,' Armitage's expression took on an air of concern. 'The attack on Miss Thorwood was a terrible event. I . . . I felt sorry, and profoundly embarrassed, that it should be an Englishman, and part of my embassy, who should have done such a thing. I would deny it, if I could, but Mrs Thorwood saw him, and has no doubt it was he.' Armitage looked pained, as if he were feeling the humiliation all over again.

'Of course,' Daniel agreed.

No one moved in the courtroom. Please heaven, Hillyer did not pick now to try to raise an objection, in order to interrupt his rhythm and the jury's concentration.

'He says it was your advice that he claim diplomatic privilege and return to England. Is that so?' Daniel asked. 'Easy enough to understand, in the circumstances.'

'Yes,' Armitage admitted reluctantly. 'There was no question in my mind that he was guilty.'

'Did he admit it to you?' Daniel asked. 'And stealing the pendant – violently?'

Armitage hesitated only a moment, then took the bait. 'Yes. He said he was desperate for the money. I believe he pawned the pendant to pay his debts . . .' His voice trailed off, soft with pity.

'Yes,' Daniel agreed. 'We retrieved it from the pawnbroker – at least, the Washington police did. They have been of great assistance to us.'

'I'm glad, for Rebecca's sake.' Armitage looked suitably grave.

'Clearly, it was taken to the pawnbroker after Sidney left America to sail back to England.'

'I dare say he asked a friend to do it for him,' Armitage suggested.

'Any idea who that might be? Such as Morley Cross, for instance? We can look into it, of course. There was a fairly good description of the young man.' This was it! Or had he struck too soon?

'I dare say it was Morley Cross,' Armitage replied. 'A nice enough young man, and they were friends.'

'That would explain it,' Daniel agreed. 'In fact, it would explain quite a lot. Was Morley Cross a gambler as well? Our enquiries suggest that he was. That would account for his sympathies. And his ability to know the ropes, so to speak.'

Armitage looked a little less comfortable. 'I suppose so. Is it important now? Sidney is the one who attacked Miss Thorwood. Mrs Thorwood recognised him in the light on the landing. And Sidney is the one who embezzled from the embassy.'

'No, actually he isn't,' Daniel contradicted. 'He did not attack Miss Thorwood, nor steal the necklace. For a start, he was aware that it was only of sentimental value, and not worth more than a few pounds. And he was not in America when it was pawned—'

'I've told you,' Armitage interrupted, 'Morley Cross would have done it for him!'

Daniel nodded. 'Yes, you did say that. And since you suggested Sidney leave, and arranged passage for him, you would be correct about the dates he left.'

'Precisely,' Armitage agreed with mounting tension. 'I don't know what the dickens you're playing at. You're supposed to be defending him!' There was a slight flush in his cheeks now.

'I am,' Daniel assured him. 'I believe it was Morley Cross who assaulted Miss Thorwood and stole the necklace, and then pawned it. I believe it was probably he who forged Sidney's name on the embassy financial records also.'

'Are you asking me?' Armitage said in astonishment. 'For God's sake, man, I don't know! This is your job, isn't it?' His voice was considerably sharper.

'Actually, my job is to defend Philip Sidney,' Daniel replied. 'And I believe the best way to do that is to find the truth about Morley Cross's part in this, and prove it.'

'Ambitious,' Armitage said a trifle sarcastically. 'I assume you are referring to some alternative truth where Sidney was not guilty?' His austere expression suggested his contempt for the idea.

'There is only one truth,' Daniel replied. 'Just several sides of it. Take a prism, if you wish.'

'A kaleidoscope would be more appropriate,' Armitage returned swiftly. 'Every time you shake it, it creates a different picture.'

'The pieces are interesting.' Daniel was not going to be shaken. 'Let us consider them, and let the gentlemen of the jury decide on the true picture.' And before Armitage could respond to that, he went on. 'You knew Mrs Sidney, and Miss Trelawny. You knew the house in Alderney. I believe you visited it, possibly several times.' He watched Armitage's face closely. He thought he saw a slight flush. 'I have witnesses. Perhaps you do not know Dr Mullane is here, in court. Still, let's go back to order.'

Armitage did not reply. The muscles were tight in his jaw. Daniel could see that, even from where he stood.

'You are stationed in Washington,' he continued. 'You are well acquainted with all the Thorwoods. And with young Morley Cross. I believe he was one of your assistants. I'll call proof to that fact, if it is necessary. I suggest that it was Morley Cross who committed the assault on Miss Thorwood, and stole the pendant. Certainly, it was he who took it to the pawnbroker. I think it was he who embezzled from the embassy also. Unfortunately, we cannot charge him with it.' Daniel hesitated only a moment. 'Regrettably, Mr Cross was murdered also. His body was pulled out of the Potomac River in Washington a few days ago. Shot in the back of the head. But finally, we have a witness who saw him alive, after Sidney had sailed for London, so that is another crime of which he cannot possibly be guilty.'

Armitage leaned back in the witness stand, as if bored. 'I see no picture yet.'

'I haven't laid out all the pieces.' Daniel gave a wry, tight smile. 'The Thorwoods have come to England to settle Miss Trelawny's will, and lay claim to the house. Someone has been trying very hard indeed to buy it. Oh, you didn't know that?'

Armitage shifted his position slightly, altering his balance on the balls of his feet.

'Yes,' Daniel went on quietly. 'I went to the island over the weekend. Just got back yesterday evening. Brought Dr Mullane with me. Excellent man. Very fond of Miss Trelawny. It was he who told me about her murder. Very dreadful. Very violent. It happened when you were over here from Washington. Not here in London, perhaps in Britain elsewhere. Like the Channel Islands, for example.'

Armitage stood rigid now.

'Never mind if you've forgotten,' Daniel continued. 'I can ask Dr Mullane. He is already present, and has a very good memory. As has the postmistress in St Anne. That is on Alderney, but of course you know that . . .' He glanced at Sidney, who was now sitting bolt upright in his seat at the dock, his face filled with anger. He seemed taller than before, bigger altogether.

'I remember what it is that I know!' Sidney said loudly.

'Mr Pitt, control your client or I will have him taken outside,' the judge warned.

'I think we should put him in the witness stand, Your Honour,' Daniel replied as politely as he could. He was directing the judge, but he did not wish to sound like it. He could not afford an enemy on the bench now.

'First we will let Mr Hillyer question Sir John, if you are

finished,' the judge answered grimly. 'And you make a claim that Dr Mullane can identify Sir John. Do you wish to call him to that effect?'

Daniel looked at Armitage, then at the jurors. 'Thank you, Your Honour, but I think that may prove unnecessary. But if not, then yes, certainly I will.'

Hillyer shook his head. 'Thank you, Your Honour, but I would prefer to question Mr Sidney on what it is that he suddenly claims to recall at this late and desperate hour.'

The judge excused Armitage, and he stepped down from the witness stand.

'I saw him in Washington,' Sidney said quite clearly from the dock. 'I went to take a message to him, and I knocked on the door. I thought I heard permission to go in. But I must have mistaken it, because he was furious. He was speaking to a cultural attaché from the German Embassy, and they had a map of the English Channel out on the table. Alderney was marked, and a lot of sea lanes. I forgot it at the time, because I was more amazed to see a scarf of Mrs Thorwood's, or one exactly like one she has, on the back of one of the chairs. I remember it, because I was with Rebecca when she chose it for her mother's birthday. It was very expensive, and Rebecca told me she had it made especially for her mother, so it couldn't have belonged to anyone else. But I know now that it was the map that mattered.'

Armitage was walking towards Bernadette Thorwood.

Next to Jemima, Patrick stood up.

The judge's face was pink. 'Order!' he said sharply. 'I will have order in court. Sir John! You have not been given permission to leave!'

At that moment, Armitage was galvanised into action. He whipped his hand out of his pocket with what looked like an open penknife, small bladed but very sharp. He grasped Bernadette by one arm, and held her immediately in front of him. 'Come after me and I'll cut her throat!' he said quite clearly.

Everyone stopped motionless.

Sidney jerked his hands as if to follow, but he was manacled to the chair and could not take even a step.

It was Armitage who dragged Bernadette out of the room, the doors opened for them by a white-faced usher.

Patrick was the first to charge after them, leaving Tobias Thorwood holding a frantic Rebecca.

Daniel left his table and dashed through the door, and past the still-paralysed usher. He could see Armitage, still dragging Bernadette with him out of the front door into the street. Patrick was only yards behind them. He caught the door as it swung back and dived after them.

Daniel reached the top of the steps in time to see Patrick sprinting along the pavement. Ahead of him Armitage stopped dragging Bernadette. It was bound to happen. He could not run holding her.

Then the impossible happened. Armitage took Bernadette by the hand and she ran with him, as fast as he did. Suddenly a whole lot of pictures in the kaleidoscope shifted and made a totally different pattern, one that explained many small details, like how Armitage knew so much about May Trelawny and the deep-water cove, why Bernadette had lied about recognising Sidney in the bedroom corridor, why Armitage had suggested so quickly that Sidney claimed diplomatic immunity and fled, leaving himself without a defence.

Patrick was racing along the pavement, gaining on them. Armitage came to an open-topped car parked by the kerb. He swung the door open and leaped in, Bernadette immediately behind him. He started the engine just as Patrick came level with him. He threw himself at Armitage, who lashed out hard, sending Patrick reeling backwards, and to the ground, blood streaming from a knife slash on his face. The knife clattered to the road and Patrick grabbed it, lashing out. It was a moment before he struggled to his feet.

Daniel skidded to a stop, ignoring the car as it jerked forward, and then sped away. 'Are you all right?' he asked. 'Here!' He held out a clean handkerchief. The blood was oozing through Patrick's fingers and running over his hand.

'Get them!' Patrick said urgently. 'They won't get far . . . I put a gash in his tyre! That'll slow him up. We'll catch them, if you get on with it.' He sounded urgent, desperate, but he was ashen pale.

'We've got to get you to a doctor . . .' Daniel began.

Patrick held the folded handkerchief hard against his face. 'Go after them. They can't get far.'

The car disappeared round a bend in the road, and a second later there was a tremendous explosion, and plumes of dark grey smoke rose in a huge billow, followed immediately by a gout of scarlet flame.

'God! I hope they didn't hit anybody else!' Patrick gasped. 'I thought it would just go flat!'

The pavement was filling with people: Jemima, Thomas and Charlotte, Tobias and Rebecca Thorwood. Jemima went instantly to Patrick, her face white. 'Patrick! Are you all right?'

'Yes. It's not much,' he said, mumbling through the handkerchief, blood now seeping through it. 'I'm all right.' He turned to Daniel, and was about to speak, when a constable in uniform came round the bend from the direction of the smoke. 'All right, ladies and gentlemen,' he said authoritatively.

'Nothing to see here. Just some damn fool who took too much to drink and drove into the bollards of the turn-off. Doesn't know the road, I expect. Foreigners!'

Daniel collected his wits. 'Was anyone hurt?'

The constable looked at him incredulously. 'Hurt? Not any more, sir. I'm afraid the car's finished, and the people inside it, too. Friction must have caused a spark, and the fuel tank had burst and went up instantly. Burned to . . .' He stopped, aware of what he was saying. 'Hope it wasn't anyone you know. Sir? Unreliable things, them motor cars. Would never have happened with a horse! Now move along, please, ladies and gentlemen.' He looked more closely at Patrick. 'Seems like you're hurt, sir. Perhaps you'd better go inside and sit down. We'll send for a doctor.'

'Yes, please,' Jemima answered before Patrick could speak.

'I'm fine,' Patrick mumbled through the handkerchief. 'We're in the middle of a trial. I'm police. For God's sake, man! What happened?'

The pavement was rapidly filling with people, including more police. Pitt and Charlotte looked at Patrick in alarm. Charlotte went to Jemima and they both stood close to him.

Pitt went to the constable. He produced his card and showed it to him.

'Yes, sir. Seems as they came round the corner too fast and ran straight into the bollards that block it off. Don't know London, maybe. Going too fast to keep control. Man and a woman. I'm sorry, sir, but there was no chance either of them survived.'

Pitt acknowledged it silently, and stepped back to Charlotte, Patrick and Jemima.

Behind them, Miriam was holding Rebecca in her arms

for a moment, and then let her go so she could comfort her father, touching him gently, as if she were the stronger.

Kitteridge came up to Daniel. He looked as if he had been close to the explosion himself, jacket crushed, tie half undone, and hair flying. 'That has to be the final defence! Armitage! Why in hell . . .? I know, don't tell me. Mrs Thorwood's affair all that time ago was with him. She never got over it. And he was a traitor all along. How long have you known?'

'About half an hour,' Daniel answered, smiling ruefully.

FOR MORE FROM ANNE PERRY, TRY
THE THOMAS PITT SERIES

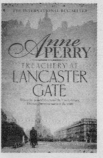

BETHLEHEM ROAD
HIGHGATE RISE
BELGRAVE SQUARE
FARRIERS' LANE
THE HYDE PARK HEADSMAN
TRAITORS GATE
PENTECOST ALLEY
ASHWORTH HALL
BRUNSWICK GARDENS
BEDFORD SQUARE
HALF MOON STREET
THE WHITECHAPEL CONSPIRACY
SOUTHAMPTON ROW
SEVEN DIALS
LONG SPOON LANE
BUCKINGHAM PALACE GARDENS
BETRAYAL AT LISSON GROVE
DORCHESTER TERRACE
MIDNIGHT AT MARBLE ARCH
DEATH ON BLACKHEATH
THE ANGEL COURT AFFAIR
TREACHERY AT LANCASTER GATE
MURDER ON THE SERPENTINE

GO TO WWW.ANNEPERRY.CO.UK
TO FIND OUT MORE

DISCOVER THE
WILLIAM MONK SERIES

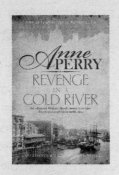

THE FACE OF A STRANGER

A DANGEROUS MOURNING

DEFEND AND BETRAY

A SUDDEN, FEARFUL DEATH

THE SINS OF THE WOLF

CAIN HIS BROTHER

WEIGHED IN THE BALANCE

THE SILENT CRY

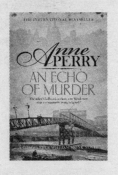

THE WHITED SEPULCHRES

THE TWISTED ROOT

SLAVES AND OBSESSION

A FUNERAL IN BLUE

DEATH OF A STRANGER

THE SHIFTING TIDE

DARK ASSASSIN

EXECUTION DOCK

ACCEPTABLE LOSS

A SUNLESS SEA

BLIND JUSTICE

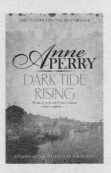

BLOOD ON THE WATER

CORRIDORS OF THE NIGHT

REVENGE IN A COLD RIVER

AN ECHO OF MURDER

DARK TIDE RISING

GO TO WWW.ANNEPERRY.CO.UK
TO FIND OUT MORE

DISCOVER MORE FESTIVE
MYSTERIES FROM THE INIMITABLE
ANNE PERRY

  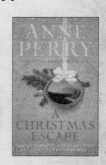

THRILLINGLY GOOD BOOKS FROM CRIMINALLY GOOD WRITERS

CRIME FILES BRINGS YOU THE LATEST RELEASES FROM TOP CRIME AND THRILLER AUTHORS.

SIGN UP ONLINE FOR OUR MONTHLY NEWSLETTER AND BE THE FIRST TO KNOW ABOUT OUR COMPETITIONS, NEW BOOKS AND MORE.